The Light Inerrant

The Light Inerrant

A novel
by
Bruce Meisterman

Author photo: Larry Kuzniewski
Front cover image: Bruce Meisterman

This is a work of fiction. All the characters, organizations, and events portrayed in this novel are the product of the author's imagination. Any resemblance to actual people, living or dead, events, and organizations is purely coincidental.

First Edition published: May 2023
Copyright 2016, Bruce Meisterman
All rights reserved.
ISBN: 9798386349998

Also by Bruce Meisterman

<u>Fiction</u>

A Coward's Guide to Living

<u>Non-fiction</u>

Arn? Narn.

<u>Contributor</u>

Giving Back

Tennessee 24/7

Gateway to Aero-Science

Acknowledgments

The word "inerrant" is often used when describing things in a religious sense. The American Heritage Dictionary describes it as such: "incapable of erring; infallible;" or "Without error, particularly in reference to the Bible."

In this story, Light is inerrant. It is pure, unfettered by dogma, and has no apparent agenda. Light is more than we comprehend.

This book could not have been written without the encouragement and support of my wife, Carla. When I first shared the idea for *The Light Inerrant* with her, I wanted to give it to someone else. She would not hear of it, saying that only I knew the story and it was mine to tell. For her to react to an idea like this speaks volumes of her enthusiasm for the story to be told. It was no small endeavor, especially for one used to telling stories with a camera. She was a sounding board for what made sense and what didn't. I can't thank her enough.

Thanks also go to early readers of *The Light Inerrant*. Thank you, Bruce (another one!), Cliff, and others who listened to my ravings about it. Your patience is very much appreciated.

So, if you like the story, credit her. If not, blame me.

It is impossible to properly appreciate the light without knowing the darkness. - Jean-Paul Sartre

Prologue

Excerpts from the True North News Interview:

"Yet, we are being cast into darkness and it is creating fear. We do know not who is standing next to us each moment. But that is just as true in the light. Is it not? We do know not where we are going. That too is true at any time. The perceived veil of certainty of which we live with each day has been removed from our eyes and we find we cannot see anything at all." – the Ajahn Khema

"Fiat Lux! What could be any simpler?" - Reverend Paxton Shea

"Fiat Lux, my ass!" – Forum moderator Lee Black

Chapter 1

Everywhere

It had been taken for granted since time began, even if early humankind knew not what it was. It was always there and not always there, punctuated by regular periods of darkness.

But after millennia, that would change.

It blinked and all light everywhere vanished, flickering back on instantly. Awake and aware for the first time, it had no memory of a past yet there must have been one.

It would not be the last such event.

And everyone would notice. And everyone would fear.

Chapter 2

Annapolis, MD

He strutted up to the lectern, polished, pressed, and preening. The studio, not far from the Naval Academy, was in standard Sunday morning mode: lights, camera, and sound systems on, awaiting its occupant to take the stage, ready for his close-up.

"Are the lights ready? Are we good to go? Yes?" Jonah Stamm was getting himself worked up for his weekly "Sacred Light" television broadcast. Others not so charitably called it "Sacred Blight" as it appeared that all Stamm did was fleece his viewers, ranting at something he believed short-changed the word of God. In his mind, he had a lot to rant about other than his ever-increasing ratings. While it was true many thousands turned off when he came on, many thousands were tuning in. He had struck a nerve with a group of people disillusioned by their own churches, spouses, government, sports teams, and in whatever else the human strain could be disappointed, just as he had.

Every Sunday morning and in its evening rebroadcast, the right Reverend Jonah Stamm railed against what he saw as that week's prevailing earthly problems. Between the music, testimonies, and sermon, all timed to last a rigid 58 minutes lest the flock grow restless, Stamm relentlessly hammered home his message. Not content with a mainstream religious message, he truly believed God spoke to him among very few others, the Pope notwithstanding. As far as Jonah was concerned the Pope was competition with an unfair advantage, one he was determined to winnow down to at least level the playing field. Hell, his church was growing far faster than any other denomination, the Pope's included!

This Sunday was to be like every other, nothing new, just more of the same very profitable sermonizing. "My friends, I want to go back to the beginning, to where and when it all began, to Genesis. Yes, after all our Lord's hard work, he spoke those unforgettable words, 'Let there be light!'"

And for a moment, in the studio and everywhere else, there wasn't... any light at all. There was only suffocating darkness.

Thinking it was only a power outage, he attempted to take immediate advantage of the odd situation. Thundering while stuttering simultaneously "H-h-he said, 'L-l-let there be l-l-light." And miraculously, it came back on at that moment. The audience's response to this was instantaneous. He'd have to find the technician and simultaneously thank and chew him out for his unplanned initiative.

He wouldn't be able to explain, nor did he have the time with the cameras back on and thousands of eyes focused on him. Oh, how much he would have paid to be able to achieve that effect on demand.

He had calmed down, his stutter under control. "YES! And there was light! Oh, yes, our Lord gave us light, His divine light! Yes! You see, He's done it again. For those of you who doubt the Word, put your skepticism away. He has spoken and you and I, we... we, were witness to it!"

If Jonah Stamm could have wrapped it up there, he would have, it was the best close of his career. But he was too early into the sermon. He continued, inspired, and charged as rarely before. He was preaching the Word and God Almighty heard it and approved. His congregation would have sat there all day long. They were convinced they'd seen a miracle, and Stamm was responsible. 'Praise the Lord' was being shouted throughout the audience and could be heard down the long hallways throughout the studio.

After his impassioned sermon, he was done and spent, having gone through the motions for the rest of the service, grateful for its end. He waited by the door in the faux narthex, thanking all the attendees, praising the Lord, and wondering how to capitalize on this. Over the years, capitalization became his trademark. It hadn't always been that way. Prior to his ministry, he was a politician but even then, he meant well.

Early in his political career, one lobby interested in limiting school bus safety regulations had pursued him for his support. Convinced by them that the buses were currently overbuilt which created 'hardships' for the manufacturers and that the proposed new design changes would ultimately not reduce their safety, Stamm took their money and voted in favor of the legislation overturning the former safety parameters.

Three years later after the legislation went into effect, Stamm had been re-elected and was running again. In a tragic accident, one of the recently deregulated buses was forced off the road by a speeding driver, crashed, and broke apart, bursting into flames and killing the driver and all but three children. Stamm was devastated, seeing the impact of his decision. Sickened, he dropped out of the race immediately and went into seclusion for over two years.

In that time, he had found God and seeking to make amends for that vote, dedicated himself to helping others. That was his plan and it worked for a while in the small urban church in which he found work and comfort. But his natural abilities and tendencies took him much further than he anticipated and thrust him back into the spotlight, leading him to recreate himself and launch his Sacred Light Ministry television program. As in politics, his greed was evident, and it was best served by his political contacts.

His 'church's' coffers grew in direct proportion to his audience, helped in no small way by those contacts whose contributions were significant. Not content to solicit 'tithes' from his viewers, he had an entire collection of books and CDs available for a nominal fee instructing his followers how to live the lives they always dreamed about and in absolute financial prosperity. But first, they had to contribute to his security before being shown the way to theirs. So, his financial well-being grew at the expense of others. If that were not enough, even his t-shirts and hats, asking the question – 'Does His

16

Light Shine On You?' were big sellers. Shameless self-promotion was
the coin of his realm.

Chapter 3

Lexington, MA

He cracked one eye open moments before the alarm sounded. Ever since Jess, his wife died, he always awoke, usually, while it was still dark outside, earlier than the alarm. He thought of that phrase and wondered, once again, if he could have beaten that damn clock just once and seen her that one last time. He wasn't there when she passed away and had never forgiven himself for that. And again, he realized the futility of that thinking.

Adam Faraday had come to hate time: time to think, time to waste, both too much and not enough time. He no longer saw time as a friend but as an enemy.

Looking out the window next to the bed, he was surprised to see in the dim light, a white owl sitting on a branch, looking back at him as if it knew what Adam was thinking. Adam returned the look, muttering, "Yeah, right, what do you know?"

It cocked its head, peering at him sideways with one black eye and as if shrugging a non-existent shoulder, flew off. Odd, he thought. The bird reminded him of the cheap cigars his father favored, White Owls, something he hadn't thought of in years. He snorted to himself, turning his back away from the window since that show was obviously over.

He stayed in bed and fumbled with the remote trying to find something mindless to watch. Sunday talking heads and televangelists weren't what he had in mind though they certainly fit his estimation of mindless. But that's what first came up. Turning up the sound, he heard another of the latest screeds from some fundamentalist preacher warning once more of the impending apocalypse. At an earlier time, he and Jess would have been doubled over with laughter at its theatricality and absurdity. He still couldn't understand why so many flocked to people of this ilk. And a flock was exactly what they were in his opinion. Sheep being led to a future that would naturally end in death but not before being fleeced. Tiring of the preacher, he flipped to another channel and found something not much better or different but mindless still.

It was a news program featuring a well-known, well-coiffed, and well-made-up news anchor and a table full of drawling, verbally drooling politicians staking their claims against whatever the opposition party currently supported. This one was the latest hopeful running for the presidency. Adam grimaced at this. Apolitical, he neither followed nor believed in any party. It was no different from religion. Though raised a Catholic, he abandoned the church early on. He was a scientist and believed in facts and theories that could be supported. Unwilling to listen to any more of the babble, he got out of bed and took a long shower. Afterward, drying himself off, he thought of the plans he and Jess had made, children, travel, and their future. So much for that.

Sundays were particularly tough. They'd stay in bed, drink coffee, read the Sunday Boston Globe, and make love. Yeah, Sundays were officially a bitch.

He was a creature of habit, making up his bed, and noticing that his side of the bed was noticeably lower, indented where only he slept, leaving the other side slightly higher. Jess died two days after it had been delivered and it had no time to conform to her body. They'd made love in it only once. It was several years ago; it was like last week. He wondered how long this pain would go on. Like many before him who'd lost a loved one, he threw himself into his work to ignore the pain. Sometimes he was able to forget it briefly, other times not so much. But that was becoming more ineffective. He was operating on automatic.

On the dresser, he noticed his wedding band in a dish along with his watch. He stuffed it into a drawer and threw on a clean sweatshirt, underwear, jeans, and a pair of old running shoes. Since her death, he had ceased running and working out and had added some weight. His tall frame disguised it, but a growing tightness in his clothes let him know otherwise. He had also let his hair grow out from the short no-nonsense/no-care cut he had favored for years. Nothing worked to get him out of this extended funk.

After her death, he accepted a new position with a small but increasingly influential organization, Aura/Sonos, an under-the-radar group working at the forefront of human sensory and development research. He hoped that change would be good. Educated at MIT, Adam loved the Boston area and wanted to stay. Aura/Sonos fit the bill perfectly for him.

However, poorly informed politicians, looking to score points back home with the constituents, often referred to Aura/Sonos as that place where nothing happens but was still happy to accept federal monies it didn't quite deserve. It was no secret, but it also wasn't common knowledge what they did, and had already discovered, so little of it was due to the federal teat. Had they known, their condemnations would have been hurled elsewhere, finding another more suitable target for their periodic election-year witch hunts.

Typical of all his days off, with no real plans, and no social life to speak of, he thought he might as well go into the lab. No sense in hanging around doing nothing but beating himself up. He'd have a coffee there along with a vending machine breakfast.

As he was getting his car keys, his cell phone buzzed. He recognized the number as his lab partner, Fran Porter.

Porter was not prone to excitement or unusual excesses, save for a constantly changing neon hair color and an omnipresent sarcasm which in the eyes of some was all too frequent and more than a little caustic. It limited her circle of friends. If one indulged her in a quixotic search for a perfect pizza, much like an orange cartoon cat, then they too could be part of an exclusive club, current membership two – her and Adam Faraday. She adored Adam, saw beneath his pain, and was determined to get him out of his funk.

Though a geek in the best way, she was firmly rooted in reality rather than video games. Video games would have been difficult for Fran as she had been legally blind since adolescence, losing much of her vision to a rare viral infection. A stereotypical Goth computer nerd, she sported all the hallmarks: nose ring, thick chains hanging everywhere from her clothing, and heavy black Doc Martens. What she lacked in sight, she more than made up for it in a compensatory increase in her other senses. One underestimated Fran at their own peril, something one usually found out after it was too late. It caught many unaware of her abilities. That said, she wasn't so much competitive as dogged, with a single-mindedness and razor focus in her determination when hunting solutions and lippy as hell when challenged. Her ego, as her senses, had disproportionately increased too.

Fran was excited, almost to the point of incoherency, "Did you see it? Adam, have you been following what's happening? Everyone's going nuts! It was only a minute long, no, a second, shit, I don't know – fuck, it happened so quickly!"

"OK. Fran, Fran, slow down. What are you talking about and why are you in the lab? It's Sunday for Chrissakes!"

"You didn't see it? What the fuck?! You didn't see it?! How could you miss it? Where've you been?"

"Fran, please, gimme a break, willya? I just got up. What the hell is going on?"

There was a long pause, the sound of someone taking a deep breath, and then finally, "Adam, the light went out! All of it! Everywhere!"

Chapter 4

Washington, DC

The theatrically named congressman, Carlton Justice from the small hamlet of Hickory Fist, Alabama, was in fine form. He was intently watching the same talking heads as Adam Faraday, making mental notes of what he saw. Shaking his head at the pablum coming out of the TV, he turned it off, reminding himself to get his chief of staff to book him more often on these shows. Re-election was only eighteen months away and he'd need all the exposure he could get. Like most in the legislative branch, he believed his voice was one of only a few clear ones and it needed to be heard. Ego was a prerequisite for running for office and the longer the tenure, the more it required feeding. And Carlton Justice's had an enormous appetite.

It was that outsized ego that got him out of his country environs. Spending the rest of his life in his father's feed store and marrying a local girl wasn't his idea of a future. Ambitious, smart, and strong, he excelled in school and football. Possessing a Southern gentleman's civility and courtesy, he was a favorite among women and farmers. Recognizing this as an asset that could be exploited, he decided to run for office. The local pols were more than happy to oblige and support.

He saw this as the way to get out of this bum-fuck town and to the big show. He campaigned on his natural homespun personality and history of sports heroics to which the voters responded overwhelmingly. His school proudly displayed his trophies. Some local businesses still had his team photo on their walls. Carlton was on his way. Paying back his constituents with his diligence, loyalty, and hard work for his gerrymandered district, his future seemed secure.

Justice knew appearances counted and he cultivated his, appealing to his voters and their tastes, favoring the look of a well-fed country gentleman whose leaner days were behind him, eschewing only the stereotypical walking stick, seersucker suits, and straw hat. In keeping with that carefully constructed image, he made sure his constituents were aware that his being in the office on Sundays was not unusual, while privately resenting it. On those days, he made sure he had at least a skeleton staff in attendance. Hell, someone had to make the coffee!

His thoughts were interrupted. "Congressman?" a question muffled through the door.

"Congressman, may I come in?" It was Trey Keenan, one of the young, faceless staffers willing to work long hours for little pay to get their foot in the door of what they believed was the greatest game in the world. The probability of their future corruption never entered their idealistic minds at this stage. It would happen, gradually, unnoticeably until they too became adept at the game or were chewed up and spit out as was more often the case. They might survive and then run for office themselves or find employment with a K Street lobbying firm, their seduction by Washington's gaudy trappings then complete.

Justice grunted, "All right, come in."

"Sir, a letter arrived."

"On a Sunday? No wonder the frigging post office is going under. Give it here. Let's see it."

The slightly built, be-suited staffer turned over the letter commenting it looked personal, the envelope hand-addressed and on expensive-looking paper. There was no postmark, postage, or return address.

The handwritten letter inside matched the same expensive paper stock as the envelope. Justice recognized it as being from that preening and pompous, publicity-seeking, televangelist Jonah Stamm. The two of them had a history together. Carlton knew a long time ago that when he threw in with Jonah before he was a man of the cloth, he'd made a deal with the devil. "Damn, just because I didn't go to church today doesn't mean I have to put up with his crap on Sundays. And he still sends letters? What's wrong with emails?"

Certainly, Stamm had heard of e-mails, but he fancied himself as being a practicing Luddite, one from another era. He was conservative where it counted and let those who mattered be aware of his bona-fides. He believed communications were best handled in a civilized fashion and e-mails were not that. And Luddite or not, he also knew e-mails never went away. This was too important a letter to be entrusted to an electronic eternity. That mistrust served him well both personally and in the pulpit in the past and he was not about to change it. Yes, a letter could be forged but it could also be destroyed. Copies could always be refuted. Stamm's conceit was the fine paper and the fountain pen he used, just as were his clothes and cars. It was obvious poverty was not a vow he'd taken seriously. These pretenses were just hallmarks of his narcissism.

Congressman Justice opened the letter and read it and then re-read it. Not noticing the lights flickering off and then back on, he reddened, gagged on his rising bile, and then vomited over himself and his desk, sparing the damned letter.

Chapter 5

Baltimore, MD

It was impossible to maintain any privacy within the confines of the crammed-together cubicles. Stories and secrets were guarded jealously. Whisper campaigns helped fuel whatever latent paranoia might be lurking around.

"I don't know. It's interesting but it just seems too out there, really. How many times have we heard this shit? How many times have we barked up this tree just to find nothing there? Yeah, yeah, I know. We both agree there's got to be something more, but we always come up dry. What makes you think this is going to be any different? Hackers maybe? If we had something more concrete, something we could hold in our hands, I'd feel a lot more confident."

Frustration had become too familiar to Edward Benton, widely known as Bennie. As a reporter for an online news organization, True North News, he'd developed the jaded attitude and cynicism common to his craft, unusual for someone his age and experience. Growing up, he was too sarcastic to be a team player yet very intelligent, intuitive, and an extremely good listener. He liked commenting on what he perceived were the foibles of others, especially if it raised him up in his own estimation. At another time, he could have been a gossip columnist.

As any reporter knows, much of what they hear is lies. His skepticism of a "sure thing" was his life raft. Believe all the stuff told and you ran the risk of getting shipped off to some weekly shopper in Montana. Cynicism was just the fate of a disillusioned idealist that Bennie had once been. There was a time when he thought he could really make a difference. The hard lesson he learned and one that would corrode his spirit was that differences were measured in inches not miles. And that could translate to on-air time, his personal golden fleece.

Lee leaned over the partition separating the desks, "C'mon, Bennie. This could be the real thing. We've heard about recordings in the past and now there's this copy of the letter," whined Lee Black, a copy editor, sometime friend, a wannabe reporter, long-time drinking buddy, self-avowed skeptic, and fellow cynic. In Benton's world, alcohol consumption did not confer genuine friendship status, but as far as Lee was concerned, it was a start and one he was happy to take.

"It's addressed to Carlton Justice and it's from Jonah Stamm or at least that's what it looks like. You've been dying to expose Stamm. You think this might be it? It's damned inflammatory."

Benton, slouching in his cheap, rumpled sports jacket, ran a hand across his unshaven face and through his dark, unkempt hair, brushing it off his face. While he had heard the cliche 'clothes make the man', he hadn't taken it very seriously, not looking much different than the A/V nerds from his high school.

"Look, that's just it. It could be real or a rumor. We don't know enough about this. You said a stranger handed it to you while you were coming into the office and just said, 'Here, you might be able to use this' and vanished in the crowd. Why you? Yeah, I will admit that does feel different from the other crap we've seen before and God knows I can't stand that motherfucker, but until we have more to go on, it's just curious. Get me more, Lee, and we'll see."

Lee continued his whining, "More? I give you this, you say it's not enough, and then you want more. Where in hell am I going to get more? From that stranger? Right. You know that ain't gonna happen. You've never even had something this serious before. And I gotta ask you this, what's your beef with Stamm anyway? He's just your run-of-the-mill huckster selling his own brand of snake oil to the believers. You know Bennie, there are bigger fish to fry. Let it go."

While Lee could be lackadaisical, he was able to parlay his street smarts and intelligence, plus a natural writing ability, to gain an internship at a local newspaper, launching his career. It was only when Lee set his mind to something that he was driven to come up with a solution. However, while Edward Benton was counting on this, Lee was in snooze mode. It was going to take something to get him off his ass.

"Yeah, I know, Lee, you're right, you're right. But I'm not alone in wanting to take this fucker down. I just don't like him or his ilk. Yeah, this letter is odd, but it's not enough. It could be the beginning of a much larger story, but we're going to need more. It only hints at something. Stamm alone will be a shit storm to deal with but throw in Justice and man, I'm going to need some heavy-duty cover, and let's face it, True North doesn't have the budget much less the credibility to run with it. It's got the balls, we know that. No, I'm going to need more, much more. I got to find a way to get to Stamm."

Benton was intrigued by the letter but stymied. Stamm represented to him everything that was wrong about organized religion. While Bennie himself wasn't particularly religious, he didn't like seeing people taken advantage of in their beliefs, religious or otherwise. To him, Stamm was the embodiment of the crass commercialism and opportunism accepted by many as religion today. How could anyone he thought keep the faith when this was how it was portrayed? In no way could Stamm be the righteous person he had cast himself as. What was he hiding?

While the letter might be real, it didn't move the needle. Bennie was not thrilled about this. Just as he was going to power off his computer, the screen went black, and all the office lights went off. It was curiously dark, in more ways than one in the newsroom for early morning.

"Damn it, not again! This shithole is going to hell. I thought they fixed those power surges a few months ago."

Reporters didn't need much to bitch about and this was just more of the same. As the lights and computers lit back up in the newsroom, reports started trickling, then cascading in about the worldwide moment of unexplained darkness. A few of the more sarcastic writers credited it to the current administration succeeding in now keeping everyone completely in the dark. But it was tinged with a little fear and uncertainty. Incoming reports did nothing to assuage that, instead creating a larger foundation for it to fester and grow.

None of the news operations could get out of their own way, stumbling simultaneously over their feet to be the first with the latest updates on what was yet a tabla rasa. It happened and that was it, no further details. The apparently worldwide "flicker" or "blink" as it was being called had not repeated itself nor had anything occurred as a result other than the hyped-up hysteria generated by the networks hungry for ad revenue.

However, it did create an enormous amount of speculation. Each group had its own idea of what had happened and its meaning. Politicians saw threats from enemies, real and imagined. Theologians saw the hand of God in it.

And the media saw dollars and lots of them. If this had been a trial, the media would be considered accessory number one. Complicit in fanning the flames, it behooved them to sensationalize the occurrences, not that any help was needed. It would only get worse.

Not unexpectedly, there were calls from multiple congressmen for investigations. Fingers were pointed at the CIA, FBI, and any other acronym-labeled agency. Some less well-hinged members saw it as a plot by the opposition party to further their climate change hoax agenda. Cooler, clearer thinkers acceded to those in the scientific community to explain it if they could. Others saw it as the end of the world and partied as such. Liquor sales grew.

The scientific community, a 'coven' as one god-fearing, mid-western congressman had labeled it, was not any more enlightened. Theories abounded and that's all they were with no understanding of the phenomenon before them. Opinions were based on nothing and consequently worthless. But scientists, like politicians, craved their fifteen minutes of fame. Whether they were truly informed or not, the news networks were happy to oblige and use them. Who knew if one of them might be right? Besides, there was a lot of time to fill and sell.

As might be expected, the new agers started forming groups to greet and honor the coming new era. The "flicker" was, for them, proof that it had begun. All that remained for them was to watch, smoke their weed, and listen to their crystals for more signs. Get out your tie-dyes, the sixties were back!

Various religious groups had taken disparate positions ranging from Armageddon to the rapture to the second coming to the devil making an appearance at the rapture. The only one not blamed for it was Elvis, but it was still early. They were all wrong and they were all right, just not about what they were thinking.

Chapter 6

Dedham, MA

Adam pushed an old R.E.M. CD into the player, adjusted the loose rear-view mirror, and pulled the car out onto the road. Since it was early Sunday and traffic was light on Route 128, dubbed somewhat self-consciously "America's Technology Highway", he unleashed his aging black Saab 900 Turbo on the highway making the drive from Lexington to the Dedham lab in near record time. Appreciating the fact that the car's manufacturer had once made jet planes before it ventured into automobiles, the Saab fit his personality well: quirky and individualist, not unusual traits for a scientist. He would keep it for as long as he could find parts and someone willing to work on it.

As he approached the gate of the research facility, he noticed he wasn't the only one coming into work. Usually, there might be only two or three cars on a Sunday and that was almost always security. Today was different, there were easily two dozen cars in the lot. Fran must have called a lot of people.

Waving through the security gate, he backed into his reserved parking spot. Adam thought once again how ridiculous the idea of a personal parking spot was. It was merely an indication of the value and importance Aura/Sonos assigned to him. He felt otherwise, believing no greater importance on him than other staff members. The hierarchy of the center meant nothing to him, which at times had him irritating the greater powers. Still, he did like the closer proximity of the spot, especially in bad weather.

Swiping his ID badge at the door gained him admittance to the main building on campus. As he passed through the large atrium and across the quad, finally arriving at the main lab, he again marveled at how quickly the company had grown. It was certainly on its way before he arrived, but the work he and the staff were doing was ground-breaking.

Funded in part by grants, both private and a couple of small but meaningful governmental ones, making it a hard organization to categorize. It was the brainchild of Peter Easton who still maintained control over it, fending off those who saw it as a desirable target for a takeover. He started it with his own money and a couple of small angels, but even that began to run thin as the company grew and demanded more to sustain it. A breakthrough would be necessary to maintain Easton's control.

As he entered his office, Adam saw Fran Porter in an adjoining lab adjusting a set of headphones, fine-tuning the amplification on a spectroradiometer coupled to a light-to-sound converter to manifest data into soundwaves. Adam smiled. If there was anyone who didn't need headphones, it was Fran Porter. Her senses had become much more acute since becoming nearly blind as an adolescent. While Fran couldn't give you an actual numerical value of a sensory event, she could almost always detect it. She was nearly canine in her abilities. But since this was an event involving light, she had it converted to register as sound.

Adam never knocked on her lab door before entering. Deaf or not, he knew that would be useless with Fran listening so intently on the headphones. Besides, Fran would sense he was there before the door even opened.

As Adam approached, she looked up and had this happy but quizzical look on her face, a sort of goofy 'this is really cool but damned if I know what the hell it is' expression. If history were any indication, she would know what to make of it before long.

He rattled off a stream of questions to her. "OK, Fran, what's going on? Why are there so many here? What did you mean when you said the light went out? And purple? That's a new color for you. Any significance?"

Fran knew Adam would always comment on new hair color, but her head was elsewhere. "Jeez. That's what you want to talk about? Yeah, OK, it's new, but Adam, the light…! I don't know where to start. This is unheard of, unseen, unwritten, un-everything, who the hell knows... oh, fuck, it's just that, the light went out. Everywhere! Here, Russia, Japan, Australia, everywhere."

Adam was still at a loss. "Hey, slow down. What do you mean? You're not making any sense."

"Adam Faraday, listen to me. All light went out. All of it! OK? Got it? The whole friggin' world went dark. No light, everywhere, nothing. It was just for a split second, but it happened. Reports are starting to come in from all over. No light! People couldn't see a fucking thing. It's as if the whole world went blind! Can't see a thing! Nada, zip, zed, zero, nothing! And where were you? You're telling me you didn't see it?"

He shrugged, "No, I didn't. When?"

She toggled a sound time check and told him probably an hour or so earlier.

Thinking back, he realized he'd slept right through it, missing light's disappearance. What the hell?

"No, I can't say I've ever seen anything like this," Adam spoke into the phone, a tinge of excitement in his voice.

"Fran had a spectroradiometer that happened to be turned on during the event. It wasn't calibrated for anything special, but it recorded pretty much what everyone saw, but nothing that would explain it. The light went off and then it came back on.

"Well yeah, Fran's on it. Interestingly though, she said she felt it before it registered with her. But that doesn't really surprise me as Fran is dialed into the world differently than the rest of us. Yeah, she is a freak, purple hair, yeah, that's her new color, but I wouldn't trade her for anything.

"No, I didn't see it myself. Yeah, OK, Peter, I'll tell her that and we'll keep on it and let you know what we find. But I got to tell you, it was so damn fast, there wasn't anything to look for, especially since it was unexpected. Fran's working on maybe recalibrating a spectrometer to better record it if it happens again. No, I don't know if it will tell us anything though. Yeah, thanks. Talk with you soon."

Looking at Fran's lop-sided smirk, he hung up the phone and turned to her. Adam grinned, something rare these days, "Well, aside from asking about your new hair color, Peter agrees with me, you're a freak! But he's a big fan, OK? Now it's out, there's no hiding it any longer, we all love you."

Fran smiled back, "Finally, it's about time you're getting around to admitting it."

She thought that Adam joining Aura/Sonos was one of the smartest moves both Peter and Adam could have made. Adam Faraday's sharp analytical and intuitive mind coupled with Fran Porter's highly honed senses made for quite a formidable and unique team. That they got along so well was an added benefit.

"So, tell me. How did you know this happened? Are you telling me you're beginning to see the light?"

Fran groaned. She wasn't sensitive about her blindness any longer, but it was an old joke.

"Too soon?" Adam asked.

"No, and yes, sort of. And not original either. When the light went out, I swear I felt the air get just a little cooler for the briefest time. I didn't give it any thought until the equipment registered the light going out at the same time and everyone went batshit about it. Since all light has temperature, I realized, well, felt it, that the lights had gone out. What I didn't know until a little bit later was that it wasn't just our lights that went out, but light everywhere. That's why it had more of a temperature change than just our lights. That's one very scary premise, you know?" Fran offered.

"Oh, and one other strange thing. An odd tingle, brief, like I felt a little buzz, a frisson, all over me." Sensing Adam would make a joke about that, was he coming out of his self-imposed humor exile, laughed. "No, and not that kind of buzz!"

"Wait. A frisson, you say? That's a sophisticated word you got there, Fran."

She turned around in her chair and responded theatrically, "Really? That's where you going to go?"

"Oh, OK. Look, you know Peter's all over this. He wants to know everything we know. Any thoughts on what we can do going forward?"

"Listen Adam, everyone's in the same place on this as we are, but we're better equipped. I'll call up a friend of mine at NASA and see if they noticed any anomalies on this. The other thing that just came to mind is I wonder if anyone has recorded any strange animal behaviors because of this. You know like how animals can sense an earthquake before it happens. Is it interrupting their nocturnal cycles? That sort of thing, you know? This is just so weird."

"Nah, this is a phenomenon, Fran, a frisson is weird."

Fran thought to herself, 'He's making jokes. That's progress.'

Chapter 7

Annapolis, MD

Usually, after a particularly rousing show, the reverend would do a meet and greet with several members of the audience singled out, the overriding parameter of importance being how large were their contributions. Using a sophisticated facial recognition program in the entryways, the staff, using earbuds, was able to identify those selected for this honor. But Jonah was not going to indulge in that today. He smiled at everyone as he bulled past staff and congregants, determined to get to his office quickly, marshaling his energies to get in front of the light situation.

He entered his office, sat down in an oversized leather desk chair, and bellowed, "Sheila, have you seen this? Get me any stories about this now! We need to get in front of this and make it ours! Now! Quickly, please."

Stamm was always ready to capitalize on any phenomenon that could be attributed to his god's displeasure or whimsy. He was convinced he had at least made a good start on owning this one with his sermon. Knowing the media would be looking for an 'authority', he was determined that he be the one they turned to.

Physically, Stamm was unremarkable save for his bright, blond hair (chemically enhanced for the TV audience), florid complexion, and a 'voice of God' delivery of sermons. His voice was such that he was once approached once to do the narration for a biblical TV series but declined when he discovered they, not him, would write the script. Of average height, he was very thin which his expensive tailors successfully concealed with clever designs and small patterns, making him appear athletic rather than sickly.

Before becoming the television equivalent of sausage (you didn't want to know what was in it), Jonah had a much different career, one not having been planned as a launchpad for his current persona. After graduating college with a law degree, he spent close to thirty years in government service, first as a public defender, then as a state prosecuting attorney gradually ascending to the position of state's attorney general. His political connections coaxed him to run for a congressional seat that he had won handily. Stamm had done well for himself and quickly.

At his core, a good and well-meaning man and nearly religious, he fell prey to the extravagances thrown at him by lobbyists. He naively believed it was one of the perks of the job. It had to be as if everyone was doing it. It would be the genesis of his fall.

Stamm could be a demanding yet not heartless employer and Sheila Weller, his assistant, was appreciative of that. When her daughter Olivia contracted leukemia, Stamm provided the resources necessary to ensure the best care possible. She was grateful for that and would easily suffer his constant requests. After all, and unknown to the public, Olivia was his daughter too. For that, she had mixed emotions: pure love for the girl, and some regrets about how she was conceived.

Like many other inner-city teenagers who had gotten themselves into drug difficulties and sought help, 'salvation' as Stamm would describe it, they could find it in Jonah's then inner-city church. Petite and pretty with startlingly green eyes, she had been taken advantage of by too many boys in the 'hood. She was also the unfortunate victim of her parent's poor choices, mostly drugs, and petty theft. Was it any wonder that she would fall into that life as well? She knew there had to be a better way for her. Jonah's church was the first step.

He took her in, got her straight and off drugs, and into believing in Jesus, exchanging one addiction for another. While his heart was in the right place, another part of his anatomy had other ideas. When Stamm saw how bright she was, he happily subsidized her education. They worked closely together until like so many before him, he succumbed to his weaknesses and the attraction of a younger woman. He was gentle in his pursuit. Sheila was not accustomed to attention from men in this way and gave in with little resistance. She felt obliged to the Reverend for all he had done for her. Maybe even love, but hardly reciprocated, and never in public. Yet there was still something of the old plantation master relationship about it that was lurking in the back of her mind. It wasn't that unpleasant, and this was, after all, a different time, wasn't it?

Had his flock ever found out about his affair with Sheila as a teenager and an African/American at that, the subsequent loss of revenue and shame would crush his aspirations. In that, he was no different from the politicians he so often counseled and cursed. The goals may indeed have been honorable if only his ego and libido didn't get in the way.

Ever responsive, Sheila asked, "Jonah, do you want them printed out or should I create an e-file for them all so you can access them anytime? I can also set up a Google alert where you'll receive a daily update on any further stories. Will that work for you?"

Sheila Weller was not the 'practicing Luddite' Jonah Stamm was. He relied on her more than anyone. She knew her way around computers better than most, courtesy of his "generosity".

He habitually wanted documents he could hold and if necessary, wave around for theatrical effect. "Sheila, darlin', would you do both? I'll take the paper copies if you can keep the electronic stuff. Oh, and please forgive me for shouting. I just want to get on top of this as fast as possible."

"And one other thing, please make a note to call Carlton Justice's office on Wednesday to see if we can have lunch, would you please?" Stamm knew what the answer would be, wanting him to stew with the letter for a few days, waiting for the inevitable other shoe to drop. And drop it would, big time. But he was certain he would hear from Justice well before then.

The articles Stamm had Sheila searching for would be his 'evidence' in whichever way he chose to use them. He believed if the Bible was subject to various interpretations, so too were heresies.

While not a man of science, he followed as many consumer-level science magazines to keep abreast of what the 'enemy' was propagating. He wasn't particular about the source of any information he received. After all, to some the Bible was hearsay. Suspending disbelief was a cornerstone of religion. Discernment had no place in his research, and he was not above using any of this knowledge for personal gain. Of course, any similarity to the written word was purely coincidental and unintentional. If it happened to jibe with science, he used it to establish credibility. If he disagreed with it, he could point to those rare areas where they were in sync and claim impartiality. Jonah saw this as a pure win-win situation. It served him well in the past and he expected it to continue.

Sheila printed out the few pieces she could find on the net, all speculative, and handed them to Stamm. He was not surprised as it was only hours or so since the 'event.' He wasn't above using that speculation to make his arguments, more than willing to backtrack on a position if he believed it made him appear thoughtful and reasonable, two qualities that his opponent energetically disputed. They should know better. Stamm was convinced his facade was one unlikely to be cracked.

That artifice did have a few faults in it, his clandestine affair with Sheila being one of them. Another is the obscene amount of money his 'church' took in, both in domestic and undocumented offshore accounts. Concealing these was no easy feat. Money laundering, even when done well, could ultimately be traced back to the source. If the affair and his finances were discovered, it would crash his whole house of cards. And there was one more element hidden very deeply, that if discovered would have distressed his base: he had a liberal social conscience and it had been borne out of the experience.

Raised in a small Alabama town like that of Carlton Justice's, his exposure to anything beyond dyed-in-the-wool conservatism would have not presaged his turn to what his family, neighbors, and friends would consider the 'dark side.' While his faith proclaimed love for all,

38

it was a beating a little black boy had endured by Jonah's schoolmates that changed him forever. They and their families, being God-fearing people, proclaimed love for everyone, but their actions demonstrated otherwise. Out of genuine pity, Jonah befriended the boy, learning much about a culture few in his town understood or cared about, and became a very private champion for civil rights, anonymously donating significant sums to minority groups, under the guise of being a good Christian. He had plans and they all rode on his ability to play his adopted role. If it became necessary to reveal that side of him, he'd make sure the media portrayed him as favorably as possible.

"Sheila, could you come over here please?" he asked.

"I seem to remember," Stamm had a nearly encyclopedic recall, "that you went to school with a young man who's now a reporter, what was his name? Larry? No, that's not it. Lee? Yes, that's it, I'm sure."

Sheila Weller was constantly amazed at how much the reverend remembered from the smallest of casual conversations. So, while this random question didn't surprise her, his recall of Lee's name did. "Yes, we did Jonah, but I haven't spoken with him in some time. The last I heard he was working for some online newsgroup, True North News I think, and he was a copy editor, not a reporter."

"Well, Sheila, maybe he's been promoted. How would you feel about maybe reaching out to him, to see how he's doing, and maybe if he'd be interested in discussing with me his views on this light thing that just happened? Be an angel and do that for me, please?"

Sheila would walk through Hell and back for the reverend, never once forgetting what he had done for her. While she was a bit uncomfortable in calling Lee Black unexpectedly, it was no big thing. She hadn't any idea why Stamm wanted to talk with Lee instead of someone else, but she would make it happen.

Going online, she looked up True North News, found the main number, and called it. It like so many companies and organizations, had an automated operator. She listened to the options, waited for the employee directory, got to Lee's name and extension, and punched in the numbers. It rang five times and was answered, "Black here."

Pursing her lips and holding her breath, she finally spoke, "Lee? It's me, Sheila, Sheila Weller."

Chapter 8

Cambridge, MA

Moderna. Biogen. Pfizer. That's just a few of the cutting-edge companies that called this place home. Include Harvard University, M.I.T., and there was no place quite as fertile as Massachusetts. It was to biotech what Silicon Valley was to computing. Perhaps a little more buttoned-up, but no less influential.

Ground zero for research companies was Cambridge. Some were start-ups funded by wily entrepreneurs, others were necessary offshoots from larger companies whose bureaucracy prevented quick pivoting, and then there were some like Aura/Sonos, founded on a real need and a quest for discoveries, pushing the boundaries of science to improve lives. It was created by Peter Easton, putting his studies aside one night to go drinking, an evening that would alter his life.

Looking back at how far he'd come in such a relatively short period of time, he wondered how much longer he'd be this content. Once again, he thought of Anna and how she had helped put him there. 'There' was a place he never imagined he'd be. Decisions made years ago had their rewards and consequences.

In the unofficial hierarchy of science wunderkinder, Peter Easton was old, if one could consider forty-three old. Born into a lower-middle-class family in Oakland, California, he had learned what the mean streets meant, and he meant to get off them as quickly as he could.

Showing an unusual aptitude for quick yet meaningful analysis and an ever-questioning intellect, his teachers pushed him into whatever science classes were available at the time. Peter found them, like sports, to be too easy, bordering on boring. Yet he felt there had to be more than met his eyes. His grades were among the top in his school and since he was not from a well-to-do family, became eligible for scholarships. Wanting to get as far away as possible from Oakland, he accepted a scholarship to M.I.T. It was there for the first time in his life, he was challenged and loved it.

One evening during his senior year, his roommate Tom, a blond jock out of a B-grade surfer movie, had badgered him to leave the books behind and go out drinking. Peter not surprisingly was ahead on his work and agreed, feeling he deserved a little downtime. He also knew that meant his roommate wanted to go trawling for women. Women were the furthest thing from Peter's mind. But it was always entertaining to see how many times Tom would get shot down.

They wound up in a little dive bar close to the school, favored by students and teachers alike. It has been joked that the teachers went there to pick up students and the students went there to pick up their grades in genuine symbiotic relationships. True to some degree, it was the intellectual challenge fueled by booze, youthful enthusiasm, and awakening wisdom that brought everyone together. More than a few times, discussions had become overheated to the point where the participants had to be separated. And who said intellectuals were no fun?

It was during one of those rapidly escalating exchanges that one of the combatants caught Peter's eye. First, it was because she was quite pretty, striking really. Secondly and more interesting, she wasn't participating in any of her friend's vices: no smoking or drinking. That set her apart immediately. Arguing loudly and passionately, vehemently even, she was a force of nature, emphatically making her points. The men in the group were all attracted to her but couldn't keep up. The other women in the group simultaneously resented and cheered her on, but no one cut her any more slack than she did them.

Peter was smitten. Reaching over to his roommate and in a not-so-quiet voice to be heard over the general din of the bar, he calls, "Tom! Hey, Tom! Who is that? The one with the dark brown hair? And who is she with?"

Tom looked back at Peter with a boozy, shit-eating grin waved his beer around, and laughed, "Petey boy, that's Anna Barth and she's out of your league. So, way out of your league, man!"

"Probably, maybe, but look at her! She's taking it to everyone in that group! Do you know her? Can you introduce me?"

Tom laughed again, "Sure, but be careful. I don't want to lose a roommate. Greater men have tried and all that, y'know?"

Peter stared at Tom for a moment and shouted, "Shot you down too, huh? No surprise. I'm going over! Coming?"

And that was over twenty years ago. It was Anna who led him to change his course of study from biology to an entirely new direction: sensory development. Growing up with a deaf father, she had shown him that a disability such as deafness did not have to prevent one from living a full life. He had become fascinated by how well her father was able to navigate life despite his disability. It made him only sharper. That opened Peter's eyes. He began to wonder what other natural resources humans might possess. It was well known that the body could compensate for the loss of a sense, but might the other senses be developed further? Could they? Yes, he learned, and ultimately, Peter Easton became the go-to expert in this field, all because of drinks that night. And it led eventually to one of the happiest moments in his life, his marriage to Anna Barth.

And that had led to this – Aura/Sonos – and now his wondering what had happened to the light.

If his plans back then were for him to have been at the forefront of sensory research, he would never have imagined it would be something like this. But then, it was beyond all imagination. Would there be a hero? If so, who would be the villain? Would there be a resolution? What would they find?

Chapter 9

Baltimore, MD

It didn't take long before the media started with wholly unfounded but sensational speculation on the phenomenon. More respectable papers such as the *New York Times* and the *Wall Street Journal* covered it responsibly. London's *Daily Mail* had a headline of "LIGHTS OUT!?" The *New York Daily News* not to be undone, similarly reported "CON ED SUCKS THE BIG ONE!" *The New York Post* typically weighed in with their expected political jibe, "DEMS HOLD LIGHT HOSTAGE, DEMAND EQUAL TIME FOR DARKNESS!" *USA Today* had a large story about it but shared it on the front page with a story of a football player's latest infidelity. Supermarket tabloids attributed it to space aliens or JFK returning to earth. Cable channels and online news outlets realized they now had their next twenty-four-hour news cycle for which they would spend the next ten days reporting. The talking heads were lining up all the 'experts' they could find. Not surprisingly, there weren't any, which didn't prevent them from creating their own.

All the televisions in the newsroom were turned to various channels. Everyone had dropped their work staring in visual captivity as Benton liked to describe it. But he too was transfixed. This had taken his attention away from Jonah Stamm and the letter. The feeding frenzy that the media had whipped itself into pissed him off. While he was of the new breed of journalists, online and typically more interested in immediacy than facts, he still tried to hold to the tenets of responsible reporting and getting the facts before writing about something. Anything else was speculation, opinion, or bullshit, and identified as such.

Of further interest to him were the crazies starting to come out from under their rocks. Leave it to the strange to worship the even more

44

strange. If nothing else, it would be entertaining. But there might be a real story here to occupy him until he learned more about that damned letter. It still bothered him. He didn't want to get off track with the letter and its possible implications. Though this light thing, this "flicker" intrigued him, just like everyone else, realizing he might have an angle into Stamm after all and was now counting on it.

In his eyes, Stamm was a self-aggrandizing SOB of the first order. Bennie figured, correctly, he'd look to appropriate the "flicker" as a sign that supposedly he and only he understood. The fearful were out there looking for something and he'd be more than happy to give it to them. All Bennie had to do was get that first interview and ask the right questions. Gaining the preacher's trust, he could start to dig deeper into the mystery behind the letter. Stamm's ego would feed on the attention, welcome, and demand it like a junkie jonesing for a fix.

Bennie, turned to his copy editor, waving his hand above the cubicle's wall in the cheaply and sparsely furnished offices of True North, "Lee?! Yo! Weren't you friends with Stamm's assistant one time? Whatshername? Shelley? No, no, something like that? Are you? Do you know how to get in touch with her?"

Bennie's question broke Lee's attention from watching YouTube cat videos.

"Huh? What's up, Bennie? Shelley? No, Sheila. And hold it, you want me to reach out to her? If you remember, I told you we sort of lost touch after she went to work for Stamm.

"We're from the same shitty neighborhood. The difference is I got out of the hood before Sheila, who had a few rounds of hard knocks before she could get out herself."

Bennie smiled at Lee. "Oh, yeah, I remember. Look, do you think she could grease the skids so I can get in to meet him? From what we know of Stamm, he'll jump at a series of exclusive one-on-one interviews, right? But he isn't taking any of my calls. Or at least he hasn't shown any inclination to. Hell, maybe he doesn't take anyone's calls. I was thinking that if you spoke with Sheila, you know, old times sakes, the hood, and all that happy horseshit, she might be able to get me in. It's worth a shot, right?"

Lee looked at Bennie, grumbling to himself 'it's probably you, he doesn't want to talk with' before he shook his head in disbelief and muttered his acknowledgment of the request.

After more of this, he figured that they'll either promote him or he'll move on. It was his time to hand out crap instead of taking it from some reporter.

"What?" Lee Black didn't like surprises and this phone call was certainly that. "Sheila? Really? Uh..." He wondered about the coincidence of his planned call and Sheila beating him to the punch.

"Yeah, Lee, I know. It's been too long. I'm so sorry. I didn't mean to fall out of touch, but the Reverend's got me so busy and, well, I know that's no excuse. But I like the work, I really do. Jonah is unbelievable. He's helped me and taught me so much; I don't know where I'd be without him."

Sheila quickly became aware of how she must have sounded. "Look, I'm sorry, Lee, how are you? How's the writing going?"

"Not so fast, Sheila. Jonah, is it? Anything I should know?" He was wary.

"Look, I am glad to hear from you, really, I am. But why after all this time? Are you in trouble?"

"No, Lee, not at all. In fact, I've got a favor to ask of you. You're still a reporter, right?"

Lee exhaled, tapping a pen on his desk. "If only. No, not yet. The powers that be at True North haven't seen the value of my journalistic skills. I'm still the same lowly copy editor I've been for the past four years. You said you have a favor to ask of me. That's funny because I was going to call you. What's up?"

46

"I'm sure you're aware that the reverend doesn't do many exclusive interviews. He's very suspicious of them, having been victimized in the past by what he calls laptop assassins. But he asked me to call you to see if you'd be interested in doing an interview with him. Exclusive, only you. Could you do that? Would you?"

She paused, uncomfortable with the conversation and Stamm's request. "Lee, it's not like Reverend Stamm to ask a favor like this from me, but I owe him, and this doesn't seem to be a big deal." Changing her tone, she continued, "Are you interested because if you're not..." Sheila had changed, she had grown up.

Lee frowned at the phone, thinking he might be being played, "Wait, slow down a minute Sheila. No need to play hardball, not with me. You haven't given me a chance to answer. I can't do the interview, I told you I'm not a reporter, at least as far as True North is concerned. But I can hook you up. With an assassin, if you'd like.

"Listen, how's this for weird? Remember I mentioned I was going to call you? Edward Benton, Bennie, one of our reporters asked if I was still in touch with you and if I was, could I call you. Weird, huh? Anyway, he wants to see if he can get an interview with your boss. Can you believe that? He's tried in the past but had no luck. Would the reverend meet with him instead?"

Sheila was hoping she would be able to get Lee to do this but saw that that part was out of her hands. "Let me check with Jonah. I know your friend has tried to reach him before, but I think he may be one of those assassins Jonah talks about. If he's good with it, how soon do you think we could set it up? He's excited about something and wants to talk about it. Can you talk to Bennie and see if they could meet?"

Lee Black was astounded. What were the odds of this? If there was a God, he had a sense of humor. If he could get Bennie to give him part of the back story he could write, he could show the editor what he was capable of and get out of the dead-end copy desk.

"Sheila, yeah, OK, I'm on it. Let me speak to him." At that moment, his cell rang. Looking at the caller ID number and recognizing it, Lee asked Sheila to hold on a moment as he took the call, quickly asking, "This a number I can call you back on? Yeah, good, I will call. Thanks."

Putting the cell phone back in his jacket, he turned back to Sheila's call, "I gotta go. I'll talk to Bennie and get back to you. It was good to see you again. Let's not wait so long next time, OK?"

He sat there for a few moments thinking about the conversation he just had. Sheila Weller was from his past and now was in his present and he liked that.

"Bennie, it's Lee, you won't believe what just happened. You ready for this?"

Chapter 10

Washington, DC

After Congressman Justice had cleaned the vomit off himself and his desk, the stench still lingering in the air, he sat down to work out his next move. That Stamm had gotten hold of this information infuriated him. If word of this leaked, retribution would be bipartisan in its effect and swift in administration. Ranking members of both parties would be taken down, Justice included. Tar and feathering would be preferable to what would happen as a result. He wondered who spilled it and how much of it was already known. The congressman had several phone calls to be made, quickly, discreetly, and on a private line.

Once the contents of the letter were known, it would be easy for certain parties, sensing blood in the water, to declare war on him. A few news outlets would have a field day with it. Journalistic careers had been made on less. Justice would have to act fast in reaching the others. If any action was required, they were going to have to enlist a particularly powerful if odious K Street resource held on retainer. He would have preferred not to but surmised correctly that that decision was not his alone to make. The rest of this group would determine that for which he was grateful. It would be a lot more than circling the wagons and holding off invading hordes. It would border on an almost full-frontal attack with no guarantee it would even work or stem the inevitably rising tide against them.

The congressman closed himself off in the small, private coat closet off his office, wiped the increasing sweat from his face, and made the first of the calls on one of the several disposable cell phones he kept for situations such as this.

"Yes, it's me. I think we need to meet. When?... Now! Tonight, if possible. I just received a letter from Jonah Stamm and he's putting

49

together the pieces. No, I don't know why he decided to do this now. I haven't spoken to him and he's not taking my calls. I thought we should all gather first to determine what our course of action should be. Believe me, I'm not exaggerating. This is serious.

"OK, agreed." He listened, biting his lip, as the voice on the other end spoke. "Yes, I'll make the calls on this side of the aisle, can you make the others? I think pretty much everyone's in town. Yes, that works. At his house? Will you call him? Good."

Carlton Justice felt better now that he'd taken some action. He knew he'd have to respond to Stamm but had no idea what to say. Did Jonah want out? Was he going to blow it all up? Why now? Ultimately, what did he want? He wasn't to have the luxury of figuring it out as the regular office phone started ringing.

If he answered the phone himself, he might never escape. Shouting for one of his aides to start answering the phone, he instructed him to say that the congressman was unavailable. He would decide later which calls to respond to and which to ignore.

Finished with his private calls, Carlton left the small closet, calling to his aide, "Trey, get in here. Would you please get Reverend Stamm on the phone? Thanks."

He had reacted just as Stamm expected but without the possibility of reaching him until Jonah was ready to talk. Justice would try his damnedest to get an idea of what Stamm wanted before the evening's meeting. Just as his aide left the office, one of his disposable phones rang.

Annoyed about receiving an unanticipated call on it, he answered it gruffly, "What? We're on? As planned? Yes. Good, good. See you then. Wait. Have you heard anything about this thing with the lights? Yeah, funny. I'm in the dark too." Justice put down the phone and tried to figure out what was Stamm's play. Justice and Stamm could have been crib-mates, almost always knowing what the other's next move would be. While he could count on Stamm for support when he needed it, he never lost the feeling, a mutual one, that Jonah was not to be trusted. The damned letter certainly indicated that.

On several occasions, he tried to dig into Stamm's past. Besides their little 'joint venture', he couldn't find anything he didn't already know. The man appeared to be as he portrayed himself, but Justice knew everyone had a closet in which their dirty little secrets were hidden. Everything had been verified multiple times about the reverend's past. He did appear to be the man of God as he professed. Yet, like running a hand over a seemingly smooth sanded piece of wood, there was an unseen splinter that one could not see but felt. Carlton Justice felt but couldn't find that splinter and would not stop trying.

For now, he had to prepare for the meeting. Whatever was behind Stamm's change of attitude scared the hell out of him. As carefully crafted was Jonah Stamm's past, so were the facades hiding Carlton Justice's activities. Were they to come to light, the repercussions would be devastating. Both required enormous opacity and worked endlessly to sustain it. So why the letter?

No less than three senators and eight congresspeople were parties to this and they wouldn't go gently into that or any good night. Whatever damage they might cause with their hidden agenda was nothing compared to the havoc it would wreak should any of it be revealed.

This meeting tonight would determine their next course of action. While all were on board for the general plan, there were still a couple who had reservations. The first order would be to calm down the nervous ones though they had the right to be concerned.

"Sir? I've tried to reach Reverend Stamm, but he was unavailable. Should I keep trying?" asked his aide Trey, exhibiting the practiced 'concerned' look his peers had utilized with good effect.

Justice looked up from the report he was reading, "Unavailable my ass. No, Trey, don't bother. I'm sure we'll hear from him in his own sweet time. Look, it's Sunday, you don't need to be here anymore than I do. Why don't you take the rest of the day off, I'll be leaving right behind you, and I'll lock up. OK? Thanks. See you tomorrow then. We've got that bill sponsorship to deal with."

But Congressman Carlton Justice had no intention of going home early as he usually did on Sundays. It was now getting past Noon and a sandwich, and a drink sounded good to him. There was a bar he frequented that poured some fine bourbon in walking distance from his office. He intended to be fortified for the coming meeting.

Approaching the bar, he cursed it being closed, its lights dark. It should have come as no surprise since it was Sunday and the places that catered to those in government often were closed. The weather was mild so he decided to walk a bit and see if he could find another place to satisfy his immediate needs. Within two blocks he found, tucked between two non-descript but probably high-priced law offices, a small bar with a chalkboard outside advertising their specialty, Italian roast beef sandwiches. That would fill the bill perfectly. It would also turn out they poured his drink of choice. He just might have to switch his drinking habits to this place since they were considerate enough to be open in his hour of need.

He entered the dimly lit bar, noting that there weren't many people in the place, mostly seated at tables. Rather than seem out of place as a solitary man at a table, he took a chair at the bar, closer to the booze. He nodded at the tall and muscular, very bald African-American bartender polishing some glasses. He stopped and came over. "So how are you today, Congressman?"

Justice was caught off guard, expecting anonymity in this place. "Do I know you? Have we met before?"

The bartender smiled, "No sir, but I make it a practice to know who our duly elected officials are. I want to know whom I'm employing. I'm Goldie by the way. So, Congressman, what'll it be?"

"Really? Goldie, is it? Hmph, Goldie. Excuse me but I don't get the name."

The large man laughed warmly, "Yeah, I understand that. Last name is Goldberg. Yeah, I know. Mom was black. Dad's a Jew. A liberal kind of thing, you know?"

"Works for me. Well, it says Italian roast beef is your specialty. I'll have that, Goldie."

"Good choice, sir. Anything to drink with that?"

"I couldn't help but notice you got some Pappy's up there," gesturing at the shelves behind the bar, "and the twenty-three-year-old at that. Not too many places carry that, hell, much less afford it. You have saved my life, Goldie. I see this as the start of a beautiful friendship. Pour me one of those."

"'nother good choice Congressman. I'll get you that Pappy now and your food will be out shortly. Welcome to Pozzi's." Goldie poured the drink, setting it down on a napkin on the bar, before walking back to the kitchen with the congressman's order.

Justice took the first sip of the bourbon and let its smooth heat run down his throat. And took another sip as an affirmation of its quality. Smiling to himself, he thought if only life could be this simple, a good lunch, a better bourbon, and nothing to do at least until the evening.

Goldie returned to the bar, "How's that bourbon, Congressman?"

"Mother's milk and I'm not ready to be weaned yet. Pour me another, would you? Goldie, how come you're open when a lot of the other places are closed? Not that I mind, I'm glad I wandered in here. My staff doesn't know about it and," and winking conspiratorially, continued, "maybe I can hide here, when necessary, you know? But who does come in here?"

Goldie smiled at the congressman. "The original owner was an immigrant who was grateful for the opportunity this country gave him. He wanted to extend the same, so he'd stayed open all week, Now, so do we." He poured Justice the second bourbon, this one more generously.

"In answer to your other question. Well, I can't say if I know that your staff comes in, I don't think I know them, but a lot of legislative staffers, regulars y'know, come here after work. It's like the internet but with alcohol and a little screwing around. It's a good crowd, respectful, hopeful, and mostly a little naive."

"Yeah, I get that. I seem to remember a long time ago being the same way. But life, this city, for sure changes all that. But what did you mean about the internet with alcohol?"

"Congressman, I'm sure some of the stuff one hears around here is probably not for my ears, but youth, hormones, ego, and booze loosen tongues quickly. Of course, how much is true and how much is BS is open to debate no different than the stuff you find on the net. Still...", Goldie raised his eyebrows and shrugged as the food bell rang, turning and walking towards the kitchen to retrieve his food order.

The congressman took a final pull on his first bourbon and reached for the second glass. Thinking about what Goldie had shared with him, left Congressman Carlton Justice smiling. This is what he came to Washington for... power, influence, and information. And if the food was as good as he hoped, he may have hit the trifecta: good food, great booze, and maybe some information. And then one more thought entered his mind before Goldie set the sandwich down in front of him, "Maybe coming here was no mistake. I just might be able to get the info I need to finally stop Stamm dead in his tracks."

Chapter 11

Dedham, MA

"Binary? Are you kidding me? How could that be?" Adam was surprised that Fran had found something so quickly. "What led you to that? Just a guess or you got lucky?"

She sat down and grinned at Adam while reaching around for her water bottle and bag of pizza-flavored chips. "Hah! I haven't gotten lucky in so long. I'd almost forgotten what it's like. But anyway, remember what I said and what I felt when it all went down? That the air felt cooler and there was almost a tingle, a very mild electric shock?"

"As I recall, you used the word frisson and buzz and I immediately thought you were buzzed. It wouldn't be the first time." He laughed.

Fran affected a wounded voice morphing quickly to a superior tone in response, "Yes, frisson for chrissakes. Give it a rest. But, my empirically challenged friend, you weren't there to see or feel it, and don't forget you too used to partake in your more carefree days," reminded Fran. "Not that you're not carefree these days, more like life-free. I know it's been hard since Jess died, but c'mon Adam, it's been... what?... three, four years?"

Adam liked Fran, more than almost any friend he'd had. But he also remembered how frustrating she could be when onto something. This was one of those times. And the last thing he needed, or wanted to hear, was about how he should get on with his life. He was doing just fine, was starting to do a little better, dealing with it as best as he could, and even starting to laugh again. He hadn't turned to drink, drugs, or mindless sex; on the contrary, he swore off all of them. Jess's death still held too much pain for him and too many sleepless nights to forget or indulge in such pleasures.

"OK Fran, just drop it and give me what you got on this light thing. You felt a chill and tingled. Is that about right? Sounds like you just had your first kiss." Adam could never get or stay angry with Fran and wasn't above throwing some of the same shade back at her.

"No, I'm still waiting for the first one, sir. You know how it is, a maiden saving herself for marriage. Want to be pure and unsullied when the right one comes along." They both laughed at that, knowing that Fran saving herself was a joke as she always seemed to be in rutting season.

"OK, this is what I have been able to figure out. I could be wrong and until, if, when it happens again, I still might not be able to confirm it.

"I checked the spectroradiometer, and it did record the incident, but it wasn't tuned to anything we can use. But, and here's the truly weird thing, just for smirks, I ran the recording at a slow speed, and all sorts of highs and lows appeared in the playback. And not in a linear line, but in multiples. At the speed of light, it was an incredibly brief 'burst', but in slowing it down, there appears to be a kind of texture to it. That's not that unusual in that kind of playback, but right now, it's nothing I can use. Remember, we weren't looking for anything. So, whatever we got out of it was sheer luck.

"What I'm thinking is that when this thing happens again and I believe it will, I'll have the equipment tuned to capture multiple wavelengths so it could record those. Even then, it still might be too fast. So, I'm planning to do is record it at a high-speed level. That'll result in a 'long' recording I can then convert that back to light and play it back maybe through some slow glass. I think that could show us what's going on. I got a feeling the peaks and valleys represent a binary language. But who knows? It's a starting point."

Adam looked at her with a mixture of awe, skepticism, and respect. This was the sort of stuff she was so damned good at. Give her an impossible, implausible scenario and Fran would as often as not figure out if it obeyed the known laws of physics. But Adam held a thought to himself: what if this didn't obey any of those laws?

"What? Hold on. Slow glass? I thought that was just some half-assed sci-fi theory. You really have some? Where did you get it? Or maybe I should be asking how in the hell did you get it?" 'Damn' Adam thought, 'I'm missing too much. Maybe Fran is right, but how do I get out of this swamp I'm in?'

She grinned at Adam. "Remember, I'm Peter's in-house freak. Someone gave him some to check out and he doesn't know if it works any more than they do. He gave it to me a while ago to play with, and see if it was for real, but I had no idea what to do with it. This seems as good a chance as any to see what it's all about. Maybe it'll shed some light on all of this. Ehhh, sorry for the pun. That was most definitely not intentional. Well, yeah it was."

"Peter just gave it to you, huh? What, you got some compromising photos of him?" Adam was intrigued. He was also curious as to why he didn't know of this addition to the lab's toys. Fran was about to tell him though.

"Look, we all know glass slows down light. Not by much, but it does. Supposedly, light enters this at one speed, the regular speed of light, and comes out later than it should. If that's true, we might be able to analyze it in real-time. Peter gave us a bunch of stuff, but you didn't care to look at it." She shrugged, "Who knows why?

"Look, Adam, put that aside for a minute. I'm not the only one worried about you. Peter has noticed too. When he brought you in, he knew what you'd been through but thought the work would help you. It wasn't a charity thing, far from it. God knows you're worth all he's paying you. Your work is great, but you seem stuck, you're missing some things that are going on here. Peter seems to think that if you can get yourself freed from this, oh, morass – whatever, who knows what you'd find."

"Peter has spoken to you about me. Why?"

"Hey, he's concerned. He is the boss remember? That's all. He cares about you. You should appreciate that."

He looked at Fran as if seeing her for the first time. "Fran, I'm good as I can be, I guess. No, better than that. I appreciate Peter's and your concern. And you're right...I'd been feeling stuck." She started to respond, but Adam waved her off.

"No, no, don't even go there. I've no interest in that sort of thing. So just drop it. But this light thing... it's different somehow. I am getting juiced about it. I've got a feeling it dovetails with what we do here, but I don't know how yet. Let me share something with you.

"First, I disagree with you. I don't think it's binary, it seems too organic. Binary would indicate, by our understanding, something artificial, or man-made. Secondly, we always look at things, and phenomena, through the lens of what we know. Laws of physics and all that. I don't think anyone thing or group has done anything to cause this. It's too different. Don't ask, I don't know what that means yet. It feels totally foreign and unique. And it feels independent, autonomous of anything we know and understand. Hell, we could consider looking at this as a virus that may have gone global. Something that could affect vision. The scope is enormous.

"At the same time, my gut instinct is telling me to consider looking outside of what we know and understand. I think that's the direction we should follow. But, honestly, what do we know?"

His partner looked at him, mouth hanging open. "What in hell are you saying, Adam?"

"I'm saying this may not be like anything else we've seen or known or... well, encountered. It's a first-time phenomenon. I don't know, it just feels different. You of all people should know how that feels."

Fran did know. "And?"

"And we wait. Wait and see if it happens again. You think it will, so we'll need to get something set up for that event. And wait."

For a scientist as intuitive and creative as Adam Faraday, waiting was not a strong suit. Intellectually he knew, clearly understood, that patience was indeed a virtue, the only thing being he wasn't feeling particularly virtuous. The light event had excited him more than anything he could remember. While he and Fran probably knew as much as anyone about it, he realized it was a pitifully small amount of knowledge. In the past, he turned to the one trusted sounding board whose insight, knowledge, and thoughtfulness he could rely on – his father, Michael Faraday whose own intuitive qualities were passed on to Adam. But the older Faraday possessed a unique sensibility in his understanding of how things operated. As is often the case, it came from not looking at a situation directly, but from an unexpected and oblique angle that led to surprising discoveries. Adam needed to talk to him.

Leaving Fran in the lab to work her magic, Adam made the short walk through the building to his office, closing the door behind him for privacy. Picking up the phone, he punched in the memorized number, hearing two rings before it was answered. He smiled to himself remembering his father never let a phone ring more than twice, that sense of urgency having contributed to Adam's impatience. "Hi, Adam, how are you? Calling about the light thing, right?"

Adam smiled at this response, at once damning caller ID while recognizing, though his father retired from actual work, was still actively interested in the world.

"Hi, Dad, yeah." He laughed. His father was a genuinely warm person, but when intrigued about a situation, cut right to the chase. This was one of those times. "Any thoughts?"

He envisioned his father: a tall man stooped a little in his advancing years, thinning hair and clear eyes smiling behind his wireless rim glasses while puffing on the ever-present cigar, no longer cheap ones, but now expensive Dominicans. He'd have to remember to get him a box for Christmas.

Michael Faraday took a thoughtful drag on his cigar before responding, "Hell yes, of course, but are any of them meaningful? I'll be damned if I know. You probably know more about this than I do. What do you guys have so far?"

His father was the one person whom Adam could confide in and know his theories would not be scoffed at. "Fran got some stuff that was inadvertently recorded on a spectroradiometer. It's a bunch of info, peaks, and valleys as she described it, nothing recognizable. However, she has a theory it might be binary in nature. I disagree. But she's going to try and play it back through some slow glass she was able to get her hands on."

There was a snort of laughter on the other end. "Slow glass, really? Adam, you know that stuff is all theoretical, and as much as I would love to see it real, I wouldn't place any stock in it. It's total bullshit. And binary? That would indicate a technological side. I'm skeptical of that too. Are you forgetting that light is omnidirectional? It's going all over the place unless it's directed. And the darkness that follows is the same. You might consider something viral in nature. I can't think of many avenues to go down on this. What else you got?"

He shook his head, amazed over his father's conclusion, mirroring exactly what he had thought. Comforted by this similar assessment, he was reminded that you followed whatever you could in a time like this.

"I thought of virus too. But it would have to be a new one that's never been seen before. We have some connections with the CDC in Atlanta. Perhaps they can give us something to start with. In the meantime, we're going to tune the spectroradiometer to a broader range of wavelengths in anticipation of a repeat occurrence. Hopefully, we'll be able to establish a baseline from which we can work. Got any other ideas?"

His father was quiet on the other end for a few moments. "Have you read any of the material written about from the Hubble? It's some wild stuff. They've detected some anomalies that are fascinating."

This was just another example of his father's intuitive leaps.

"I've seen the images and yes, they are breath-taking, but nothing more than that," Adam admitted. "What does that have to do with this?"

"OK, let me bring you up to speed. Using Hubble's Cosmic Origins Spectrograph, these guys have determined that light from nearby galaxies is missing. That's 'missing' Adam, missing with a capital M. The light from further, much older galaxies, billions of years in the past, is consistent throughout. Measured as ultraviolet, it makes sense. But when they look at the amount of ultraviolet from closer, younger galaxies, it doesn't make sense."

"I'm not sure I follow. I must have missed that class."

"Yeah, uh-huh. There was never a class you missed. But let me give you a primer then. We know that the younger, hotter stars shoot off ionizing rays that are almost always absorbed by the gas in their own galaxies. They never get to affect hydrogen outside their own environment. When these guys performed simulations of the amount of intergalactic hydrogen compared to what the Hubble showed them, they discovered the amount of light from those quasars is considerably lower than what has been observed elsewhere. There is an unexplained deficit of ultraviolet rays. It makes no sense. There are some who believe that the missing photons are emanating from an exotic new source, not their usual galaxies or quasars at all. It might be dark matter capable of decay, generating this extra light."

It was Adam's turn to pause before responding. "OK, I understand dark matter constituting eighty-five percent of the universe's matter, even though we haven't been able to see it, touch it, measure it. It is all theory, right? You're not suggesting this is something entropic?"

"Adam, you know better than most, it's all theory, or bullshit until proven otherwise. It might be or not. But it is an avenue you may want to check out. If it is indeed happening out there, could it not be happening here but on a totally different scale, you know the light disappearing? What is the source of it? And if that is what is happening, I can't even begin to think about what it might mean for our world. But look, it's an idea. So, let's not jump the gun and start predicting the end of the world.

"So, Adam," pausing to take another long draw on his cigar, "how are you otherwise?"

If asked, Adam felt a lot more confused than before this call. But he knew calling him was the right thing to do, even if he now knew even less. "I'm good, Dad, doing better. Let's get together for dinner soon. I miss you. I'll call when we know something. Thanks for your input. You know how much it means to me."

Chapter 12

Great Falls, VA

Carlton Justice drove up the long, dark, and heavily tree-lined drive to the large Georgian-style home of his host, Thaddeus Pingry. Pingry was from a family whose lineage stretched straight back to Jamestown. Like many other families before them, they had risen to respectability and riches on the backs of others. His family had done quite well for itself despite having started its considerable fortune in a very desirable commodity of its time, the actual backs of others: slaves.

After abolition, Pingry's companies operated in somewhat less objectionable but no less questionable sectors. His holdings included media properties whose ownership was hidden by a well-constructed veil of corporate camouflage, shipping companies under foreign flags, and immense commercial real estate properties throughout the US. The family's reputation was cleansed and burnished by time, short memories, and large contributions to politicians, charities, and other organizations, discerning only how those might serve them.

Of all the members in their shadow organization, Thaddeus Pingry was the only one, not an elected official, who preferred to work behind the scenes. At one point earlier in his life, in his middle years at the University of Virginia's Darden School of Business, and interested in running for office, he'd been advised his family's history might prove to be a hindrance in getting elected.

Subsequently, he found more power and influence in dealing from behind a meticulously constructed facade. A side benefit was not having to pander to voters. Pingry was also a major, but a silent, principal partner in one of the most powerful lobbying firms in DC, exerting influence from near obscurity in multiple corners.

Located in the sparsely populated area of Great Falls, Virginia, s short fourteen miles from DC, his house provided the seclusion yet quick accessibility necessary for these meetings. Backed up against the Great Falls Park, each of the adjoining estates was comprised of large tracts of land. Watchful neighbors were not an issue. Even if they were, Pingry's security system was nearly as good as the CIA's. No expense had been spared to protect his home, his privacy, and the work which had been conducted almost exclusively from this residence.

Justice lusted for such a residence. Not that his current home was an embarrassment, far from it. But he felt that after all his years of service, he should be rewarded appropriately. A home like this would meet his requirements as a reward and if all went as planned, it would soon be a reality. If not, well, he grimaced at that thought. First, he had to deal with Stamm and that damned letter. This meeting would help determine the group's course of action. What had been devised years ago was now threatened. The carnage that would ensue if their activities were made public was immeasurable. Governments had been sunk on less.

Driving up the wide circular white brick driveway and parking in front of the house, he was among the first to have arrived. Justice was hoping Congressman Neil Lucey from Texas was among the early arrivals. This was a group of supposed equals, but as with any organization some were perceived as more equal than others. It would be helpful if Virginia Senator Bell Williams was there as well. Between the three of them, they wielded an unusual amount of influence on their committees, those being Homeland Security, Foreign Relations, and the Appropriations committee conveniently chaired by Congressman Justice. Carlton wanted to speak with them and Pingry privately before the entire group convened. While all were of the same mind on their self-appointed mission, these meetings could still dissolve into a wild discord. Justice wanted to head that off if possible. He believed they needed to see Stamm's threat clearly and be prepared to deal with it in any way necessary.

Before he could even ring the bell, Thaddeus Pingry, while wealthy enough to employ household staff, opened the door, seeing no need to employ people uselessly. Though his empire had been subjected to much speculation, it remained as opaque as a stone wall. Looking down at Justice, he ushered him into the foyer with casual indifference, guardedly, and with a hostile undertone. "Carlton, it's good to see you, but I wish you had given me more notice. Is this meeting necessary? I thought everything was proceeding properly."

The tone caught Justice off-guard. Pingry was usually the picture of restraint and gentility. Standing well over six and a half feet tall, patrician, and cadaverously thin, yet vigorous looking with a full mane of graying black hair, he cut an imposing figure. The congressman knew of Pingry's formidable temper but had the good fortune to have never witnessed it firsthand. "Thaddeus, I am truly sorry for the inconvenience. But something has come up that I didn't want to trust phones. I felt it was in our best interest to meet and discuss this together. Are Neil and Bell here yet? I would like just the four of us to discuss this together before everyone else is here."

Pingry looked at Carlton with obvious displeasure. "Carlton, I'm sure what you're bringing us is important, but if you remember, there would be full disclosure among all parties. There would be no opportunity for plausible denial. Do you remember that?"

Justice knew his usual bluff and bluster would not work here. Pingry did not suffer fools gladly. "Of course, Thaddeus. But I'm concerned that what I'm about to share might lead to a division in our group. I wanted to line up those whom I felt would follow our lead through this if the contention I expect materializes. That's all Thaddeus, really, that's all."

"I will mention this once again in case I was unclear, Carlton – no plausible deniability for anyone. All will follow. If we go down, we all go together. Each of us has much to lose, but no one more than me. Do not interpret my civility as an indication of favoritism. We will talk about this only when everyone is here. Do I make myself clear, Carlton?" The foyer had suddenly gotten cold, very cold.

"Now let's hear no more of this until the rest of the group arrives."

The congressman was not used to being dressed down. But if there was anyone who could do it and make it stick, Pingry was it. He had contributed much to his and everyone else's campaigns and expected access, accountability, silence, and most of all complete loyalty. That was to be understood from the outset upon requesting and receiving his help. Justice foolishly believed any group will naturally develop factions within itself and he had seen himself as the de facto leader. What he had not counted on was Thaddeus' insistence upon uniformity of purpose and position. In Pingry's eyes, flexibility was an indication of a weak commitment to one's goals. It led to compromise which was not in his vocabulary.

What Carlton had helped start was now out of his hands. He thought to himself, power does corrupt, but it's money that really corrupts absolutely. He was in with no escape and would have to present to the entire group and accept their consensus, regardless of any personal loss.

Within thirty minutes, all the invited gathered in the dimly lit den. Pingry welcomed the group simply stating that Carlton had called the meeting having something urgent to discuss. By this time, Justice was more than a little nervous hoping that no one had noticed the copious sweat now staining his shirt collar. "Thank you, Thaddeus. And thank all of you for coming with such short notice, but I felt this was something that had to be shared with everyone.

"All of you know the Reverend Jonah Stamm. He's been an important part of our endeavors for a long time. You may also know that he and I go back many years. He has been a strong supporter of my campaigns over the years and a fuckin' pain in the ass for much of that time." Remembering the women present he apologized. "Amy, Nina, please excuse the language, that was uncalled for, but he always wants something from me."

Both women smiled at him. "Carlton, remember I'm from New Jersey, that should be the official state word. Now please fucking proceed," Nina Parsons, a short, grey-haired, somewhat over-weight woman responded, laughing, and breaking some of the tension Justice was feeling.

"Thank you, Nina. I was in my office this morning, a Sunday of all things, and received this letter," holding it up in the air for all to see. "I knew immediately who it was from, hand-written on expensive paper with no return address but I knew it was from Stamm. We got ourselves a problem, a damn big one."

Justice was warming up and trying to keep to a minimum the theatrics for which he was famed, "He seems to have grown tired of our venture. He wants to talk with all of us, especially with you Thaddeus. There is a veiled threat in the letter, and he does allude to what that might be. We can't ignore this. I tried to reach him after I received this, but he was conveniently unavailable."

Pingry quietly asked to see the letter, "May I, Carlton? How bad is it?" He read the letter, paused, read it once again, and stated simply, succinctly, and entirely out of character, "Damn." He then passed it around to the group, each reader expressing a similar sentiment.

Carlton Justice felt only a little relief at this, Pingry's response validating his own fear. "Exactly. That's why I thought we needed to meet as soon as possible. But what action should we take? As I said, I tried to reach Stamm, but he wasn't available, or more likely not taking my calls, whatever."

While Thaddeus Pingry could be glacial in his movements, his mind was not. Perceptive and decisive, he would just as soon strike someone down both figuratively and literally as shake their hand. "He's playing with you, Carlton, and therefore, us. His avoidance of your call is a little game. He'll call you when he's ready and I don't think it will be before too long. Let's sit on this for a few days, he won't act first. Should we not hear from him this week, I'll call him, and he *will* take my call. But I don't think that will be necessary. Agreed?"

Justice was about to protest, but Pingry froze him out with a laser-like glare. The group nodded murmuring their agreement. He continued, "This is a serious matter, no doubt. When we find out what

Jonah is up to, we may be able to turn this to our advantage or at the very least, minimize its effect. Should that not be possible, other measures may be needed. Understood?

"In the meantime, we need to bring the Vice-President up to speed on this."

Chapter 13

Dedham, MA

When she got into something, Anna Barth was a force of nature. Speaking as rapidly as an auctioneer, she was the first in the company to recognize that Aura/Sonos would need a spokesperson. She also believed that going public too soon would be as harmful as too late. Since they still knew nothing of what was happening with light, this was not yet the time.

"What do Adam and Fran have to say about this? Surely, they have some opinions on what's going on. Is there anything you know, Peter? Tell me!" Anna had two speeds – fast and faster.

"Slow down! Save the passion for later." Peter laughed. He was never surprised by the fervor she brought to her work. While she had worked for a prestigious PR firm in Boston, she found the work meaningless. She had recently resigned, telling Peter, 'How many legislators can I bail out from their, um, indiscretions, before I lose it?' She was a full partner in Aura/Sonos, though not on the payroll. That didn't mean she wasn't involved.

Peter marveled at her, "Yes, I spoke with Adam and he and Fran are setting something up to measure it if it happens again. Do I think it will happen again? I don't know, Anna. No one does. But Fran thinks it will."

Anna responded impatiently, "Yes, you do, Peter. Yes, you do. I know you! You believe it will happen again, just not when. Am I right?"

Peter Easton threw up his hands in the universal gesture of 'I give up.'

"Yes, Anna, I think it will happen again. I hope it will, but that's probably based on wishful thinking rather than factual evidence. Truth is, we have no facts or anything approaching what could be called evidence.

"It's a phenomenon that's got everyone wondering what the hell is it. We're probably as well situated as anybody to figure it out, maybe better, but do I know if it will occur again? No, not at all. Fran and Adam are preparing for it, if, and when it happens."

Anna, like a dog with a bone, wasn't letting go. Pointing at Peter, Anna pressed on, "Have you given any thought to what will happen when it happens again, and you are supposedly at the forefront of knowledge about it? Who will speak for Aura/Sonos then? You?

"Look, I love you, you're one of the smartest people I know, but you suck in front of the media. You know your stuff, that's for sure. But with people not at your level, with your understanding, you lose them fast. And let's not forget this, you don't like talking with them either."

Pausing for a moment, she continued, "This is what I think we should do. Let me be your spokesperson." Peter started to protest, but Anna cut him off quickly. "Just listen. While I may not know your work like you or Adam or Fran, I won't need to know the details as deeply as you guys do. You tell me what you know or want to disclose, I'll do the rest. If it's technical, I'll call in Adam. He cleans up pretty good. With all due respect for the media, I can handle them. You know that as well as I do.

"Oh, and one more benefit to that: as a partner, I'll have built-in credibility that a typical PR flack wouldn't. This is as much my baby as yours."

Peter had to admit she was right; it made sense for Anna to act as the primary Aura/Sonos talking head. Besides her natural telegenics, she was whip-smart and quick on her feet. The other underlying reason for Anna becoming the face of Aura/Sonos and not Peter was borne in his pre-adolescent years. Due to a lousy orthodontist, he'd been left with a sibilant "S" which appeared only under pressure such as appearing on camera and he was still acutely aware of it, even in adulthood. Anna Barth was indeed the right choice.

Peter laughed, waving his hands in mock surrender, "OK, OK. You win. It does make a lot of sense and it is out of the box. We'll look good and I like that. I pity the press or whoever decides to try and take you on. Is our liability insurance paid up?"

Anna laughed, and saluted Peter with a raised middle finger, "Love you too!"

Chapter 14

Baltimore, MD

"Un-fuckin'-believable! You did it! Stamm has agreed to meet with me. His office asked for a list of the questions I'm going to ask. I'm not too happy about that and he also wants to use a prepared statement. But still... and it won't be until next week, maybe Monday. But dammit, Lee, you did it!"

Lee Black grinned back. "Look Bennie, much as I'd like you to believe I'm a miracle worker, remember Sheila reached out to me. But we're both on the same page. Don't worry about the questions. You can always go off-script on his answers. What's your starting point?"

"Hell, Lee, I don't know. His single life, his dedication to that church, his charitable work, that friggin' TV show of his. Got any ideas?"

"I think you should start off with something safe, like his children's home in Southeast Asia. He's very proud of that and you know he'll have a lot to say on that one. You can move on from there. Of course, you'll want to get into the TV show, maybe its finances, contributions, profitability, and the good work it contributes to. He might be a little tight-lipped if you go too deep. On the other hand, it might be the opening you're looking for.

"On the personal side, and this could be a softball for him, why has he never married? You know, an answer such as he's given his life to the work, etc. Let him preen a bit."

Bennie smiled at Lee. "Shit, why haven't they given you a reporter's gig by now? You could do this as well as me, maybe better, damn it."

Lee shrugged. "OK. So, you tell me why in hell won't they give me a shot? I've been here long enough to gain their trust." Then laughed, "I mean, who d'ya have to blow here? It's just like any other organization, it's not what you know, but... right? I admit I can ruffle some feathers now and then. But, just like you, I thought True North would be different though. Shows you what I know."

"Look Lee, I want you to work closely with me on this. If we get something good, I have no problem sharing the credit and the byline with you. Screw Tim, our fearless editor. If it doesn't work, it's on me and you're clear. That work for you?"

Lee Black nodded, "Where do you want me to start?"

"Start by getting me all the background data we have on Stamm, his history, education, all that. You know the stuff we know we know. But what don't we know? It's probably a lot. Maybe something will turn up that informs that letter. I need you to go as deep as you can. See if you can talk with some of the members of his church. Are there any who've left because they got pissed off? Any indiscretions? Whatever, you know? Are you willing to get closer to Sheila without tipping her off?"

"Bennie, you know I'd walk through Hell for you, and I'll try to get closer to Sheila. But is Tim going to clear this?"

Edward Benton was never about kissing ass. And certainly not Tim Siegel's. "Let me worry about him. He's been a little too quiet anyway. We need some excitement around here. This'll rattle his cage a bit.

"Also, find out about this school, this children's home. How did that come about? Has he really helped them? Where does all his money really go? Does he pay his taxes? Does he kick his dog? We need to know as much as we can before I talk with him. Are you good to go? Yes? Great. Unless something comes up big, let's meet again Friday morning. I'll buy the donuts."

"Donuts, great, you cheap bastard."

Since the initial "flicker", nothing else had happened. With no other information forthcoming other than the now tired and tedious analyses, all of which were wrong, the media had to turn somewhere else to feed its beast. If they could not find a story, then a well-planned and "researched" piece on the health effects of GMO-engineered foods would be dusted off once again, presented as new until something else came along. For the time being, the hype behind the Reverend Jonah Stamm's first-ever exclusive interview was story enough.

The media gurus were dumbstruck at how Edward Benton of all people could have snagged this one. They had no way of knowing, and never would, that it was pure luck. Neither Stamm nor Benton was likely to divulge that information. They had their own agendas that just happened to be in sync at this time. Each would use the other best as they could to gain their ends, not giving a damn about the other. When either's use had been played out, they'd be tossed with no more concern than a bad card in a poker game. Stamm had no concerns about Bennie being a wild card in the deck, he was just another hack.

Each geared up for the interview like two fighters. Bennie knew he would have to approach Stamm gently and with a little forced naivete. Stamm, on the other hand, saw Edward Benton as a lightweight and a means to his end, ready to steam-roll him if necessary. He would as convincingly as possible, as non-threatening and understanding as plausible, position himself and his views as the answer and solution to the meaning of the "flicker." He was armed with biblical quotes, lines from scripture, and a folksy demeanor that was all too often mistaken for simple-mindedness. Benton, in his mind, was just some clay to be molded to his needs.

Conversely, Benton saw Stamm as a man with clay feet, one who had, and would continue to, exploit his "flock" and was nothing more than a dollar store charlatan. He would relish taking him down.

Both the Reverend Jonah Stamm and reporter Edward Benton would learn just how wrong they were.

Chapter 15

Three days after the light flickered, the media was still milking it for all its ratings' worth and ad dollars. Experts, real and otherwise, were recycled continuously, regurgitating the same things but attempting to put a different spin on them as if something new had been discovered. Which it had not.

In the meantime, the administration had quietly reached out to Peter Easton and his group to weigh in on this and do some research for them. This hadn't yet been made public much to the relief of his staff and the administration. No sense in creating a story where one did not yet exist.

But that never stopped the media from its appointed rounds. It found, created, or conflated stories from meaningless actions such as the effort by a few well-meaning but entirely misdirected legislators calling for congressional hearings on this. As if it were something they could fix.

The crazies were painting their faces, coming out across the planet in a Woodstock-type inspired movement, camping out, playing music, and indulging in their baser, sometimes carnal instincts wherever they could to receive media attention. Traffic jams were caused by people gathering at the reflecting pool in DC. If there was one thing the capitol did not need, it was more traffic, though it did make for interesting TV.

One of the more anticipated side shows was the upcoming interview with Reverend Jonah Stamm. He'd notified every conceivable media outlet as to his exclusive interview the following week and all wanted a part of it. He had something to share with the world and wanted as many to know about it. True to Stamm's word, Edward Benton was designated for the exclusive role of interviewer. It was to be simulcast and streamed continuously, and available on any outlet that wanted it. To soften the blow to True North's ego, they would be the sole provider and get logos and interstitial advertising on all broadcasts. Stamm wanted to manage this media circus and not let it get ahead of him thinking Edward Benton and True North News would be the perfect foil for this.

If all went as Jonah anticipated, he would continue to dangle exclusive access as a carrot to Bennie and his network. He realized what it would mean revenue-wise to them. True North would welcome the ratings boost in addition to the much-needed income. He also knew it would create a jealous feeding frenzy among the other networks and publications. Each was begging to get a piece of the action; each was offering the moon, and he was more than willing to accept it.

Other news organizations were not happy they were scooped on this. They had little respect for True North, less for Bennie, and were pissed. Having ruled the media roost for years, they were not accustomed to giving up their exalted perch. No one could figure out how that came about, ceding their exclusive position without any gain. They also knew that if one played the game long enough, it would eventually come around their way once again.

Benton knew this as well and was intent on owning it. He also knew Stamm would make him jump through hoops for it. If that's what it took, fine. The good reverend could be his ticket to greater things, that coveted Swedish prize maybe. First, he had to manage the balancing act sure to follow. If Lee was able to come through with some dirt, Bennie just might achieve leverage. It was a long shot, but still worth chasing down.

In the meantime, those news organizations refusing to cooperate with Stamm, and True North were attempting to create or redefine what was happening. Speculation was becoming their new currency. Those who pursued such a course ran the risk of being D.O.A. should they be wrong. Weighing the alternatives, it was a gamble they felt compelled to take.

It wouldn't be long before they learned how wrong they were, and they wouldn't be alone. Others who played it down would be left by the roadside. Once the story broke and started picking up speed, it would be unstoppable and unpredictable. At this point, it was like an enormous corn maze with no indication of which way to go. No one had a map for what path it was to follow, but leading the pack was True North of all groups.

Chapter 16

Dedham, MA

That Fran was upset was no surprise. Raging would have been a more accurate description. "Sonofabitch! I can't believe he's getting in bed with them! I thought our independence was what we and the work were all about! How could he? Adam, talk to him, he'll listen to you. We'll never get anything done now with them sticking their fingers into everything. Damn it, Peter!"

"Take it down a notch, Fran. I'm as surprised as you and I don't like it any more than you do. But you know there are more people out there who've become aware of what we're doing. We will have competition. That the government was the first to contact us on this before anyone else may not be a bad thing. If it was another company engaging us, we could lose all our independence and autonomy. In the long run, maybe Peter did the right thing. Let's wait and talk with him when he gets here."

As if on cue, Peter Easton walked into their lab, "OK, what've we got?"

Wasting no time letting her feelings be known loud and clear, Fran started spouting off, glaring as best as she could. "Peter, damn it, what the hell have you done!? This is not what I signed on for! I thought more of you! And now..."

Adam, always the calmer of the two, interrupted her, "Careful Fran. This isn't personal, don't make it so. Give him a chance to talk, will you?"

Peter looked on, both bemused and concerned. It was not his intention to create chaos with his staff, but if he had to admit it, watching Fran riled up was kind of amusing.

"Thanks, Adam. Like anything else, there's more to this than you know. And if everyone, and Fran that means you, can remain calm, I'll fill you in on what's happened.

He sat down on one of the stools by a counter and took a deep breath. "First, what you already know is we'll be doing some work for the government on this light thing. They recognize we're uniquely positioned to get a handle on this.

"Secondly and this is important, we're hoping to keep this below the radar for as long as possible, so the lowest of all profiles is necessary. That means no one outside of this lab, Adam, Fran, your staff, or anyone, is to know of this. No spouses, significant others, drinking buddies, no one. Not that it's top secret, it isn't. Though we don't even have any government clearances and no idea of what we're dealing with, we still need to keep our mouths shut. OK?"

Fran the pacifist, and not at all pacified, interrupted, "Peter, which part of the government? If it's the goddam military, I quit. I mean it! I'm not going to do work for them. You know how I feel about that."

"Yes, I do Fran and I respect that. Really, I do. But you need to realize that ultimately whatever we do and accomplish here, whatever we discover will probably find its way into the military whether you or I like it. So, accept that as a fact of life. But it's not the military if that makes you feel any better."

"So, who is it? I'd feel a hell of a lot better if you said it was the Girl Scouts."

Peter smiled, "I'm sure you would. No cookies though, it's the NSA."

"Oh, shit, like that makes it any better! C'mon Peter, do we really have to? You know it won't stay below the radar for long."

Easton was not pleased with the resistance he was meeting. "All right Fran, let me spell this out to you and anyone else who may have a problem with this. As you know, I started this company with some very generous yet low-profile grants and my own money. Thanks to all your hard and incredible work, we've learned things we could have never anticipated. We have genuinely pushed some boundaries and made some new and unexpected discoveries. We've created some enormous research on sensory processing disorders that's going to make life a lot easier for kids with autism.

"But we're only scratching the surface. Don't think for a minute that it has gone unnoticed. Outside companies would love to get their hands on us, they've made contact in the past and will continue to do so. They also know what you don't is we do not have much capital left and no new grants are pending. That doesn't mean we're in financial trouble, but this did come at a good time.

"But as of now, we have the kind of support we could never have hoped for. We remain autonomous, free from raiders, and best of all free to do our work. The NSA will want whatever we find. Will they be a silent partner? For now, yes. Going forward, your guess is as good as mine. However, for now, we'll be free to pursue this wherever it leads us. That work is not the NSA's. And we can go with that wherever we want."

He rubbed his hand across his face, "And when it becomes known, I've enlisted Anna to be our front person on this. She'll handle all media relations.

"Going forward though, since we are now a contract vendor, the NSA will be conducting background checks on all of us." Peter attempted to lighten the mood, "So hide your grass, wipe your computer histories clean, and pay all your parking tickets. Any questions?"

Of course, there were, but all Easton received were a lot of shrugs and raised eyebrows. "OK, then. Let's make sure we've got all our equipment calibrated and running. I don't want us to miss this if it comes around again."

"Peter, are you sure about this?" muttered Fran.

"No, Fran, I'm not. Not at all."

Leaning over Fran's shoulder, Adam, with some uncertainty, continued, "So, you're sure we're ready to go?" He knew there was no good answer to his question.

Fran looked at him, sensing Adam's doubt. "Sure, we're ready if you mean are we going to be able to catch or measure something we have no clue about. Absolutely. No problem. Sure thing. Why do you ask?"

Adam knew he could always rely on information, data he was able to see, and material that resulted from empirical work. This was far from it. They *were* in the dark as far as he was concerned.

"Look, Fran, we've gone over this before. It's unlike anything we've ever seen. We have no clue what we're doing, or what we're looking for. Nothing. You seem awfully sure of yourself. Doesn't this bother you at all?"

She could tell he was baffled. That was natural at this stage. "Adam, chill. You sound like you're going on your first date. Which, by the way..." Fran halted her thought recognizing Adam didn't want to go there. Again.

"Look, we know we're not alone in trying to solve this thing. Gaspard in France is chasing this thing too. The goons in Russia and China also want to be first as well. Good for them.

"But y'know, we will be the first. We are so far ahead of them on sensory phenomenon, we'll kick their asses."

"Yeah, Fran, I know, but that's not it.' Adam was not convinced. "This defies everything we know. How could it have happened? There's so little we know. No, that's wrong, there's nothing we know. And we really don't know if it'll happen again. I can't shake the feeling that it will… and not just once and we may still not know a damn thing."

There were so many emotions, and stimuli, bombarding it though it could not have identified them. There were also questions it had but

did not know what questions were. These were unknowable.' It 'knew'
language, all languages, and what those words meant. It was present
and it felt – strong? It felt alone yet also as one, all concepts still
beyond its rudimentary understanding.

And then it blinked again, and all was dark as all light vanished.
Not just the light from the sun and stars, but man-made light,
televisions, reflections, all gone, plunging everything into a total, all-
encompassing, stygian darkness. It was as if light itself had decided
to leave all responsibilities behind. It blinked again and it was light
once more.

Fran's equipment, now set up to sound an audio alert should the light blink again, went off in a fury. "Adam? Guess what? You were right. It happened again," she said in the dark.

The light returned in just a few seconds, finding Adam and Fran just standing there, slack jawed. She was the first to grasp what happened and let out a shrieking "Yeah! Adam, c'mon, I assume you're just standing there with your mouth hanging open. Well, close it and just don't stand there, we got work to do. Damn, this is so cool!"

Though Adam was as prepared for another incident, the suddenness, without warning caught him off guard. It took him a few moments to catch up with what just happened.

"Fran, did we get it?"

She was already at the equipment, listening to the audio conversions of data. "Damn straight we did, Adam. There is something there! I can't tell you what it means yet, but you and I aren't going home tonight, and probably not for the next couple of days. Hope you got a spare toothbrush on your desk! Oh, and order some pizzas, will ya? I think we're going to be here for a while."

Adam felt a sense of relief. Not so much for the recording of the data but that it happened again. Now they could start to analyze it. A nagging feeling remained, suggesting what they might eventually discover would not be easily understood. Something else about this 'flicker' gnawed at the back of his mind. It was plain as day if he thought about it, but it wouldn't come. Not just yet.

The second event created further havoc, sending people to their homes, their churches, and wherever they felt safe. Predictably the media jumped all over it. A new, greater feeding frenzy had begun. The talking heads were ecstatic. Governments were concerned. People were becoming a little fearful and Reverend Jonah Stamm couldn't be happier. The invitations had gone out and the party was on.

Chapter 17

Annapolis, MD

Reverend Jonah Stamm looked forward to this day with childlike anticipation. He had two important calls to make: the first was to Edward Benton of True North to confirm the interview. It would launch the opening movement on securing his position in the media on this light thing.

The second call was going to be delicious. He was going to call Congressman Justice and set up the confrontation only alluded to in his letter. Justice had already tried to reach him, just as he anticipated. He also knew he was probably fuming over his unavailability. Good. Let him. He was not about to let the congressman's activities get in the way of his plans. Such was the ego of Jonah Stamm. Such too was the ego of Carlton Justice.

Stamm picked up the landline phone and dialed Bennie's number. As with his aversion to e-mails, he felt the same way about cordless phones. He preferred older, tried and true, reliable technology. If he could have relied solely on written communication, delivered by a personal courier, he would have been a very happy man.

Benton's phone rang three times. He put down his coffee and before he had it to his ear, he could hear Jonah Stamm's voice booming on the other end. "Edward Benton? Good morning, this is Reverend Jonah Stamm. I understand you've been trying to reach me?"

With a mixture of surprise and frustration, Edward Benton looked at the phone before responding. Benton did not like playing games unless they were of his own making. Stamm was a master game player, and he knew Bennie would be on guard.

"Yes, good morning, Reverend. Thank you for getting back to me," swallowing what he really wanted to say. "Your assistant has informed us that you would like to offer us an exclusive interview. Is that correct?"

Jonah smiled to himself as he set the hook. "Yes, Mr. Benton. That is correct. I know the terms of this have already been discussed with your company as to being the lead on the interview and sharing it with others. And we are all in agreement on fees and rights.

"There are two things I would like to discuss with you though. The first is the date for our interview. Would next Tuesday, the 13th be a suitable time? Say perhaps 10:00 AM. I'm prepared to allocate three hours for taping including lunch. Will that be satisfactory?"

Edward Benton was stunned. This was far more than he expected or even dreamed about. He steadied himself, "Yes, Reverend, that is. Thank you. You said there were two things you wanted to talk with me about?"

"Yes, that's right. At our interview next week, I want to make a statement in the first part of the broadcast, sort of setting the stage for our conversation. Then we can get into your questions. I trust you are agreeable to this?" Moving on before Benton had a chance to answer, "If all goes well, and we have, what do you call it, chemistry, I am prepared to grant you further interviews, Edward, if I may call you that. I trust this is satisfactory as well."

Satisfactory? Hell, this is unbelievable thought, Bennie, shaking his head in disbelief, realizing that if not careful, he could become Stamm's media lapdog. How in hell had Lee pulled this off? "Yes sir, it is. I look forward to meeting you next week. Thank you, Reverend."

"No, no, thank you, Edward. And please call me Jonah. My assistant will let you know where," and the phone clicked off.

As Reverend Jonah Stamm hung up his phone, he sneered, "Easier than shootin' fish in a barrel."

Bennie was charged and more than a little apprehensive. How did Stamm gain the upper hand so quickly? He was going to have to play at a much higher plane if he was to keep up. He thought of the cliché,

'Be careful of what you wish for...' Then he smiled to himself and thought that could as easily apply to the good reverend.

He picked up the phone quickly, nearly knocking over his coffee. He had to reach Lee and formulate a new game plan. Things had changed fast in just a little time.

In the meantime, Stamm was placing the second of his planned phone calls. The phone rang in Carlton Justice's office and Trey Keenan, his aide, answered it, sounding more like a retail sales associate taking one's order than a congressional aide, "Good morning, Congressman Justice's office, this is Trey. How may I help you?"

"Trey, yes, good morning. This is Reverend Jonah Stamm. Is Carlton in? I think he may be expecting my call."

Trey knew full well Justice had been waiting for three days for this call. "Just a moment Reverend, I'll see if he's in. He's been awfully busy this week. Please hold," now sounding more like a congressional aide this time, playing the importance game. Walking into Justice's office, Trey announced Stamm's call to the congressman.

Carlton, pissed for having to wait this long to hear from Stamm, was debating playing his own waiting game but decided against it. He picked up the phone, struggling to remain cordial,
considering the increasing pressure Stamm's letter had created. He decided to attack the situation head-on. "Jonah, you're a busy man. I've been trying to reach you. Let me say that that was quite a letter. What were you thinking? It's created a bit of a furor. It's quite a change of heart on your part. I hope you know what you're stirring up. There are a few who haven't taken kindly to what you wrote."

Stamm smiled to himself, "Carlton, what are you saying? That sounds very much like a veiled threat. I can imagine the few people you mentioned."

While Stamm could be disingenuous with the best of them, coy at a time like this would not work. "I ask you, are you denying it? I shouldn't think that would be the best course of action, would you?"

The congressman's necktie was beginning to feel tighter as his blood pressure rose. "Now I would have to say, Jonah, you're the one issuing a threat. Don't play games. What are you up to? What do you want?"

"Congressman, what do I want? What am I up to? Really, do you have to ask that? You're aware of the good work my church does. It is not an easy labor, no, but one I am called to do. You supposedly answer to your constituents. I answer to a higher power. I cannot in good conscience continue to look the other way while you persevere in your, ahem, endeavors. This partnership must end. It can't go on any longer this way. People, and media, are starting to ask questions, which I am extremely uncomfortable answering.

"So, in answer to your question, what do I want and what am I up to. That's simple. I want out, that's it. I've learned more about what you're up to. I cannot condone it. Nor can I believe I've been party to it. No further cooperation or involvement, and in exchange for my silence, I would expect your group to continue its same level of support."

Carlton was astonished. Stamm had balls for sure. "Jonah, do you really expect that to happen? If you were to reveal what's going on, you'd suffer the same consequences we would. Are you serious about pursuing this? You know you'll get screwed now whatever you do. Pingry will be out for blood, and it'll be yours."

"Yes, I imagine he will. But truthfully, that will be the least of my worries."

Chapter 18

Fort Meade, MD

Grace Perez sat alone in her office wondering, based on her phone conversation, what to make of Peter Easton. He was unlike most of the people she usually encountered – self-assured without the preening ego commonly associated with such types. Nor did he seem intimidated by her or the agency. When someone was summoned by the NSA, their fear or trepidation was akin to that of an IRS audit, only with more dread. Easton was one very confident individual with no obvious fear. After he was thoroughly vetted and found to be what they believed him to be, Easton could prove quite a valuable partner. At the very least, he and his company would be an asset in investigating the light event.

Aware of the problems experienced in the past with outside contractors, she needed to determine what liabilities presented themselves because of the NSA's association with a quasi-private group such as Aura/Sonos. The similarities between her agency and Peter's company were not lost on her. One or two different decisions in her life might have led her there instead of the NSA. Both were involved in discovering what was not there, only suspected. Publicly, Aura/Sonos's track record was a hell of a lot better than that of her agency. Behind closed doors where few spoke of it, the NSA had a better record than commonly known, but still not as good as Easton's organization. Grace was looking forward to learning more about him firsthand.

She had not arrived at the NSA through a familiar route. The only thing traditional in her ascendance was her time in the military. As an Army brat, structure, rules, and familiarity were attractive to her when younger. She was 5'6", with black hair (a gift from her biological father, a loser who'd abandoned her and her mother when she was quite young.) She'd had few relationships, one being a failed marriage.

Her time in the Army, though successful in the military police, saw limited upward progress due to her strong sense of independence. There had been other well-placed females, but they were more inclined to follow the rules of which she bridled. She knew better but realized there wasn't much room for her individuality in the service. When her first and only enlistment was up, she decided to pursue another course, a formal education. She realized that while she had useful experience, it would only take her so far, and going back to school would take her even further. Much further than she ever dreamed.

Growing up in Michigan, Grace Perez was fascinated by her uncle's foundry. She loved the heat and the clamor, the men managing raw materials into something useful. She learned from her uncle that before any of this could happen, it had to have come from a designer, or an engineer. That led her to engineering and the University of California – Berkeley. Her fascination for engineering was shaped in the crucible of the foundry but her politics, while formed at home and honed in the military, were to be tested there.

Being brought up in a military household, it was not surprising she'd lean in a conservative direction. But an interesting thing happened in Berkeley: her conservative bona fides were at the same time hardened by what she saw while simultaneously being moderated by arguments she heard put forth. She'd learned the value of seeing both sides.

Older than the other students, she had no social life. The same dedication and determination she applied in the Army served her well in academia. She graduated at the top of her class, bringing her to the attention of several corporations.

Her engineering degree along with her military experience led to a rapid rise with a defense manufacturer. She subsequently made a name for herself when she was asked to testify as an expert before Senate and House committees investigating equipment malfunctions and failures that led to the death of eight soldiers. Resolute in her testimony, she gave as good as she got, taking no quarter, frustrating her inquisitors to no end. She could be disarming or when necessary, vituperative. Small talk was not really her bailiwick, believing directness was more meaningful. After the hearings were over and her company was exonerated, her stock was never higher. She could have chosen from any number of jobs, but she still wanted to serve her country. When she was unexpectedly approached for the NSA position, there was no hesitation in her decision. That was four years ago. And now she thought of Aura/Sonos.

Peter Easton seemed amenable enough but how far she could push him when they needed recommendations was yet an unanswered question. She was reserved in her dealings with him, wary that it could either alert him to their other intentions or steel his resolve not to cooperate at all. Grace knew he was not a fool, nor would she play him as such.

It was all speculation at this point. If this light thing did not repeat itself, it would be chalked up as an unexplained phenomenon. If it did, things would move ahead with incredible speed. Before that happened, she'd have to arrange a visit to his research center after the vetting had been completed. There was no sense in allowing the good people at Aura/Sonos to put a face on the NSA yet. There was also no need at the present to introduce them to her boss, August Ashe. That would come later, if necessary, which she thought was a real possibility, more likely a probability.

"Yes, Peter, tell what me you've found. What are the details?" Grace Perez was abrupt.

He was getting accustomed to her abruptness. "Good afternoon to you too, Grace. Not much, but something interesting. It's going to require a lot more study and a few more incidences to create a database before we can start to draw some conclusions."

Peter wasn't being purposely obtuse, but he did not like being subservient to anyone, including Grace even though her agency was playing the role of an angel. "We've found what appears to be, for lack of a better description, some sort of data pool, a communication maybe, we don't know yet."

Grace suddenly sat up straight. The innate paranoia that pervades any intelligence operation went on full alert. "What do you mean a communication? From whom? Where? Is it a message? A code? Easton, you're not helping me here!"

Though not his intention to stonewall, by not helping Grace Perez immediately, he wanted her to subtly know that a short leash would not be tolerated. "Grace, slow down, please. You now know almost as much as we do. Here's the rest of it. Fran Porter discovered something that looks like multiple data streams within the light flickers. They, it's weird I know, appear when the light comes back. She felt it on the first event, and you've got to hear me out on this, a tingle, almost a buzzing sensation on her skin."

"Whoa, wait a minute. You're telling me with all that expensive high-tech equipment, her skin tingled? That's it?"

On the other end of the line, Peter was smiling. "It's not as simple as that, but yes, her skin tingled." He proceeded to fill Perez in on Fran's unusual qualities. "It was from that sensory experience that clued her in. She thought it might be like turning a light switch on and off very quickly, you know, ones and zeroes. The measurements from the second flicker confirmed that. There are some irregularities that might point to that. We've learned that when Fran speaks, we'd better listen."

The Deputy Director wasn't happy with this information. There was nothing here she could take this to her boss. Nor would she cover for Peter Easton and his group. "Peter, that's not nearly enough to report. A tingle! For chrissakes, that's it? Is there a technical term for that? Uh-uh, no, there's got to be more." Grace's patience, while famously long, was wearing thin quickly.

"Grace, you're not listening to me. We think it might be communication. Yes, we're still grasping at straws, I know what you're going to ask, who, what, why, and all that. Well, we don't know. We're certain it's not man-made. Adam and Fran are working on this. I wish I could tell you more, but that's all we've got right now, and it'll have to serve until we learn something else. I'll call you as soon as we have something else. Is that all right?"

"No, it's not. I'm flying up there," slamming down her phone before he finished.

Chapter 19

Dedham, MA

Peter Easton's phone rang continuously. None of the calls were terribly surprising, they were anticipated, and most of all, one from Grace Perez. Peter, looked at the caller ID and knew he couldn't ignore it. "Grace, hello. I think I can guess why you're calling."

Grace bypassed any pleasantries, and fired off questions like a machine gun, "Peter, are your guys on this? What have you found? Is it something we should be concerned about? Who did it? Peter, tell me something you found from it!"

Calm and relaxed, he responded, "I'm fine, Grace, thank you. How are you?" He was not about to be bulldozed by Grace Perez.

"Slow down. It just happened and I haven't even been able to talk with my people yet. I'm sure they're on it. Give me a couple of hours or so and I'll get back to you with what we know. Will that work for you?"

"All right, Peter. I'm sorry. It's just that I want to get in front of this before anyone else does and get an idea of what we're looking at. I don't have to tell you Director Ashe is an impatient man. So, yes, two hours are fine. I'll be waiting. Thanks."

He looked at the phone in his hand, shaking his head in disbelief. The new 'flicker' just happened, and Grace already wanted a report on it. There was no denying her drive.

He got up from his desk and made the long walk to Adam and Fran's lab. Usually, the research campus was a quiet place, but after this latest incident, the halls filled with staff speculating on it. While normally he would have stopped and talked with them, he wanted to get to the two people he knew were most closely involved in this.

Approaching the lab, he stopped to look inside. Fran was hunkered down over a table, oblivious to anything around her, earphones fastened to her head. Adam was running back and forth between computers and printers, snatching up printouts and comparing the data on screens. If it hadn't been such a serious activity, it would have been comical.

He approached quietly and with a smile on his face. "Fran, Adam, looks like you're kind of busy. Anything I should know about?" Unusual for Fran, she didn't hear him approach and Adam nearly jumped out of his skin at the interruption.

"Damn it, Peter, don't do that again! And yes, we are 'kind of busy' and there's nothing at this point we can tell you except we captured a hell of a lot of data. I don't know what any of it means, there's just so much of it." Waving to the active equipment all around, he added. "It's hard to believe that just a few seconds generated all this. It's going to take some time to make some sense of it."

Easton looked at Adam and then Fran who was still oblivious to his presence, "I don't think we have much time. I've already received a call from the NSA wanting to know what we've got. I told them that it was a little early, but I'd give them an update in a couple of hours."

Adam started to protest, but Peter waved him off, "Save it, Adam. I know what you're going to say. What do you think you can give me that I can share with them now?"

"Hell, your guess is as good as mine. You could tell them we got a lot of data and we're going over it, but I'm sure that won't hold 'em. Look, I haven't even spoken with Fran yet. If I can get the 'phones off her head, maybe I can get some sort of picture of what we're dealing with. Look, I can't tell you we'll have something that soon, but I'll call you, OK? Two hours, huh? Shit."

Peter nodded in agreement and left, quietly closing the door behind him. Fran looked up from her table and asked, "Was that the pizza guy?"

Adam, laughed, "Yeah, the main pizza guy, that was Peter, and he needs to let the NSA know what's happening. So, what's happening?"

Fran on the other hand did not think that was funny. "That's just what I was afraid of. It happened only minutes ago, and they already want to get in our pants. I told Peter. Damn it, damn it. Damn it!"

Adam put his hands up as if surrendering. "Fran, listen, I know this pisses you off, and I must state that there may be a good reason to be upset over this, but there's nothing we can do about it but be very cautious in how we release the information. I think at the end of the day, Peter would probably side with us. But he does have the NSA to deal with. So again, what's happening?"

Fran looked at Adam, tears forming in the corners of her eyes. She refused to believe that by extension she was working with a government agency, much less the NSA. "OK. It appears the equipment worked perfectly. We have all sorts of data on this. But what, I don't know, and that's a lot. Was there more out there that we may have missed? Take a guess. Since we don't know what we're looking for, we don't know yet where to look.

"So, I was thinking as I was listening to it that there are so many different wavelengths of light, we only recorded a set number. And while it was a large set, I don't know how many or which wavelengths were involved, and if so, we missed a lot. There's just so much there and so much I don't know yet."

Adam sat down on the counter next to Fran, "The info I got doesn't make any sense yet either. It's all over the place and it isn't. I'm wondering what the key would be. Can you run a quick comparison across all the wavelengths and see if there's any aberrant info on some and not others? Similarities, maybe. That way we could answer one of your questions. Then obviously going forward, we'll have to be prepared for either all wavelengths or just a select few which would sure as hell make our jobs a little easier. Can you do that?"

Fran nodded. "I'll get on it right away. Thanks, Adam. This is what we're paid the big bucks for, right?"

Adam grinned back at her, wondering if she was up to what they might find. He wondered if he was up to it. He answered her, "Right. What do you want on your pizza?"

Forty-five minutes later with a mouthful of pizza almost flying out of her mouth, Fran lets out a shout, "Fuck, fuck, fuck, I knew it! I knew it!"

Adam, startled, looked up from his table, "What Fran? What did you know?"

"Remember when I thought that the 'buzz' seemed like they could be like peaks and valleys, sort of like a hidden transcript? Well, there is something there and it might be binary."

Adam's eyebrows shot up in surprise, "Really? You said it might be binary. Is it, or isn't it? Can you read it? Peter's gonna want to know about this."

"Right now, I'm not sure where it starts and stops. It could be a repeated message or a very long one. I'll have to run it through the binary translator to make some sense of it all." She was stoked.

"This is so cool," almost frothing at the discovery, cheese dripping from the corner of her mouth.

"If it's repeated though, it's really long and I haven't seen anything yet that looks like a repetition."

"Look, Fran, we've got to give Peter something for his report to the NSA. What do we have? What can we tell him?" While early in their analysis, he could feel the pressure mounting. What would that be like if this happened again and again? What would Grace Perez want from them then?

Fran looked at Adam as if he were speaking binary himself, "Adam, I don't know yet. It could just be gibberish, or it could be something else. Those two things both point to the same thing, whatever this is or may be, it doesn't feel accidental. This feels intentional. But of what and from where. I got no clue.

"And there's one other thing. Do you recall we talked about which wavelength this might be operating on? That idea was not a bad one, it was pretty good but not in the way we thought. Something is going on, but I don't know if it's across the spectrum, a couple of wavelengths, or a simultaneous occurrence.

"OK. What in hell are you talking about?' Adam asked with not a little frustration over Fran's vagueness.

"Adam, it doesn't sound like just one, for lack of a better description, 'message'. It could be, and this is an imperfect analogy, sort of like stereo. I think it's coming across multiple channels."

Chapter 20

Washington, DC

Rainy nights in Washington had their own special feel, something almost magical when it wasn't depressing, one that Congressman Justice liked, not wanting to go home. He found his way back to Pozzi's and Goldie, his new friend. Goldie, representing the best of his craft, remembered Justice and was pouring a Pappy before he even sat down. Looking up, he slid it towards him, "Congressman, how are we this evening?"

Justice took a long pull on the expensive whiskey, paused, took another, and drained it, licking his lips to get the last of the spirit. "Better now, Goldie, better. Again, please."

Smiling and nodding at the congressman, Goldie refilled the glass. "What brings you out in the rain this evening, sir?"

Justice stifled a snort, giving voice to both a universal half-truth, "This is a shitty town, Goldie. You know that? We come here hoping to do some good, make a difference, and change things for the better, and what do we get? Screwed and corrupted if we don't do the screwing and corrupting first. How does that happen? You've seen a lot of what happens, what do you think?"

Goldie put down his towel, looked over at the Justice, and clucked, "What I think? Hell, despite what you think, you guys do get some things done. Not all of what you want of course, not in the time you or your voters want, and hardly ever the way you want, but from what I've seen, things do get done. That doesn't mean it's all good, far from it, but you know that. The quest for power distorts s much and sometimes, you all work too hard at cross purposes. That said, I think you're being a little hard on yourself and the whole process.

"The way I see it, any forward movement is progress. Nothing comes easy. I learned that from my mother and life. Don't get down on yourself, there are plenty of other people who'll do that for you and for free. Congressman, it always gets better, just never on our time frame."

Justice looked at Goldie and responded with a tight smile, "There's so much crap to put up with. You find yourself in places you never thought you'd be, much less imagining such places even existed. And the lies you hear and the lies you tell. Goldie, I tell you, the only thing there's more of lies in DC are agendas. And half of them are lies too."

The bartender looked at Justice puzzled, "Not sure what you mean, Congressman."

The two bourbons were starting to influence Justice, and they were about to be joined by a third. Nodding at Goldie, Justice grunted and slurred, "You know, the people whom you think are doing good stuff, aren't. Not only that, but they also want to suck you into their schemes." Carlton Justice didn't realize at the time that he too was guilty of the very thing he was complaining about.
"No, I've just got to figure something out before it bites me on the leg or higher.

"Screw this, Goldie. Let's talk about something else. Hey, what do you make of this light thing? Any ideas, or theories? What're you hearing about it from your regulars? Are any CIA types coming in and spilling state secrets? C'mon Goldie, talk to me."

Goldie laughed, "No, Congressman, haven't heard anything but the usual Hill BS. It does seem everyone has a theory, but pardon the language, they're all like assholes, everyone's got one, but no one wants to hear from them. You know, the usual conspiracy theories, end times. The Chinese. Donald Trump. Global warming, that kind of stuff. Lights go on. Lights go off. But, no, nothing. How about you? Got any ideas?"

"After the couple of days I've had, I'm afraid my ideas ran out a long time ago. Right now, I'm having some trouble trying to figure out which way is up and which way to go. There's no road map for that that I know of." With the help of the bourbon, Justice's fears were starting to percolate to the surface. A close friend might have recognized it. Goldie just saw a worried politician, par for the course.

"Well, Congressman, there are a lot of people up here who profess that they've found it. They have the answer. You know what I mean? Now, I don't personally subscribe to that or much of anything in that area, coming from where I come from, but... Good answers are awfully hard to come by, right?"

Justice, eyes getting glassy and tongue thick, looked at Goldie and slurred, "Yeah, you're right, and that's the source of this crap. And there are more than a few people willing to believe and follow it."

"Different strokes, y'know? What are you gonna do?"

"How 'bout one more of these?" sliding his now empty glass forward. Goldie suggested coffee instead, Justice nodded in agreement. "Yeah, OK, and then please call me a cab. 'Preciate it," his slurring more pronounced. A thought entered the congressman's mind, "Goldie, I know this is probably a long shot, but speaking of those people, does anyone from Reverend Stamm's group ever come in here? I don't suspect they would, but you never know, you know?"

"Congressman, if one of them came in here, that would be the proverbial cold day in Hell, they probably do their partying on the down low, you know? I mean we get all kinds for sure, but not from that group. I would most definitely know that. Why do you ask?"

Taking the hot coffee cup in his hands, Carlton Justice spoke over the steam, "Just a thought, nothin' more 'n that..."

Chapter 21

Annapolis, MD

With the latest flicker, Jonah Stamm was loaded for bear with his interview with Edward Benton in four days. Whether or not there would be another before then was only incidental to him. It would only add to his new message. Prior to that though, he wanted even more background on Benton. He wanted personal info and thought he had just the way to get it.

He looked up from his desk and called for his assistant, "Sheila, swee...", and remembered there was other staff present, stopping him from calling her the endearment he used when they were alone, "Sheila, could you please come in here?"

Sheila Weller was entering his office before he had finished. She was at his beck and call, loyalty seemingly absolute. "Yes, Reverend?" She would call him Jonah privately, never in public, seeking also to keep their true relationship secret. She too knew the risks, the damage that would occur should it become known.

Stamm smiled warmly at her. His affection was real. "Sheila, again I'd like to thank you for reaching out to Lee Black for me. It was perfect. I'd like you to call him again and see if he'd meet with you. I need to know more about this Benton guy, any skeletons, and bad history we should know about. He'd tell you, wouldn't he?

"I realize it might make you uncomfortable, but it's necessary or I wouldn't ask you. Maybe meet for lunch, coffee, whatever, or something like that, completely innocent. Be entirely open about this when you meet him, but not before. Just tell him I want to know a little bit about Edward Benton. Can you do that for me please?"

While this was different from any other requests the reverend had made, she saw no reason to refuse. It would be a little odd to seeing

Lee again after all this time, but nice to catch up in person. "How soon would you like me to set this up, Reverend?"

"As soon as possible, tomorrow? It does have to be before Tuesday's interview, though. Tomorrow, Saturday would be the best, Sunday we're always busy, and Monday will be a little too late. Yes, it'll have to be tomorrow. Will that work for your schedule?"

"Not a problem, Reverend. I'll get on it. Olivia will have homework, so she'll be at home or at the library. I'll call and let her know." Sheila returned to her desk and placed the call to Lee Black, using her cell phone, punching in his number only to get his voicemail. Frowning since she would rather have spoken with Lee, she left a brief message, "Lee, Hi. Could you please call me? I'd like to see if we could meet, maybe tomorrow if that's OK. Call me. Thanks." Hanging up, she felt a small twinge of discomfort, unable to identify its source, probably just the prospect of seeing Lee for the first time in so long. That must be it.

It was only minutes before he called her back, curtly responding, "Lee Black, you called?"

Sheila was a little surprised at the brusqueness of the answer but realized it wasn't personal as Lee might not have recognized the number. Trying to sound casual, Sheila spoke into the phone, "Lee, it's Sheila. Thanks for getting back to me so quickly. How are you?"

Lee laughed, "How am I? Like trying to load mercury with a pitchfork. Bennie's got me doing all sorts of research and background crap for the interview. Other than that, fine, really. What's up? I didn't expect to hear from you until maybe after the show when the reverend would want to rip me and Bennie new ones."

She laughingly protested, "Lee, the reverend would never do that. Curse your soul to damnation maybe, but nothing physical, Lee, I was wondering if we could meet, maybe tomorrow, Saturday?" Knowing she was about to lie made her uncomfortable, "It would be on the QT, you know? Can you do that? Coffee, maybe lunch?"

He was thinking 'on the QT? what's that about?' He would have preferred she had suggested dinner. "Yeah, I can do lunch. I know just the place, not far from the capital, it should be quiet at lunchtime tomorrow, nobody should know us. Let me know when and where I can pick you up."

It was unseasonably cold for mid-June. As he got ready to go to the studio for the interview, Bennie laughed to himself, "I got the damn interview, so this must be that proverbial cold day in Hell." It was his intention to create such a day for Stamm. He realized he might jeopardize further interviews but thought it would be worth it if he could expose Stamm. He had some ammunition but was undecided if and how he'd use it.

Conversely, Jonah Stamm was prepared to be as cooperative and accessible as he could be, provided it fits his agenda. He had, for the first time in his ministry, a national platform and didn't want to blow it.

In truth, he had more to lose than Edward Benton. Benton, if he failed, would sink back into a deserved obscurity much like the one in which he was found. Stamm could not afford a mistake. He couldn't lose it in front of a large audience. He had to be comforting, reassuring, reasonable, and most of all safe. Unprovoked, he was all of that. But if one got under his skin, he could be prickly. Benton might be the kind who could.

He'd have to appear guileless, his guard down, though ready to rise at a moment's provocation. He asked Sheila to call for the limo. Minutes later, they were both getting into the back seat of the car for the drive-over, Jonah taking the time to center himself.

"Sheila, let me get this straight. Does this Benton guy claim to have a copy of a letter I wrote threatening a US congressman? Is that correct? Did your friend show you anything or are they just bluffing?"

She shook her head. Sheila hadn't shared anything of consequence, but he still wondered how that letter had gotten out. Would they really use it? This could destroy everything. But and this could be huge, he might be able to make it work to his advantage though a long shot at best.

As Jonah's limo pulled into the studio parking lot, they arrived simultaneously as Edward Benton. Both men eyed each other warily before meeting to shake hands. The reverend was the first to speak, "Edward, it's good to see you again. You're looking good. Is that a new jacket? Well, it's the big day, right? I hope you'll go easy on me today."

Bennie looked at Jonah Stamm, thinking 'new jacket, my ass' and laughed, "You know, Reverend, I might say the same."

Jonah turned on his charm and the well-practiced thousand-watt smile, the one that charmed white- and blue-haired matrons, eliciting record contributions this year, "Edward, I can tell you're ready. Let's just make a small pact that both of us will still be standing when this is over. No mutually agreed on destruction, all right? Does that work for you?"

Using a similar analogy, Edward Benton grimly replied, "Yes, Reverend, it does, provided of course, there's no first strike," issuing his own not-so-subtle warning.

"Good, good, shall we enter the lion's den such as it is? I'm eager to get going," Stamm offered good-naturedly.

The show's director watched the monitors in the control room, counting down to the start, "Three, two, one... and we're live!" The show would also be recorded and edited for repeated airings later that evening.

The commercials, titles, and opening credits rolled and the voice-over announced with its usual faux gravitas, "Today, the Reverend Jonah Stamm, in his first prime-time worldwide interview, will speak with Edward Benton of True North News. The reverend will be answering questions and addressing what he believes to be the problems facing society today and how he believes we can deal with them.

"Edward Benton has been selected to conduct this interview which will be available live and streaming online. And now, the Jonah Stamm interview."

Nothing was said about Bennie being Stamm's personal choice to do it, Benton being in Stamm's eyes nothing more than cannon fodder.

"Reverend, thank you for taking the time to speak with us today. There are many watching who are looking forward to your thoughts," Bennie opened innocuously. "I understand you've got a statement you'd like to make before we get started, is that correct?"

"Yes, Edward, thank you. That is correct. There is much I do want to share with you and all our viewers this evening. I'd like to talk about the state of the world, its people, and the alarming amounts of stress put upon our hearts and souls. We all know about rising drug use, we all know about the increase in immorality across our nation, and we all know about the loss of faith in our elected officials, and I might add, a general loss of faith, yet we just seem to stand by and watch helplessly. But, truthfully, I'm not that alarmed. And I'd like to share why with you."

Warming to his topic, Stamm continued, "You know, much has been made of this light thing, these flickers, or blinks as some have come to call it. The media, the politicians, everyone, and anybody has a theory about it. And no surprise," smiling benignly, "so do I. But, if I may say so, I believe mine makes the most sense. I see this light thing as a word from above. It is the Lord speaking to us directly in a language we don't yet quite understand. It has certainly gotten our attention, wouldn't you agree? I believe there are more messages yet to come and it will be incumbent upon us to listen and discern what is being told to us. This may be our opportunity to end all our problems, to heal, and to live together in harmony for the first time in human history. One message may indeed be that without our Lord, we are now or will soon be blind."

Bennie was dumbfounded. He did not expect the reverend to address that at all. But he would go along to see where it took him. "Reverend, you appear to be optimistic about our future where the light situation is concerned. I could take that to understand you believe this is perhaps theological in nature. Am I correct in that appraisal?"

Tugging on a button on his vest, Stamm looked at Bennie as a proud parent might of their child. "Bennie, in my world, everything is theological in nature. I believe everything springs from the Almighty. Though we may pray, we sometimes don't clearly understand His answers. That doesn't mean we can't."

"But what do you think the implications of this are? Do they favor any one belief? Help us understand this, please."

"I think the implications are rather obvious – as I said a moment ago, we need to listen more carefully. God favors those who follow His word. It's not complicated, it's simple – we are to follow his word as written in the Bible and devote ourselves to serving Him."

Bennie did his best not to roll his eyes over Stamm's sales pitch. "Does that mean only the Bible and not the Torah or the Quran? Are you preaching exclusivity of favor then? Does God play favorites?"

The reverend, realizing that was a trap he could fall into, backed off. "Well, Edward, I'm sure there are those who believe God does indeed favor them. I believe God favors those who follow His word. Is that exclusive as you say? His word is not exclusive, it's interpreted in many ways."

Knowing a continuation in that direction would take him away from his goal, he shook his head and instead threw the reverend some softball questions. After a short period of a meaningless give-and-take on the light situation with no further solutions or answers provided, Bennie was able to get to more substantial questions.

"Reverend, thank you for that. It is certainly food for thought. Before we continue, we need to take a brief commercial break." The commercials came on, advertising the latest in Priapus treatment, bowel disorders, and an incongruous spot for Mr. Clean. Bennie thought of the irony of those placements when he was signaled to resume.

"We welcome back our audience. Reverend Stamm, you're known far and wide for your own television show and your own brand of evangelism. In fact. It's been quite successful. It has support from many." Bennie wanted to avoid the mention of money at this time. "What would you like to share with our audience about that?"

"Edward, you're correct. My worship program has been the cornerstone of our ministry and the engine that helps us do our good work. And it has been successful, thanks in no small part to those who want to see the good work we do continue. But please, don't categorize it as my own particular brand of evangelism." He smiled, almost a leer at Bennie, "We are all doing the Lord's work, whether it's a gardener, a carpenter, or even" chuckling, "a reporter."

Bennie looked at him back at him, and nodded, returning his own leer-like smile. "Reverend, you mentioned your good work. Could you please tell us more about that?" He would waste no time in setting the reverend up. And Stamm did not see it coming. At all.

"Of course, that's one of the reasons I wanted to come and talk with you and all the good people out there." Stamm was already in his Sunday-best performance mode. "Edward, you know there's a lot of hardship in the world today, not just here, but all over. My ministry is all about trying to ease some of that pain."

"Here in the US that means trying to feed the homeless, give them shelter where possible, and hopefully find them jobs. And a lot of them have children, we mustn't forget them. It's hard work but it's what we've been called to do. I'm not ashamed that my church receives generous contributions from its members and friends. In fact, I'm extremely proud and grateful for those who see the value in what we're trying to do. We're able to accomplish this because of their generosity." As if on cue, Stamm's face took a somber yet grateful, sad but contented countenance.

"But Bennie, know this, it's not just in the US where we till the soil. As you probably know, there has been a lot of turmoil, and conflict really in Myanmar. And of course, who bears the brunt of such violence? Yes, the children. The ethnic tensions are off the chart, families are being destroyed, and the children, well the..." Stamm paused to theatrically wipe away a nearly non-existent tear.

"Excuse me, Edward. Please let me continue. We learned about this some time ago and decided to go there and see how we could help. That help materialized into building a home for displaced and needy children. Some we've been able to reunite with their families. Others haven't been so fortunate. So, with the permission of the prevailing government, we are trying to find them homes here in the US. Edward."

Pausing again to wipe away another imaginary tear, he continued, "If you could only see these kids, it would break your heart." Stamm was pouring it on, and Bennie thought he'd throw up. But it unexpectedly went right in the direction he wanted.

"Reverend, you mentioned generous contributors. Is that all from private contributions? Do any other organizations help? Corporations, perhaps?"

Stamm smiled, "Yes, these contributions come from all over. There's no government involvement at all. Were that to happen, there would be no separation of church and state. We are very mindful of that. And Edward, truth be told, I'm glad there isn't any participation from them. We do not have a bureaucracy to deal with nor do we want one. Our budget is ours and not subject to any political needs or restrictions. We are good just as we are." And there it was, the opening he dreaded making and realizing it too late.

"Reverend, I must admit to a little confusion as to what you've just shared with me. You stated there is no government involvement in your work, but... I am in receipt of a letter you sent to Congressman Carlton Justice about your joint involvement in Myanmar. Can you elaborate?"

"Are you seeing any of this?! He's fallen right into a trap! Damn it, damn it, damn it! That stupid sonofabitch! How in the hell did he get that? And who in hell gave it to him?!" Carlton Justice was furious, and he was going to have to get on the phone with Thaddeus Pingry and start damage control. If Pingry hadn't seen this, it would only be moments before he was aware of it. And Justice could not afford to receive the call from Thaddeus, he had to be the bearer of this news. There was no fan large enough to handle the shitstorm about to happen.

"What the fuck?" Lee Black just about fell out of his chair. Bennie had shared the questions with Lee and had not intimated any real desire to disclose their knowledge of the letter. Yes, they had discussed it, but not knowing what was behind the letter, he decided to let it rest for now. And now? "Damn it, Bennie, what in hell are you up to?"

It made for good TV. Bennie was about to be an overnight celebrity, welcome in some parts, reviled in others, all while True North News' ratings skyrocketed.

Stamm was momentarily caught off guard. He didn't think Benton would go with the letter so soon or even today. Damn it, he had to find out how that letter got out. He knew Justice would not have let the letter out of his sight, it was just as damning to him as it was to Stamm. So, who?

Regaining his composure, he smiled naively at Bennie, stalling, "What letter are you referring to, Edward? You can imagine the amount of mail we receive and answer. And by the way," attempting to put some spin on it, "we answer every piece we get. It's certainly a large undertaking but again, part of our ministry. If a member or friend feels compelled to write us, we must in all good faith respond."

"As I said, it's a letter, hand-written, seemingly by you to Congressman Carlton Justice. Is it or is it not real?"

Pinching his brows together seemingly confused, he stalled, a bluff to be sure, but one that usually worked. "I don't understand why you think a hand-written letter is so important, Edward. The congressman is an old friend of mine, why he's even a member of our congregation. Why would a personal letter from me to Carlton be of interest to you or anyone else for that matter?"

"Well, Reverend, as you said, there's no government involvement, yet here you are," holding up a copy of the letter, "communicating with a US congressman about some possibly mutual involvement in Southeast Asia and it did mention the Vice-President. Once again, can you elaborate?"

Suddenly Stamm was not happy he'd insisted on a live interview. The pause that followed revealed him as uncomfortable at the least and insinuatingly guilty at worst. He faked a coughing fit knowing they'd stop the cameras only to resume when it was over. They could fix it in the editing booth before rebroadcasting, but right now he'd have to think fast. "Well, Edward," pausing to cough again, "as I said earlier, the congressman and I go way back. And not surprisingly, we share many of the same viewpoints, not all I assure you, but enough to have strengthened the bonds of our friendship over the years.

"As a member of our church, he has supported our efforts over there almost from the very beginning. Why wouldn't he write to me about it? He is so much in favor of the work we do he's elicited support from a group of very influential businessmen as well." And there, once again, was yet another opening and Reverend Jonah Stamm realized too late what he had done.

Chapter 22

This circus knew no bounds. And it was coming to every town around the world all at once.

Reports were coming in from around the world. Riots in Jakarta, cults springing up in Southern California and Germany, an increase in suicides in the Scandinavian countries, traffic accidents all over as drivers could not see in the total darkness, rampant graffiti, and increasing fear were headlining the news. The media was treating it as a starving man might when confronted with an all-you-can-eat buffet.

In the absence of facts and a clueless free press, nothing was off-limits. Speculation was the new coin of the realm. Theories were abundant. The conservative media was blaming it on liberalism and ungodliness. The liberal media was trying to 'understand' it. Approaching the election, many candidates on both sides were positioning themselves as 'hard' on this intrusion or whatever in hell it was. Bloggers were the worst of them all, advancing lunatic ideas of interplanetary invasions, government conspiracies, AI running amok, and climate change among others. One even went so far as to suggest a vampire cabal was behind it, darkness being their friend. All were wrong.

In less free countries, governments were setting the tone, naturally blaming it on whoever was their enemy du jour. Plans were being put in place to shut down the internet should these occurrences become more frequent. The last thing those governments wanted was an informed population.

Politicians not wanting to be left at the gate of all this free coverage were wrestling to get as much airtime as possible. They were no better than the bloggers, attempting to solidify their base as if this was a reelection campaign. It made for great TV and was absolutely no help in calming the burgeoning fear.

The scientific community was as happy as a weatherman during tornado season. Speculation wasn't limited to the media. Now scientists were as much in demand as other talking heads, bolstered by the perception of actual expertise. In this, Peter Easton and his group refused to participate in the feeding frenzy, both by good sense and their involvement with the NSA. That didn't however prevent speculation within the confines of the Aura/Sonos labs. After all, when confronted by an indefinable situation, theories would naturally arise.

While fear of darkness is a common phobia among children and to some degree adults, none of that could compare with worldwide darkness. Psychologists had nothing available to address this. Night terrors, while an extreme form of nightmares, did not occur every night. Now, they were happening daily, multiple times per day. There was no clinical diagnosis for day terrors however rampant they now were.

Odd was that while nearly every group in the world, governments, companies, denominations, you name it, were aware of this growing crisis, they were doing virtually nothing to assuage the increasing terror experienced throughout the world.

Cliches, platitudes, and banalities were offered up to pacify the masses to no effect.

In government, it was stated once again that elections had consequences. The inability of the current congress to effectively address this issue was proof positive. So next election, if there is one, you'll know whom to vote for. At least that's what they hoped for.

Companies were held to the same standard. After all, if progress was their most important product, as General Electric used to say, what in hell were they doing right now? The stock market when the lights were on, tumbled drastically, reflecting that lack of confidence in that product.

Nowhere was confidence at its lowest level than organized religion. And those organizations were fraying quickly. To some true believers, it didn't matter. To many others, the promises made were not promises kept. If anything, it echoed a loud hollowness which in turn cost even more conviction. Where was one's God in all of this?

Families with small children were affected particularly hard. Small, developing minds, oftentimes naturally afraid of the dark, were nearly impossible to soothe, unraveling whatever calmness remained in their parents.

The circadian rhythms of all life were thrown off completely. The impact of that on the food supply had yet to be realized, the implication being that if bees couldn't pollinate, food yields would drop precipitously. When coupled with plant life's need for light, a recipe for global catastrophe loomed.

Along with the rest of the world, sea life was in peril. Mammals such as whales would be able to find their way into dark seas, but their food sources would be tremendously diminished. Nothing could survive without light.

Chapter 23

Washington, DC

Sheila was waiting outside as Lee pulled up in his red, six-year-old Corolla. He leaned across the passenger seat and opened the door for her. Nervous but unwilling to let Lee know it, she tried to keep it light, "Nice ride Lee, bet you have to fight off all the sisters with this."

Lee laughed, "Yeah, I got to beat 'em off with a stick and change my cell number. C'mon, get in, and let's get something to eat and you can tell me what's up."

Sheila didn't know why she was so anxious; this was Lee after all. Though out of touch for the past few years, they had known each other since childhood. She wanted to be completely open with him but didn't want to do anything that might betray Reverend Stamm. Hesitantly and stammering slightly, "It's the interview, Lee. Jonah... uh, the reverend, wants to know, you know, a little more about Edward Benton beforehand.

"He doesn't want to be blindsided but wants to be as candid and forthcoming as he can be. He does have something to say but doesn't want his 'message', this is him talking now, in his own words, 'corrupted'.

"A lot depends on what happens next week, and he wants me to stress that if all goes well, there could be the follow-up interviews we already discussed. I need your help, Lee. Would you happen to know what Mr. Benton is planning on asking?"

It was now Lee Black's turn to feel apprehensive. "That's a good and fair question, Sheila. Bennie doesn't want to appear as if he's shilling for Stamm but does want to give him an opportunity to say what he has to say." Lee knew there was more than that but was hesitant to say anything else. Fortunately, they just arrived at the restaurant, granting Lee a short reprieve before he had to answer Sheila's questions.

"This is it, we're here. Let's talk inside."

They left the car in a parking lot a short distance away, walking to the restaurant. Lee was surprised as the restaurant was crowded for a Saturday afternoon. The only seating available now was a table by the bathrooms or seats at the bar. They chose a couple of seats at the end of the bar against a wall, ensuring a small bit of privacy. The bartender welcomed them. "Hi. What can I do for you? Lunch, drinks?"

Lee exhaled while raising an eyebrow, "Lunch for sure and I got a feeling I'm going to need a drink or two as well. Sheila, what about you?"

Barely audible, Sheila mumbled, "Just lunch, Lee, maybe a ham and cheese sandwich." Not a big drinker, Sheila thought to herself a drink might help but not now, not with Lee, and not today.

The bartender slid a couple of menus over to them telling them she'd be back in a few minutes. Lee and Sheila looked over the menus, silently making their choices. Sheila looked up at Lee and smiled tightly.

"OK, Sheila, what's up? What was so important we had to meet today? What's got your Reverend Stamm so concerned?" Lee's reporter's instincts were attuned to something he couldn't quite yet identify.

"And why are you so nervous?"

"Lee, I told you. He just wants to be properly prepared and for him, that means knowing everything he can. As I said, he doesn't want to be surprised. Is there anything you can tell me, you know, what kind of questions, anything about Mr. Benton that would help the reverend?"

That answer could put him on a path that could lead to glory or disaster. Whichever way he responded to Sheila's question could lead to a betrayal. That of Bennie or of Sheila, neither option is particularly attractive. "Sheila, Bennie doesn't want, as you said of Stamm, to be blindsided either. He believes Stamm..."

At that point, the bartender came back for their order. "Have you guys made your decisions yet?"

Lee looked up and said, "Yeah, ham and cheese on rye for my friend, I'll have the turkey club on toast with fries, and a Dewars, a double. Thanks."

Lee returned his attention to Sheila, "Bennie thinks Stamm has a hidden agenda and wants to use him to launch it. He thinks the reverend is dangling the possibility of further interviews to achieve this. Look, Sheila, Bennie has been trying for months to get close to Stamm and hasn't gotten anywhere. Now, out of the blue, you call and say Stamm wants to talk. You know, I gotta be suspicious of that, don't you think?"

Sheila swallowed before speaking, "Yeah, Lee, I got it. That's not unreasonable. And if we're going to be on the level here, we're going to have to trust each other, OK? I'll go first.

"The reverend is concerned about what this light thing, you know, the flicker, is all about. He believes he may know what's behind it and that it's a much larger thing than we know." Lee was about to interrupt when Sheila held up her hand, "Wait. Of course, he'll preach what he usually does, that's him, but he is sincere. He's a good man, Lee, really. I know, I've seen his work." Sheila did not tell Lee of the depth of their private relationship.

"I want to believe you, Sheila. The light thing I get. Everyone wants in on it, it's weird, all right. And I know of his good work too, the children's home in Southeast Asia. That's good stuff, almost newsworthy if it weren't so old. I get that too."

Their lunches arrived, brought in by a different bartender. He smiled at them both and placed their meals in front of them. "Enjoy. Please let me know if there's anything else we can do for you. Again, hope you enjoy your lunch," and went back to refilling the beer coolers.

Lee waited until the bartender was out of earshot, and continued, "But here's the big one, Bennie has a copy of a hand-written letter seemingly from Stamm threatening Carlton Justice, the congressman.

We don't know if it's real and we don't know who it's from. And the threat has only alluded to if an action or response isn't taken. Will Bennie use it in the interview? I don't know. He is a reporter and he'll dig into it. He feels caught off-guard by the reverend and is determined not to let that happen again.

"So, it seems all we've got, you and me, is speculation. Absolutely nothing we can use. Do you know anything more about this letter from Stamm or something to do with Justice?"

Sheila was reluctant to share much more with Lee but felt a growing need to confide in him, "Lee, I'm aware of a letter and I think it may relate to Congressman Justice, but I don't know anything more than that. Reverend Stamm doesn't tell me everything and really, he shouldn't."

These last few sentences caught the bartender's attention. It was typical of the conversations he heard too often. But it involved one of his newest customers. He would, as he normally did, file it away in his memory. A good bartender, in addition to making drinks, succeeded when he remembered his customers' names, their jobs, and their favorite libations. And Goldie was one hell of a good bartender.

Chapter 24

Dedham, MA

In anticipation of Grace Perez's visit, Peter had asked Anna Barth, his soon-to-be public face on the light issue, to join them. He valued her opinion and perceptions over all others. Grace Perez's visit was the last thing he wanted to do. Except for the initial investors, few visitors had ever broached the doors of Aura/Sonos. Now, not only a visitor but one who was going to be holding Easton and his group accountable. The good news was whatever they had wasn't very much and was completely out of their control. Unfortunately, that was also the bad news.

He and Anna walked from his office over to the lab in which Adam, Fran, and their staff were working. "OK, ladies and gentlemen, and that will be the last time you hear that phrase from me today, Grace Perez from the NSA is on her way here and she doesn't sound thrilled. What have you found since we last spoke? Anything new?"

Fran turned her head in the direction of Peter's voice, and waving her hand was the first to speak, "OK, maybe, maybe not. First, the slow glass didn't show us anything. I don't even know if it works because we still don't know what's going on. Also, my friend at NASA came up completely dry with one very odd exception. Their satellites show the light disappearing and then returning, but nothing beyond that. They went blind like we did and were in the dark as everyone else.

"But in a few places, there were thunderstorms when the light went out. With that came lightning which was heard. But not seen. Even that has gone dark. How's that for strange? It's almost mythological you know, the gods, Zeus, being angry and that stuff raining down invisible fire on his subjects."

Adam looked at Fran, simultaneously entertained and interested in her off-the-cuff comment about Zeus. Not that he believed in such stories, but it planted a tiny seed in his mind.

"And we're still waiting for the CDC to get back with us on some protocols for looking into the possibility of this being viral. Nothing yet though." Fran wrapped up her presentation.

"Once, if, and when," Easton started to talk but was halted by Fran waving her hand to stop his questions.

"Yeah, yeah, I know I'm sounding like a stuck CD on this. If it happens again, we'll then have two measurable and comparable incidents with which to study. We'll be able to measure duration, intensity, and anything else. It'll still be a rather small sample to work on."

Adam interrupted Fran, "By anything else we mean, for lack of a better description and knowledge, the 'messages' as we call them, seem like rapid-fire pulses really. Based on what we have so far, we're thinking that there's not just one message or communication going on but several. Remember we described it in terms of stereo? Well, we're thinking it's much, much more than a couple of channels. It may be a lot. If we can isolate just one or two, that might be the key to getting a read on this. I know it's not much, but we're slowly eliminating things it isn't."

Easton frowned, "Things it isn't, are not going to make Grace Perez happy, not that that's my main concern here. I want us to figure this out first. It would go a long way to helping secure our future independence. Let me ask you something... do you think this is something that you could replicate here in the lab?" Peter was staring to grasp at straws.

Fran felt her way over to the wall, sliding her hand to a light switch and shutting it off and on several times. "You mean like this?"

Anna laughed at Fran's action until Peter told Fran to stop. She then broke out into a broad grin, laughing even louder. Fran's remark got a tense laugh from the others in the room, including Peter Easton, "Yeah, just like that Fran. Who did you say paid for your scholarship?" reminding her in a not-too-subtle way of their relationship. That too elicited a laugh, easing the growing tension among them. "Let me ask you a question though. Did your skin tingle that time? Was it as good for you as...?" He was in the select group who could sling sarcasm back at her.

Peter gathered Adam, Anna, and Fran into a conference room for their meeting with NSA Deputy Director Perez. This was to be a face-to-face introduction and expectations were not very high. That out of the way, everyone settled down at a conference table: Easton at the head, Anna to his right, Grace Perez at the far end, Fran and Adam split up on either side of the far end of the table, demonstrating their reservations by their seating choice and not unnoticed by the others.

Before he could open the discussion, Perez took charge, "Adam, Fran, please don't think I'm not aware of your apprehensions, your reluctance to work with us. I understand that. But know we are not the enemy, not yours at least."

"We are all being confronted by a phenomenon of which none of us has a clue, well, maybe apart from you two, which is why we're here today. Peter has shared some of your thoughts, perhaps you can tell me them in your own words?"

Fran, arching her eyebrows, tilted her head to Adam who in turn was nearly staring at Perez. She wasn't what was expected, but they would display caution with what was about to be shared. Fran was not about to lead off, given her normal paranoia, so Adam spoke first. "Ms. Perez, we really don't know that much at this point. But let me start at where we are now and work backward. It's a little unconventional, but so is this thing. I think we're going to have to rely on, trust even, our intuition." She started to speak, but Adam continued, "I know that's not the way you would approach this, but we've found intuition to be a powerful tool. Is it always right? No, of course not. But we almost always learn something from it.

"We believe, hope, this will occur again. How often, we've no idea. But once we do have another incident to measure, we'll have something to compare it to the previous one. I view the first incident as more of an alert to us and not much more. But we've detected some 'information' in it, particularly the last one. I'd like Fran to elaborate on that. She's got some interesting, perhaps intuitive, thoughts on it."

Fran, scowling, again turned her head back in Adam's direction. She didn't want to be here, but her inner geekiness and the desire to show off easily overcame whatever mistrust she was feeling. But that didn't prevent her from petulantly displaying her disdain, almost contempt, for Grace.

"Thanks a lot, Adam. Well, Grrrrace," drawing out her name, "can you promise me you won't weaponize what we find? That you won't use it against some poor, helpless little country that you happen to dislike today."

Peter slammed his hand on the table, "Stow it, Fran! Tell Ms. Perez what you've found and no more of this childish bullshit. OK?"

Anna frowned at Peter's sudden change but knew it was borne out of frustration rather than anger. She signaled for him to take it down a notch.

Fran loved Peter and reacted like a chastised little girl, which in this instance she was, but still impudent, drawing out the first word of her response, "Yesss, Boss. Sorry, *Ms*. Perez. As Adam said, we'll have a better idea after we record the info from the next incident. But we do have some interesting thoughts. We are getting indications of information possibly buried, encoded, encrypted maybe, we really don't know yet, inside our measurements. We don't know if that's normal or interference of some kind. I thought it might be binary in nature but have since moved away from that theory. And, yes, there is something there, but you're going to have to wait until we know more."

"That's it? Your boss already told me that. Peter, why are you wasting my time?"

122

Easton stifled a smirk, "Grace, please remember, it was your idea to come down here."

"Well, there may be more, but it's only a hunch," Adam offered. "We're thinking it might be communication or communications to be more specific. The source is what we're completely in the dark about. I don't even know how to explain this... but, at this point we think it's of this earth," pausing for a very long time, "and simultaneously, may not be. There's nothing that indicates anything off-world. We just aren't sure. It defies everything we believe we know of light."

Both Peter and Grace looked at Adam dumbfounded, both speechless. Peter was the first to break the sudden silence, "What? Adam, I need you to clarify what you just said."

Easton didn't like things kept from him especially if they were surprises like this. This was the unseen angry side he kept in check most of the time. "Tell us what you know and don't skip a damn thing!"

Grace Perez was surprised by this outbreak. Easton's reputation was of a buttoned-up leader. His response belied that characterization.

Fran jumped in before Adam could respond, "Peter, he said 'we believe', not 'know'. It's pure speculation and very peculiar. Parts of it seem to be identifiable but then it goes off into something else that sounds like gibberish. It's almost, for lack of a better description, like a two-way street. You can see traffic moving both ways but you've no idea where it's ultimately going. Another way of looking at it could be a conversation, a dialogue but with many people, but right now it's still all speculation."

Grace Perez started impatiently hammering Fran and Adam with questions for which they had no answers, "Are you saying it's not from another planet? Another country? Is it hostile? Do we know where it originated? Can we..." only to be interrupted by Adam.

"Ms. Perez, please understand, you now know as much as we do. You've heard what we're speculating it might be. And that's it, speculation. We're starting to eliminate things, but it's way too early to draw any conclusions. We're sure it's not little green space aliens.

Nothing indicates that. We don't know if it's hostile and we don't know yet where it's from. We are sure that the more often it occurs, the more info we'll get and the more we can figure out."

Perez was not satisfied, "Could you *speculate* when the next incident will happen?"

Fran, Adam, and Peter looked at each other, unwilling to make a guess. Finally, Peter spoke, "Grace, you're just going to have to wait along with the rest of us. It's not like it's on a schedule. We don't know when it'll happen again..."

It was a new mind, an ancient mind, filled with too many thoughts and ideas, emotions, and memories. It had seen peace and it had seen war. It felt fear, hatred, love, kindness, temptation, hunger, cruelty, and so much more and it was all an overwhelming confusion. The only thing that gave it rest was darkness.

Once again, the light disappeared. And once again sensing the light had disappeared, Fran, feeling a now familiar tingle on her skin, was heard to say, almost gleefully, "Ms. Perez? Is now a good time?"

Adam, in total darkness, realized something no one else did, "Jeez, how can that be?"

Chapter 25

Great Falls, VA

Thaddeus Pingry was livid having watched the damned interview. How in the hell did that reporter get the letter? More problematic was how Jonah Stamm was going to respond to that last question. Pingry, while maintaining adequate staff to do his menial day-to-day work, did not ask his assistant to make the call. He wanted the first voice Carlton Justice heard on the phone to be his. Before he could pick up his phone, it rang with Justice on the other end. Justice started, "Thaddeus…" only to be sharply cut off.

"No…" Pingry's rage was arctic. Cold and clipped, he spoke slowly, glacial in speed and temperature. "Do. Not. Speak. Listen to me carefully. I want to know how that letter got out. I want to know what you and that charlatan preacher are going to do about it. And I don't care what it takes for you to reach him. Even if you fly to Myanmar. Just do it and get back to me as soon as possible. We do not have the luxury of time on our side. Do I make myself clear?"

The congressman could only manage a weak and pitiful, "Yes, Thaddeus."

Hanging up abruptly, Pingry picked up the phone and placed a call to Bell Williams, the senior senator from Virginia and one of the members of their small private group that he expected to be more fruitful. "Bell, it's Thaddeus. Have you been watching this debacle? Yes? I concur. The liability to us could be immense. We're going to have to reconvene much sooner than I thought. Would you please make the calls to the group and let them know we must meet by tomorrow evening at my home? They'll know why. Oh, one other thing, do not contact Carlton. Please let the others know he is not to be made aware of this meeting. I'm afraid he may be part of that liability. We'll discuss it all then. Thank you, Bell."

Bell Williams knew better than to question Thaddeus. Having the entire group's contact information on his phone, he started to dial when suddenly he couldn't see. The light had vanished. "Sonofabitch, again? What the hell is this all about?"

Theo Garcia, a young congressman from New Mexico, was wondering what in hell he'd gotten himself into. When initially approached to join Pingry's group, he was more than flattered. The son of a naturalized Mexican immigrant, he had risen from near poverty outside of the Indian reservation of Shiprock to a rising star in his party, to even having his name tossed about as a future vice-presidential contender.

But the call from Bell Williams for this secret meeting had unnerved him. With Bell requesting that he keep any knowledge of it from Justice, Theo was experiencing something akin to betrayal. After all, it had been Carlton Justice who had approached him about joining the group. He knew better than to go against Pingry or anyone else in the group. Still, he approached the meeting with growing apprehension.

He followed Cullen Peters, the senior senator from Pennsylvania, up the long driveway, and exiting his car, approached the senator. Deferentially, Garcia spoke first, "Cullen, how are you this evening? Do you know why we're here again so soon?"

Peters was a hardened politician from the rough and tumble streets of Philadelphia, capable of legendary glad-handing with one hand while simultaneously stabbing someone in the back with the other. A fearsome campaigner and politicker, he operated behind the image of a blue-collar worker happy to have a beer with anyone after work. And he was as likely to be found playing poker, smiling gratuitously, as pressing the flesh of voters. That was the face he now put on for Theo.

"Hola, mi amigo. Como Esta? No, Theo, I'm just as much in the dark as you are." Putting his hand on Garcia's back, gently propelling him forward, "But let's find out, shall we?"

As usual, before they could even ring the doorbell, Pingry opened the door and greeted them, "Cullen, Theo, thank you for coming. Everyone else is here, let's get started," ushering them into the large, dark-paneled library.

After the two new arrivals were greeted and drinks were offered, Bell Williams, as previously arranged, was the first to speak.

"I won't bother with niceties or small talk this evening; our discussion is much too serious for that. Considering what has transpired and what threats we may be facing, Thaddeus felt that we need to close ranks around those we can trust, and that unfortunately no longer includes Carlton, and I concur.

"His inability to shut down the threat from Stamm's letter has endangered our venture and each of us individually. I would suggest that from now on, we have no contact at any level with him or any representatives of his. He must be isolated from us, and we must be insulated at all costs from him.

"However, that does beg the question of how we deal with that letter now that he's been removed from our group. I'm open to suggestions."

Neil Lucey, the senior senator from Texas, was the first to respond. His West Texas twang stood out from the rest of the group, "Thaddeus, people, whatever direct action we take might leave us open to discovery, that being the last thing we want. We do have a significant influence though. As you know, some of us are up for re-election next year. That's already occupying much of our time. I think that's where we have an opportunity to isolate and ultimately remove Carlton.

"We know who his largest contributors are, many of them are ours as well. It's not unreasonable to think we could influence them to withdraw their support. Without it, Carlton will be hard-pressed to do anything but scramble for money while trying to hold on to his seat much less deal with us. Hell, we know he can't even hold his booze.

Look, he's been ineffective at quashing that letter, let's see how effective he'll be at this threat to his office." Snorting a laugh, the Texas senator finished with, "That'll certainly get him drinking again. Shit, it would get me drinking for sure and I'm on the wagon. Ha!"

There were murmurs of agreement and some laughter among the members in the library. Thaddeus, standing silently the entire time, nodded and spoke, "Are we in agreement on this course?" Receiving agreement from all, he continued, "Cullen, get on that. And of course, discretion is paramount.

"On the other front, we will need someone to reach out to the good reverend and attempt a rapprochement with him."

One hand went up, that of the senator from Arkansas, Douglas Condon, "Thaddeus, I'd be happy to contact Stamm. I don't think he would see me as a threat."

"Thank you, Douglas. No, you're right, he wouldn't perceive you as a threat and that's a good thing. You would be good at it. But I have another idea. One that would appeal to his sense of helping others.

"Theo, I think you should reach out to him. We know about his 'good work' and I'm relying on his ego to help, please forgive me Theo, some formerly down-trodden, dark-skinned New Mexican who has pulled himself up by his own bootstraps. He'll be well-inclined to give you an audience. When he does, this is the message you'll give him."

Chapter 26

Annapolis, MD

Just as Jonah Stamm was about to answer, he and the entire world was cast into darkness. Total and complete, again. Naturally, the broadcast, now more radio than TV, continued for a few moments before everyone involved realized what had happened. The viewing audience was treated to a stream of curses, some shrieks, and overall chaos before the sound was cut off. Even the reverend was heard uttering profanity in the darkness. It made for television, or rather radio, at its best, live, unedited, and totally unscripted.

Moments later when the light returned, the viewers were treated once again, this time with visuals, to the confusion and its resulting disarray. They saw showrunners looking helpless, Edward Benton still with a pencil in hand and mouth open, and the Reverend Jonah Stamm in his chair bending over as if in prayer. All were genuine reactions. Stamm was indeed praying, not for God's intervention, but for an idea on how he could capitalize on this latest incident. He was grateful as it took the emphasis off that damnable letter. It was no surprise he was the first to recover.

"Edward, Edward, are you all right?" Stamm was now in his element. "Is everyone all right? Please don't worry, everything will be just fine. That is exactly what I was talking about earlier. This is one of the messages from our Lord I described. We must listen and listen carefully because His Word is being spoken! He is reaching out to us, he wants us to live by his word, he..."

And as if on cue, the light went out yet again.

###

Feeling a respite from the jumble, it was learning that it could calm some of the noise on its own. And when it came back, it wasn't as bad as before. But it still didn't know...anything. Words entered its consciousness. Not yet knowledge, but thoughts. What? Am? I? Why am I?

Each time the light disappeared it was a surprise. It could not be predicted and this time it nearly caused a worldwide panic. The previous incidents had been days apart, not minutes. And the duration of each was a little bit longer as well. People were demanding answers and for their leaders do something about it as if that were possible. Some thoughtful politicians were admitting they were at a loss to determine what it was, much less acting on it. That was a small benefit.

Could there be something to what Stamm was saying? Were the cults on to something? The questions were increasing, and the confusion and fear were, and would, continue to grow exponentially.

It was like trying to pin the tail on a donkey for the scientific community. Their speculation was oftentimes as wild media's. A growing concern was if the light remained absent for days, weeks, or longer, crops would start to be affected and possibly die, eventually starving the entire planet. Human and animal cycles would be disrupted, leading to what? It was a worst-case scenario, but still...

Outside of Boston in the labs of Aura/Sonos, there wasn't confusion so much as almost restrained joy. This is what they were working for, to solve the unsolvable. Fran was beside herself. Darkness didn't frighten her, she lived it in every day. But when the light disappeared and her skin tingled, she knew she was getting that much closer to solving whatever this was.

It was also the first time that Adam, Fran, and Peter were together when it happened. It would have been better in Fran's opinion had

Grace Perez not been there, but she knew in the scheme of things it wouldn't matter anyway. And what did Adam's comment 'Jeez' mean?

In Great Falls, Virginia, Pingry's anger grew exponentially. It wasn't enough that he had to deal with Justice and Stamm and the damned letter. This light vanishing was not something he had time to confront, yet it confounded him less than the rest of the world. Pingry held himself above most people and didn't attach much significance to the light, believing that this was a problem with which others should deal. At one point in the past, he might have even contributed to its solution. Possessed of an enormous intellect and an inexhaustible curiosity, had he been otherwise focused on life, he would have found a kindred soul in Peter Easton. But his family's history, his upbringing, and his current position would have never allowed it. As if to exacerbate his fury, the light went out again.

Unlike a child with a new toy who quickly loses interest in it, the media intensity was increasing as the frequency of the flickers grew. It drove TV anchors into a deeper frenzy, contributing to the same fear on they were reporting. Despite that, they were already looking for the next new thing to feed the ratings beast. With no answers from those in power, people were becoming more and more paranoid about what did this all mean. Bloggers were more hyped than ever and with each occurrence, more theories sprung up. Some even had "proof" of what was going on. Add to that the mushroom-like growth of podcasts devoted to the mix and there was no escaping this fever. In that respect, they all might as well have been on Jonah Stamm's payroll. No one had a clue.

When the light returned this time, the cameras in the studio were pointed in all directions but the right one. Had they been aimed at the set, they would have recorded the priceless expressions on Benton and Stamm's faces, Bennie both confused and concerned, Stamm sharing the concerned part but mixing it with smugness as he saw another opportunity to further capitalize on the light occurrences. His main concern now was who in hell leaked that letter. He knew Benton wouldn't let go of it. But then, he thought of a way in which he might stall on it.

The cameras eventually located their subjects and repositioned them to continue the interview. Bennie was the first to speak, "Are we back on? Are we live?"

The director responded, "Believe it or not, we were never off. No picture of course, but the sound continued." Laughing, "We were radio. And very good radio at that."

Stamm realized a very large audience had heard him curse, not that there was anything he could do about it. In times of stress, he knew men often resorted to such language as a release and he was after all a man and a man of God. He would play that up as well, asking for forgiveness for his outburst, and asking for mercy always played well.

Bennie attempted to take charge. "Reverend, as I was saying before," trying to inject a little levity into the tension, "we were so rudely interrupted, please tell us about that letter."

Stamm smiled in the way a tolerant parent might at a naughty child. "Edward, I don't think that when the Lord speaks to us, we should categorize it as 'a rude interruption.' Do you? And I do believe that was God speaking to us, once again trying to get our attention in a most innocuous way. Remember, it was He who said, 'Let there be light.' Why could he not say just the opposite as well?

"I would much rather talk about that than some letter of mine you say you have, and...", stopping in mid-sentence, mouth still open, realizing that he just admitted to the world the letter was legitimate. Recovering quickly, Jonah offered a deal, "Edward, I know you want an explanation of the letter and I want to give it to you.

"But right now, we are seeing something wondrous happening and I think it's certainly more important than a minor correspondence of mine. Let me offer this to you... let's talk for whatever time we have remaining today about this incredible thing, and I promise to make myself available to you for another interview in the next week or so provided the networks are willing. Does that work for you?"

Bennie had the reverend in his sights and lost the upper hand when the light went out. But Stamm did admit the letter was his. Now he was experiencing a slew of unexpected emotions and wasn't sure how it was coming across on TV. He was feeling frustration, anger, and some helplessness because if truth be told, he had no opinion on this light thing, he really didn't want to get into that with Stamm. But he realized he also had some hope as the reverend had given him another shot. He'd just go along with this one to get to the next.

"Yes, Reverend," almost choking on the words, "thank you. That will be fine. Tell us why you think this light thing is a message from above."

And for the next twelve minutes, Bennie listened to what he thought was the biggest pile of crap he had heard in a very long time.

Chapter 27

Dedham, MA

During the darkness, the silence was the first thing noticeable in the Aura/Sonos lab. When the light returned, the sound followed, a lot of it. Etiquette was the first thing to go as everyone started talking, even yelling all at once. It was a mixture of consternation, frustration, fear, and of all things, joy which largely emanated from Fran Porter.

Not one to shrink from sticking it to others, Fran leveled a snotty shot at Grace, "Ms. Perez, I felt a tingle, I did!"

Peter responded quickly leaving no room for doubt as to how he felt about Fran's barb, "Stow it, Fran! Drop it, now!" Once again, Anna motioned for him to remain calm.

Grace Perez was genteel. "It's all right, Peter. I understand where she's coming from."

Addressing Fran directly, Grace offered, "Fran, look I don't suppose we'll ever be best friends, friends even, but I would like your respect. I've done nothing to elicit your response except work for an organization you disapprove of. That's all well and good. I'm sure I would disapprove of some of your activities were I to investigate them. Please do not take that as a threat. It isn't. You've been vetted as has everyone else and we know where your sympathies lie. And that's fine. We do not see you as a threat to us.

"However, we are, at the end of the day, all working towards the same goal – that's to find out what is going on. What I've learned about you and the rest of the Aura/Sonos staff demands my respect. That is all I would ask of you. Is that reasonable?"

Fran turned to Grace warily, with growing respect borne out of contentiousness. She knew she gave people shit and respected those who stood up and gave it back to her. Grace Perez passed that test. "Yes, it is. Do I call you Ms. Perez, Grace, Your Grace?" once more sticking it to her. Turning away from her, she leveled another parting shot, "Next time you come, would you mind bringing some pizza?" To the rest of the staff, they saw that as Fran grudgingly accepted Grace.

Grace smiled back at Fran, something she'd be unable to see but would hear, "You are a real ball-buster. You sure you weren't in the military?" which was high praise from her. "And please call me Grace, all of you, and Fran, I suppose you'll want extra cheese on that too?"

All preconceived notions were now tossed out. Fran and the rest of the Aura/Sonos group now accepted Grace as a fellow human. She in turn saw them as earnest and focused, trying to do their job amidst an increasingly difficult environment. Looking back towards Peter, she asked, "So, what do we have? Is there anything new from this? Is it possible to predict when this might happen again? Was this different from any of the other incidents? What about..." only to be cut off by Adam Faraday.

Adam appreciated anyone who would stand up to Fran. Grace Perez was one of them. He became aware of another kind of appreciation for her, one of which he thought might never occur again.

He wasn't sure he was ready for that kind of thing. "Ma'am, uh, Grace, slow down. These are all good questions and ones we are looking for the answers to. Before we know anything, we're going to have to look at the data we recorded and analyze it. So far, everything we've got has been speculative. There is data but it's unlike anything we've seen. The binary translation came up empty as we'd been advised it might."

Adam wasn't ready to share the info his father gave him. He had yet to process what it might mean. He continued, "There are some markers that might make sense, but everything else seems to be an anomaly. Hell, we don't even know if it's an anomaly since we've no idea what that could look like. We may have to rely on intuition as much as facts since there aren't many of them yet.

"The timing of that last incident or blink or whatever you want to call it has a different feel to it. Prior to that one, they were separated by days, not minutes. I don't know how to describe it with what we've seen, but if I had to draw an analogy, it would be something like a bear waking up after a long hibernation. The blinks would become more frequent as the bear woke up."

"Wait a minute! Are you saying this thing, whatever it is, is alive, a being?" Grace Perez's impatience was showing again.

"No, Ms. Perez, uh, Grace, not at all, I don't really know. Think about it like this... when you wake up in the morning, sometimes you're a little foggy, right? Who hasn't felt that? But once you move around a bit, and have some coffee maybe, your thought processes become a little clearer. That's what this seems like a little. It might be experiencing, uh, what? for a better word, clarity.

"Each time the light blinks, the messages, or whatever you want to call them, appear on our measurements to become less jumbled, more cohesive if you will. But again, we still don't know what's going on. However, this may well challenge our notion of what is light.

"I don't know if anyone noticed this during the last blink but when it was dark, it was totally dark. Yes, the lights went out, but even the monitor lights on the equipment went dark, yet it all kept functioning. Electricity was still evident and apparently in its regular state. We've seen that when lightning strikes. We couldn't see it, but we could hear it and see the destruction it caused.

"When it normally goes dark, there is usually some ambient light present. Not so when this happens. All light disappears. I think this is far broader than what we may think. If all light is vanishing and we experience it simultaneously, then we don't need to look for a viral agent. It's got to be much bigger if it's affecting nature itself."

Grace Perez was not thrilled with that explanation. "Adam, you're not giving me much confidence in what this group has done. If anything, it seems like you're all working on hunches. And I'm not a fan of hunches. This isn't the time for idle speculation."

Adam brushed his now longer hair out of his eyes, "You're right, we are working on hunches and speculating. In the absence of facts, that's all we've got. But keep in mind, that's how many breakthroughs start. Can you live with that for the time being?" hoping she could.

Everyone including Peter Easton at Aura/Sonos breathed a little easier after the NSA Deputy Director left. While she had yet to lower the boom or make any tangible threats, the prevailing feeling was it would only be a matter of time. It didn't help that while Fran had agreed to a truce with her, she remained loudly paranoid about the NSA's involvement. It would ultimately fall to Adam, not Peter, to rein her in.

Fran was about to launch into one of her impassioned but entertaining rants when Adam brought her up short, "Don't start Fran. Really. I don't think Grace is the enemy. And we need her and the NSA to do this."

She respected authority to a degree, after that all bets were off. But with Adam, that respect went deep and while she could kid him, she knew when to rattle his cage and when to leave it be. Few people commanded that level of respect from her.

"Peter, there's more to this than what Fran and I have shared with you and Grace. I'm sorry, but maybe I'm getting a little paranoid too, certainly proprietary about it at the very least."

Easton looked over at Adam and then Fran, not hiding his consternation, simply asking "Why?"

Adam quickly took the lead, "Remember what I said about this being of, and not being of earth, and challenging our notion of what is light? First, we're pretty sure its origins are here on Earth, not anywhere else. Nothing indicates otherwise, but that could change. The more times it happens, the more info we get, and the more likely we are to determine what it is, what is its originating source, and lastly, who. That seems simple, but trust us, it isn't at all.

"Do you also remember when we theorized it was like a 'conversation', a two-way street? That part is still in consideration. But here's what else we've discovered – some 'conversations' are 'louder', than others. It's like a strong signal versus a weak signal. And they all vary in intensity, duration, and strength. The best analogy I can give you is this: if you take sounds of equal level but put them at different distances, some will sound louder while others softer. That's what we've determined.

"Yet, they're all going on simultaneously as we said before, all at once. It's as if all the radios in the world were turned on listening to different stations at the same time. We hear something, a lot of something, but we can't yet separate them. Right now, it's just a lot of babble." He realized his father may have been correct about it being omnidirectional. But what that meant was still beyond him.

Fran was fidgeting through Adam's description and could hold it no longer. "Adam, if you're not gonna tell 'em, I will. Peter, Adam is right, it is a lot of babble, but here's the big thing. In it, we got lucky and heard some languages or words we think we recognize. We haven't been able to isolate them to translate, but when we slow down the recordings and transcribe the info, that's when we were able to pick some stuff up out of the garble. But there is just so much of the damn stuff going on, it's like trying to watch a film playing of ridiculously high-speed traffic patterns and then trying to pick out the red 2008 Toyota from New York with the driver wearing one argyle sock in it. Now, how in hell are we going to find that?

"We're working on it. We've already come a long way in a short time, but man, we've got an even longer way to go. Who knows what the hell we're going to find?"

Peter wasn't happy he'd been kept out of the loop. Looking at Anna who shrugged, then at Fran, then Adam, his anger was obvious, "Why haven't you told me this? You can't continue to parcel out your findings as you see fit. Are you both clear on that? Now, is there more I should know?"

Adam and Fran looked at each other and she nodded, while Adam hesitated before speaking, "Uh, yeah, there is. It's going to sound a bit like a moonshot of an idea. It's pure speculation, but it's an idea we should consider. Remember I mentioned our notion of light? It's always been there. We rely on natural light from the sun. We learned how to make our own light. It could be considered a mimicry of the sun. Ancients referred to the sun as a god. Light came from them and if the gods were angry, could take it away, as an eclipse. Learning how to imitate it, we, in a sense, made ourselves gods.

"Think about this... it, light, as an idea or a thought even from within. Writers for centuries have depicted people as "bright", 'shining', 'radiant'. What if there is something more to that? What if those descriptions weren't just artistic license?"

"I hope I misunderstand you. Are you saying light is God?" Easton was more than skeptical on this statement.

"No. Hardly. We think it could be us, all of us, the whole planet made manifest. Almost like a loop, but not. All meaningful babble. I admit it's out there, but so is what's happening."

Chapter 28

Baltimore, MD

Editors get upset when stories aren't turned in on time and are further pissed off when interviews get off track. Tim Siegel, True North's chief editor was more than pissed, he was furious, thinking to himself, 'no wonder I've got no hair anymore. Dammit, Benton.'

"What the hell happened, Bennie? I thought you weren't going to go with the letter, at least not that soon. And then you let him off the hook! Fuck it, you're better than that, but you looked like a damn rookie out there and on national TV no less. I expect that shit from a cable network, but we're supposed to be different."

Edward Benton was not taking this dressing down well. He knew it had gotten out of his hands, but what could he do when the light decided to toss its two cents into the mix? "Tim, I'm sorry. He's good, very good. We knew that but you gotta admit, we weren't ready for another one of those flickers. He pivoted damn fast on that one, but he did confirm the letter is real. Don't forget, he's going to give us another interview though. We're not done yet."

Tim looked at Bennie with disgust. "Then you better be prepared for that one. This was a coup for us to get and some legitimization for what we do. Another performance like that and whatever reputation we do have will be crap. Clear?"

"What if I can't get the info we need? Do we have a fallback on this?"

"Fallback? Yeah, we do. You'll be looking for a new job."

"C'mon, Tim. This thing came up on us so fast, we're doing the best we can. Stamm's always been slippery and now we may finally have some traction. Give me a chance to build this, will ya?"

"Bennie, listen to me. We don't have the luxury of time. Who knows what this light thing is all about? We're going to have to move as fast as we can on this and if that means improvising, then that's what we'll have to do.

"Besides, there are other issues involved, ones I haven't shared with anyone yet."

Bennie, looking at his editor, was about to ask the question whose answer he was about to receive.

"If you leak this to anyone, you might as well pack up your desk now. We're about to lose our backing…"

Staring at his reporter ready to interrupt, he motioned with his hand to stop.

"Yes, our revenues have increased with the light deal, but that's not nearly enough. We've been hemorrhaging cash for the last eighteen months and the well has just about run dry. You can consider this Stamm thing a last-ditch effort to save True North. Now, do you understand?"

Bennie nodded numbly at Tim and walking off to his cubicle, signaled to Lee Black to follow him. Lee trailed along several steps behind him. "Bennie, hey, don't let this thing get you down. There's no way you could have predicted the..."

His hand shot up to stop Lee, "It's more than just that. I should have been ready for anything, even that. Shit, it caught me off-guard, but he did provide me with an opening. Did you catch it? The thing about a group of influential businessmen behind his 'work.' Let's find out who they are and what kind of involvement they've got. We'll reopen with that, OK."

"What do you mean more than that? What are we missing?"

Benton ignored Lee's first question. "I don't know what we're missing. If I did, we'd be in much better shape."

"We're going to have to be ready at a moment's notice. We just don't have much time. While the good reverend said he'd do another interview, we don't know when. We can count on him to start off with the good work, the good word, and whom the hell knows what else. In the meantime, I want to have as much background on the effects this light thing is having on people, countries, whatever, around the world. From what I know it ain't all good and I'd like to see what spin he'll put on it."

Meanwhile, in Stamm's study, he and Sheila were looking over a spreadsheet documenting the increase in tithes. Since the light incidences started, they'd increased 23% over the same period last year, a welcome turn of events. However, after the interview, there were signs of it tailing off, indicating he did not come across as positively as he would've liked. That would have to be corrected on the next interview which would now be sooner than later.

"Sheila, would you please reach out to your friend and Mr. Benton again and see when they would like to conduct the next interview? I don't think we can wait longer than a week from today," he asked, absently reaching out for her hand.

He didn't notice Sheila reflexively wince, refraining from pulling back her hand. The reverend had been so occupied that she was beginning to feel isolated from him. But the isolation was due not only to his absorption, She and her view of the world was changing. It was aided by growing feelings towards Lee Black, something from a long time ago. She hadn't given conscious thought to that.

She nodded absently at Jonah, "Certainly, Reverend," maintaining the formality in the office Stamm demanded, protective as ever of his and her own privacy and their secret.

Picking up her phone, she called Lee, letting the phone ring for what seemed a long time before moving to voice mail. "Lee, it's Sheila. Could you call me, please? The reverend would like to discuss the next interview, next week if possible. Call me please." Putting it down, she felt apprehension about these interviews. That was not the only reason. She was now beginning to sense that she was only a means to an end. Was Stamm all he portrayed himself or was he deceiving Sheila or was she deceiving herself? It wasn't the first time such doubts had entered her mind. It had happened the first time she slept with him, but he picked up on her unease and reassured her there was no cause for such discomfort.

Standing in the doorway to Stamm's office, Sheila spoke, "Reverend, he wasn't in. I left a message on his phone." He nodded without looking up and returned to the spreadsheet, trying to figure how to get the numbers back on the upswing.

Chapter 29

Dedham, MA

Everyone was holding their breath, waiting for Easton to blow up. Not that he had a temper, but they realized how preposterous was this idea. They would be disappointed.

"Really, that's it? You've got to be joking. What evidence do you have? What would support that premise? And what the hell does it have to do with the light blinking on and off?" Easton was astounded. Twice in a few minutes, he felt his team had misled him.

Adam paused once again, then spoke, "No, we're not joking. It is preposterous. It is out there. We know that, but so is this situation and we haven't figured it out yet. We do believe the two are connected in some fashion though and until we can analyze the data we have and hopefully get more, we're still theorizing... in a big way. I know that too is more than a reach, but…

"Peter, I wish we could give you more, but can you see how Grace Perez and the NSA might receive this? They'd think we're nuts. It is an outrageous theory, I admit. So is what's happening. Hell, even if we're correct, I don't yet know what to make of this. But I believe the light's behavior and the translations we have may be one and the same, a key perhaps.

"I also think Grace Perez could be an asset to us. I trust her. If it's OK with you, I'd like to work with her."

Fran turned her head in Adam's direction, mumbling, "Oh yeah, even without eyes, I can see that." Her spidey sense picked up on that.

The chief of Aura/Sonos was astounded as was everyone else. Easton knew they needed to keep a lid on this for as long as possible, even if it meant stalling the NSA, something of which he was not keen.

"Adam, Fran, I don't like that you held this back. We are supposed to share all discoveries we make. That said, I understand why you did what you did. I don't condone it at all. I do support it though."

Fran was ecstatic, "Finally!"

"Stow it, Fran. We could get our asses in the proverbial sling if we're not careful. The question is how do we sit on this until we know what we got? And then, to avoid that damn sling, what kind of excuse do we have for doing so? You know I've always required ethical behavior from all of you. This may seriously compromise what this company is all about. Not to mention me personally. We're placing ourselves in jeopardy with a group not famous for mercy.

"Adam, it's not a bad idea you work with her provided you remember who signs your paycheck. You might even be able to get some insight into where they're going as well."

Anna had remained silent throughout this exchange. "Peter, I agree with Adam. I don't think Grace Perez is the enemy. She may have a different agenda than ours, but it doesn't mean we can't work with her. I also like the idea of Adam working with her.

"But" she continued, "I don't think you, Adam, should be dealing with her alone. Let me join you. I think I have a much better idea of where she's coming from than the rest of you and she won't see me as quite the adversary." Looking over at Adam and smiling to herself, she too saw noticeable changes in him when Grace was nearby.

"That's fine with me. Hopefully, by the next time we speak with her, we may know something concerning any viral aspects of this as well. You got to admit, this is the strangest thing we're ever faced. You know Occam's Razor – all other things being equal, the simplest explanations are usually better than the more complicated ones. Well, this is like that. I just don't see any explanations to this yet – simple or otherwise."

###

145

Things were starting to slow down for it. Clarity was being achieved but through no effort on its part. Confusion was ebbing. There were so many voices heard, so many emotions and experiences, it was all at once overwhelming yet oddly comforting.

It was rested and restless, alone in a crowd, one among many. Lifetimes of memories flooded its consciousness while it slowly became aware of the past, the now, and the present which were still meaningless. And fear for the future for which it had no reference.

It observed all around it while at the same time experiencing it. The most powerful feeling was one of curiosity. It held no opinions nor animosity towards what it was learning. And it was learning at an unbelievable speed. Eons of history, cataclysms – natural and human-made, hopes and dreams, evil and good, prejudices, and beneath it all an underlying desire for peace among those many voices. Not from all, but from most, so many. And there were some, whose desire for peace was secondary to... what? Greed? 'What is peace? What is greed?' it thought for the first time. It was facing concepts for the first time.

None of it made sense but it was not as overwhelming as before. It did not know what it was experiencing for it did not yet know what it itself was. Yet an awareness was being realized and that too was foreign.

It reached out as if involuntarily stretching, not yet fully comprehending what it was doing, and saw things, again for which it had no reference. The accumulation of new memories would inform and shape it as more thoughts formed. With it came more questions. It reached out once more, this time intentionally. And once more the light winked out.

And it was glad.

Chapter 30

Washington, DC

Years of Alabama backroom politics had given Carlton Justice a keen sense of when things were working against him, and his alarms were blaring. He had tried reaching Pingry with no luck. The same happened when he reached out to other members of their group. That told him all he needed to know he was being shut out. He knew why, it was that damned letter from Stamm, and feared what the consequences might be. Justice was certain he wouldn't be thrown under the proverbial bus but knew it wouldn't be pretty.

The congressman figured that Stamm wanted to meet with Pingry and the group, but because of his newly imposed isolation, didn't know how to proceed. He was unaware of the initiative in setting up that closed meeting. Either way, the outcome would be dire. Stamm was no longer available to Justice as well. Could things get any worse?

Whatever capital or leverage he once had was now lost. He pulled out a legal pad and attempted to draw up a list of options available. After several false starts, the pad remained unmarked. He had forged his strongest alliances with these people and those were now in shambles. He saw no options at all.

Realizing he couldn't stand being in his office any longer, he ventured out to his now favorite refuge, Pozzi's. Walking a few blocks to his destination, he stopped in front of a few stores, mindlessly window shopping. He realized that unless he was able to pull the proverbial rabbit out of a hat, he'd no longer be able to patronize these shops or others. Nor would he be able to partake in his favorite libation. He thought he might as well indulge now while it was still available to him.

It was only a few minutes before he arrived at the restaurant. Walking over to the far end of the bar, he looked around but didn't see

Goldie there. That was just another disappointment in a rapidly deteriorating day. The bartender in attendance, a young, attractive Hispanic woman, walked up to him laying down a napkin on the bar in front of him. "Hi! What's your pleasure today?"

In his current mood, the question seemed to be providing a choice between freedom and crucifixion, laughing to himself over the Monty Pythonesque absurdity of that. He looked up at her, "Isn't Goldie here tonight?"

"No, not yet. He should be coming on in about an hour. I'm Pilar," smiling and offering a handshake, "what can I do for you in the meantime?"

Offering a small, tight smile but not taking her hand, he pointed to the bourbon shelf, "Let me have a Pappy 23, please. And leave the bottle out. Thanks."

Anticipating a good tip from an obviously upscale and desperate drinker, she was intent on making sure Carlton was well taken care of, giving him a generous pour of the liquor. "Just let me know if there's anything else I can do for you. OK?"

The congressman nodded, yet eying her warily. While not Goldie, she admittedly was a hell of a lot better looking. He'd have to watch himself. Congress was filled with stories of roving eyes *and* hands bringing down the mighty. Too many more Pappy's and he could find himself in new trouble on top of everything else.

The next hour went by slowly, aided and abetted by the bourbon and the attentiveness of the attractive Pilar. As he was getting ready to order his third drink, Goldie arrived behind the bar. "Evening, Congressman. How are we this fine night?"

"Well, Goldie, better because of this," waving his now empty glass. "But it is in need of resuscitation."

While not as good-looking as Pilar, he was a superior bartender, hardly ever forgetting a customer's preference. "Pappy's, right?"

Carlton was impressed, "Indeed. Goldie, you are a godsend. What do you hear these days?"

Goldie looked at the congressman, "Funny you should ask. The last time you were in, you asked me if anyone from Reverend Stamm's office ever came in. Until then, not that I knew of. But, last week, Friday I think, there was a couple sitting pretty much where you are right now. I couldn't help but overhear a bit of their conversation, you know?"

That got Carlton's attention quickly, "And?"

"I only heard a part of their conversation, they were there when I started my shift, but I think one of them worked for a news organization, a reporter maybe, the other worked for Stamm. She, the one from Stamm's office, was answering the guy's questions about a letter Stamm may have sent, uhh... to you. It seemed more than a business relationship if you catch my drift. That mean anything to you?"

Justice felt as if he had just lost his best friend and won the lottery all at once. How this all fit together was still a puzzle, but if he was able to piece it together, he might come out unscathed. If not, he may as well pack his bags and skulk back off to Alabama. Right now, he had to get his arms around this and fast. To make things worse, the media was now involved. He realized there was little or no time remaining, and he'd better leave Pozzi's quickly.

"Goldie, it might, it just might. Can you throw together some sort of sandwich to go for me? I can't stay."

When Goldie returned, Justice took out a roll of cash and peeled off some bills, "The twenty is for Pilar, this, the hundred, is for you. Thanks. See you soon."

"Sonofabitch! Trey, get the fuck in here! Now!"

Carlton Justice was pissed and was about to do physical damage to anything or anyone nearby. Fortunately for Trey Keenan, one of Justice's aides, he was in the hall speaking with Parks Denton, a friend,

149

and a congressional staffer from congressman Neil Lucey's office. He heard the boss's bellow and decided to make himself scarce for a while. "Parks, let's get some lunch. I don't want to be around for that," nodding to Justice's office.

The two young aides walked quickly and quietly down the hall and outside, making their way to the Longworth Cafeteria. The lines would most likely be lengthy ensuring a longer-than-usual lunch which suited Trey perfectly. While trying to figure out what they would order, Trey's cell rang. Looking at it, he saw it was the congressman. He debated upon answering it, ultimately deciding to take the call.

Justice's wrath would be better to receive through an earpiece than let it steep, festering until his return. "Yes, Congressman?" Wincing and pulling the phone away from his ear, the congressman's anger could be clearly heard by any standing nearby. "Yessir, I was out getting us some lunch," Trey rolled his eyes and lied. "The usual, yes. And a diet iced tea. Yessir. As soon as I can."

"Justice?" asked Denton.

"Yeah," Trey laughed, "the perfectly named congressman from the beautiful state of Alabama. You know, he's OK, but when he gets pissed, stay out of his way. And this is one of those times. I don't know what this latest thing is, but for the past few days, all I've been doing is throwing raw meat into his office and closing the door behind me. He's got a wild hair up his ass, and he can't reach it to pull out."

The line moved more quickly than normal. Both aides were able to place their orders and received them in minutes.

"You know Trey, I've been seeing some of that same stuff at my office but not as bad as this. But I think it may something to do with your guy. Lucey won't take his calls, but I've heard his name mentioned several times."

Trey hesitated before speaking, "Look, Parks. I got to get back to the office before he torches the place, but let's meet after work for a drink and talk. Usual place, that work for you? 7'ish? Good?" Both agreed and walked back to their respective offices.

When Trey made his way back to his desk, he found the congressman fuming but now under control of his emotions. "Trey, when you leave, let me or someone know. I can't have you running around when I need you most."

Handing over the takeout container with his lunch to Justice, Trey responded apologetically, "Congressman, I saw you were buried and just decided to get you lunch knowing you had no appointments and thinking you wouldn't break for it. I apologize. It won't happen again."

"Fine, fine. Look, I want the entire staff here at three. Shit runs downhill and it seems like I'm at the bottom of a mountain of it! We're running into some major fund-raising problems, and I need everyone here to figure out what's happening and what the hell we're going to do about it."

His aide had learned the most valuable currency in Washington, DC was information, and he might just now have some. He thought about what Parks had shared with him and wondered if there was any connection. He also wondered if he should share that with Justice. Trey also learned that timing is everything, especially in DC. "Yessir, Congressman, right away."

He would wait until after his drinks with Congressman Lucey's aid deciding if there was anything worth sharing with Justice. Or anyone else for that matter.

Chapter 31

The increasing number of flickers was starting to take a greater toll on the populace around the world. What had been curious, and peculiar was now becoming more and more frightening. Each time it occurred, the media drumbeat became louder and more strident with calls for governments to do something. Obviously unable to do more than offer platitudes and empty reassurances, governments tried fruitlessly to keep their citizenry calm. Not surprisingly, that void was filled by others who believed they had the inside track on this.

Were they honest with themselves, they would have admitted uncharacteristically they were in no better position to address the problem than the governments who happily ignored their schemes. That said, they persisted, exacerbating the situation, one charge being led by Reverend Jonah Stamm, who was rising to the top of an already rancid pool of fear-mongers.

While Stamm was fanning his own flames, the media was unintentionally doing its best, contributing to the rising fear and impending hysteria sure to follow. As with any crisis or catastrophe, the media continued to feed itself and its audience on the 'what we know at this time' pablum. Oddly, among all the news outlets, the one organization keeping largely above this fray was True North. Not that they were the most scrupulous of operations, but they were understaffed and were maintaining their sole focus on Stamm.

Around the world, the demonstrations and cult-like groups grew rapidly. People were losing confidence in their leaders and their churches. Main-stream denominations, which in uncertain times people historically turned to, saw a precipitous drop in attendance and consequently their contributions. There was no solace nor safety to be found in their platitudes.

In such times of increasing fear and growing apprehension, any answers were better than none. Turning to those who appeared to be able to make sense of it provided a small level of comfort, no matter how badly misplaced it was. In the end, they would be no better off than had they sought solutions elsewhere. There were too many voices offering too much babble and the overload was approaching a critical mass.

Beyond the psychological toll, it was beginning to take a physical toll. People were afraid to travel as the likelihood of an accident was increasing. As the periods of 'darkness' increased both in duration and frequency, people were reluctant to leave their homes. The effect on business was calamitous. Employees were not showing up for work, productivity was crashing, sales of goods were drying up, and economies were starting to feel the growing effects of a cowering citizenry.

Work-from-home as a solution was a joke. Gun sales however were doing quite nicely, thank you. While there was no comfort to be found outside the home, at least that would now be a "safe" place.

Speculation was rampant in the scientific community. Peter Easton and his group deliberately kept a low profile primarily because it suited their natural position to remain below the radar and secondly that's the way Grace Perez and the NSA wanted it. It wouldn't be long before that was no longer possible and when it broke, they needed to be out in front of it. A preemptive, preventive course would have to be devised. Easton knew this but understood that the NSA's agenda was probably far different from his. It would require delicacy and assistance and he knew whom he would turn to for that.

Adam Faraday couldn't remember the last time he was this excited about work. Until now, his work at Aura/Sonos moved at tortoise-like speed, methodical, almost plodding. True, it was fulfilling but not something he'd take home. That changed with the light phenomenon. He wasn't ready to call it a breakthrough, hardly, since he had no idea of what they were dealing. Yet, it was entirely new ground, never explored, much less considered. He was in pursuit of something so unknown whose outcome could not even be speculated upon.

He was surprised to realize, he might be attracted to Grace Perez and her no-nonsense, cut-through-the-bullshit attitude. It was that same quality that had attracted him to Jess. Now for the first time since her death, another woman interested him.

Those thoughts would have to wait as he was to meet Fran at a coffee shop on the square on the main street in town. He found a parking spot about a block away, fed the meter, and walked the short distance to where he saw Fran waiting outside the shop. "So," he offered, "come here often, sweetheart?"

Fran almost dropped her cane and jaw simultaneously, "Adam? I could swear I heard a smile in your voice. Is that really you?"

Adam smiled at her though she couldn't see it. "Yeah, it's me. Got a problem with me being happy? I know that's been in short supply, but I'm stoked about what we're working on. You got to be too, aren't you?"

"Let's go inside and talk, Adam. I'm hungry and I need some coffee."

Adam opened the door for Fran and led her to a booth in the back of the restaurant. Sitting down, Fran started, "Adam, what do you think we're into here? This light thing I mean?"

Keeping it easy, Adam responded, "Whew, Fran, for a moment I thought you were breaking up with me. The light thing...yeah, right. Good question. Look, you know as much as I do, more maybe. Are you holding back on anything I should know about? And even more importantly, from Peter?"

At that moment, the waitperson came to their table for their order. Adam ordered just a coffee while Fran went full tilt, OJ, coffee, three eggs over easy, bacon and ham, toast, and home fries.

Laughing, Adam commented on Fran's order, "Wow, you miss your last feeding?"

"Hey, I said I was hungry! Holding back? I don't think I could call it that. How can you hold back what you don't know? What about you? What are you holding back? I got to believe you've some ideas you haven't shared with us."

Smiling, Adam cut in quickly, "Whoa! That's both of us! I know you too well Fran to let a comment like that go by. What's up?"

Fran was about to speak when the waitperson came over with their coffee. When their cups were filled, the carafe left on the table for them, Fran spoke. "Adam, you know I've been dealing with hunches on this since it happened, right? And really, I don't know if any of them are any good or just dead ends. I've got a few hunches though and one wild ass idea which if real scares the shit out of me.

"First, as we get more occurrences of this, they seem to be changing, evolving even, maybe. Shit, it's too weird. But and this is a big one, there seems to be a clarity developing. That would support what you're theorizing. Not specifically where I can determine what's happening, but it looks like what could have been described as a clamor, is starting to coalesce, for lack of a better word. Again, not into anything I can figure out, but...

"Remember when I used the multiple radio stations as an example? I think that's still a good analogy. It's like finding a stronger signal amidst many. There's still so much going on in the data, but there's a certain cohesion I sense building, but can't describe it yet. It's something I feel as much as I, uh, think about. Yeah, but, that's not it really either. It's like the difference between logic and emotion, youth and age. I experience it beyond just thinking. Weird, huh?"

Adam just looked at Fran, not touching his coffee once. "Yeah, weird doesn't begin to describe it. What in hell are you saying, Fran?"

"What if it's not many channels after all? What if it's only a couple? What if it's only one?"

Staring at Fran as if seeing her for the first time, Adam took a long pull on his coffee before speaking, "One what, Fran? Can you be any clearer?"

"Look, and this is a hunch too. Each time the light blinks, we've been able to record data. Do we know what we've got, no, but you know that? Yet each time, there appears to be a little less jumble and more clarity in the data streams. It's almost like someone learning a new language, which in this case we are. But I think the learning is on both sides. Whatever is going on, this thing, whatever is causing this, it appears like it is learning to speak. Too many things that sound like words, lousy syntax, mixed metaphors, and different languages even. Maybe? You name it. I think it may be an attempt at communication. If so, we're dealing with an intelligence completely foreign to us"

Adam was grateful for the arrival of Fran's breakfast. It gave him a moment to think about what she had just shared. Meanwhile, Fran felt for her plates, found the toast, and shoved a piece in her mouth. Chewing, she was about to speak when Adam started, "OK, I can accept that. I've learned to respect your hunches. They're usually a little otherworldly, but, hey this one is no different. Any idea who might be behind this? Us? Them?"

Fran was eating rapidly as if this was indeed her first meal in days. "It ain't us. It can't be. And I don't know who 'them' is. It could be a 'what'. You ever hear of a Dyson Sphere?"

Holding back his own theories, Adam responded to Fran's statement. "That was not an answer I expected. What's a Dyson Sphere? Sounds like you renewed your subscription to *Popular Science* or your vacuum cleaner broke."

"Damn, Adam, you're no fun. Look, think about what I've told you. Initially, I only felt a tingle, a coolness on my skin the first time it happened, right? Now, in addition to that, I'm intuiting, feeling something. For lack of a better description, I've sensed mixed emotions and none of them are mine. They are all tied up in the blinks.

"I've also a feeling of reaching out and learning as I mentioned. That's it. But can you see why I wanted to talk with you offline first? Yeah, yeah, I know. I'll tell Peter, but do we have to let Grace know?"

Glad that Fran couldn't see him, Grace's name brought a small but genuine smile to Adam's face. Still smiling, "Yes, of course, we do, you know that. I know you don't trust her, but we are working with and for them and will continue to. I got to admit I enjoyed seeing Grace stand up to you. It was pretty funny. So, what's your second hunch?"

Fran paused, waiting to finish the large forkful of potatoes she shoveled into her mouth, "So, you *enjoyed* seeing Grace stand up to me, did you?"

"Yeah. So?"

"It's no longer a hunch, you just confirmed it."

"Confirmed what, Fran? Give me a break here, will ya?"

Wiping her mouth, Fran offered, "You Adam. You got the hots for her. That was one of my hunches, now a fact."

Adam looked at her with admiration, only Fran could have picked up on that. Neither denying nor confirming, Adam responded, "That's real funny, Fran. More theory, huh?"

"Funny? And are you smiling again? Oh shit, Adam. Grace? Really?"

"No. But I can't deny that there's something about her I find attractive. And that's the first time since Jess died. But put that aside if you can, OK? Now, what's a Dyson Sphere?"

Fran took a deep breath before speaking quietly. "Look, it is a wild ass idea, but so is this thing that's happening. OK, a Dyson Sphere. Back in the '30s, a sci-fi writer, Olaf Stapledon, conceptualized a mega-structure that can completely encapsulate a star and harness its power. It was later theorized by others that not only could this be done to a star, but to planets as well, for survival and colonization. It could explain why all light disappears. It's blocking out the mother of all light, the sun. What if someone actually built one of those?

"I'm not saying that's what this is, but it's something we might consider."

"Jeez, Fran, that's too much. It wouldn't explain why we can't even see equipment lights. No, it's too out there. Scratch that idea now. It doesn't explain why light goes on and off. And if that's what it is, and I'm sure it isn't, then there's an alien invasion going on and we would have noticed that kind of construction. No, I think I'm on solid ground saying it isn't that."

"God, you're such a wet blanket. I didn't think so either but thought it was worth a giggle and I'd put it out there. Got to laugh at something, right? So back to the important issue at hand... you and Grace? At least tell me what she looks like so I can hate her even more." She didn't need eyes to hear Adam's mock pained groan.

Chapter 32

Washington, DC

The apprehension Theo Garcia felt upon arriving at Pingry's home was nothing compared to the considerable trepidation he felt about his call to Jonah Stamm. While publicly he'd never taken a stand on religious issues, he had a problem with what those of Stamm's ilk did in the name of their proprietary deity. Some of them did good work, but overall, when it came to matters involving Native North Americans, Theo had nothing but contempt for them. Now he had to deal with them directly. He knew this was what Washington was all about and reluctantly made the call.

It rang for a long time before being picked up. A breathless Sheila Weller picked it up and gasped lightly, "Reverend Jonah Stamm's office, it's another blessed day. How can I help you?"

Flustered and confused, Theo introduced himself, "Uh, yes, hello, uh, I'm, this is Congressman Theo Garcia for Thaddeus Pingry, is the Reverend Stamm there?"

Garcia was taken aback, by the greeting and the unexpected breathless, huskiness of the voice on the other end. Had he called just a few minutes earlier, he would have interrupted the strenuous sex between Stamm and Sheila, instead now just hearing her post-coital breathiness. He would have also received an altogether different response had the sexually satiated Stamm answered.

Replacing her glasses and gaining a bit more composure, Sheila continued in an uncharacteristically brief manner, "One moment please, I'll see if he's in." Happy to get off the phone, Sheila entered his office to inform the now nearly reclothed reverend of the call, "Jonah, there's a Congressman Theo Garcia on the phone for you. He said he's with Thaddeus Pingry. Should I just take a message?"

159

Stamm looked up and with a Cheshire cat grin, answered, "No, no, Sheila, not at all. Please put him through and close my door, would you please?" his public unction now permeating even his personal life. "Thank you so much, dear."

Closing the door behind her, she leaned back against it, thankful for the interruption.

Not wanting to seem too eager or even familiar with the caller, though it was his action that precipitated this call, he picked up the phone and spoke, "Jonah Stamm, how can I help you?"

"Reverend Stamm, this is Theo Garcia, congressman from New Mexico. I hope you're doing well today. I'm pretty sure you don't know me, but..."

Stamm interrupted him, troweling on the smarm, "Oh no, I am very aware of the work you do Congressman, it's an honor to talk with you. Now again, how can I help you?"

The New Mexico congressman hated this. Stamm sounded just as he thought he would, reinforcing his not incorrect impression. Hiding his disdain and couching the purpose of the call behind some useless double-speak, Theo addressed him, "Reverend, I've been asked by Thaddeus Pingry to reach out to you. He believes that the two of you, and perhaps some other like-minded individuals, share some common ideals and values. It is with that in mind he would like to meet with you. Mr. Pingry also desires, his word, that this meeting take place sooner than later. We hope you agree. Could you possibly join us this evening, for dinner perhaps? 8:30? We'll send you directions."

Before he could respond, Garcia hung up as instructed. Stamm was not to be given the opportunity to hedge on time or place. He had fired the first salvo in this. Pingry was now returning fire. He might only get one shot at this.

The brusqueness of Garcia's call wasn't lost on Jonah. He knew Thaddeus Pingry to be a formidable individual, one he would rather count as an ally than a foe. Either way, he felt he had the upper hand.

Calling in Sheila, Jonah struck an apologetic tone, "Sheila, I'm sorry but something has come up and I must deal with it. Is it all right with you if we reschedule our dinner? I know today was to be special, but I need to address this issue immediately. Forgive, please?"

If the truth were to be spoken at that moment, Sheila would have admitted to no small amount of relief. Their lovemaking had been pleasant, it always was, but she felt somewhat detached, an almost illicit feeling, during it and was happy that Stamm hadn't noticed. Though there was no way he could have known, her thoughts were now increasingly of Lee Black. And why in hell should they be, was a confusing question as nothing had happened between them. Sheila Weller wondered if it was just indulging in a fantasy. Or was something happening there? Perhaps the past wasn't over after all.

"Jonah, of course. Not a problem. It's probably just as well, I'm beat. You wore me out," addressing his ever-present and fragile male ego.

Stamm ate it up, "Thank you, Sheila, When I get through this, you choose where you'd like to go, anywhere. Is that OK?

"In the meantime, I'll be working on this, but go home and spend some time with Olivia. I know you haven't seen much of her lately. It'll be good for both of you. Oh, before you leave, would you please get me, Carlton Justice, on the phone? Thanks so much."

Sheila placed the call through to Stamm, gathering her things to leave when she heard the reverend pick up the phone, "Carlton, wait, wait, wait, yes, yes, I know. No, no. I can imagine I'm the last person you expected to hear from, but..." Stamm walked over to his door closing it and muffling the conversation, not realizing that Sheila had not yet left. What she had heard was enough for her to reason out an accurate assumption as to what Stamm would be up to that evening.

Meanwhile, Stamm was trying to calm down the very angry Alabama congressman. "Carlton, look, I know you're not happy with the way this is going down, but I had nothing to do with it. They reached out to me. When? Earlier today. A Theo Garcia from New Mexico. You know him?"

161

Stamm now knew who some of the players were with whom Justice had been involved and that was not good. That he had been contacted directly confirmed what he'd feared, he was about to be called out.

"Yes, of course, I know him, we're in congress together. What did he want? And Jonah, don't bullshit me."

"They want to meet with me tonight. I'm sure it's about the letter, what else could it be? But that's the reason I sent it to you. I do need to talk with them. But it now seems like you've been cut out from this, and they want to meet directly. Care to tell me why?" Stamm was suspicious of anything he didn't arrange and would always look for an advantage. There might not be such a thing this go-around.

Stamm was not the only suspicious one on this call. Justice too was on full alert now. The group whom he felt he could trust had indeed shut him out. Who knew what else they might be up to? And now they had contacted the reverend directly behind his back. The fact that they wanted to meet with Stamm was evidence of their concern. "Jonah, are you really that naïve? They want what I tried to find out from you concerning your damned letter. Don't play innocent. You've created a shit storm and I'm only the first to get hit with it.

"You pretty much told me you wanted out, what the hell else do you might think it is? Remember? You're threatening Thaddeus fuckin' Pingry. Did you expect him to welcome you with open arms? And now you're calling me? Come now, Jonah, we've known each other way too long to indulge in this kind of crap. I can't help you, no thanks to you. My ass is now on the line too."

Chapter 33

Baltimore, MD

Tim Siegel, the managing editor of True North News, was again waiting impatiently for the habitually late Edward "Bennie" Benton. Since the original interview, Siegel had been champing at the bit for their next shot at Stamm, now scheduled only four days away He needed to see where Bennie was on it and called his cell phone, getting instead his voicemail. Just as he was unhappily hanging up the phone, Benton, smiling broadly, walked into his office. "I hope that stupid grin on your face is telling me something good for a change."

Bennie had hoped to be a little more subtle but couldn't pull it off. Affecting a wounded attitude, he held his hand over his heart and frowned at Tim Siegel, "Stupid? Really? I'm hurt, Tim. I've always spoken well about you."

Siegel frowned at this remark. "You never let up, do you? Why do you have to break my balls, Bennie? Just get to the point."

Bennie's grin got even larger. "Tim, look, I've got something but I'm not sure what it is yet. You know the source of the original letter? Well, I just learned Justice had an intense phone conversation with the good reverend. They wouldn't tell me what it was about, but I'd bet good money it was about that letter.

"I think there's an angle we can play we haven't considered: Lee's relationship with Stamm's assistant, Sheila Weller. I think Lee might be able to find out more. Up until now, it's been rather one-sided. What do you think?"

The editor leaned back in his chair, closing his eyes for a moment before speaking, "I think we've got a few things to talk about. First, how good is your source, and by that, I mean could it be a setup? The last thing we need is to be blindsided again. If you're confident this is an opening you can exploit, do it. Providing Lee is willing.

"Bennie we can't afford to screw this up. The networks are eating our breakfast, lunch, and dinner everywhere we turn. If you're right on this, it'll go a long way in saving our asses, and you know what I mean. Obviously, we don't have the resources they do, but I think we're hungrier than them. Before you make any other moves, make sure no one else knows anything about this letter.

"The other thing there is a lot of speculation on the light thing. We're getting calls from some religious groups about it, end times, and all that stuff. I was thinking it might be a good idea for you to host a forum, round table sort of thing about it on a Sunday morning. Unscripted except for opening questions. Get some religious types, different denominations, and maybe a few from the scientific community. It could be interesting and would position us as more than a one-issue network. What do you think? It might also garner us a larger audience."

"Tim, I'm up to my friggin' eyeballs trying to corral Stamm for the other stuff. How about giving Lee a shot? He should have been online a long time ago. He's smart, comes across as sincere, and is knowledgeable, give it to him."

Frowning at this rebuff, Tim saw he had no other choice, "All right, find Lee and have him come see me."

Bennie was out the door in search of Lee Black before Tim could finish. It didn't take long to find him, hammering away on a vending machine that had appropriated his seventy-five cents for a Famous Amos cookie package. "I can't afford to lose any money in a friggin' machine with what they pay here! Sonofabitch! Hey, Bennie, what's up?"

"Lee, I gotta talk with you. Got a minute? It's about Stamm."

He ceased his assault on the defenseless machine, vowing to return another time to wreak revenge. "Stamm? I thought we were good to go on that. More questions? Or are you dropping it?"

Bennie grinned at Lee, "Drop it? Hardly. But it's a different angle. I got some intel that the honorable Carlton Justice just had a rough phone conversation with him and from what they could tell, it didn't go well on either end of the line. They said if they had to guess, Stamm was hanging Justice out to dry."

"Holy shit, Bennie! Is there anything else we can use? Can you use it in the interview? Wait, you mentioned a different angle…"

Benton would have to proceed with caution. From what he had seen, Lee seemed to have growing feelings for Stamm's assistant that might have some history. "Lee, how would you describe your relationship with Stamm's assistant? Sheila, isn't it? Do you trust her? Even more important, does she trust you?" Bennie was attempting to manipulate Lee and not very artfully.

Lee's eyes narrowed and he didn't answer for a few moments. "What's this about Bennie? What's your interest in Sheila? You know I knew her from a long time ago and… oh, no! No. You're really going to go there? Fuck! What're you digging for?"

Now Bennie's eyes narrowed, but not in suspicion, but in an implied conspiracy knowing how to hook Lee quickly. "Listen, we've been looking at this letter from one angle. Obviously, there's got to be more to it and others are involved. We need to find out who they are and what Stamm's got on Justice. We figure that out and they'll be making movies about us.

"I need you to talk with Sheila specifically about that letter. None of the nonsense we'd been looking for earlier. This time you got to ask her to go behind the reverend's back. Maybe make something up. Look, I'm sorry, you're going to have to lie to her, but it's going to be all we got unless Stamm has Edward Snowden's brother working for him and that's not likely. You in?"

Lee, like Sheila, had not yet shared his feelings with her. If he did what Bennie was asking, it could end the possibility of anything more. He sensed she had some sort of relationship with Stamm but knew nothing certain about it. Lee saw himself between the proverbial rock and a hard place, knowing he couldn't refuse what Bennie asked without endangering his job and the possibility of moving up. He didn't really want to use Sheila to that end. In his argument with himself, Bennie's side won, and Lee wasn't thrilled about it.

"Yeah, OK. But I'm not happy about this. There must be another way to do this. It's not right and you know it."

"Uh-huh, I get it. But there's no time for 'right' right now. It's the only way in.

"Oh, and Lee, Tim wants to see you. This could be the break you're looking for. I think you'll be happy about that. You might even consider going to church more often. Hah! But call Sheila first, will ya?"

Since it was only four days until the next interview, Lee did have a reason to contact Sheila. However, it would now be with a different agenda. Reluctantly, he picked up the phone and called her, mumbling the words that usually signified the end of a relationship, which wouldn't be lost on her. "Sheila, hi, it's me, we need to talk."

Chapter 34

Annapolis, MD

It dawned on Jonah Stamm how deeply entangled he was. He misjudged badly how many tentacles this thing might have. Believing that tweaking Carlton Justice would bring him to heel quickly, he found himself as the likely one being brought to heel by masters of whom he knew little. He'd now been made an avowed enemy of Justice and his friends. If Thaddeus Pingry was involved, that was an adversary he'd rather not confront. But until he met with him, he could only speculate. There was no information and consequently, no leverage. Stamm would find out tonight, too soon and not soon enough.

To compound matters further, he had that damn interview with Edward Benton scheduled in four days, also too soon and not soon enough.

Jonah thought he pretty much knew what Bennie would be looking for. It would be that damned letter.

Benton would be the proverbial dog with a bone. And it would be difficult to catch him off-guard this time. Jonah thought to himself, "Heaven help me if he finds out about my meeting with Pingry."

But then, slowly at first, the beginnings of an idea started to form. All the elements were there, they just needed to be arranged.

"Sheila! Sheila! Where the hell are you? Get in here, now!"

She was conditioned to drop everything when he beckoned, especially in that tone. Speaking quietly into the phone, she whispered, "Lee, he's calling me. Yes, I'll meet with you again. Same place where we had lunch last week, right? OK, see you then." She finished the call and entered Stamm's office.

"Yes, Reverend. What can I do for you?"

Using his sweetest tone, usually reserved for congregants about to be separated from some of their money, "Sheila, sweetheart, I need you to make some phone calls for me. Here's the list and please make them in that order. Do not make the next call on the list until you have spoken with the person at each number. And here's the message I want you to tell them." He hoped the calls would give him the lifeline he believed he would need.

###

It realized that all the sounds, all the voices, all the noise were one and the same and yet individual, making up its own self. But 'self' would have indicated an awareness not yet realized.

While in its own light, it could see and hear and experience. When in darkness, as if blinking or not 'awake' it felt nothing but peace. But in truth, it preferred light over darkness even though sometimes it brought discomfort.

If it knew what questions were, it would understand what it was thinking and feeling. Still the same questions...What am...? Who...?

The concept of self was not yet a thought. It was like a new baby receiving an overload of stimuli, but unlike the baby, it was learning at a much faster rate, increasing its knowledge exponentially every few minutes. Yet it had what would appear to be an unstructured mind of eons of history and knowledge to process. And with nothing to relate it to, or put into a perspective, the internal confusion was enormous.

It began to feel certain things – emotions as if it were human. It saw that some of them made it feel uncomfortable while others brought it peace and pleasure, emotions while not readily identifiable as such, it could and would remember.

As it started to remember, thoughts formed. As it did, each created a simultaneous cacophony, starting and ending all at the same time. If analyzed by a human, the analogy would have been like listening to the same speech at the UN being broadcast simultaneously in many languages.

It was overwhelming, a little less than before, but still all engulfing and tiring. It didn't sleep so much as adjust and change, never really leaving. But when it blinked, and it did blink again, all light disappeared.

The noise would stop for a while and then return, even in the darkness, coupled with fear and uncertainty. Languages did not matter so much when this happened. Emotions were far more powerful. There was also a difference in the noise when it was light and when it was dark. That too was confusing, but its curiosity was growing.

Chapter 35

Washington, DC

Justice had hardly touched his lunch. He was focused on some ideas of how he to proceed regarding Pingry et al. They were what he originally came to fight against, only to find himself sucked in, co-opted, and swallowed up by them, only to later be unceremoniously regurgitated. Justice did not take kindly to such action. His main concern was how to save his skin, both figuratively and literally.

He knew it was Pingry and his cadre that had been able to shut off the taps that provided his reelection funds. He knew he now had no allies on that front. In the past, he could have relied on Jonah Stamm to watch his back. Now, that too was in question.

Justice had always been among the most resourceful in his circles, whether it was school, his election class, or the House of Representatives. He could find a way to make things happen when there appeared to be no alternative. That didn't mean all deals were above board, but in the tradition of LBJ, he got things done. Faced with his most daunting adversary – isolation from those things he could so adeptly manipulate, he was pissed and energized by what confronted him. Confident that not only would he endure this he might ultimately prevail. By what means was still unknown. In the meantime, he'd have to take some action, any action to shake things loose. Whatever fell out might give him what he needed.

Bellowing behind his closed door, Justice called for his aide, "Trey, are you still here? Get in here, now!" The congressman knew his aide had made some friends among his counterparts on the hill. Perhaps he could discreetly inquire about anything involving his newly imposed exile.

Opening the door cautiously, Keenan stuck his head into the office, "Yes, Congressman? What's up?"

Softening his tone, Stamm addressed his aide, "Trey, come in and close the door behind you. Sit, sit.

"Trey, you've made some friends with some other aides here, right?" Keenan was about to answer when Justice waved his hand to stop him from speaking, Troweling it on rather thickly, Justice attempted to appeal to Trey's naïve altruism. "Please hold on for a minute. I know why you came to Washington. It's the reason many of us do. We want to do good. But you know there's some, um, how would you say it, some obstacles if you will be thrown in front of us that make it very difficult to accomplish what we'd like to.

"It would be very helpful to me and to you if you might be able to speak with some of your friends here. You know, casual-like, what're they hearing, gossip on the hill, anything about me. I think you get it. Can you do that for me?"

His aide smiled at him. "Congressman, absolutely." He debated whether he should share that such a meeting was already set up, then decided against it. "Let me ask around and see if there's anything I can dig up." Keenan had often fantasized about such an opportunity and here it was. He'd do his best to make sure it wasn't wasted.

After his aide left, Justice tried to determine how to make him the fall guy should anything go tits up, which most assuredly it would. The kid would survive, just not in Washington.

Nowhere is ambition more obvious than in the young. And nowhere than in DC was a more pure and unleavened ambition to be found in greater supply than among congressional aides. So, it was no surprise that Trey Keenan and Parks Denton, similar in size, appearance, and dress, had formed a friendship. From redder parts of the electoral map, they shared much in common, ambition not being the least of it.

As the two often shared drinks, dinner, and sometimes even women, it wouldn't surprise anyone to see them out together after work. A congressional aide who could trade in cloakroom secrets had a very bright future. For Trey Keenan and Parks Denton, unlike many of their counterparts, working behind the scenes held a far greater attraction than just mere civil service.

This meeting had an entirely different agenda. One had knowledge that the other wanted and needed. The other was all too willing to owe a favor that could be paid back when necessary. There would be no currency involved other than the expected quid pro quo somewhere down the road. It was basic – everyone in Washington, DC wanted something from someone. Sometimes their goals meshed, other times it was pure warfare, and occasionally the plots were the same, only the names changed.

Parks Denton was already at the bar when Trey arrived. "Hey. Kept a spot for you here. What'll you have?"

Trey looked around at the gathering crowd at the bar and suggested they find a table with more privacy. After securing one in a corner, Keenan spoke first. "Parks, you're not gonna believe this, but Justice suggested I meet with you and get a feel for what if anything's going on. Weird, huh? Do you know anything that would involve Jonah Stamm?"

Before Denton could speak, a server came over and asked what they'd like. Both ordered gin and tonics. The other aide looked at him for a moment as the server left before speaking. "Trey, this is confidential, as usual. I'm not sure what we could be getting ourselves into, but my guy was in a meeting with Stamm and a bunch of others."

Shaking his head, he interrupted his friend before he could ask a question, "No, don't ask, I don't know who the others were. I'm pretty sure they've met before, but it's always been off the record. I tried to track it once but came up empty."

The other aide shook his head, "The congressman must be making contacts on his private cell or has an e-mail account I'm unaware of. I wish I had more, but I'm afraid that's it."

Frowning, Trey looked at his friend. "Parks, let me share something with you. Justice has been on the receiving end of some potentially nasty shit. We all know which direction shit travels, and in this case, on me. First, he received a letter from Stamm that just about sent him off the deep end. Then he makes a short trip one night out to the suburbs and might even be with the same guy Lucey met with. You know thinking about it, I'd bet it was them because the day after he was burning up the lines to whom the hell knows.

"I heard him mention Stamm's name several times on one call. He was furious. A lot of phones slamming down, people not taking his calls, and cursing someone called Thaddeus. And then, suddenly, his campaign contributions start to dry up. There's got to be a connection somewhere in all of this, don't you think?"

As Denton was about to speak, their drinks arrived. Taking a small pull from his drink, pausing to savor its freshness, he spoke, "Have you seen that letter? Actually, really read it?" Keenan looked back at his friend with a sideways glance, raising an eyebrow.

"Shit, Trey. Be careful. I don't know if my guy is like yours, but anything he does is to be entered into the schedule record and that includes correspondence. Supposedly everything is logged in and accounted for. *Supposedly*. But as I said, there have been a few unscheduled meetings I was unaware of. His wife must have radar, because she calls, looking for him at those times. And he's always been nowhere to be found at those times. You think he might be screwing around?"

It was Trey's turn to think for a moment before answering. "Really? I thought Lucey was as straight an arrow as there was. Man, if he isn't, his wife will gut him alive on TV. Nah, I don't think that's it, but in this town, who knows? And if he was, what would that have to do with any of this?

"You mentioned someone named Thaddeus. Thaddeus who? The name doesn't ring a bell to me. You?"

Parks shrugged his shoulders, "No, not really. But from what you've just told me, whatever this is is heating up. Why don't we sort of root around, off the record right? And see if there's any spillover elsewhere. Maybe something will turn up."

"And if it doesn't? And my guy loses his seat, then what?"

Parks looked at him, laughing, "Then jeez, you'll have to get a real job."

"Not funny. Not funny at all. Let's see what we can find out. It might be something or nothing, just DC bullshit as usual. Let's meet up here tomorrow, same time. That work for you?" The aide nodded in agreement. They both finished their drinks and headed out of the bar, not noticing the very attentive, bald African American man watching them.

Chapter 36

Great Falls, VA

In most groups, Jonah Stamm would be the center of attention. This group was no exception, the difference being it was not his agenda. Confronted by a group in command of so much power, if he was honest, reminded him of his former career and all he disliked about it. That was the past. He had been introduced and was asked, rather commanded, to sit down by Thaddeus Pingry.

"Reverend Stamm, do you know why we requested you to join us this evening," demanded Pingry in his usual wintry fashion.

He was far more formidable than Jonah realized, recognizing immediately he was out of his league, Playing the innocent and resorting to his hopefully disarming charm, he smiled, "Please, Mr. Pingry, call me Jonah. No, I'm not sure I do."

Pingry got right to it, curtly asking "Reverend Stamm, are you in the habit of blackmailing others? If so, you will find you're treading on very dangerous ground. What did you expect to accomplish by sending that letter? Please tell us, we are all very interested in what you have to say since you are no less culpable than any of us."

Looking around for an ally, realizing there were none, he spoke softly, as to assuage an angry opponent. "Mr. Pingry, gentlemen, ladies, please. Blackmail is the furthest thing from my mind. I reached out to some of your colleagues in hopes of perhaps clarifying our alliance."

Pingry glowered at Stamm. "Clarify? Alliance? You must be joking. And I am not in a humorous mood. You've no idea of what we're trying to do here. Did you or did you not tell Carlton Justice you wanted out? Tell me, Reverend, what does that look like? Because quite frankly, those are the utterances of a turncoat, and I will not deal with such. Please tell us, we are waiting, and we are impatient."

"I might have spoken a little crassly when I said that. I was merely trying to impress on the congressman and some others how I thought our interests now may ultimately be in conflict." Stamm was starting to realize he overreached when sending that letter, not to mention the phone calls he had Sheila make, but there was nothing to do but press on.

For too many years Thaddeus Pingry had played such games with adversaries far more formidable than Jonah Stamm. Yet this fool could quickly bring down everything if not handled properly. But Pingry was not quite ready to reveal anything. "And just what might those interests be? You have told me nothing but allusions and stalled."

Stamm knew this was it. Pingry called his bluff, refusing to reveal anything first. Poker had never been his game and that was painfully obvious. "Sir, I believe you know of the good work we do in Southeast Asia with our children's home there. There are so many sad stories, we do what we can. But once they're old enough and they leave the home, there is nothing else we can do for them."

Not taking the bait, Pingry glowered at him, "Yes, a very noble endeavor, Reverend. But exactly what does that have to do with us?"

Jonah took a very deep breath before speaking, wondering how to get out of this in one piece. "Mr. Pingry, it's no secret how well your family and its corporations have done over the years. Everyone knows it has been around since before the civil war." He was about to take a step from which there was no turning back. "Many have also forgotten how it got its start, the slave trade, am I correct?"

Pingry reddened noticeably at the mention of this, "Yes, thank you Reverend for the history lesson." Now it was his turn to bluff. "What has that got to do with us tonight?"

Stamm saw the blush, realizing his information had been correct. He would have to proceed cautiously, "Mr. Pingry, I apologize if this offends your sensibilities, but... I have reason to believe you are still in the slave trade. Sex slaves to be precise. In Southeast Asia. And you are taking my children for that purpose. Am I right, sir?"

176

"Reverend Stamm, Jonah, isn't it? I'm sure I don't have to remind you of your namesake in the Bible, do I? Please consider this, I am your whale. And please keep that in mind. You will be nothing more than krill to me. Now please remove yourself before like that whale, I swallow you."

As Stamm left the room, Pingry gestured to Theo Garcia, "See that he is followed. We need no further surprises from that weasel."

Once again light blinked off and on, this time longer. Each time it happened, fear increased exponentially across the world, with real and lasting panic after each occurrence. The world's leaders, unsurprisingly, continued to be completely ineffectual in calming their citizenry.

Those who thought it was only an aberration were now seriously concerned. In the face of an unknown adversary, apprehension had grown. Solutions were suggested with no real belief in their effectiveness. Consequently, none were attempted, not that they would work. They were being confronted by an extraordinary entity. Had they known what it really was, that panic would exceed all others, meaning the loss of control, imaginary or not, which had been carefully marshaled over the years. A genuine understanding was still some time away.

In the meantime, there were those who sought to profit from the growing terror. They, like their leaders, would in time learn what they were facing but not before everything got worse.

Most pernicious were the fear-mongers, purporting to know what was happening, creating cults to save the masses. The number of their new disciples grew daily, more after each event. That too created more fear. As those fears increased, so did their membership. It was the ultimate pyramid scheme with as false a payoff as ever existed. Still, they came.

Organized religion wasn't much further behind. While attendance of regular members continued to decline, it was harnessing record numbers, of new members who sought the kind of reassurance and comfort they'd not had before. Confined to their specific dogmas, there were those not above creating new interpretations to suit their needs. Nowhere was this more apparent than in fundamentalist groups. Fear was a featured part of their menu, and that recipe could feed millions.

The group most attracted to these occurrences was the televangelists. Even though Jonah Stamm was preoccupied with his new situation, he was positioned to lead the charge, taking a greater role on this stage. If not him, then someone else would quickly fill that fissure and it wouldn't take long for them to try and wrest the opportunity out of his hands.

And it heard all this too. Confusing and confounding and distressing and... amusing? There was something about this posturing that gave it... amusement? If it could have laughed, it would have. There was so much to absorb, to sort, to balance. It came to the realization that some things it felt were wrong and other things felt were...correct? So many questions and no answers were offered. Slowly, it was achieving...knowledge?

It heard pain and pleasure, joy and sorrow. It witnessed deceit and truth. All concepts were new to it. It was growing, not so much in size but in discernment, yet had so far to go before...what?

And why were some voices it heard louder than others? And why did they cause it pain?

Chapter 37

Dedham, MA

As usual, Adam had the TV on as he got dressed. Thankfully it wasn't the typical Sunday morning fare of televangelists or political talking heads, only the same old morning news shows, nothing new, just the usual talk about the economy, the environment, and a particularly brutal recounting of the most recent atrocities in Syria. And of course, the latest in no further developments concerning the light. But it was still scaring the shit out of people. No news *was* news, and the media would make the most of it. One more typical day. Finished dressing, he quickly knocked down an OJ and walked to the garage in a rare happy mood.

He was looking forward to seeing Grace Perez again, even if it meant dealing with Fran's comments. He loved her, but what a pain the ass she could be. He laughed to himself, maybe if he kept her mouth filled with pizza, she'd shut up for once. 'Fat chance of that,' he thought.

At Aura/Sonos, energized about this mystery, they were theorizing about what was happening, being no closer to an answer. More theories had been ruled out, mostly on what they felt rather than knew, discarded about what it was instead of what it might be. They were now certain there was no one or no one group generating it, yet there were peculiar human qualities about what they were, for lack of a better word, deciphering. This was not the report Grace would be expecting, but it was all they had.

Getting into his car, Adam rummaged around for his sunglasses. Looking through the glove box, he found an old movie ticket, a sad reminder of the last film he and Jess had seen together. He quickly shoved it back in, eventually finding his glasses lodged under the passenger seat. Putting them on, he started the old Saab and drove off to the lab, while R.E.M.'s "It's The End of the World as We Know It."

played on the CD player. Shaking his head in disbelief, he thought what were the chances the song was right? Damn, he was going to have to his shit together.

Putting that fatalistic thought out of his mind, he concentrated on driving until he found a Starbucks. He bought a plain coffee, nothing fancy like Jess would have ordered, and walked back to his car. As he climbed back in, he noticed another white owl. It could not have been the same one from a few days ago. Yet, it too stared back at him as if recognizing him, making the same peculiar shrugging motion as before, and flew off.

Looking out the windshield, he saw the bird hadn't flown that far, just onto another tree, still staring at him. It flew off once again, this time out of sight and it was now Adam mirroring its odd behavior, shrugging his shoulders.

That owl intrigued him. In all the years he'd lived in this area, he'd never seen one in daylight, and now twice in just a few days. It looked at him as if it knew something he didn't. His mind worked best free of imposed restrictions such as the laws of nature. Consequently, connections could be made uninhibited. He began to think of the raptor as a symbol, a metaphor for something, but what? What did owls represent? Wisdom? "Holy fucking shit! Could that be it?" Adam cursed and laughed nervously both at the same time. He couldn't wait to get to the lab and catch up with Fran and her work. This time, the last thing he wanted to do was give Grace and Ashe a half-assed report.

He approached the gate, flashed his employee ID at the guard, and pulled into the Aura/Sonos parking lot noticing an unfamiliar car in a visitor spot, probably a government-issued vehicle. He smiled to himself, thinking it must be Grace Perez's, getting in a bit earlier than him. That pleased him.

Climbing out of the car and carrying his coffee, he walked the short distance to the main lab, swiping his pass key to gain admittance. Once in, he took the stairs to the second-floor lab where his and Fran's offices and labs were located. As he approached one of the larger conference rooms, he saw Peter, Fran, Anna, Grace Perez, and a man he didn't recognize. Judging from who was in attendance, he thought he should be there as well. Not bothering to knock on the closed door, he entered, nodding to each of them, "Peter, Fran, Grace, how are you? What's up?"

Grace was the first to respond as Fran and Elliott nodded back at him. "Adam, I was just apologizing to everyone about showing up unannounced, but Director Ashe wanted to talk with all of you himself. Adam, this is August Ashe, director of the NSA. August, this is Adam Faraday, lead researcher on the light phenomenon."

Ashe looked like someone straight out of central casting had they been looking for the stereotypical military officer: late middle age, average height, frameless glasses, black hair cut dangerously close to his scalp, and wearing an expensively tailored suit cut to accent his still trim Navy Seal hardened body. Tilting his head and dropping his glasses down on his nose, he looked over the rims at Adam, then the others in the conference room, "Grace has told me what you've found so far, and it doesn't seem like much. Would you agree?" Before anyone could answer, Ashe continued.

"We've agreed to help fund you on this and possibly other projects but so far, you've come up with zero. From what I can tell, you've been able to determine what it isn't. That doesn't help us at all. Do you have any idea what it *is*? And spare me your speculations. We don't have time for those. Have you seen what is happening? Right now, for the most part, our citizens while worried, aren't going off the deep end…yet. But each time this happens, they get a little closer. Do you know what is the source of this? How do we combat it? Can someone here please tell me what in hell we're dealing with?"

Peter Easton, Anna, Fran, and Adam looked at each other, raising their eyebrows, remaining silent. Peter broke the awkward silence. "Director Ashe, as we've told Deputy Director Perez, we've nothing we can relate this to. Nothing like this has ever occurred, therefore we are figuratively stumbling around in the dark.

"Adam and Fran have been working 'round the clock on this. We look at the evidence after each occurrence and compare them with the previous ones. Each time, there appears to be a further clarification if you will, of data. That's why we're finding out what it's not. Each time, we believe we're getting a bit closer to an answer or an understanding of it. But and this is significant, don't minimize that simplification. We're beginning to get a better sense of structure though none of the parts fit together...yet."

Adam was standing silently through all of this, debating whether he should share his latest thoughts. Finally, he spoke. "Peter, I'd like to share a new thought with all of you. Even Fran hasn't heard this. You're right. All we've done so far is determine what it's not. Though you may not agree, that is progress. But it hasn't identified what it is.

"One of the techniques we've been using when the light goes out, you've probably noticed the periods of darkness are longer with every occurrence, is we record the light and translate it to sound. While that may not seem an orthodox method, we have a very unorthodox tool, sorry Fran, at our disposal. And that's Fran, who," smiling in Fran's direction, "is definitely not a tool. Her hearing abilities as well as other senses are off the charts. Her blindness has permitted her or rather her senses to evolve differently. They are all more developed and acute than ours. Yes, we can measure this electronically, but Fran's peculiar ability and discernment bring another level of assessment that technology can't match. Plus, I can't speak highly enough of her intuition.

"Fran, why don't you share with the Director what we know? When you're finished, I'll jump in with what I believe this might be. If I'm right, this is an entirely different ballgame. But you do need to know what background we must understand the leap I'm talking about. Fran?"

Fran turned in Adam's direction, mouthing the word 'Tool?' "Well, General, it's like this..."

Both Adam and Grace suppressed small smirks at this. Ashe was not amused, and Peter spoke up, "Fran, once more, cut the crap and get to it. I apologize Director for Fran's disrespect. That is just another of her peculiar abilities, that of pissing people off. Can you please enlighten the Director now without your customary insolence, now?"

Not contritely, Fran continued, "Sorry. The first time this happened we were not prepared, no one was, so whatever we had, we got by chance. But it did help us as a starting point. When we analyzed the quality of the light as translated into sound waves, it looked like just a lot of noise, coming from all over. Different directions, different levels.

"We've kicked around some ideas. First, we thought of it as a binary sequence. That led nowhere. Then we theorized it might be disparate channels, sort of like stereo. That was too simple and led us nowhere. After the second occurrence, we threw that notion out because we detected a familiarity, not one we could really identify, but it just seemed like something we might have heard. Hell, we even discussed it being a Dyson Sphere."

It was obvious that no one else knew what that was, questions were written all over their faces. Adam put up both of his hands, "No, don't even ask. It's another dead end.

Fran picked up where she's left off, "So after the third blink, the familiarity became a bit more pronounced. It was like everyone was in a large room, speaking in different languages, all at once. A lot of jumbles, and a lot of noise, but every now and then it sounded somewhat recognizable. We even played it backward, but no 'Paul is dead' moment either. I also noticed, sorry about this Elliott and Adam, I haven't had time to share this with you, there were periods where it seemed more rushed, or urgent like. Almost like emotions. So, that's it. It's a bitch and all I got. Adam?"

What Fran had just shared stopped Adam cold before he could speak. It made sense considering what he was about to share. "Uhh, I don't even know how to proceed after that. Fran without even knowing it has come to a similar conclusion as I have. But I'm about to take it further and I ask for your patience. If what I'm to say sounds a little far-fetched, keep in mind that what we're dealing with is far-fetched itself.

"Fran said she felt an urgency, a speeding up and slowing down of the info. Let me pose a few questions. Might that be described as emotion? If so, are we dealing with a being? If we are, what kind of being? Here's where it's going to sound a little bit out there. We believe there is no one or no one group behind it. It's also not, we think, an extra-terrestrial entity. From what we can tell, it is light itself, all light – man-made, natural, reflections, ambient, everything. When it goes out, there is no light of any kind, anywhere. So, we can discard this as being a directed human effort.

"So…what if it's not human?"

Ashe, having heard enough, cut in, not prepared to listen to any more such babble, "If it's not..."

"Please wait, Director. I know this sounds absurd but hear me out. This activity, or more likely actions, are those that are commensurate with a living entity. We think we hear things that sound like mimicked emotions, but I don't think it's mimicry. I think we're dealing with a living thing, maybe a new thing, maybe a sense just coming into its own realization... Oh, oh, and…" with that, the image of the white bird came to mind and a connection was made.

Ashe was ready to explode. "Just what in hell are you saying, Doctor? I don't understand what you're getting at."

Adam paused briefly, "I think light may becoming sentient, thinking for itself. Becoming… something… a being. I think it's alive."

Though there was plenty of light, not a sound was heard in the room.

Chapter 38

Baltimore, MD

Neither Lee nor Sheila could have predicted it, the attraction was obvious, with an awkwardness permeating their conversations. So, Lee's call to Sheila was filled with unspoken meaning which both sensed but would not respond to, not just yet. Lee, too, found himself frequently thinking of Sheila. If he was to have a chance with her, his deception could shatter that opportunity. Picking up the phone with apprehension and anticipation, he placed the call to her. After a few rings, she answered. Trying to sound natural despite the desperation he was starting to feel, he spoke, "Hi, Sheila? It's me. Lee..."

Before he could say more, Sheila responded brightly, "Hi Lee. I was just thinking of you. You know, the next interview is coming up and I hadn't heard from you. What's up?"

He fumbled for an answer. Lee wanted two things from Sheila, each exclusive of the other. Get one and say goodbye to the other. Either way, he'd lose. "Uh, I was just wondering if we could get together.

"I need to talk with you about... uh... the... interview. You know? You doing anything after work today? Maybe we could get a bite to eat or something..."

"Or something?" Sheila asked teasingly. She was more than pleased Lee had called. "Yeah, I'd like that but I'm working a bit late. I've got a bunch of calls to make. How about nine? Will that work?"

He fumbled again, "Uh, yeah, that's good. Pick you up then?" It was set.

#

It was a rainy evening, so Lee was waiting with an umbrella for her outside her office. Lost in his conflicting feelings, he greeted her casually, "Hey! Hi! How was your day?"

Pulling up the collar of her coat, she smiled at him, "Long. And tiresome. It's so good to see you again, Lee. Where are we going?"

"We can drive somewhere, or we could walk to someplace close if you don't mind sharing an umbrella. And place around here you like?"

There were a few places Sheila did like, but more than anything, sharing an umbrella with Lee would be first on her list. While she too was dealing with mixed feelings, she let her guard down this night. "Yes, let's walk. I don't mind the rain that much. Let's go this way."

They walked together, side-by-side, for several blocks before they reached Sheila's choice. "We're here, hope you like it, Lee."

Lee looked around. It looked like a typical DC restaurant, decorated smartly for its fussy patrons with a menu priced accordingly. "Really? Looks a little out of my league."

Sheila laughed at Lee's reaction. "You were expecting what, Waffle House? Not this girl, besides, this isn't what it looks like. C'mon, you'll like it. If it'll make you feel any better, we can go Dutch."

Still standing outside the restaurant, Lee protested, "Oh no, I asked you to come out. My treat. Besides, I need to talk with you, and ask you something. You down with that?"

Sheila looked at him, wondering if there was more to this meeting than she had anticipated. "What's going on Lee? What's this all about?"

"Look, I feel weird doing this. I didn't mean for it to go this way. We only needed to get a foot in the door with Stamm. But now...

"Forgive me, but over time I'd forgotten all about you, your family and how close we all were. But seeing you again, talking with you, you know, brought back a bunch of stuff, nothing I expected and... Sheila, I want to be with you. Not just this way, but to really be with you. Does that make any sense?"

It did. If she went down that road, she would likely jeopardize her position with Jonah Stamm. But she also knew that nothing would ever come from that besides Stamm's generosity and the occasional intimacy. She saved her money wisely and really didn't need Stamm for security, other than her job of course. And there was Olivia to think about too.

Smiling, happy, though feeling a little uncomfortable, she responded, "Yes, Lee, it does. I feel the same way. But there's something more, isn't there?"

He looked down at his feet. "Let's go in and I'll tell you what's up." They entered the quiet restaurant and were seated almost immediately. A waitperson came over, rattled off the specials, and took their drink orders.

And for a moment, everything was plunged into darkness again.

It was now feeling and beginning to understand things about itself as an entity, a being. It felt...huge. No, omnipotent. Omnipresent. It felt things in all those different places. All at once and now discretely and in the early stages of its discernment, able to separate all it was hearing and seeing, receiving so much with its understanding beginning to crystallize.

Some of it was good, other not as much. It was starting to feel within itself as much as what it experienced from outside. Since there was nothing else like it, it would be hard to communicate with an "other". It began to identify with some of those feelings, almost like an agreement with some and hostility towards others, a feeling almost akin to pain. It wanted some to continue and others to stop, to go away. All it could do was blink.

Other 'noises' brought what could be construed as pleasure. It would learn that this was laughter, love, a human response. To what, it didn't know. But it liked it.

Another 'noise' made it feel 'sad.' It would blink at this, almost as if it was trying to blink away tears if it was possible. Which it wasn't. It didn't like 'sad'.

Still not yet realizing who or what itself was, frustrated it. It began to realize that when it felt the things that brought it pain and angered it, it blinked more. That brought it fleeting relief. Then, eventually, sooner than later the pain always returned.

As a child learns from experience, so did it. And this "child" was a fast learner. Just simple cause and effect. Other than the pain to go away, it didn't want anything as it had no reference for such a thing. It didn't know what 'want' was. Desire had yet to be experienced, much less understood.

And like a child, it was experiencing a host of emotions with no guidance on how to cope. Transitions were difficult. If it were capable of tantrums, it would have thrown them, often. All it could do was go dark. Which it was starting to do with increasing frequency without any understanding of the effect other than to achieve something akin to peace.

Conversely, the effect on all other living beings was creating recurring and greater chaos that did not add to its peace. If peace brought people pain – how? Why? Understanding would not come for some time – either by it or those affected.

Chapter 39

Dedham, MA

"Sometimes a leap of faith is what's needed to gain some understanding." Adam held up both his hands quickly, seeing that there were objections to this statement.

"Please, wait a minute. That may not have been the right way of putting it. It was a leap, maybe not of faith, but of intuition. A 'what-if' moment. And why not?

"There's nothing in the human experience that fits the description of this. The data, while interesting so far is only telling us what it's not. So why isn't grand speculation considered? We've nothing to lose at this point. If it is light, we still don't know how to communicate with it. It's certainly not talking to us in any language we understand other than off and on. Yes, that appears to be binary in nature but in no way significant. It would have to be blinking with enormous intensity and frequency to be anything meaningful.

"I would suggest we look at what's happening before, during, and after each blink to see if there is any correlation. Could these blinks be not a message but a response?"

The director of the NSA, August Ashe, in a near parody of the George C. Scott character from Dr. Strangelove, was nearly gaping at Adam. "Dr. Faraday, what you are saying is that this thing, this blinking, whatever the hell it is, maybe, what, alive? A thinking thing?"

"Not quite Director, but you may be on the right track. What I'm saying, and I agree it is a bit far-fetched, is that I think this may be a sensing entity. If we can establish that the blinks correspond to stimuli, it might lead us to a rudimentary understanding, a starting point which we may be able to use."

189

Ashe was not buying it, "Grace, is this the kind of bullshit you've been getting all along? And you've been accepting it? Covering for them? Why are we wasting our time with this?"

She looked back at him and spoke in a measured tone, "August, I understand your impatience, but this is not something that we, no, make that no one has any experience with. It is extraordinary and I think we need to think accordingly. And that's what Adam and the rest of the Aura/Sonos staff are doing. We may find otherwise, but until we do, let Peter and his group pursue this.

"Just because it doesn't fit known parameters doesn't mean it's counter to what their speculation is. And yes, it is speculation, but that's all we have at this point. It's all we ever have when we're confronted with something new."

Ashe was not placated. "So, what you're suggesting is that we sit on our asses until it happens again? And then what? Look, Mr. Easton, Dr. Faraday, I get that this is your bailiwick. But I'm charged with protecting this country from threats, inside and outside our borders. And hell, if I know where this coming from any more than you do, and I do not like it."

Ashe was clearly frustrated, "Every time this occurs, shit happens. People are afraid to use their cars for fear of crashing into something. The same is true of air travel. Do you have any idea what this is starting to do with our economy, not to mention the world? What if light goes out for an extended period? Do you have any idea what that will do to crops? Electricity will be meaningless as we won't be able to see a damned thing, much less find the on and off switches. We'd be as good as blind.

"Everyone around the world is becoming more and more fearful every time it happens. They're looking to their leaders for answers. And, no surprise, none of them have a clue. Do you expect governments to tell their citizenry what you've just shared with me? No, I don't think so."

It was now Peter's time to throw in. "Director Ashe, we all understand your concern. But consider this: Adam and Fran are the best at what they do. The type of intuitive leaps they make is responsible for many of the breakthroughs in science for years. I can't say I know how they do it, but they do, and I'll stand behind them any day. I recommend you do too."

Ashe was not mollified. "Mr. Easton, recommendations are all well and good if they're based on facts. You're asking me to suspend disbelief for what seems to me a crackpot theory. We don't deal in science fiction. You say you've got your 'best' people on this and this is what they've come up with. If that's your best, then the NSA might have to reconsider its involvement with you."

Silent during all of this, Fran could no longer keep quiet. As she started to speak, Adam, Peter, and Grace held their collective breath, expecting a sudden downturn in direction. "Director, it's no secret here that I've been pretty vocal about the NSA's involvement with this. Ask Grace. From where I sit, you're not in any position to question what we're doing." Peter started to speak and tried to cut her off, dreading where this might go, when Fran threw up her hand, signaling him to stop. He knew that when Fran started in like this, it was a crap shoot which way it could go, very good or very bad. He was a gambler, he let her toss the dice.

"Hold on, Peter. Director, you came to us, remember? You sought our help, remember? Because you didn't know how to approach this, remember? I do. And you called us because we're the best at what we do. That was a good move. But this isn't something you can bend to your will. Neither are we. We research and develop theories, prove, or disprove them, and then come up with conclusions and that takes time, probably more than you're comfortable with. So, tell me how you would affect that. What would you do differently?

"So, when this doesn't meet up with whatever your expectations are, you're ready to pull the plug. Let me ask you a question since it looks like you're ready to book. We've got nothing to lose, right? How many

191

of the decisions made at the NSA are based entirely on facts? All? Some? A few? None? I'd be willing to bet at the least, it's only some."

Ashe started to speak, but Fran once again raised her hand to stop him.

"And how do they turn out? No, no, don't bother answering that one, we all know the answer. So why in hell won't you cut us some slack and let us do what you've asked us to do? You don't know any more about this than we do, even less actually. You're no different than we are – we both deal in speculation until we know something definite. So please back off. Oh, and I say that with all due respect. Sorry Boss, I thought someone had to say it."

The room was quiet, waiting for Ashe's response. The reactions ranged from Grace's raised eyebrows, and Adam's small smirk, to Peter's grin and August Ashe's mouth hanging open. "Ms. Porter, I see that timidity is not an issue for you. Your hair tells me that. I trust you bring that same intensity to your work. I admit it, you're right… on all counts.

"But as you are obviously protective of what you do. So am I. The difference is in our charges. You are responsible to this company. I am responsible to this country which in turn is responsible for giving your company an environment in which it could grow and prosper. Don't forget we are working on the same thing and maybe even for some of the same reasons. Territory has no place in this situation if either of us is to proceed."

August Ashe, while military to his core when it came to structure, was also flexible when necessary, seeing both sides of an issue. "Maybe you view it as an issue of scale or philosophy or even motivation. That's fine. But it doesn't mitigate those responsibilities, yours or mine. I appreciate your candor. But we need each other's help. If we're to continue together, then we are all going to have to question each other openly and without rancor of which, yes, I am guilty. I realize that might be difficult for you, Ms. Porter. It might be difficult for all of us, but it's all we've got. And yes, that means we're still in this... together."

Anna had held her silence throughout all of this. "Director, thank you. That's good to know. But I've been thinking about this in a different way. Yes, you are right, there are ramifications to everything that's happening. But look at it this way. Everything we do is informed by light. Without it, we're blind as you just said. We need light as much as we do air. But the word I used was inform. If you can accept as theory what Fran and Adam have told us, could it be that light is, perhaps, trying to further inform us?"

As Peter was about to speak, all the cell phones in the room started ringing. A moment of silence followed this surprise and then the simultaneous answering filled the room with disbelief.

All the conversations were brief but astonishing. No one wanted to speak first. Finally, Adam broke the impasse. "I assume all the calls were about the same thing. The light went out again, but this time in just one place. Am I right?"

The mood, previously serious, was now grim. All nodded in silent agreement. The light had blinked off in only one area, the Middle East, Syria. It came back only to blink off and then on once again.

Adam looked questioningly at Peter, and reached out to touch Fran who then nodded, "I think that one was intentional."

Chapter 40

Baltimore, MD

The media-feeding frenzy picked up. Fueled largely by reports from Syria and speculation elsewhere, fear and doubts were now rampant in government halls as well as the streets. Fanning the flames even higher was the Reverend Jonah Stamm, again claiming knowledge and insight exclusive to him. Expectations, at least his, were that he would claim the reigning position on this once the next interview aired. Though others were preaching some of the same fiction as he was, he believed the total effect of his interviews would give him center stage. He was both wrong and right on this.

In the meantime, Bennie was getting ready to do battle again with the reverend. He was irritated he hadn't yet heard back from Lee about his meeting with Sheila Weller and that pissed him off. If Lee came up empty, he'd have to find something else. The calendar would start to work against him. When he was in that mood, he tossed sharpened pencils into the ceiling tiles. Looking up, he noticed that a small area of the ceiling was virtually invisible due to the sheer number of pencils sticking into it. Occasionally, they would drop down on him, reminding him that in physics, what goes up does come down, furthering his aggravation. Finally, his phone rang. It was Lee Black.

"It's about fucking time! I hope you got something. I've been sitting here numbing my ass waiting for you. Did she tell you anything? Anything I can use? C'mon, help me out here, Lee! I'm drowning!"

Lee took a deep breath before speaking. "Bennie, I couldn't find out anything along the lines you were looking for, but…" Another deep breath, "But, Sheila did tell me something that might be even bigger than we thought."

"Bigger than Sasquatch, I hope. Please, Lee, tell me. I need something good."

"OK, I don't know what to make of this but here goes. Just before Sheila and I met up, she said she had to make a bunch of phone calls for Stamm. She thinks they're the result of a meeting he had earlier. She said he seemed distressed by it when he got back."

"So? What else? You gonna keep me in the dark before you tell me who it was with?"

Knowing how impatient Bennie could get and taking some small pleasure from it, he prolonged it before the inevitable blow-up. "Sheila said it wasn't on his schedule so she couldn't know for sure. She did hear him cursing, yes, the good reverend is capable of the expletive deleted, someone named Pingry and she quoted him, 'that motherfucker Pingry and his two-bit congressional whores.' Pretty strong stuff from a man of God, wouldn't you say? Any idea who this Pingry might be?"

Holding the phone away from his ear for a moment, Bennie's eyes went wide. "Lee, did you say Pingry? Any first name by chance?"

"No, just that name. Nothing more. You know the name?"

"The only Pingry I know of, and not that much, except he's not one to screw around with, is Thaddeus Pingry. Old line, Mayflower type. S.A.R. kind of stuff. Rich, a real puppet master from what I've heard. Stays out of the public eye big time, about as stealth as you can get. And she said he was cursing some 'congressional whores'. Which ones?

"Look, Lee, let's keep this on the down low, but follow up on Pingry and see what you can find. If he's got Stamm spooked, then there may be some sort kind of holy trinity going on that isn't the kind the reverend preaches about. Can you do a Lexis/Nexis on him? Get a family history, and SEC filings, anything. I would love to spring this on the reverend in the next interview."

"Bennie, look, I got to be upfront with you. I didn't expect this, but I think something's happening between me and Sheila and I'd like to see it through. But, if I do, I'm not going to use her to get information. I just can't do that. You understand. You all right with that?"

Subtlety was not one of Bennie's strong suits. "No, I'm not all right with that. Are you sure of that? It's not a good idea to get involved with a source. You know that better than most. Every newbie hears that every day. If you are, you're an idiot. Someone always gets hurt. It's not a good idea."

"Yeah, Bennie, I know. And I am sure of it. So, what's next?"

"You're going to need to do more digging. What you just told me may open the door, but it may not be enough. What it is, is anyone's guess, but if it involves Pingry and some government types, it'll be juicy, and a lot of money is sure to be involved and maybe illegally.

"The interview is in a couple of days so let's get on this. And for those next two days, I suggest you stay away from Sheila. Just sayin'. Give me a call when you've found something else and don't screw around. There'll be plenty of time for that kind of crap later.

"One other thing… how's it going with the religious forum thing? You got that squared away yet?"

"Damn it, Bennie, it's not going to go anywhere if you keep unloading shit on me. It's a handful and if you don't leave me alone, it'll never get done and that's my ass on the line. OK?"

Bennie hung up the phone and sat motionless for a few minutes, wondering what in hell was going on. He pulled his laptop over and Googled the name Thaddeus Pingry. Over 4,400 hits came up. Shit, he thought, where in hell have I been? And only two days until the interview. Damn!

Bennie was eager for the next go-round with Jonah Stamm. He realized he would need more than he had. The conversations he'd had with Lee had been tantalizing yet nothing substantial. Now Lee wasn't returning any of his calls again. What in hell was that about, he worried.

For the first time, this light thing was appearing on his radar well after the rest of the world whose fears had been building daily for some time. Not prone to conspiracies, his paranoia was alive and well, masquerading as skepticism. He wasn't paranoid in the black helicopter sense, no more than other reporters, but he was becoming interested in the light phenomenon. While he didn't believe it was the work of an evil axis of corporations or a cabal doing it, he also didn't have any theories of what it was. Bennie was anticipating that in the next interview, Jonah Stamm would bring it up as further evidence of God's will and power. How to refute that bit of crap? Where in hell was Lee?

As if on cue, his cell rang. He was relieved to see Lee's number. "It's about time you called. You know I've got this thing with Stamm coming up in less than forty hours and you go AWOL. That's no help, Lee! I hope you got something, or this will be just another of the good reverend's plea for cash. Tell me you got something, will you? Please."

When Bennie finally stopped, there was a long pause on the other end of the conversation. A deep breath, then, "Bennie, this is some pretty messed up shit. Lemme give you a little history if you don't know it already. You've heard how Pingry's family started their whole big empire, right?"

After hearing a 'no', he continued. "I think you'll understand it when I say I now have skin in this game. Pingry's family started out as slave traders back in the 1600s. They supplied the workforce that built this friggin' country. And I'm pretty sure if confronted with that little bit of info, we'd get it was a necessary evil crap. These are my people, my people, mine. Now *I* got a reason to hate this Pingry dude."

"So?"

"So? It looks like he's still in the business. I haven't been able to find out if it's been non-stop or a recent addition to his corporate portfolio of companies, but he's involved. But this time it's the sex trade. How do you like that?"

A long exhalation, an extended "S-h-i-i-i-t" and then a moment of silence, then a torrent of questions that Bennie needed to ask to verify before using it. "Lee, are you sure? Are you fucking sure? That's about as big a bombshell as we could get. Where did you get this? Who gave it to you? Can we verify it? What's the connection to Stamm? Are you willing to risk everything on this? If we're wrong, we're toast."

"Bennie, slow down. If we're wrong, if I'm wrong, that'll be the least of our problems. First, am I sure? Hell, no. I've got no documents. I'm putting one and one and one together and I'm coming up with, not three... I dunno, something that ain't two, that's for sure. But the connection to Stamm is interesting. Remember, the good reverend has got that little orphanage in Southeast Asia. Which just happens to be where Mr. Pingry fought and won a lawsuit over illegal aliens, prostitutes, underage and all that. A real all-American, apple pie kind of guy, this Pingry. It's amazing what you can find out with Lexis/Nexis and Google. Short of private documents, maybe even then, it's out there. But it's been hidden behind so much smoke and mirrors, it went largely unnoticed.

"There was also a sidebar article about missing children, all of whom happened to have been guests at that orphanage. I don't know if there's a connection, but it caught my eye.

"Beyond that, we have a connection between Stamm, Pingry, and Justice because of the letter. Sheila told me that Stamm was on one end of a heated but short conversation with our Congressman Justice."

Bennie tried to interrupt but was stopped by Lee's continuing, "Wait, there's more. I was out with Sheila and a couple of congressional aides were there whining about their jobs and the hours. Well, turns out one of them works for Justice and he was saying that he'd had been in a bad way because contributions were down. No one was calling him back, that sort of shit. Sounds like he's been shut out from their private treasury.

"Then he gets a call from Pingry calling him into a private meeting, like immediately. The reverend doesn't say much but books fast out of the office. I guess to this meeting or whatever. But don't you think it's all rather strange?"

Bennie was quiet for a few moments, trying to take in all that Lee had shared with him. "Strange doesn't even begin to describe it. But you know, there's an angle we might try, and who knows, maybe we can work it into the interview. You know anybody in Congressman Justice's office you can call?"

"Funny you should ask. Ever been to a place called Pozzi's? That's where Sheila and I were when I overheard those two guys at the bar, and one was from the good congressman's office. We made some small talk and even exchanged cards. You want I should call him?"

"Ya think?"

"And that's got to be it, Bennie. Don't forget, I've got that damn forum on Sunday."

Chapter 41

Great Falls, VA

Thaddeus Pingry was furious. The appearance of Stamm's letter and subsequent demands, a possible public revelation, Carlton Justice's ineffectiveness, and the prospect of the whole thing blowing up in his face was the type of situation he dealt with ruthlessly. He would have crushed a competitor in this situation. Jonah Stamm would not be so fortunate.

The country which Pingry loved in his own way had abolished slavery a very long time ago. It also abhorred those countries who had condoned it. If one of its favored sons was found trafficking in it, the blowback would be devastating. Everything he and his family had worked hard to build would be destroyed before another news cycle could even begin. He understood the liabilities and would have to prepare a contingency exit plan in the event.

All his family's achievements could be documented by their daring and unconventional thinking. Where others may have seen pitfalls or obstacles, the Pingry's would perceive them as part of a larger road map to their ultimate destination of wealth, influence, and control. Closer in their prosecution to Machiavelli than Mother Teresa, they were dogged in the pursuit of their goals. Enemies could be dealt with accordingly and friends were only conveniences that could be dealt with later.

Trust was parceled out to only a few among his group. It took a long time, inch by inch, for someone to gain that trust. Errors were unacceptable. If he was to act, it would have to be on his own and directly so. Characteristically, he was unpredictable in his decision-making. From the outside, his next move would have appeared irrational and foolish. That assessment would have been an imprudent mistake others made too often when dealing with him. That would result in nasty consequences, detrimental to them and beneficial to him. In doing business with the Pingry's, it was wise to remember Dante's words inscribed upon the entrance to Hell, 'Abandon all hope, ye who enter here.' As in Hell, all that would remain were tortured souls. Thaddeus Pingry exemplified that philosophy.

Picking up his phone, encrypted so only perhaps the NSA could decipher, he placed a call. It rang continuously without a response. As he was about to replace the phone in its cradle, it was answered. "Good afternoon, Congressman Justice's office, this is Trey."

Eschewing social niceties, he responded curtly, "Where is he?"

"I beg your pardon. Are you referring to the Congressman, sir?"

Now more curtly and impatient, "Where is he? Do you not understand English?"

"One moment, please. I'll see if he's available." Trey hurried to Justice's office and knocked on the closed door.

"Sir, you've got a phone call and I think you ought to take it. He wouldn't say who he was, but it sounded like he knew you."

Justice cocked an eyebrow, puzzled, and nodded to his aide. "Thank you, Trey. I'll take it." He waited for Trey to leave, motioning him to close the door on his way out. "This is Carlton Justice. Who's speaking and how can I help you?"

Pingry didn't bother to identify himself. "Are you ready to come in from the cold? Be at my house tonight at 10:00. You do remember how to get there?" And hung up without waiting for a response.

Justice stood there, mouth agape. Thaddeus was the last person he expected to hear from, much less summoned. While he was hopeful no harm would come to him there, it didn't lessen his apprehension. He'd been on the receiving end of Pingry's dissatisfaction and was under no illusion that anything had changed. But he could not fathom what Thaddeus wanted with him now. He had already been made persona non grata among his donors and the group, what in hell more did he want?

He had originally planned to spend the evening at his new home away from home, Pozzi's, having dinner and knocking back some bourbon. It was still early enough for one, maybe two fortifying drinks before his command appearance.

The rain that had plagued DC for the past few days was gone and the evening was mild and typically humid. Justice decided to walk the few blocks over, maybe clear his mind and try and get an idea of what Pingry wanted.

Entering the restaurant, he saw the usual amount of DC wannabe hangers-on who fancied themselves, powerbrokers, congressional aides hoping to score with the small amount of info they might have to trade, two or three maybe actually wielding some power and influence, and a few couples hoping to see some of the real movers and shakers. Disappointingly, the latter group conducted their affairs out of the public limelight and certainly not in a place such as Pozzi's. That said, Justice hoped he might be able to pick up some useful information.

In his past visits, Goldie didn't disappoint, at least when it came to providing the congressman's sustenance of choice. He hoped maybe tonight there would be something, anything else the bartender could provide. He was desperately needing to have a little leverage in his meeting with Pingry. Approaching the bar, Justice didn't know it at the time, but Goldie had more than food and booze waiting for him.

Congressman Carlton Justice, reinforced by bourbon and the sharing of Goldie's intel, got into his car for the drive to Thaddeus Pingry's estate. He loosened his collar and his belt, noticing they were getting a little tight. Much like he was at that moment. While he would have rather fooled himself that he was prepared for anything thrown at him, he knew better. He was now aware of Stamm's meeting with Pingry. He was also pretty sure it had to do with their joint and now conflicting interests in Southeast Asia. What he didn't know is why he was being summoned. It had been made damn clear that his involvement in the group and probably politics was over. There would be no membership and no further contributions.

He couldn't bluff Pingry; he had no such capital. Asking for mercy was out of the question. Pingry never sought mercy, nor did he ever grant it. There was no time for greys, only the black and white of the matter in front of him. Justice realized that in his eyes, he had failed him and in a spectacular fashion concerning the letter and its author. That had to be it. Shaking his head, he realized for all intents and purposes, he was dead meat.

The drive, even without much traffic, still took more than an hour, giving Justice more time to mull over the eventualities of this meeting. Approaching ten o'clock in the evening, there was still just a little summer light left in the sky so when the light went out again, everything including Carlton Justice in his car was plunged into total darkness. As the light blinked out, Carlton Justice, traveling at a good clip and not able to see the curve in the road, plowed his car into a large oak tree not a mile from his destination.

Shortly after, the light returned, revealing a large, misshapen black Ford Crown Victoria intimately hugging the tree. Its horn was blaring, a turn signal was flashing, and no movement from within the car.

Chapter 42

Dedham, MA

He took a deep breath before continuing, knowing full well that his theory might be perceived as sci-fi geek crap, certainly with incredulity if not laughter. Still, Adam pressed on.

"Please let me continue. We may be on the verge of discovering a new entity. I hesitate to call it a life-form at this point, but hell if it isn't lifelike. So, what would the normal procedure be in approaching something like that? Caution. We need to get an idea of what it is responding to – good and bad. It's a crap shoot and we may not have much time."

Adam paused for what seemed like an eternity but was less than a minute. He was going to explain his latest hunch, knowing that it would either be accepted or, more likely, he would be branded crazy.

"All right, the rules we've gone by, which we've followed rigidly in the past, are not applicable any longer. At least not in an accepted way. This flies in the face of Newtonian and Einsteinian science big time. Both theorized about light and its properties. But neither predicted this. They saw light as elemental. As I said this theory does fit. I do think the light, no, Light itself, is becoming sentient. If it is an entity, it's one we've never acknowledged as such. Why would we since we've always taken it for granted? There's never been any indication otherwise.

"But", taking another deep breath before continuing, "it's exhibiting an almost human-like response to stress and..." He could not continue as the room exploded with questions, disbelief, and skepticism.

"Look, hear me out. I know this is out there, but please let me continue. I don't know that I'll convince any of you but please wait.

"The latest incident happened in one spot. That's a first, right? Prior to that, it's always been global. Now it happened in Syria, correct?

Think about it. Was anything happening in Syria at that time? You don't have to respond as the answer is yes. There's a large migration to escape the government. Nobody wants them. Then a particularly brutal put down of a peaceful demonstration occurs and the light goes off. What happens? The confrontation ends as nothing goes on without light. Coincidence? Maybe, but it got me to thinking. What if we were to plot the incidences of blinks on a calendar against the occurrences of, what, war, famine, violence, whatever? Is there a correlation? It would be simple enough to do that. I think we'll see that it lines up. That's also in keeping with what Anna just shared with us. Was that an intentional sign? Yes, light does inform everything we do. Was light attempting to inform us of something?"

"Dr. Faraday, do you expect us to believe that? That light is a thing? A thinking thing? Come on, now." Director August Ashe was not impressed.

"No, Director, I don't expect you to accept that light is a thinking thing, not yet at least, though it might be. Hell, I don't... yet. But I do think at this point, light might be a feeling thing and, in my theory, it's responding to pain, a pain we've all felt in our own lives."

Grace Perez admired his intellect and intuition but had refrained from speaking during his speech, waiting until he finished. "Adam, if what you're saying is true and I'm not saying I buy it, then how are we to deal with it? Have you any thoughts on that? Are these blackouts or blinks an attempt to communicate with us? And why now and not before? Has something reached a critical mass, if you will, that is creating this... uh... aberration?"

"Actually no. No thoughts yet on how to deal with it. Remember, I said I think it's a feeling thing. Feeling is usually a response, not premeditation. We don't know its language if even it has one. And I can't say for certain if this is an attempt at communication. I mentioned previously this might be omnidirectional when the blinks were global. Now, it seems to have focused on one area, indicating something more akin to bi-directional. If that's the case, it might provide insight on how to converse with it. Even then, I don't know if we'll know how to talk to it or if it's even possible. At this point, we're going to have to wait and see what the next few blinks correspond to. I wish I could tell you more but again, it's just a theory that I believe will be proven to be correct."

More questions came from those attending. Peter Easton's was the first to be taken. "So, Adam, what do you suggest we do now?"

"Peter, all we can do is wait until we can see if there's a developing pattern. Not much more than that I'm afraid. Director Ashe, you have a question?"

"I'll allow that we're dealing with something out of the ordinary here. I think that's clear. And it's a hell of a stretch. But you are convinced that this is not a man-made... uhh, thing? Am I correct in assuming that?"

"Yes, you are correct. The blinks fit no discernible pattern and exhibit no known ability we're aware of to make it happen. It is a stretch. But we've nothing to lose pursuing this theory."

"No, you're wrong Dr. Faraday, we do. Remember each time it happens it's costing money, lives, and is creating widespread fear. It will, it already is, have a cumulative effect on people. Unstable governments could be toppled by this. Even stable ones. There are a lot of bad actors out there and you can bet they'll seize on this opportunity to move. Does it think about that? How does that fit your theory?"

"Director, you're right, there is a lot at stake. Everything has a cause and effect. You of all people know that. Your own department operates daily on that very assumption. There are always unintended consequences from even the best intentions. Since we assume we're powerless on this issue, that's all we can do. And all theories have a few loose ends until proven otherwise."

Fran butted in, "Damn, Adam, that is way out there, even for me. I got to tell you, that even I think you've lost it. Next thing you're going to say is a little birdie told you this."

Grinning broadly, he answered, "Actually, it was a rather big bird, a white one."

###

For the first time, it began to realize the consequence of its action. It saw a correlation between its pain/fear and its source. This understanding was not complete, but it was more than enough to identify things that made it unhappy if such a concept was even possible.

It heard/felt the pain so clearly in many places, but especially in a place called "Syria". Experiencing that pain caused it further pain and it did not like that. It had to stop, and it did. When it focused and blinked, the pain went away in that one place, for the first time as did the light in that one area. Not forever, but it did cease. But what was "Syria"? It, "Syria", had entered its consciousness unbidden. It wanted to close its eyes on it all.

But it couldn't keep its 'eyes', its awareness closed all the time, and the entirety of the stimulus was too much to ignore. For while that would have stopped the pain/fear completely, it would have also prevented it from those things which, for lack of any description, pleased it. It also had yet to realize that were it to continue along the randomness of its blinks, more unintended pain consequently would occur as well as a cessation of its 'pleasure'.

There was so much to learn and no teacher. There was no one or thing to turn to for guidance. Like a child left to its own devices, it would learn through trial and error. Some errors would be minor and without much in the way of repercussions though there was no way to administer discipline in that event; others would be devastating and pain-causing.

And despite all that, it would learn. It had so much more to learn. And as it learned, it would teach, not with intent, but with a yet unidentified goal of calm. It did not like discord and anguish.

207

It blinked again and all light disappeared again for a moment. Peace. Welcomed peace.

Chapter 43

Baltimore, MD

Lee was listening to the police monitor when a report flashed on the net of an automobile accident in the Virginia suburb of Great Falls. He paid it no attention until the driver was identified as Congressman Carlton Justice. The car was reported as likely traveling at a high speed when it smashed into a large oak tree. The preliminary report mentioned the smell of alcohol, but until a blood test could be administered, it was not conclusive. It continued by speculating that the accident may have also been the result of another of the light blinks and the driver consequently driving blind. Again, that too was not stated as definite.

Yelling over to Bennie, Lee Black summoned him over to share the news with him. "You're not going to believe this. The Virginia Highway Patrol has just reported an auto accident out in Great Falls."

"And that's important, because?"

"Because? Only because it was Carlton Justice in the car. There's no info as to if he's hurt, but alcohol is mentioned in the report. Also, it's timed to have occurred during a blink."

"OK, you've got my attention. Was he alone? Where did it happen?"

"Nothing about if anyone was with him but it happened in Great Falls, less than a mile from one Thaddeus Pingry's estate if you're interested."

Bennie's mouth dropped open a bit. Squinting his eyes in thought, "OK, yes, that is interesting. I thought there might be some bad blood between the two of them but why in hell would Justice go over to Pingry's? The letter maybe? Let me think a moment.

"First, Justice is asshole buddies with Pingry. There's a falling out. Stamm comes back into the picture and his staff gets wind of some shit going down. Then suddenly Justice seems to be on his way to

Pingry's. Oh, yeah, it's the letter. There's some heavy-duty shit going down. Let's start listing what we know, what the connections might be, and a timeline if possible, and put some pressure on the good congressman's staffers, and that includes Sheila, I'm sorry about that but I've got a feeling this is going to be much bigger than we thought. If we can get something on it before the interview, we might be able to break the whole friggin' thing open.

"Oh, and hey, have you read anything more about this light thing? I know I'm coming to it late, but what can you tell me about it? Is it serious or just a pain in the ass thing? Do you think Stamm will start on that again?"

"Bennie, once again, the forum. Give me a goddamned break, will ya? Oh, shit! Remember when I said putting one and one together? I think I just did."

"Five, four, three" then a silent but visual hand countdown of two, then one. "You're live"

A stentorian voiceover introduced the program, "Good evening, and welcome to part two of the exclusive Reverend Jonah Stamm interview. And now True North News correspondent, Edward Benton."

Bennie, in a new sports jacket and tie purchased specifically for the interview, started, "Reverend Stamm, it's good to see you again."

Turning to the camera and addressing the audience while simultaneously baiting the hook, Bennie looked into the camera and continued, "I'm glad you could join us for the second in this series of interviews exploring Reverend Jonah Stamm's ministry and its connection to the political arena, the condition of spirituality in our country, and other things that may come up in our discussion.

"Reverend, the last time we spoke, you were…" only to be suddenly interrupted.

The reverend was pissed, and it showed and showed rather poorly on camera. Trying to rapidly regain his vanishing composure, Stamm stuttered a bit before finally getting his emotions under control. "Edward, I'm not sure what you mean by 'connection to the political arena.' We've always taken precise and unambiguous measures to ensure we remain unsullied by politics. While of course, we accept contributions from voters of all political parties, we are in no position to offer any favor. We've no favor to grant. Rather we are trying to do the good lord's work. You know that. We've discussed that before. Why are you insinuating something of that nature? I find it offensive and insist you immediately cease that line of questioning and get back to what is important. Could we do that, please?"

Edward Benton took a deep breath, this was it. It would either blow the lid off Stamm's deal or spectacularly blow up Bennie's career. He wondered briefly before starting if Walmart was hiring.

"Reverend Stamm, we've learned that you've had some dealings with one Thaddeus Pingry and Congressman Carlton Justice. One is obviously in politics while the other works behind the scenes in that arena among others. What can you share with us about your relationships with them?"

Feigning relief he did not at all possess, Stamm tried his best smarmy tone and posture. "Well, of course, I know of Thaddeus Pingry, but not much personally about the man. And Carlton Justice, heck, he's an old and valued friend of mine. We speak quite frequently and go back many years. I don't see anything particularly heinous about that. Why do you ask?" Bennie was starting to like where this was going.

"Reverend, did you know your old and valued friend was in an auto accident late last night? His condition has not yet been reported so we don't know how he's doing." Stamm shook his 'no.'

"Did you also know that this accident was less than a mile away from Thaddeus Pingry's estate? Do you have any idea why he would be going there at that time of night? It's certainly not anywhere near where he lives. And that it happened after the meeting you had with Thaddeus Pingry."

Uncharacteristically forgetting the cameras were still on, Stamm blustered "Mr. Benton, I find this direction of questioning to be quite insulting. We'd agreed on the topics to be discussed and you are in visible violation of that agreement. If you insist on continuing in this manner, I'm afraid I'll have to terminate this and any further interviews with you."

"Reverend Stamm, I can understand your discomfort. Certainly, when one is attempting to avoid an uncomfortable topic, a good defense is a strong offense. But clearly, no one is attacking you. All I've done is ask some questions. Do you have anything to hide that you feel might embarrass you or your ministry? Such as a letter from you to Congressman Justice regarding Southeast Asia?"

TV screens all over the world showed Jonah Stamm, crimson-faced, profusely sweating, and mouth hanging open, nearly drooling.

Watching this spectacle was Thaddeus Pingry, his mouth also hanging open, his face turning an even deeper shade of red.

"What the fuck? What in hell is he doing? I thought he was going to wait on that! And why the fuck didn't I know anything about it?" Tim Siegel was pissed off and ecstatic. Bennie had gone off script. Hell, he was off the reservation as far as Tim was concerned, but the ratings would be phenomenal.

Standing next to Siegel was Lee Black, barely hiding his astonishment over Bennie's balls. He thought Bennie might go for the jugular but had no idea what that might have looked like. Now he knew and was watching with the kind of morbid fascination usually reserved for train wrecks. In truth that was what was happening with no indication of who the survivors would be.

"Lee, get your sorry ass over here. Now!" roared Tim. "Did you have any idea this was what Bennie had in mind? And don't bullshit me!"

"Tim, look, Bennie's on to something and we really don't know at this point what it is, but he thinks it's big. Every time he pokes at something, it's like chewing on a sore tooth. They're instinctively protective and, well, you saw how Stamm reacted. If anything, it was proof of something bigger, and the letter certainly validates Bennie's gut instinct.

"But no, Bennie hasn't shared any secret agenda, besides I've sort of had my hands full with that forum you gave me."

The managing editor wanted badly to break a story big, bigger than his mainstream competition had. He had worked elsewhere but was stifled in his ambitions. Going to True North was his last chance to make a name in the business.

"Lee, when that shithead is done with his grandstanding, get him on the phone and tell him this: I said, 'As soon as your Sunday forum is wrapped up, the two of you are to work on nothing else but this.' I want scalps. I don't care whose scalp, just bring them to me. And if they're still wet with blood, so much the better. As soon as the telecast is over, OK?"

The copy editor looked back at Tim with rare respect. He'd never seen him fired up about anything. He liked it but didn't know how hot that fire burned. But taking a page out of Bennie's book, he would go full tilt.

He didn't have to wait long to make the phone call as Reverend Stamm walked off the set during mid-interview, thinking how in hell had this rank amateur hack reporter discovered all of that? Some of it might have been a bluff, but it cut too close to the truth not to be genuine. He was in trouble and knew it. To make matters worse, he appeared disconnected about his friend's accident near Thaddeus Pingry's home. He sensed the sharks circling.

And they were. Given the go-ahead by their managing editor, Lee and Bennie could smell the blood in the water.

213

###

Neither Bennie nor Lee had any idea of what they were about to get into. If asked, both, at this moment, wouldn't have traded their jobs for anything. Since Watergate back in the '70s, every reporter fancied themselves, Woodward and Bernstein. This of course led to ridiculous non-stories but occasionally turned up a gem. Both believed they had a diamond but just needed the proper setting to place and present it.

Now that the Kraken had been released, they realized the interview format on this was dead. Jonah Stamm, swearing under his breath as he left the studio, would have agreed that it would be a cold day in hell and other unmentionable places before he subjected himself again to such an inquisition.

Now denied the arena provided by the interviews, Bennie and Lee had to dig deeper into the very same allegations to which they contributed.

"So, Bennie, where do we start? What's next? Photos of Stamm with farm animals? You're the point person on this."

Edward Benton looked blankly at Lee. "Really? Uh, I didn't think that far. I thought Stamm would try and stonewall in which case I would have pushed even harder. I never thought he would book. But now, I don't know. It sure looks like he's hiding something. Let's see where there might be some soft spots we can exploit. That sound good?"

"By soft spots, you're talking about Sheila Weller, right? I don't think she's gonna be predisposed to talk with me after the hatchet job you did on her boss"

"No, I wasn't, but now that you mention it, yeah. Look, with Justice being his old friend, in the hospital, there might be an opportunity to apply some pressure. And no, I don't know what that might be but there's a connection. You saw his reaction. You've got to believe that with this information coming out, her job might not be all that secure anyway."

"Bennie, you're asking me to do something that I'm not comfortable with. You know that Sheila and I may have something going on. Aww, shit, we do have something, and I don't want to screw it up. Can you understand that?"

"Yeah, I do. And Lee, I'm sorry but I don't care. This may be the biggest story of the year if not the decade. If you don't want to get your fingers dirty, I understand. If we break this story, we'll be able to write our own ticket out of True North. I've got to believe you want that as much as I do. Right?

"So, are you in?"

Before Lee could answer, Bennie's cell phone buzzed. Looking at the screen, he frowned at the unrecognizable number. He swiped it on, "Benton here."

He didn't speak again for a few moments, the contents of the call registering on his face as quickly as it did in his mind. "Are you sure? Did you verify it? You have copies of the documents? Good. Can you get me them? Even better. Yes, I do owe you. Big time."

Ending the call, he turned to his copy editor. "Lee, you're not going to believe this and I'm not sure you'll want to."

"What now? You the father of some baby?"

"Something like that yeah, but no, not me. Jonah Stamm. And here's where it's going to be rough for you. The mother is Sheila Weller."

Lee Black must have felt as Reverend Stamm had in the interview, caught in the crosshairs with no place to hide. "What? No. Where did you get this? Olivia is Stamm's daughter? When did it happen, the birth I mean?"

"OK, I don't have all the info yet, but my source has proof, a birth certificate with both names on it. As soon as I get it, I'll share it with you. But now we know why Stamm's been so generous to Sheila and her daughter.

"Given his history, it's obvious he couldn't marry Sheila, her being black and much younger than him, but he did do the honorable thing if you can look at it that way.

"The more I think about it, you may not have to talk with Sheila. Stamm will want to keep this under wraps big time. I'll reach out to him. But ask yourself this, how will it affect your relationship with Sheila? Are you comfortable with Stamm being a de facto father-in-law if it comes to that?"

"Bennie, you are a world-class shit."

Chapter 44

Dedham, MA

No one in the Aura/Sonos conference room was amused by Adam's 'little bird' comment, least of all August Ashe. "Dr. Faraday, I'm sorry if I'm not entertained by your little joke. We are confronted by something of which we know nothing and seem to be powerless to respond. Do you find that funny?"

"Well yes, I do, but that was not my intent. Look, Director Ashe, we've been running around this planet for thousands of years doing whatever the hell we want without worrying about any consequences. Wouldn't it surprise you if there were no consequences for this behavior?

"I'm not saying this is a great karmic event, the one some say we've got it coming, but I feel it's in response to us on this planet. Do I find that amusing? No, I don't, not at all. Do I find it odd that we've always felt we were at the top of the food chain with no one to answer to? Yeah, I do. We, as a species, practice hubris daily on a worldwide scale. If we were children, and to some degree we are, wouldn't it make sense that a 'parental unit' would take us down a notch or two?

"We know there are many who feel there's a greater being to whom we will answer. If you're interested, we can debate that at some other time. As matter of fact, I would love to. I may be a scientist, but there are too many things that defy our analysis. Given time we might figure it all out. Or not. Right now, I don't think time is on our side."

Among all the mouths drooping open at Adam's speech, Grace Perez's was the first to close and then open again with a question. "Adam, I don't know what to say. Do you think this thing, uh, is benign, or, for lack of a better word, bad intentioned? I'm at a loss. Help me here."

"I wish I could, Grace, we're all at a loss. So far, none of the incidents have been anything more than blinks. While those have consequences and will continue to, there's nothing that indicates malevolence. Could that happen? Yes, of course. Will it? I don't know."

The Director stood up quickly, "Dr. Faraday, what are you thinking of doing if it's not benign? Any thoughts on that?"

Adam just stared at Ashe. "Director, let me ask you a question. What if it isn't? Benign, that is. How would you go about attacking light?"

Silent throughout the conversation was Fran. "I can't believe I'm going to be the voice of reason here. But I think Adam was on to something when he suggested we correlate the incidences with happenings around the world. If they line up, then there is a cause and effect indicated. If that's the case, then the next few times it happens will corroborate the theory.

"It really won't help us much in how to deal with it, but it's a start and that's more than we've had. Everybody around the world is being affected by this and all the incidents are being recorded. So far, there's only been that one isolated blink. That might prove to be our baseline for determining more.

"And, I can't believe I'm saying this either, but Adam's theory may be right about another being, not a god, at least I hope not. How the hell I became a scientist after having been raised a good Catholic girl, is beyond me, but some of that stuff may have stuck. Is someone, or thing, reaching out to us? Shit, I really can't believe I just said that. Just don't call in that Stamm dude for advice. That's the last thing I want to hear."

That got some laughs in the room as Grace responded. "I must admit I agree with you, Fran. We could mark those down as a phenomenon we may never see again, but like Adam, I doubt that. We can get our people to do the correlations on these. Is there anything else we should look for such as time of day, duration, or any other aberrations?"

"Shit, they're all aberrations," chimed in Fran.

Adam responded quickly, "I think that's a good start. The weather perhaps, but that may be a dead end. See if there are any indications of warning elements or signals that might be a herald of sorts."

Fran jumped on that immediately, "Herald? Really? As in 'hark the herald angels'...? You didn't mean that, did you? Adam, did you? And a little bird? Really?"

Grace looked at Fran realizing that she was starting to like the little wiseass, after all, laughing "You don't cut anyone any slack, do you?"

Director August Ashe sat in his car in the Aura/Sonos parking lot, tamping down his frustration and anger. He had held it in check with much difficulty, during the meeting. His Deputy Director had seen him this way before and knew that silence was the best action taken until he was ready to speak. It didn't take long.

"Grace, I can't tell you the last time I heard such a load of bullshit. Light thinking? Was this group thoroughly vetted? What am I supposed to do with this? How do you think the president will receive this? They've no idea what they're messing around with."

Perez waited until he was through with this thought. She waited again a little longer before speaking directly. "August, yes, you're right, but if the truth is told, neither do we. Adam told you we can't approach this with methods used before. This is entirely new. I think they are making progress, slow – yes, but really, it is out of their hands. They can only wait, record, measure, and then speculate. What would you have them do? Bomb someone? Tell me, what would you do?"

August Ashe had a deep respect for his deputy director. Grace Perez had come up all on her own, no favors asked, and none was given, not that she would have accepted them. He had become her mentor, seeing in her both the son and the daughter he never had. Barring any political games played by others vying for the position, he would have Grace as his successor.

Well before she was aware of it, Ashe had been grooming her for that ascension. He believed that any competition for the position would be crushed by Grace if they attempted to prevent her climb.

"I am frustrated. Everything you said is true, it's reasonable but it doesn't make me feel any better about the progress or lack of it that they've made. Throw in helpless along with the frustration if you'd like. In the past, we sort of knew what we might be up against and could deal with it accordingly. We had personal and historical experiences we could call on for foundation. Now? Christ!"

Taking a deep breath, she asked Ashe quietly, "What else is on your mind? That can't be all of it."

"No, it isn't. it's obvious we don't have a goddam clue about what's going on, only speculation. If it is what Faraday and his people think it is, we've got some heavy lifting to do to prepare for what will be an entirely new world.

"You know I'm a religious man, but I don't buy into the religious angle you hear in the media. If what Faraday says is true, I, and every other god-fearing person, am going to have one hell of a reality check. There are far more serious implications to this. This will affect all life, everyone. There'll be a shitload of political ramifications to this. It'll be just like all those shamans on TV claiming they have the answer. They don't and the politicians won't either. The one thing both have in common is the desire to control and neither has proven adept at it.

"The President will want to know what happened today and he'll have the same questions as I do. Where will the government as we know fit into this? Will it become obsolete, a relic that may have outlived its usefulness only to be relegated to history books? Again, if what they're speculating is accurate, we could become a self-governing species. Imagine, self-government as the rule. Not necessarily a bad thing – on paper – but you and I have both seen what mob rule can do."

He looked at her, an expression she'd never seen before, sadness and perhaps frustration. While he was a fierce warrior, he was always in defense of his country. He was now confronted by an opponent for which he had no tactics.

"That's only the beginning. Everything we know and value will be turned over on its ass. And it won't just be us. The whole world will be going through this as if there aren't enough problems to deal with. Think about it, Grace. Cultural, social, governmental, and religious values will all be called into question, much more than they are today."

Shaking his head, he continued quietly, "But it won't stop there. You already see different groups and people claiming this as their own. One can only imagine what that will look like on a global scale. I wonder if we have the temperament to handle this. Someone is going to have to lead and we're going to need to be damned careful on that front."

Grace had never seen Ashe so overcome. "August, we don't know. Those are all good questions. But until more is revealed, we're going to have to follow Adam's lead on this."

He looked up at her, "*Adam?* Since when is he Adam?"

"For Chrissakes, August. I don't have time for this and certainly not for that. Give me a break, will you?" But she did admit to herself that it was an interesting prospect. Putting it out of her mind for the moment, she continued, "Let's get back to the office. I'm sure we'll have some debriefing to do." 'Adam,' she thought, smiling to herself, 'Hmmph.'

Chapter 45

Baltimore, MD

No sooner had the forum's director signaled they were live when faux fire and brimstone erupted: "FIAT LUX! What could be clearer than that? It is the word of God. That's all we need to know. All we need to believe. Discussion ended!" The fundamentalist preacher Paxton Shea then sat down, smiling smugly at his preemptive declaration, having none of the free-wheeling discussion planned.

Lee narrowed it down to five clergy people, three representatives from mainstream denominations, Islam, Judaism, Presbyterian, one Christian fundamentalist, and a monk from the Buddhist school, Vajrayana. Including himself, he believed that six talking heads would represent a broad enough view of things. Lee knew all he would have to do is feed some innocuous questions to the group and hopefully avoid the tendency of some towards self-aggrandizement. The hard part had been winnowing through a large and very willing group of clergy people desperate for facetime. He had not counted on such a fiery start though, unable to make the scantest of introductions.

He took a deep breath, "Thank you, Reverend Shea. We appreciate the strength and fervor of your beliefs, but please before we start, I'd like to introduce the other participants to our audience.

"Good evening, my name is Lee Black of True North News and I welcome you to this hopefully engaging and thoughtful discussion of what has the entire world simultaneously fascinated and fearful, specifically, the odd behavior of light. This has many around the world beginning to question their own beliefs. In response to that, True North News presents a forum addressing this subject.

"My guests tonight are from a wide range of religious beliefs who, and no pun intended, will attempt to shed some light on the situation, according of course to their own beliefs. Our goal was also to have representation from the scientific community, but we were unable to secure that. It was apparent to us that no one there was willing to participate in tonight's forum. We can only speculate why. Hopefully, that will change as time goes on and we have a more complete understanding of this phenomenon. So, with that said, let's proceed.

Before they could start, Reverend Shea interrupted once again. "Science! There are no answers there. That's why they're not here today. They finally know they're phonies!"

Fortunately, Lee was off camera as he glared at Shea. Taking one more breath, he proceeded.

"Starting from my right and moving around the table are, Reverend Bonnie McFarland, Presbyterian Minister from the Second Street St. Louis Presbyterian Church; Rabbi Jacob, or Jay, Roth from Temple Beth Abraham in Atlanta; Iman Hassan Al-Haq of the Islamic Freedom Council in Washington, DC; the famed Buddhist teacher, Ajahn Khema, visiting the US from Thailand; and of course, the Reverend Paxton Shea from the Crystal Spirit Church in Denver.

"Our intent this evening is to open a discussion about what these esteemed religious leaders believe is happening regarding the phenomenon of light's behavior. It is not a debate, but an open-ended dialogue about what they believe is going on or what this represents, and what it means. So, who would like to start?"

Sitting opposite Lee, the Reverend Paxton Shea, very short with his feet barely touching the carpet, leaped at the chance to dominate as he tried earlier, demonstrating his insecurity. "I do appreciate all coming out here, but I have to restate what I said earlier, perhaps a little too enthusiastically."

Lee mentally rolled his eyes at Shea's obvious ploy. "Fiat Lux. It's that simple. It is God who is giving us his word, made manifest in the behavior of light. He is trying to show us his way."

Rabbi Jay Roth was quick to respond, "Reverend, please, you're assuming we all believe as you do. Yes, I think we all here believe in a god, and while they all have similarities, my god is not your god.

Please do not project your beliefs upon me, or the others for that matter and I will reciprocate the consideration."

Shea's immediate dislike toward the rabbi was apparent though for no understandable reason other than the civil dressing down just administered. The slender, intellectual Jew represented all Paxton Shea believed was wrong - liberal thought: religiously, socially, and politically. But he understood this was not the time nor place to confront such an adversary.

Rabbi Roth continued, "As Jews, we believe God speaks to each one of us individually. Look at Abraham, look at Moses and the Burning Bush. That was God speaking to only one person. His actions upon that may have affected many, but directions were given to just one. But I do agree with you about the first words, 'Let there be light.' The Midrash asks, from what was light created? An answer is said softly, 'God cloaked Himself in a white shawl, and the light of its splendor shone from one end of the world to the other.'"

In his best rabbinical tone, the Rabbi continued, further pissing off Reverend Shea. "So, what are we to take from this? Plainly said, light does not belong to this world. Consider it a radiation
of an entirely different quintessence, from an altogether different side of reality. This light acts symbolically as all that is good and beautiful and positive. But it does beg the question, what does this odd behavior mean? I would like to…" And once more, light removed itself, and once more made itself the center of attention.

And it did just that again and again and again.

Interrupted by that example of light's 'odd behavior', blinking several times before re-establishing itself again, the Rabbi paused before calmly continuing. "As I said, and here it was displayed, what does it mean? I think that is the crux of the matter. There are a multitude of meanings for light in Judaism. Which one are we to use? Which one is applicable? I would say, in agreement with the scientists, we do not know enough yet. And if we did, how would we meet this challenge?"

Paxton Shea was about to speak out when interrupted by the moderator. "Reverend, please, we've yet to hear from the other participants. Reverend McFarland, where do you come down on this? What is your interpretation?"

The presbyterian minister was the only clergy not wearing anything closely resembling clerical garb except for the small cross on a chain around her neck. With a minimum of makeup save what was needed for the cameras, she looked more like a businessperson, conveying an austere no-nonsense yet friendly demeanor. "Lee, thank you. And to the others in this impressive group, I'm honored to be included. Please let me open by saying this: I do not speak for my denomination. True, I do speak as a member of it, but we follow Scripture alone as the source of our truth. That is our guiding principle. Neither the Bible nor church tradition governs our way." This 'blasphemy' elicited a gasp and a few raised eyebrows from the panel.

She allowed herself a small smile, continuing, "that said, I, and again this is only me speaking, do believe this may be interpreted as an epiphany. The word epiphany comes from the Greek word Phos, meaning light. It is the light coming on, a revelation, an understanding of which we've not had before. I think we are being given a chance to see and experience something we've never seen previously and certainly do not understand. It indeed may be an epiphany that transcends all religious beliefs. If it is that, then I see an unbelievable opportunity to build bridges that have been wholly unimaginable before."

"Exactly! He is showing us His way!" Paxton Shea was obviously not above blatantly co-opting someone else's message.

The Reverend McFarland cast a steely eye while smiling sweetly at Shea. "No, Reverend Shea, that is not what I'm saying. Yes, in the Bible, Fiat Lux as you said, Light appears as the first of all creatures. It is thought to be a symbol of God's Being and Goodness. But I see this phenomenon as an end to the Dark Ages which in a sense never really ended. If one thinks of this in a theological way, then this may very well be the Light of the World, the whole world, while not corporeal, no longer ethereal, but manifested as intentional.

"I think we are being given the occasion to finally think holistically for ourselves, to build our own way, working together, all of us, to create a better world. Personally, I see that as a positive thing, believing in the inherent good of humankind." Raising a hand to stop Shea's next interruption, "Yes, I believe evil things happen in this world and no, I don't know why. But I do believe there is far more good than bad."

Lee Black sat there, pleased with the answers from the rabbi and the minister, but knew he had to intercede to get the other viewpoints included before it was dominated by any one of the others. "Reverend, thank you. We've yet to hear from Ajahn Khema and Hassan Al-Haq. But before we do, we need to take a commercial break. When we return, we'll continue with this very enlightening and spirited discussion and what light's behavior portends for all of us. Be back in just a few moments."

With that, the broadcast shifted from the studio to commercials including one touting the latest in lithium battery technology, the irony not lost on Lee Black. Craven though that placement may have been, it was those dollars that made this possible.

And what was *this?* He wondered if it would make a difference to anyone. While it was enlightening (his word), what would it change? Just like everyone else, these people too had their theories and positions and none of it made a dime's worth of sense. It was not the action that could be taken, rather it was the same-old centuries of posturing that may have contributed to the world's problems.

But receiving the alert in his earphone the broadcast was about to resume, he banished those thoughts to concentrate on getting through this. If only Paxton Shea would shut up.

"Thank you for being patient until we could return and welcome back to our forum on the issue of light's disappearances. Iman, Ajahn, what are your thoughts and response to what's been said? Agreement? Disagreement?"

The Buddhist teacher Ajahn Khema, sitting peacefully, raised his hand first, and spoke calmly in soft, accented, almost melodic tones, "We believe that the God Almighty resides in all humans as Light, a fact maintained in all scriptures. Consequently, we can meditate on that indefinitely, forever perhaps. We believe we can find the Creator within.

He made for a startling contrast to the rest of the clergy present, his appearance in a flowing saffron yellow robe and bald head portrayed him as almost otherworldly. "Now again, how does that differ from what everyone here has stated? Our writings reference a Divine Light, a celestial being, a Buddha. Many of our texts comment on Buddha and light. Let me quote an excerpt:

the world of the ten quarters;
and those sentient beings
who are mindful of the Buddha
are embraced (by that light),
never to be abandoned.

"May that be what is happening now? Reverend McFarland, I think you and I have a lot in common and even more to discuss." Her smile in response was much warmer than the one offered Paxton Shea.

"That is truly beautiful and hopeful, Ajahn," responded Reverend McFarland. "But, if one is not mindful of Buddha, are they to be abandoned? Please know that I am not challenging you or the sutra. But during this, what, a phenomenon? Isn't that what some, maybe many are feeling, abandoned? Life without light leaves no room for hope. And it each time the light disappears, so does a little more hope. Cast into the darkness as it were.

"I think we in this forum and our brethren need to be cognizant of the dilemma facing the world. Our work has for centuries been the source of hope for many. And yes, it has also brought much pain, let us not forget that. But I know from my own experience, people are looking to us for reassurance which truthfully, we may not be able to give, not knowing what is happening. It may be that time our faith is to be tested as it will those who follow us."

The Ajahn listened attentively. Raising his hand, he spoke, "Reverend McFarland, you are right. I think when the sutra speaks about abandonment, one could easily substitute their own god for Buddha, and it would still apply. Yet, we are indeed being cast into darkness and it is creating fear. We do know not who is standing next to us each moment. But that is just as true in light. Is it not? We do know not where we are going. That too is true at any time. The perceived veil of certainty of we live with each day has been cast from our eyes and yet we find we cannot see anything at all. All we have is our own faith. For some that will be enough. I'm afraid for the others, they will only have their fear and maybe terror with which to deal."

This was met with assent by the others, manifested in nods and quiet thought and agreement, except for Paxton Shea. "I'm sorry. All of this is second-hand nonsense. There is only one true God, and his name is…"

Lee needed to keep it going, making sure all had an opportunity to speak before it devolved into a posturing theological competition for time.

"Reverend Shea, please. Your interruptions are not helpful to this discussion. As with everyone here, you're entitled to your beliefs, but not at the cost of others' time. Please refrain and let other participants speak.

"Iman? Have you any thoughts on what's being discussed? We would certainly like to hear your position on this."

Looking more like a prosperous oil baron than a cleric, the Iman was dressed in traditional Muslim garb, a loose, ankle-length shirt, topped by a colored kufiyah over hand-made Najd sandals. He was slow, almost reluctant to answer, pursing his lips as if in deep thought. In heavily accented English, finally answered, "It appears Light is an important part of all our beliefs. In Islam, we too see Light as sacred. There is a famous parable in Islam called Ayat An Nur. Much has been written about it, countless volumes in fact. Consequently, there are also many interpretations as with almost everything theological.

"It is known as 'the Light Verse' or "The Parable of Light" and is rather brief, but very meaningful. If you would permit me, I would like to share part of it."

"As you'll realize afterward, there is much that can be interpreted, subject of course to an interpreter's particular leaning." Warming to his subject, his eyes gleamed in anticipation of his recital,

"'Allah is the Light of the heavens and the earth,
The parable of His Light is as if there were a niche,
And within it a Lamp: The Lamp enclosed in Glass;
The glass as if it were a brilliant star;
An Olive, neither of the East nor of the West,
Whose oil is well-nigh luminous, though fire scarce touched it;
Light upon Light!
Allah doth set forth parables for men: and Allah doth know all things.'"

The Iman's recitation was met with silence, not of disbelief, but of its implications. The other clerics could find parallels within their own faith. At that moment, Lee Black realized that however qualified he might be to moderate a forum, he was way in over his head. How in hell did Tim Siegel expect him to add anything to this? Nothing he had in his life was comparable to this when growing up, reserved only for going to Sunday school and a strict, family-fueled belief in Jesus which to his parent's dismay did not take root.

The silence was broken by the Rabbi Jay Roth. "Iman, I want to thank you personally for that. I profess to a shallow knowledge of Islam, and I apologize. You've given me yet another course of study to follow which I assure you I will.

"I find the line about the oil comforting, the oil being luminous, well-nigh luminous I think it was, and it reminded me not a little of Hannukah, our Festival of Lights where there was scarce oil in the lamps, but not being consumed by flames as it would normally have been, lasted for eight days. I have much to learn from you.

"It's also heartening to see that we all appear to have a similar interpretation of light.

And so it went, agreement and 'understanding' by all throughout the rest of the program until the end when Lee tried to wrap it up. Everyone had had time to illustrate what light means to them in their own faiths but talked around what light was doing with no conclusions. They did not know.

The broadcast ended as it started with the now frustrated Reverend Shea, loudly blurting once again, "It's so simple, it is God talking to us. I don't know why you all can't see that. We could have all saved a lot of time."

Lee took a deep breath and thanked everyone and closed the broadcast thinking, 'Oh well, nothing ventured, nothing gained. What a cluster fuck.' But he was wrong on several counts, the first being the phone call he received immediately after the broadcast.

Picking up his cell, he saw it was his editor Tim Siegel, surprisingly effusive for the job he'd just done. "Lee, I got to hand it to you. That was a good job, juggling all of them. I'm surprised and impressed. Look, I've got something else I'd like you to do."

Lee started to protest, "Tim, c'mon, I thought you wanted me to work exclusively with Bennie on the Stamm thing. What now?"

"Well, you're going to have to find a way to juggle both. Who knows, they might even be connected in some weird way.

"It's this… we haven't given any coverage to the light thing. I heard some talk about a group called Aura/Sonos who's doing some research on this thing. Everyone is talking about it, but no one else has talked with them... yet. I want you to contact them and see what you can find. Maybe it'll just be filler, background stuff, who knows, maybe you'll find out something. It'd be a feature, not a program as soon as we have it.

"And I want to keep it clean, no sensationalism, no tawdry crap, let's see if we can, God forbid, elevate the conversation. OK?"

Lee frowned, ending the call, thinking to himself, 'Fiat Lux, my ass!'

Chapter 46

Washington, DC

He knew it would be a long shot but hoped that the combination of the accident, drugs and the fear of being exposed without a backup plan would loosen Carlton Justice's tongue. First, he had to get through the guards by the hospital room door. Aides he felt would have no trouble running that gauntlet. He was right in more ways than one.

"Excuse me, is this the congressman's room? I'd like to see how he's doing. Is he all right?" His insincere concern was instantly recognized by the congressman's senior aide Trey Keenan.

"Yes, it is, Mr. Benton. How may I help you?"

Surprised at being made, Bennie took another tack – that of conspiracy. "Well, in this case I think you really might be able to help. First, how is the congressman doing? Has he regained consciousness? What's the prognosis? I want to make sure I get it right, you know?"

Trey looked at him and smirked, thinking, yeah, this guy wants to get it right. Seeing an opportunity to advance his own personal goals, he decided to speak with the reporter, but not before placing a few jabs of his own. "As you did with Jonah Stamm? What was the basis for your questions, Mr. Benton? Besides your own ego, what did you hope to achieve?

"That said, I will talk with you, but not here." Motioning with his head towards the left, he continued, "Meet me in the stairwell at the end of the hall in fifteen minutes. We'll talk."

Not at all the response he expected, he was silent for a moment, then asked once more if he could see the congressman. Denied, he walked the opposite way down the hall in search of a coffee machine to kill some time until his meeting with the aide.

Finding a large wooden, box-like structure masquerading as a hospital bench, he sat down, enjoying neither the seating accommodations nor coffee. It would be a long fifteen minutes.

Surprised at the aide's response, Bennie speculated on what he might have to share with him. He thought it was a waste of time. Whatever he might come up with would probably be no closer to the actuality than what he currently knew. He'd be surprised a second time this evening and by the same person.

The reporter decided to wait in the stairwell, sitting on the stairs would probably not be any less comfortable than the bench. It was only a few minutes before Justice's aide arrived. "Mr. Benton. What can I do for you?"

Bennie, not really knowing Trey Keenan, viewed him as a lightweight and approached him accordingly. "Look, I don't know you. I assume you work for the congressman, an aide or something, right?"

"Yes, or something. As I asked, what can I do for you?" Though young, the aide had ambition, drive, and no problems with confrontation. That was made clear by his tone.

Bennie picked up on that quickly, realizing he was going to have to try a different tack. Enlisting Trey's help, perhaps as a confidant who had the congressman's best interests at heart would be his tactic. "Look, it's clear you know who I am. But I've not had the pleasure of your acquaintance. Can we start with that?"

Trey Keenan was unaccustomed to being in the driver's seat and it he liked it, a lot. Even at this stage in his career, he knew he had to handle it carefully, especially with the media. "Fair enough. Trey Keenan. And again, now that we've introduced ourselves," somewhat impatiently this time, "what can I do for you, Mr. Benton?"

"It's like this, Trey. And I'm going to be upfront with you. I don't know if there's a story here. Maybe the congressman had a little too much to drink and went off the road. OK, I can buy that. Or maybe it's because the damned light went off again. Who the fuck knows what that's all about anyway? Right? But and here's the big question, what in hell was he doing right outside Thaddeus Pingry's house that night? What was that all about? Or are you just gonna stand there and blow smoke up my ass?"

The aide looked at Bennie for a long time, not saying anything. Finally, he spoke. "Quite an unattractive image that is. I need to know what you're up to before I tell you anything. If it sinks the congressman, so be it. He's an asshole anyway. But if it can blow up in my face, and that's a real possibility, you know where the door is. And not to sound too opportunistic, but what's in it for me? There's got to be a quid pro quo. One worth my time and risk."

Benton had underestimated the aide. He was young but possessed the ruthless qualities of a good politician. He'd been taught well and learned his lessons. Bennie wondered what this kid really wants. It was simple, what all politicians and up-and-comers wanted, media exposure, power, and influence. Played right, Bennie might be able to cultivate a productive source with Trey Keenan.

"Trey, I got to believe that being a congressional aide is not where you think your career ends. You're obviously too smart for that. You probably want to run for office someday, right? And what everyone on the way up, or even down for that matter, wants is access to media exposure, sympathetic exposure. You want that? I'll give it to you.

"Now, I won't lie for you. I won't even cover up for you. Comes the day though, and it will, I just might look the other way. That work for you?"

Congressman Justice's aide looked at him the way a starving dog looks at a raw piece of meat. "Yeah, it does. What do you want?"

"Good. First, what was Justice doing outside of Pingry's estate that night? I don't care about drinking and whoring or even the light. What in hell was he doing out there? We heard of a blow-up between them, over who knows what, and now they're doing late-night booty calls. C'mon."

Trey Keenan looked at Bennie and laughed. "A booty call? Nah, different from the one I intimated to you before." Bennie's eyes opened wide.

"No, not that kind. Worse. How familiar are you with Jonah Stamm's children's home in Southeast Asia?"

"I am, a little," he lied. Was this going to be a corroboration of Lee's info? If so, the chips wouldn't fall, they'd be flying.

"And just one more thing... that letter you had on TV...?"

Its realization was growing. Seeing that what it did had an effect, it wondered what to do next. It knew that when it blinked, the noise and the pain and the discomfort went away…still, only for a little while, but it did relent. While it still felt alone, it also felt a growing sense of belonging to something while being apart from everything. It did not know how to reconcile that. It was at once very young and still very old.

And its assimilation process was unbelievably fast. If it had had a reference point for all it was experiencing, it would have been even faster. Still learning, exponentially faster.

It was starting to see what specifically caused it pain. What hurt it? And it was beginning to realize it had the power to stop it. It possessed a native curiosity and intelligence. And as such, had a very basic and simplistic idea of what in a civilized culture might be considered 'right and wrong'. 'Right' was peaceful, restful, and comfortable. 'Wrong' hurt. It did not like 'wrong'. There was no nuance in its thinking. It did not, could not yet recognize or identify individuals.

Rather than everything at once, it found that it could focus on one thing at a time and isolate it. 'Syria' was one thing and when it focused on that, the pain and the crying it heard went away. Did it do that? Could it do it again? There were so many tears and cries. It was not asked to do anything about it. For what could anyone ask of it? It had no peers, nothing and no one to lean on. It felt required to do something if only to turn off all the hurt it experienced, to preserve itself.

And as it felt compelled, it experienced emotions, welcomed peace, started to realize its own being, it became fully sentient.

Chapter 47

While light's unpredictability was becoming commonplace though disturbing, the world was not ready for what came next. Syria had only been the first instance of light disappearing in specifically one place. That was about to become the norm.

Like a traffic light system, light was regularly going off and on in only certain areas. And not just for a moment or two. It would vanish for hours at a time while the rest of the world remained unaffected. Those looking out from the darkness could see no light; those looking into the darkness saw just that.

Each time it eased the pain and suffering and conflict, it would resume at a lower level. It didn't take long for astute observers to recognize a developing pattern. First among those were the researchers at Aura/Sonos. The re-occurrence of light vanishing could be a vindication of Faraday's theory, no matter how preposterous it had first sounded.

Through much arguing, cajoling, and simple pleading, Adam was able to convince Ashe and Perez there was nothing to lose by publicizing their theories. They realized that there'd be a lot of skepticism, ridicule, and fear over such a pronouncement, but arrived at the conclusion that if they were able to identify the issue, it might reduce the fear and uncertainty around the world. There was no other course to take. The worst could be ridicule – the best, well, who knew that?

As with any action, benign and innocent, there are always unintended consequences. Their announcement was met with incredulity and denials from the clergy, the Vatican first among them. The proclamation was viewed as just short of heresy, right up there with Galileo. They urged their members not to be swayed or seduced by such fanciful and dangerous thinking. There was only one God and only they had his private number.

Several steps below that were the televangelists with Jonah Stamm leading the charge. He saw this as the equivalent of a certified letter straight from the lord and was not above milking it for all its worth.

Not restricted to dogma as the Vatican, he was free to make it up as he happily went along. Not that he had no other concerns, but they, in his estimation, paled in comparison. Were he to have really believed what he preached; he could not have conjured up this future. For the moment his difficulties with Justice and Pingry fell by the wayside.

The politicians were among the most reluctant to wade in on this. While they all voiced nonsensical opinions, none were surprisingly willing to take a real position on it until they figured out how to generate political capital from it. Unintentionally, this would not hurt them.

At the end of the day, it was the scientists and the NSA promoting this idea, who became the equivalent of the messenger, the target for which many wanted to shoot, an old lesson yet to be learned by many.

"I say it's the Lord! He has made himself manifest, yea! Visible now, visiting us in the one true form, the light in which is only him! We have waited for this for so long and now our reward is here!

"Do not believe those who would say otherwise! Only God can be light! God is light! I beg you, read John 8:12, 'I am the Light of the world'! Jesus himself said that. Do you doubt it? Yes, you do. Does it get any simpler than that? No! He has come and only you, the true believers will ascend with him to heaven!"

Working up to his conclusion, he pleaded, "Call right now and help fund our ministries in sharing the light of the world! He is speaking to us now, as we must speak to each other. Please call, our brothers and sisters are waiting to talk with you. God loves you and peace be with you as we walk together in this new and uncertain time."

Jonah Stamm was wrapping up a taping of his next show in fine form. "How was that? Can you believe what's happening? He has come back. We are blessed."

While a believer, the reverend was also an unremitting cynic. "I could not have scripted this any better. Let the Vatican do its thing, they're entitled to their share. I've, uh, we've got ours and it's about to get bigger. Oh, yes, the lord does work in mysterious ways."

The sedation was beginning to wear off and Carlton Justice was regaining consciousness for the first time since the accident. He lay quietly and alone in the hospital room, remembering Pozzi's and the couple, and maybe the three or four bourbons he had before leaving for his meeting. He seemed to recall slowing down as he approached the turnoff for Pingry's estate and the crash, then nothing else, just darkness. He didn't realize that that was not a lapse in memory but in fact what really happened.

Reaching for the carafe of water on the small table before him, he knocked it to the floor. The noise alerted the nurse. "Congressman, how good it is to see you awake. I'm Rosie,' she chirped, "your nurse. How are we?"

She looked at the monitors, seeing nothing alarming. "Well, Congressman, we've been waiting for you. It was touch and go for a while, but the docs took great care of you. I'm sure they'll give you a complete rundown of what you've gone through. Let me go and tell them you're awake."

Still a little disoriented, Justice weakly waved his hand, "No, don't go. Rosie, right? Rosie, please tell me this, what happened? How long have I been here? Excuse me, I'm a bit confused."

She gave him her best nurse smile, "That's all-right Congressman. You were in an auto accident, no one else was hurt. But a bad one. You've been with us for four days now. I'll be right back with the doctor. Just try and take it easy. Don't go getting worked up over anything, OK?" And once again alone, he was alone.

Thaddeus Pingry knew almost immediately when Carlton Justice crashed his car outside of his estate. As was happening more and more frequently these days, light's behavior was yet another element out of his control, a situation he detested. While not alarmed at the increasing regularity of these aberrations, he was not happy. Usually, whatever he touched fell under his control and that started to unravel with Jonah Stamm's damned letter.

Now this with Justice. Gritting his teeth, he would have preferred Justice be killed in the accident. That would have easily eliminated one problem. Now unbelievably, it had been exacerbated. He had no idea when Justice would be released and what he'd be able to do afterward.

In the meantime, Stamm as a minor nuisance had grown to a major problem. How he had learned of the details of Pingry's activities in Southeast Asia was troubling. Making matters worse, the damned light went out over there as well, halting all his activities. They had ground to a complete standstill during the outage. To compound matters, none of the workers over there would continue, superstitious that the disappearing light was punishment for what they were doing. Ignorant fools! What nonsense!

Light or no light, he could not stop. Business had to be conducted and his clients were demanding. Hell, most of their business was figuratively managed in the dark. This should suit them well enough. He would find a solution where others could not, he always did. It was how he and his family had built their empire and saw no reason to deviate from that now, nor would he plan any changes. Still, the light was beginning to concern him. He understood he had no control over it. Like the rest of the world save those at Aura/Sonos, he had no idea what was going on or how to deal with it.

He also knew that sooner than later he was going to have to deal with Jonah Stamm, a vulgar man whose base motivations weren't all that different from his. One hid behind faith while the other hid behind walls, both offering a level of secrecy that only obscene wealth could provide. Light knew no such walls. It reached everything and it apparently could do so at will.

Chapter 48

Great Falls, VA

Pingry, attired in a severely cut, dark gray worsted suit and a stiffly starched white shirt with a subdued print tie, opened the large ornate front door and blocked the entrance to the house, as Bennie approached it. He immediately took the lead, "Mr. Benton, I presume? You should know, I don't usually speak with members of the media. And…" gazing at Bennie, with his rumpled sport coat and pants, was treated to a look Pingry normally reserved for unwelcome garden insects, "certainly not the likes of you."

It wasn't the first time did Bennie wish he dressed better. Driving up the long access road to the immense house, Bennie was once again reminded of his own beginnings and current situation and how far removed he was from such wealth. He'd wondered how Pingry would receive him and now he knew. The man was, as his reputation was known, imposing, and intolerant of small nuisances himself. He'd have only one shot. "Mr. Pingry, thank you for seeing me. I…"

"Mr. Benton, your social niceties are a nuisance, they've no place at this moment. Get to the reason for your visit. You mentioned something about Congressman Justice. What could possibly be your interest in him and further, by extension, me? Only as a courtesy to the congressman's condition, have I agreed to see you. Get on with it, please."

Taking a deep mental breath, Bennie rattled off multiple questions, "Sir, what can you tell me about your business in Southeast Asia? Do you deal in exports? Do you support Reverend Jonah Stamm's orphanage? Mr. Pingry, is it true you're taking children from them and selling them into sexual slavery?"

If it were possible for Thaddeus Pingry to simultaneously erupt volcanically while remaining glacially cold, that would have been an apt description following Bennie's queries. "Mr. Benton, you may leave this house immediately. Such accusations will not be tolerated and certainly not from someone like you." And in a very measured cadence, "Now. Get. The. Hell. Out. Of. My. House. Do I make myself clear?"

This was the reaction that Bennie expected and rather enjoyed. He'd learned, the hard way, that such responses signaled cracks that he might exploit. "Mr. Pingry, are you denying this? Because if you…"

Pingry's response was quick and completely uncharacteristic, he back-handed Bennie across the face, knocking him into the large urn that stood to one side of the door. Bennie stumbled and fell into the urn, shattering it. "Get out!" growled Pingry, "Now!"

Bennie still dazed from the sudden confrontation, had his confirmation.

He did not tolerate well anything out of his control. His ego was such as to believe he could bend most anything to his will. So, what in hell was this light thing, but an unwanted complication? Why hadn't anyone figured out what was going on? He was sure if he had put his best people on it, they'd have solved it and found a way to exploit it. Not often was he wrong, this being one of those times. He mused that if he were a spiritual person, he might have construed it as a sign. But that was for weak-minded people and Thaddeus Pingry was anything but weak.

His staff had retired for the night, yet still available should they be summoned. But Pingry was in no mood for dealing with anyone even those who were at his beck and call. He walked over to his bar and opened one of his last bottles of Chateau Margaux '64. Wine was one of the few vices he permitted himself.

Pingry needed to be alone as he worked on his next move. He was exasperated with Justice's incompetence, intolerant of Stamm's

243

obsequiousness and failed attempt at extortion, and fumed over the reporter Benton from that childish, ersatz news organization. Remembering years long ago when if one had enough money, news could be bought, written, and sold like the commodity he viewed it to be. Not so these days and the world was, he believed, all the worst for it. Would Benton jump at such an inducement? Possibly. He doubted that Bennie had such scruples. But it was obvious he wanted a bigger prize: that of bringing down the powerful. Pingry took a long pull of the expensive wine and thought, maybe, but not this one, not this time.

Reaching for his phone, everything went black. Pingry was blind in total and complete darkness. He didn't believe it. Again? It shook him and seemed to make all these other issues greater in magnitude, the darkness amplifying the implication. For the first time in his recollection, he felt a small tinge of, what, fear? Used to casting fear, not being on the receiving end, he didn't like it. What in hell could do that? And as suddenly as everything had gone dark, the light returned, blindingly bright. He was now experiencing something almost everyone on the world did: worry. He'd have to marshal his energies and act.

Realizing that more people besides himself were in jeopardy, though not really giving a damn personally, he thought they should have an opportunity to try and save their ship or go down with it. He picked up his landline phone and called Bell Williams, the senior senator from Virginia. Williams had been in the group from its inception and was his de facto capo. "Bell, I just sat here in this confounded darkness wondering what the hell is going on with it. It's unsettling. But the hell with that, we need to get the group together as soon as possible. No, Justice has not ingratiated himself back into our good graces as he had expected to. All but him. Yes. Call me when it's all set up. And Bell, not here. We'll meet at the backup. Thank you.

"Oh, and Bell? We go back a long way. You're one of the few people I trust. So, trust me when I say this is something we've never considered. This might have to get a little, how would you say, messy.

Please make a call to our media group friends first and let them know we may need to engage them without much notice. Again, thank you."

Bell Williams, standing quietly alone in his study, hung up the phone and stared at it, shaking his head, thinking about the uncharacteristic uncertainty in Pingry's voice. He picked up his phone to start the calls and hesitated, putting it back down. He couldn't delay making the calls, but he wanted to have his wits about him. It would be no trouble calling the members of their private group, but the last thing he wanted to do was show any apprehension.

It was the call to the euphemistically named "media group" that made him very uneasy. They were used to being summoned at a moment's notice. Making it would be tantamount to pulling a fire alarm, they'd rush in to put out the fire. They could clean up messes as efficiently as they could create them. He'd have to be very clear and succinct that no action was to be taken yet, only that they were needed on a stand-by.

He hoped he could sell that to them. He knew he should have no trouble as he was representing a powerful group that didn't do these things lightly. But from stories he had heard, this group didn't measure things by weight, just immediacy, and the faster the better results. Waiting wasn't something they liked to do, people of action usually don't. It would be like leaving a steak outside a pit bull's cage. He was going to make sure that when that door was finally opened, he wasn't between the dog and the meat lest he becomes part of the feeding frenzy certain to follow.

Nervously, he made the call. It rang four times before being answered with a barely audible, "Yes?"

Using the brief identification of "You know who this is?" He continued, "I have a message for you. Be ready," and hung up the phone worrying where this would go and how it would end. Pingry had never lost a battle and seldom called in outsiders. This was different but how? The senator was certain he'd find out soon enough.

Looking up the numbers on his smartphone, Bell Williams made all the necessary calls without issue until the final call to Senator John Marchand of Maryland. "John, Bell here. We need to meet with Thaddeus at the other location. No, he didn't say why, but he sounded worried. I'm not sure since I've never heard him sound the way he did." Williams paused while listening to the questions from the other end of the call.

"No, I don't know why he wants to meet there. What? You think you do? Why?'

The senior senator from Maryland was silent for a long moment. "Bell, I know you're a longtime friend of Thaddeus and you keep his confidences. I respect that. Whatever I share with you now has got to be completely confidential, do you understand that? Yes? Are you sure because you must be completely silent on this to any and every one? Yes? Good. Bell, it might be the time our little group should break up. And not by his hand. I think this thing with the letter and those buffoons attached to it may spell the end of our endeavor. I would suggest making some contingencies... just in case. It's probably me being overly cautious, but still. Please, don't share this with Thaddeus."

He wouldn't. But it wouldn't matter, nor would he have time to act on it.

Chapter 49

Dedham, MA

Laying down his cell phone, a small smile on his face, Faraday addressed the group in the conference room, "I know this might seem repetitive and a bit farfetched but let me explain how I came to this. And it *was* a white bird that led me to this. An owl in fact. Do any of you remember what Peter said when you first came here? We make leaps. Sometimes we can explain them logically. Other times, we might have difficulty in describing how we got there. But they're no less valid. Intuition is real but immeasurable and unpredictable. It can't be summoned up like a gypsy with a crystal ball." Laughing, "At least I don't think so.

"But we've had way too many instances where intuition, that leap of knowledge into an unknown, has proven to be the right direction. None of us knows how it works, but it does. And this is one of those times.

"Here's what I see as a stumbling block in my own theory. If indeed light has become sentient, is it trying to communicate with us? If so, why? What is it saying? How do we answer it?"

Peter, quiet through his monologue, broke his silence. "Adam, you know I'm right there with you on intuition, but suppose your theory is wrong. It's not like there's a solid foundation of research backing up your idea. We'd have to go back to square one and we don't even know where that is."

Following quickly on Peter's line of questioning, Grace Perez spoke. "Adam, Fran, I know you've discounted the human element as causing this, but what if you're wrong? Is it at all possible that this whole thing is a human creation? And if so, how? It could be an incredible technology that could change the world."

Fran sighed, "Grace, no, not at all. If it were…"

Adam interrupted her. "Hold on, Fran. Yes, we've pretty much ruled it out, but let's face it, anything is possible. We live by that credo. But I still doubt that humans have created this. There's no technology we know of, and I'm sure you guys at the NSA would have an even better handle on what's out there. So, the human element as you put it isn't I think a factor in this. No... unless..." and he paused, a faraway look in his eyes.

"Unless what? Another little bird, Adam?" Fran was joking, but she knew for Adam, at a subconscious level, that is exactly what he saw.

He didn't answer immediately. There was much more going on in his mind. As if coming out of a brief trance, he spoke, "In a matter of speaking, I did. I think for this conversation, a little bird is as good a description. It's another leap."

Fran grinned, Grace Perez cocked an appraising eyebrow, and August Ashe, fixing his shirt sleeve cuff, groaned impatiently, "Dr. Faraday, uh, Adam, with all due respect, this is not a goddam aviary. Can you please stop with the damn birds and leaps and get to the point?"

"Well, Director, you're probably going to think I've lost it. Hell, maybe I have. But did you hear about that broadcast on True North with the religious types talking about their take on this? No? Not a big deal. I didn't watch much of it as I'm not a religious person. But they, those I heard, talked about the significance of light in their faith. In one way or another, they saw light as a manifestation of God realized in us. The gist of their discussion was that light was imbued upon us by their deity. It was a one-way communication, directly from God to us. It got me to thinking, what if it's the other way around? Just the opposite.

"What if it's the human condition causing this? What if this is a manifestation of humanity itself? And light is responding to that? That's a bunch of what-ifs, but and here's one more, what if that's it?"

In the ensuing silence, the only thing heard was Fran's "What the fuck? Are you gonna start sending those quacks money now, Adam?"

248

"Yes, what the fuck?" Ashe was not used to speculation of such magnitude. Relying on data and information that could be trusted, was a frivolous guess as this was not appreciated.

"That's what you've come up with? You're suggesting that light is, what, the zeitgeist of humanity? What in hell is your basis for that? Please tell me, I can hardly wait for the next hair-up-your-ass premise."

"August, please. Let Adam finish. Antagonizing everyone won't help a damn bit," Grace interrupted.

"That phone call I just finished? The light went out again, in only one place, again. This time it was Ukraine. Violence and rioting have broken out there, only to be halted by the light going out. Will the chaos resume? Your guess is as good as anyone's, but don't you think it's odd that each time the light went out in one area, that place was experiencing hostilities and disruption? What if this is a *response* to human behavior, human activity?"

Fran was the first to respond, "Holy shit, boys, and girls, it's a cosmic time out. Better behave or I'll shut off the lights and you'll go to bed without dinner. Something like that, maybe?"

Ashe sat there, shaking his head at the nonsense he was hearing. He was about to drop the hammer on all of this when Adam answered.

"As I said, your guess is as good as anyone else's. But yes, that does seem like what's happening. Those two incidents have got to be intentional, not coincidental. It does point to a certain sentience. Or at the very least an emotional reaction to the hostilities, yes, the zeitgeist as you described, Director. It feels like a warning or at the very least a response. My question is, how do *we* respond? Can we instigate a dialogue or is it one-sided? If we agree on the premise at least, and I admit it's a bit out there, then we need to figure out how to talk with it. Any ideas, anyone?"

Fran again was the first to answer, "How about 'Children, stop your fighting now and be good.'" Meant as a small joke to lighten the mood, it had the opposite effect. 'What if' was on everyone in the room's mind.

###

It blinked again and felt relief, a sense of well-being, and a surge of ... what? Something. Power? And when the darkness went away, it was calmer for longer. It was starting to associate blinking and its results with a developing cause and effect.

There was no shortage of pain and suffering and hurt. It was beginning to realize that when it blinked without discrimination, still not understood, it could cause itself pain while stopping it. It now knew instinctively that it had to proceed with specificity and intention. That, it learned could stop a certain area of pain while not affecting others.

While learning and dissimilating an incredible amount of knowledge and information, it was not yet sophisticated enough to understand the collateral effects of its actions. So, while it did accomplish some of what it longed for, it still created fear. Fear disturbed it almost as much as did pain, hurt, and suffering. It would come to learn how to deal with that in time.

It was also learning that the blinks took a toll of sorts, a draining of its energy. It found itself weakened and tired after the longer and more directed blinks. Rest restored it. If only the cries it heard would cease. Did they not go away when it blinked only to return there or elsewhere? What else could it do?

After a blink, everything looked more intensely brilliant, hopeful even, for a while. Was that a result of returning from its darkness or was it something it else? Could it make things brighter than before as well as dark? Would that create more hurt and cries? Would it feel better doing that? It would try to do that.

250

Chapter 50

Reston, VA

The cleanliness, the sterility of the hospital room was in stark contrast to the deeds of the man in the bed and the other sitting by him. There were no antiseptics or antibiotics to combat their heinous behavior. The wounds they inflicted would not heal with drugs or time. Their victims were innocent who now faced a lifetime filled with unimaginable scars, both physical and psychological. What was to be those men's fate was only fitting, only to be realized as their liability became clear.

At first, he thought he was hallucinating, a side effect from the drugs pumped into him. But as he slowly awoke, he realized that was not the case. Jonah Stamm was indeed sitting by his bedside. If he was dead, this could not be heaven. He would be right. But instead, he was alive and waiting for the hell about to be delivered.

"You are the last person I expected to see here of all places, Jonah. Come to give me last rites or something? Gloat, maybe?"

The reverend looked at his old friend and new adversary. He had not expected the reception he received from Thaddeus Pingry and was now forced to mend fences. "No, I'd have to be a Catholic first. Carlton, you are still my friend. We go back too far to be at each other's throats. I admit I did the wrong thing. I thought I was doing right. Hell, I still think it was the right thing to do, but I threw in with the wrong people. Do you know what that monster is doing to my kids?

"He's dumping them into the sex trade. They're children for God's sake. Yes, I wanted a better life for them, and I thought that's what they would get. Pingry lied to me. He said he would place them in good homes. That was the lie. The man is a monster. I was wrong, so wrong."

Justice remained silent.

For a man of the cloth, confession was never a strong suit for Stamm, but he soldiered on, "And I went about it the wrong way. Greed is a terrible thing. My own greed for righteousness was far exceeded by his greed for money and power. But one doesn't negate the other. He always held the upper hand. I must take responsibility for my role in this.

"This was never a fair fight. It was never a good fight. Now I find myself in a situation for which I am completely unaccustomed and totally unprepared. I've come for forgiveness which you may think I don't deserve. You're probably right. I'm hoping I can mend things between us, and we can help each other. I'm asking for mercy from you. Is that at all possible, Carlton?"

Justice coughed, slowly wiping spittle from his lips, "Mercy? Help each other? Help you? Jonah, I don't trust you. Do you know what you did to me? Was I on the wrong side of this? Hell, yes. But your meddling, your interference cost me dearly. My reelection is in doubt. Enormous doubt. I've no money to campaign with, and my support in the House has dried up. Pingry saw to that, no thanks to you. And you say you're my friend? How does any of what you've done constitute friendship? Tell me, why in hell are you here?"

"Forgiveness, Carlton, your forgiveness. I need and want your forgiveness. I am truly sorry, I am. I need your help and I think you can use mine. There's too much at stake and we both know it. Pingry must be stopped before this goes any further. I believe you and I can do this if we have any chance of stopping him. But we're going to have to able to trust each other if we're to get past this."

"Past this?" Justice coughed, "Are you mad? And trust? Do you think it's really that simple? Why are you suddenly ready to throw in with me assuming that's even a possibility? Because you need my help, that's why. What happened with you and Pingry at that meeting? Hah, I can tell by the look on your face you didn't know I knew about it. Good. Did Pingry hurt your feelings? I'm sorry. He does that to everyone. Deal with it.

"So, he threatened you? He does that too. He'll make good on it too. What happened, Jonah? If you expect us to be friends again, you've got to tell me everything. If not, get out and let me rest and figure out what to do with what remains of my life."

The minister swallowed uncomfortably, smoothing his coat, summoning up whatever real courage he still had, completely different from his television persona. "Carlton, he scared me. I mean terrified me. I've never felt that kind of fear before. It wasn't anything he said, heavens no, he didn't say much at all. He didn't have to. That is a dangerous man, and an evil man, and I'm now on his radar."

"Yes, he is a dangerous man. Very. I know that as well as any who've crossed him. If it's any consolation, we are both, as you say, on his radar. I guess misery does love company. He will do everything within his power to stop us, destroy us if necessary. He gives no quarter and takes no prisoners. You need to realize that.

"Jonah, look, I can forgive you, but it will be a long time before I trust you. You'll have to earn it and even then..."

"Thank you, Carlton. I do appreciate that. You've no idea how much. Where do we start?"

"Jonah, the only way I think we can stop this is to go straight at him. There will be collateral damage, more on your side, the damage has already been done to me. But if we play our cards right, at the very least we can make things awfully uncomfortable for our friend.

"It's interesting that this is all coming apart while we're wondering what is going on with the light thing. The old chestnut, 'light is the best disinfectant' may be the exact thing we need to do. Shine some damn light on it. In this case, that would be the media.

"First, we'll need to get them involved, but only as an anonymous source. We can both work on that. Secondly, we're going to need money. Lots of money."

Jonah smiled, a small weak smile, "Carlton, *that* is not a problem. What else?"

"I'm talking Pingry type money here. You don't have that."

Stamm smiled again, this time larger and genuine, the first in quite a long time, "Actually, I do. The lord's been very good to me."

Chapter 51

Annapolis, MD

"You want to do what?" Lee Black was astounded and confused by this latest turn in events. He couldn't believe this was coming from Sheila. "Where is this coming from? And maybe more importantly, from who and why?"

She looked down at her feet, sheepish for she was now trading places with Lee, asking him for something. "I know it sounds weird, maybe, but he asked me to call you. The reverend and Congressman Justice want to meet with you and Bennie."

Before Lee could interrupt, she continued, "Wait, Reverend Stamm had just come back from the hospital where the congressman was, and he was very focused. It was different, not like he is after a good show, but a combination of anger and purpose. Purpose... that's the right word. He seemed to have a purpose in mind and was ready to pursue it."

Lee thought he knew what might be going on. Bennie shared with him the gist of his meeting with Thaddeus Pingry. Whatever it was, it caused Justice and Stamm to mend whatever fences had been broken. He thought, this could be good.

"OK, Sheila, look, I've really got my hands full with other stuff, but you've got me interested. Hell, more than interested. But do you know what this could mean? It could blow up in your face, lose your job, maybe more. You've got responsibilities, Olivia and all that. You sure you want to go this route?"

"Lee, it's not like I have a choice and besides, he asked me to do this. I haven't done anything wrong." Sheila, obviously upset, was full of questions for Lee he might not be able to answer.

"Why do you ask? What do you know? Is there something I should know, Lee? Tell me! What's at stake here?"

He paused, taking a deep breath. He knew that what he shared with Sheila, she might not want to be involved any further, with Stamm or him. "Sheila, what do you know of Stamm's involvement in Southeast Asia?"

It was Sheila's turn to take a deep breath before speaking and when she finally did, it was with anger bordering on indignation. "Lee, I can't believe you're asking me that. You know the work he does there. I've already told you that. His mission over there has been so helpful to so many of the homeless children living on the streets. He gives them a safe place, food, clothes, and schooling. Even finds them good homes. What's wrong with that?"

Gazing out the window, Lee debated on how much he was willing to reveal. Still looking away, he muttered, "Nothing. If that were all it was."

Turning to her, he continued, "You're right. There's nothing wrong with that. Nothing at all. If that's all it was. Did you know why Stamm went to see Thaddeus Pingry the other night? No? He's been involved with Pingry and some politicians, yes, Justice is one of them, are in some pretty shitty business.

"It seems that Stamm started out doing the right thing, his heart was in the right place, but somehow, he got turned around. He thought he was sending them to good homes. Thaddeus Pingry was instrumental in their futures. That's the bad news.

"Pingry wasn't placing them in good homes. He saw the orphanages, or whatever you want to call them, as his private stock, his inventory. He was selling the children into sex slavery. Pingry was a very large, undisclosed contributor to his ministry. From what we can tell, Stamm went along with it or looked the other way, denying to himself what was going on. He believed or wanted to believe Pingry's denials. Stamm was blind to everything else. Apparently, he had finally had enough and sent that letter to Carlton Justice asking that it stop. Maybe he does have a conscience after all. But they have no idea how that letter got to me.

"Thaddeus Pingry was not about to kill his cash cow. Did you know that's how Pingry's family started, how they got so rich? They were slave traders and apparently not much has changed over a few centuries. Justice took the letter to Pingry and his group of politicians and got the expected response. He was then charged with getting Stamm under control. Obviously, that didn't happen. So, Pingry acted on his own. He reached out to your boss. And here we are, so why does Stamm want to meet with us?"

"I think he's scared. Nothing he's said, but that's my impression. And… maybe a little desperate. Will you and Bennie please meet with him and the congressman?"

Before Lee could answer, the light flickered a bit. Not complete darkness as in previous times, more an intermittent dimming and brightening.

"Aw shit, again? Yeah, yes, tell him we'll meet. I'll call Bennie and see when we can do this."

"Lee? Soon, please. I don't like this."

Realizing she might be forced to take a side, Sheila confusedly looked around. Sitting in a group comprised of Carlton Justice, Bennie, Lee, and her boss, she was wondering where her allegiance lay. Fireworks were still bound to break out with this group, ostensibly meeting with the same goal whether they liked it or not. The only ones happy to see each other, though they couldn't show it, were Lee and Sheila.

Carlton Justice was the first to speak. "Thank you all for meeting out here, I thought it would be best to be away from anywhere we could be seen together. I'm sure you've all heard that chestnut about politics making for strange bedfellows, well, this has got to be amongst the strangest. I would love to say we're all patriots here with the common good at heart, but that would be a little disingenuous, don't you think?

257

Whatever our individual agendas may be, I think, since all of you have consented to meet, that there's an underlying and common element in all of them. That said, is there anyone who would like to speak, to open this thing up?"

Glances were exchanged. Bennie sensing if he didn't jump in quickly, he might be lost as this thing moved ahead and got out of hand. "Yes, I do. It seems to me there are some conflicts of interest going on and while I don't want to carry anyone's water on this, I certainly do want to hear what this is all about. This meeting alone is newsworthy. So, why are we here?"

"Bennie, let me cut to the chase." Looking at the Congressman for agreement and receiving it, the reverend spoke. "Look around you. There are three parties here with diverging needs and agendas. Yet, circumstance has brought us together and you've had no small hand in accomplishing that. Simply put, we do want you to, how did you put it, carry our water. Especially since you had such a large hand in spilling it."

One of the few times he had no response, Bennie, looked on, eyes wide open in disbelief.

"Your digging around has uncovered some unseemly activities that would have been better, as far as some of us are concerned, left alone. That however is not where we find ourselves today, no thanks to you and your friend here.

"Now, we don't need to point fingers, offer apologies, or even issue denials, here or anywhere else. It's much too late for that. There have been some things done that are horrendous in nature. While I directly have had nothing to do with them, I am just as culpable of the congressman as I have looked the other way until I could no longer. I cannot speak for Carlton about contrition. Personally, I think he is more worried about being found out for what he contributed to than the actual activity. He will have to deal with that at another time, may God have mercy on his soul. That aside, he agrees with what action needs to be taken, now and quickly.

"The last thing we want to do is bring more unwanted attention to this. We cannot sit still and receive what we expect to be a hostile and possibly violent response to what has been unleashed. Outside of this room, there must be no knowledge of what we're proposing."

Bennie knew he and Lee were the people being addressed and that Stamm and Justice had more likely met prior to this gathering to rehearse their plan. Sheila was there for what? And he thought once again, why was he here?

"Why does this have the feel of a conspiracy? And what are you two co-conspirators hatching now? And you want me to be your water boy, right? I guess Reverend, there will be no more interviews, right?"

Jonah Stamm and Carlton Justice both smiled wolfishly at Bennie, the reverend speaking first. "Oh no, Bennie. You're wrong. There will be one more interview. If it's done well, hopefully, we'll all get out of this somewhat intact. If not, then you'll probably be the only one standing."

Justice then chimed in, "Bennie, in media terms, this will be like you earning your mob button. Interested?"

Lee had remained silent the entire time, stealing sidelong, questioning glances at Sheila. "Bennie, do you know what they're asking? We've had an idea of what these guys were up to and now they want to suck you, us, in. Bennie, do you hear me?"

Edward Benton knew exactly what they were asking and he in fact did want a piece of it. He liked the idea of being the last one standing. Earn his button indeed. "Yes, Lee, I do. And yes, Congressman, I am interested, very interested. What are you proposing?"

Justice and Stamm looked at each other, weighing who should speak first. Stamm nodded at the congressman who spoke, "Bennie, how familiar are you with a man named Thaddeus Pingry?"

It was then Bennie's and Lee's turn to look at each other before responding, simultaneously and silently mouthing, "Oh, shit!"

Chapter 52

Dedham, MA

Anna Barth was adamant about going public, but Peter Easton was not. Walking forward to the head of the room, he cleared his throat, not as a theatrical gesture, but out of need, then spoke to all in the room, "Do you realize what we would be saying? And what the reaction would be? Governments across the world would be made irrelevant. Churches of all kinds would be calling for our heads claiming blasphemy and heresy at the very least. If we're wrong, Anna, and there's a good chance we are, *we* would quickly become irrelevant. We can't talk about this yet, we just don't know enough to support what we're claiming. And people will find out fast enough. You want to deal with that because I sure as hell don't."

Holding her hands up in a placating gesture, Anna responded, nodding at him as she responded. "Well, yes, I do. But do *you* realize the implications of this? No, I think you're missing it. If this is what we think it is, it's a game changer for all of us. Not just us in this room, but all mankind and that's no exaggeration. Do you want to be the obstacle or an implement? The longer we remain silent on this, the more chaos there'll be. Personally, I find this unbelievably exciting. This could be the change we've all dreamed about but had no clue on how to bring it about.

"There are issues that have gone unaddressed for way too long. But it's out of our hands, and probably a good thing since no one can claim a hidden agenda. So far, none of us here have figured out a way to answer this. Adam, am I wrong?"

Adam had been silent during the conversation. "No, Anna, you're not wrong, but truthfully and even though it's my theory, I'm sort of in the same camp as Peter. All we've got is speculation based on some data that any good researcher could rip apart. That said, what we do have points to the conclusion we've come to… that light is reacting, responding maybe, to human behavior, particularly bad behavior. But, why? And why now? Yes, no one likes what's going on in some of these places. Yet still they continue. Worldwide condemnation may be growing, but it's having no effect, it's not stopping anything."

Anna's eyes lit up, her eagerness apparent, "Adam, you said the light is reacting to human behavior. If that's true, then it's a response, right? What if, and hear me out, and yes, this is out there, what if the light itself is not responding? What if the light is something else? What if," taking a deep breath before continuing, "what if light's response is a manifestation? A manifestation of humanity reaching its limits, and this is unsophisticated I know, saying, we've had enough. Director Ashe may have been right as describing this as the zeitgeist of the planet."

She heard nothing in response to her statement, the silence being complete. It was several moments before anyone spoke. Both Grace Perez and August Ashe looked on incredulously as if a newborn had just recited the Constitution in Esperanto. Fran sat there, mouth hanging open. Peter sat stone-faced, not believing what his wife had just shared. Adam grinned.

"Anna, that's ridiculous. We are not going public with that." Peter was steadfast on that.

Adam jumped in quickly, "Wait Peter, I think Anna has given name to what I've been trying to get my head around. Anna, correct me if you think I'm on the wrong track. What she and Director Ashe were both describing, in their own way, is light as a manifestation of humankind's collective consciousness. Am I right so far?" Anna nodded. Ashe looked on in complete puzzlement.

"If she's right, then humankind is starting to speak out about its own behaviors, and it apparently doesn't like what it's seeing."

Warming to the subject, he continued, "We've been looking at the flickers, the blinks of light, whatever you want to call them as something independent, another being perhaps, unconnected, it being sentient, or least aware. Not necessarily of itself, but like an animal. It doesn't realize it's a dog or whatever, but it reacts to its environment, its needs, as we recognize it the way a dog does.

"In one way it may be a thinking, feeling thing, but not as an entity alone, on its own. It's not self-aware. I think it's as if the entire planet is speaking out. Not the planet per se, but its inhabitants, us. So that presents questions. Is it intentional with a predetermined goal? I don't know. At least not yet. Maybe never. But it poses several questions. Is this for the greater good or an aberration? Does it have intentions? If so, that would indicate a level of self-awareness and then a whole new set of questions. Can it be directed? I hope not as that could lead to someone trying to take it over. Is this a permanent situation or a quirk? Assuming we believe this premise, we're in the same place we've been all along.

"Also, think about this. Nothing changes when the light goes out other than the obvious. Everything still works. Electricity still powers appliances, phones, whatever. There's just no light to see them or indicate they're visibly working. And that may be the key – visibility. What are we seeing and more importantly, not seeing? I think if it were a malicious effort, everything powered by electricity would cease to work. That's not the case.

"Other than the expected results of operating in the darkness, it doesn't appear to be inflicting pain intentionally. It's almost as if the blinks are a warning.

"Look, we don't know what we know, and we don't know why. But personally, I can't wait for the next blink."

Contention bordered on hostility. There were those, Peter Easton for one, who still thought it was too soon to go public. He perceived more risk than reward, not to mention the strong possibility of losing their hard-earned credibility. He was joined by NSA director, August Ashe on that position. Though he inadvertently helped to put a face on this, he was fearful of a panic resulting from such an announcement. Compounding that, it would embolden those who perceived this as opportunity for further aggression.

On the other side of the argument, led by Anna Barth, they believed that announcing and identifying it for what they believed it to be would start to personify it and make it, hopefully, a more understandable and less threatening situation. More a humanist argument than a military or political solution, it was nonetheless joined, under Ashe's extreme consternation and surprise, by his second in command, Grace Perez. "Grace, I can't believe you're buying this horseshit. This is only one step removed from those Roswell crackpots." Ashe was turning bright red, in danger of losing his composure. "What in hell are you thinking? It makes no sense. Light thinking for itself? Really! We should have vetted this group better."

Smiling at her boss, Grace tried not to adopt a patronizing tone, but failed. "August, first we did vet them and you approved of them… whole-heartedly, remember? Secondly, you wanted someone who could think out of the box, and you must admit this is certainly out of the box. I'm not sure what box that is if any, but it's what you wanted, and I think what we need. So please calm down.

"We're dealing with something of which we have no clue, no history, nothing. So why is Adam's theory so far out there? It is a phenomenon the likes unheard of before. There is no evidence to the contrary of an origin familiar to us. Aside from issues occurring from the general panicking, which really is to be expected given its visible nature, we've seen nothing that suggests hostile intent. The biggest issue is fear because we don't know what it is. Maybe now we do. Adam, do you have anything to add to that?"

Hesitating before he answered, Adam looked around the room, "Well, maybe this. Director, let me ask you a question. You believe history is important, right? I'm sure you do, but why? Essentially, history is our collective knowledge or memory of such written down,

263

right? Before writing, and cave paintings for that matter, it was passed along by stories told to succeeding generations. It entered their collective consciousness. It became part of their DNA. It informed how they would behave, believe, and ultimately respond to their world. It was their connection to their past, present, and future.

"And now, we, our whole planet, is more connected than ever. Is it such a stretch to believe that a collective intent could exist? Especially if there's a critical mass forming around an issue or many issues. Were this a problem that could be identified as a physics question, a collective intent could certainly fall under the realm of quantum physics and its subsequent reaction. That's what string theory is all about.

"You know, for an issue to take root in our minds, it takes only about five percent of the population to start believing and talking about it. That doesn't make it right, but that's all it takes. Pundits call it a groundswell."

The director of the NSA didn't like where this was going. "Are you saying this is a mind over matter thing? All we got to do is think it and it comes true? Sounds like more of that new age crap. I don't buy it and Grace, neither should you."

His assistant director was about to speak when Adam loudly interrupted. "Director Ashe, no, it's not mind over matter. I think its minds over matter. Look let's use a football team as an imperfect analogy. When everyone plays for themselves, nothing good happens. When they all pull together, they accomplish so much more.

"Remember when this all started? Light went out universally around the planet. Then in an evolving way, it became selective and only in places that were experiencing hardships, hostility, and more. Those are just the places that we have heard about. I'd be willing to bet there've been more incidences like that that haven't been reported. If we knew of them, we could be more certain of what we're postulating. But I'm on record as saying I believe that's exactly what's happening. On a scientific basis, it's fascinating. On a socio-economic basis, it's troublesome for obvious reasons. At your level, I'm sure it's terrifying."

"What the hell are you talking about? Terrifying? Why do you say that?"

Adam smiled grimly at Ashe, "Because it means whatever illusion of control you imagined having no longer exists. You're no longer in charge. We're not in charge, if we ever were. No one is. I think that's a conceit whose time has come and gone, and now we've got a hell of a lot of questions. If this is what some of us think it is, the idea of us being in charge is no longer a consideration. We may have to answer to a higher power, one that none of us ever dreamed of.

"So, Director, what do you think of that?"

He didn't want to think of that. He'd been brought up in a time when diplomacy, coercion, or if need be, brute force exerted control. He didn't want to think of losing to anyone much less something he couldn't see. "I think you're full of shit. You've nothing to support this crackpot idea. Nothing! Grace, we're through here. Now!"

Silent throughout this dialogue, Easton spoke up. "Director Ashe, wait. I agree, it is a crackpot theory, even for us. But what do you have to refute it? Do you, other than your life long held beliefs? But as you've seen, none of those can explain this. I agree this is a hard thing to get our heads around, but you've got to admit, or at least I hope you will, that when all the other avenues turn into dead ends, this is what we're probably looking at, as outrageous as it seems."

He continued, "Manned flight was outrageous until it was done, going into space, the same thing, a cure for polio, lasers, I could go on. We've seen outrageous, wondrous things. Why resist considering that this may be one of those?"

"August, you've got to back down on this. Stubbornness is not going to get us anywhere but spinning our wheels and losing time. I think we need to listen to Adam and Peter on what they propose our next move should be. Can you be patient with that?" Grace Perez could always calm Ashe down. It was this pragmatism and cool-headed demeanor that helped her move into her position. And it worked once again. Again, asking a familiar question, "Adam, Peter, what do we do next?"

Adam grateful for Grace's effect on her boss, took the lead, "We should wait a bit before going public with this. Let's start by going over what we know, empirically, and then what we suspect. If it is what we think, then we might be able to reach out to it or affect what it does. But we are going to need to get a hell of a lot of cooperation. Grace, Director Ashe, you're going to need to get on the phones and fast."

Anna held up both her hands, almost shouting, signaling, "Wait."

Everyone in the conference room stopped talking and looked to Anna Barth. She responded, "I don't think everyone is on board and on the same page. Until we are, then only one of us should speak outside this room, and pardon me Director, that's not you. Come to think of that, that's the way it should be going forward even when we're all in agreement. We won't have any need to gloss things over or make any politically correct statements. Just tell it like it is and we'll let everything else take care of itself. Pretty radical, huh?"

August Ashe immediately and loudly disagreed with her, "Radical, yes. But, no, young lady, I am not going to let you or anyone else speak for the government. You people are our employees. We will dictate who speaks, when they speak, and what they say. Is that understood?"

Ashe's outburst was met with shock and amusement among the women in the room. Anna stood there, mouth hanging open. Fran smirked, raising her eyebrows in disbelief, mumbling "Misogynistic asshole."

Grace Perez, caught completely off guard by her boss's comment, wasted no time in responding, "Fran, I never thought we'd agree on anything, but you're right, he is being a misogynistic asshole. 'Young lady', really?

"August, when in hell are you going to get over that old world mindset? You're quickly becoming an embarrassment revealing yourself to be a dinosaur. At least they faded into extinction without making fools of themselves. I can't say the same for you though. Now you either get over yourself or get someone else to do my work. As your second, I can handle this... and apparently a lot better than you."

Before anyone could respond, Easton's phone rang. He answered it quietly and moved off to a corner to continue the call, waving to everyone to keep talking.

The NSA director hesitated – embarrassed, realizing she was right, spoke first, "I apologize Grace, Miss Barth, and everyone else. I find it difficult to buy into this. I've nothing to compare it to and to put it bluntly, I'm feeling a little helpless. Your theories are disconcerting even if correct. I'm not prepared to deal with a threat for which I've no experience. Speaking candidly, I do not like the loss of control. It's as simple as that. Again, my apologies."

Easton finished with his call, returned to the discussion in time to hear Ashe's last comments, "Apologies accepted. Director Ashe, none of us do. But in some ways, you're better prepared for this than we are." Peter was in an arena he was well equipped to handle.

"You've seen technologies develop and implemented that none of us could have ever predicted. You learned how to use them in ways never expected. Yes, this is unusual. Very. We're all trying to connect the dots in a way that makes sense. Adam and Fran have come up with something that appears to make sense, no matter how outlandish it may seem.

"We will need your expertise, means, and experience on how to deal with this, both militarily, politically, and socially. But I don't think that you're the person who can portray the reassuring
public presence we're going to need. If I may, you come off a little too much like Patton, when in fact we're going to need someone like Mr. Rogers."

That elicited a few laughs, Ashe instead frowned. "Alright Peter, if not me, and I'm going on record as not liking this, who?"

Adam, smiling nervously, asked, "Well, yes, Peter, who is our 'Mr. Rogers'?"

A long pause, followed by a mischievous smile, "Why, Adam, I agree with Anna...you of course. And not a moment too soon either. That was a reporter from True North News who would like to interview you on the light phenomenon. You're up, Anna. Schedule it after the press conference. In for a penny, right?"

Chapter 53

Washington, DC

The interview was scheduled to start in less than three hours. Hovering over it was a heightened sense of anticipation mixed with a foreboding of things to go wrong. Everyone knew that could happen fast and no one wanted to talk about that, not openly, not privately.

"Are you sure you want to go through with this, Jonah?" Carlton Justice was understandably apprehensive about Stamm's plan. It was audacious to say the least, risky at best, and almost certainly suicidal. But he did see the beauty in its inherent danger. It was the only play they had.

Jonah Stamm smiled tightly. "If our friend Bennie is willing to go along with us, the way I spelled it out, yes, I'm sure. We'll have only one chance to do this. There's no sequel. We've all got to be on the same page, the same motivation, and we can't deviate from the plan. I can't stress that strongly enough."

Turning to the True North reporter, "Bennie, are you and your crew ready? Your editor?"

"He's not thrilled with it, he's apprehensive too, but yeah, he'll go along with it. He sees it as an opportunity to expand True North's credibility. His position, and I never thought I would agree with him on this, is that this really isn't news. It's us inserting ourselves into the story. It's smacks more of a vendetta and a human sacrifice, but I don't see a way around it. We're good."

The congressman jumped in, "Bennie, you're right. We are truly throwing someone onto a sacrificial alter, I'm not sure who. It might be me, but we'll see. It's the only way out of this.

"And yes, it isn't news as we plan to do it, but once it's done, it will be. Don't think of it as True North News inserting itself into the story, even if you are. You're only the vehicle for this. Trust us, you'll be only a footnote to this, if that when all's said and done."

Trust was the last thing Bennie expected to hear Justice or Stamm espousing. He had begun to believe he had fallen through the Looking Glass.

Bennie could not have been any blunter. "Congressman, Reverend, with all due respect, I don't trust either of you. At the risk of sounding self-righteous, you've fucked over a lot of innocent children for your own gain. Now you want us to get into bed with you and fuck someone else over. Mind you, I have no problem with you screwing Thaddeus Pingry or anyone else of his ilk, yourselves included, but trust? No, I don't think so.

"We agreed to go along with this for our own reasons and don't have to be reminded of our own collusion in this. Altruism isn't at the top of anyone's list here. So go sell your ideas of trust to your viewers and the poor voters who elected you, not us. We're in this with you for reasons as base as yours. Let's keep that straight and get this charade over with. Oh, one more thing," pointing his hand at them, "I'll have no problem throwing all of you under the bus on this too. Understood?"

They all looked at each other, nodding, knowing they were about to embark on their own version of the emperor's new clothes. With nothing left to discuss, they retreated into themselves until airtime, Bennie and Lee, Justice with his aide, and Stamm and Sheila who wished she was over with Lee.

Sheila had heard the reverend preach about the devil but never gave it much thought. She was now thinking that the reverend despite his preaching was in league with him. She said a short, silent prayer for him and a longer one for herself and Lee, hoping they would get out of this intact.

With no one saying much of anything, time passed slowly. Finally, as airtime approached, grim smiles and nods were exchanged. Everyone knew what was at stake and took their places on the studio set, Lee, Sheila, and others remaining offstage. Once the lights and cameras went on, there'd be no turning back. Stamm and Justice looked coolly professional on camera despite what they were about to reveal. Bennie, powdered and made-up, was fidgeting, shuffling his feet back and forth trying to keep his nerves at bay.

The on-air countdown began. The video came up with the titles and voice-over announcing the program. Before the introduction could finish, it was interrupted by a network special announcement. Made with the usual sonorous tones, it started, "We interrupt your programming with this…" And the lights went out again, plunging the studio and the world into a familiar yet fearful darkness. But even in darkness, the interview continued.

###

No longer was its world as confusing. It was seeing things more clearly than before. It also realized that it was a part of everything it saw, felt, experienced, heard, smelled, and tasted. Much was good, in fact very good. There was also much it did not like that it thought was wrong, harmful, bad.

It realized that its actions affected what it saw and felt. It felt, what? Empowered? An odd word, but it did have a basic and growing concept of power and knew that it possessed it. Still learning, it had yet to understand how much power and influence it had, but that would come quickly and with it change.

What was once a universal darkness visited upon the world, could now be far more finite. It recognized that it could wield that influence specifically not just globally. In that realization, it discovered it could halt actions in one place that caused it pain and distress. And in doing so, it helped reduce the same elsewhere. It also began to wonder what other effects its action had. Sometimes in stopping the pain one place, it created hurt in another. And it felt that as well and realized in its confusion something new – inner conflict.

There was so much of that pettiness, mean-spiritedness, and anger… so much anger, so much fear, hatred, greed, jealousy, the entire spectrum of what it was discovering was humanity, realizing just what part of it, it was. And the final element fell into place, "I am humanity, rendered visible. And I serve."

Chapter 54

Great Falls, VA

Stalking impatiently through his empty home, he wandered into the media room to watch the damned interview. From there he could, with multiple screens, watch over most of his ventures, either through closed circuit television, or whatever broadcast entity might be reporting on them.

As luck would have it, he tuned into the introduction of the latest Stamm interview. Sitting down on a large leather couch to watch, almost immediately everything was plunged into darkness. Instead of the picture he expected, his screens had morphed into extremely expensive radios.

"This is not amusing, not at all. What in hell is going on?" Thaddeus Pingry thought to himself. What he could never admit was fear. Not just at what might be revealed, but a deeper secret. As a child he was terrified of the dark, a fear that never completely left him. In a lifelong attempt to control and conquer it, he kept his home lit by few lamps. Windows were always curtained. This situation was out of his purview and experience, something uncontrollable, consequently intolerable.

Unlike any other time in his life, he had no one to turn to for help. None of his minions would be any good on this. No, he thought, I'll have to deal with this on my own. Even though he took little comfort in that, a small shudder of fear remained.

Under normal circumstances, this would have been a minor distraction, remedied by changing the channel. Upon further listening, he realized that changing the channel would have no effect on what he was hearing. This interview, as with the earlier ones, was available on multiple channels. The big difference was that in addition to that damned reporter from True North News and Stamm, they were joined by his former cohort, congressman Carlton Justice.

273

"What?! Damn those idiots!" Pingry's anger increased exponentially. Speaking loudly to himself, he growled, "What are those two idiots up to? Don't they know they'll go down with this ship if they continue this course?"

It became obvious. There was no need for speculation. Were they that completely foolish and reckless? It wouldn't take long to discover the answer.

The sound of the broadcast continued while he remained in darkness. Edward Benton started with a very brief introduction of those on stage. "Good evening and welcome to what is the final of three interviews with Reverend Jonah Stamm and a special guest tonight, the esteemed congressman from Alabama, Carlton Justice.

"In the past two interviews, we discussed the work your church does Reverend. We also talked about what you felt is a message from God in the form of the light blinks. If we have enough time tonight, I would like to talk about that further, but I'm hoping you can tell us more about the good work you're doing with your children's orphanage in Southeast Asia."

Bennie hated having to do such a crap set-up, but knew he had no choice. It didn't prevent him from injecting a small amount of sarcasm into his questions. "How are those kids doing? Are you finding homes for all of them? Where do most of them go to?"

Jonah Stamm took a very deep breath, pausing dramatically before answering. While all of this had been scripted, he knew this next step would likely end his ministry, such as it was. He knew a similar outcome awaited Justice when he spoke his part. "Bennie, thank you for asking. You know that the orphanage has been a cornerstone of my ministry and our church's mission. The conditions over there are deplorable and we have always tried to provide shelter, safety, food, and education to these wonderful children.

"Like so many other endeavors, we have had our victories and our defeats. When we see one of our kids, some of them now adults, succeeding, working in jobs, raising families, contributing to society, we are guilty unfortunately of one of the seven deadly sins, that being pride. While that is not a good thing, I would happily be guilty of more pride of these kids making something of themselves.

"But" taking another deep breath, "the defeats can be overwhelming. Disappointing for certain. But when we fail, we've only to blame ourselves. And I'm very sad to say we've failed some of these kids in a big way. First, we are guilty of looking the other way. Looking the other way when others took advantage of our well-meaning nature and gullibility."

Tears came to his eyes, an old and effective ploy. He was the consummate showman. "Bennie, yes, we've failed them and not in a way you might imagine. We…" and more tears materialized, halting Stamm for the moment. Bennie knew at this juncture he was to have appeared moved by this outpouring of emotion and he was. He also knew what came next and waited for it as agreed.

"Jonah, it's OK. You're doing the right thing. We're doing the right thing. It must stop," offered Carlton Justice.

Stamm tried to continue, sobbing almost, and was unable, prompting Justice to pick up the narrative, as planned. "Bennie, if I may? I think I know what the reverend was going to say, and I'll try to fill his shoes on this, though I'm sure I'll fall sort. Pardon me if I start to cry as well." Smarmy as all hell, he continued, "We've got a terrible thing to share, an admission. Please bear with us.

"The reverend has been shaken to the core by this. You asked about the children's home. And Jonah, my oldest and dearest friend, alluded to the successes he's had. That is all true. There is much to be proud of. But…" and now came Justice's tears, "we've failed in a far greater way than our success. As you know, his church has been blessed by very generous contributions that helped enable this work. And I've helped to push through legislation to help grow this effort. So, I too am guilty. But the reverend has just discovered that this money is blood money. There was no generosity involved. It was for lack of a better word, seed money for a horrible agenda to keep the orphanage open, filled with innocent children."

Before Justice could continue, Jonah, seemingly in control of his emotions, interrupted. "Thank you, Carlton, but I must be the one who says this. Yes, the congressman is right, we'd been given blood money and that is exactly what it was. We didn't know that at the time the contributions were made, it has only come to light in the past few days. Unhappily we've been able to verify that it is indeed true.

"You see, we believed the money was donated by people who felt and believed as we do to continue the good work we started. Except someone else saw it as an opportunity to make even more money. It was, please excuse me, this is very difficult to admit. The children did indeed find new homes, but not the ones we thought they were going to. They were being sold into sexual slavery around the world. Yes, human slavery. And I confess, we were complicit in this. Not in that we condoned it, no. But we failed to look beyond the money and the motives. We are as guilty as those who trafficked these kids. I failed. I don't know that I can ever continue doing what I felt was my lord's work. I have much to repent for."

As agreed, prior to the interview, Bennie let that admission hang in the air a good long time for theatrical effect. His look of amazement, rehearsed, was genuine. He did not really expect this to come off, much less on live TV. Waiting for what seemed like an eternity, Bennie resumed the interview. "Reverend Stamm, Congressman Justice, I'm...astonished. That is quite an admission. Are you prepared to share with us where this money came from?"

Then suddenly as the light disappeared, it illuminated everything.

Justice and Stamm looked at each other, their practiced worried looks on their faces. "Yes, I think we must," answered Jonah Stamm.

"And who or where did this money come from?"

"Only one person... Thaddeus Pingry. He used his fortune, influence, and government contracts to make this all happen."

No longer in the dark at his home but now in full light, only one word issued forth, a loud and emphatic "Sonofabitch!"

And as if laughing at him, the light disappeared once again, this time only in his Virginia home.

Chapter 55

Dedham, MA

The expectation was the interview with Justice, Stamm, and their interrogator Edward Benton would eclipse everything else, dominating the news cycle. What was revealed was enormous in scope and impact. It possessed all the requisite elements of a made-for-TV movie: betrayal, sex, politics, religion, and unbelievable hubris of those involved. And with a cast of such a film, the ratings would be off the charts.

In a plot twist worthy of O. Henry, that was not as significant as what was about to happen 400 miles north of their studio. No one, least of all those three, could have predicted the competition they would face for attention. Their interview would not be overlooked, but it was about to become the secondary story of the day.

Inside the large auditorium on the Aura/Sonos campus, the media was setting up for a press conference called jointly by Peter Easton and the NSA. Speculation was rampant with unfounded rumors ranging from a terrorist cell discovered nearby in Framingham to ET being discovered. No one could have believed that the ultra-secret NSA would have anything to do with something so apparently mundane as Aura/Sonos. Nothing had been revealed. Consequently, no dots were being connected which was the way it had been planned.

It had been managed perfectly. Once revealed, management of the story and speculation was out of their hands.

Peter had sequestered his small group in a side office off the auditorium. They all agreed that until the press conference started, no recognizable faces were to be seen, preventing any prior speculation which might dilute their story. The conference would be introduced as breaking news.

When all in the makeshift green room were ready, they walked out on to the stage, facing cameras, digital recorders, and an eager group of media types wondering why they were there. For one of the few times in their careers, the media was about to be rewarded with a story unlike any other imagined.

The head of Aura/Sonos walked up to the podium and introduced himself, "Good afternoon, my name is Peter Easton and I'm the CEO of Aura/Sonos. Joining me on stage are NSA Director August Ashe, NSA Assistant Director Grace Perez, Director of Public Relations Ms. Anna Barth, sensory development expert Fran Porter, and our lead researcher on sensory research, Dr. Adam Faraday.

"Now, I'm sure you're all wondering what kind of odd couple is this, the NSA and Aura/Sonos. And more to the point, why? We'd like to talk about a situation that affects us all. But rather than me talking in circles about it, I'd like to have Dr. Faraday step forward and talk with you. He'll do a Q&A after his speech."

Nodding to Adam, he announced, "Everyone, Dr. Faraday."

"It's show time folks! Break a leg, Adam," Fran whispered to Adam as he stepped forward.

Adam turned his head in a sideways glance and shooting a wink at Fran, whispered, "Yeah, thanks." He stepped up to the microphone.

Looking at the press immediately in front of him, stealing another glance at Fran and Grace sitting next to each other, he started, "Thank you all for coming on such short notice, especially since you've little information on why this conference was called. Usually, the work we do here doesn't merit much public attention. Certainly, sorry Director Ashe, the NSA wishes theirs didn't. But they've called on us to do some analyses of the light phenomenon we've been witnessing.

"You're all aware of what's been happening around the world concerning this, so I don't think there's any need to go into its effects. That's been well-covered by you and your friends. What we are here for today is to share with you some of our findings and our thinking on what's happening. I do ask that you hold your questions until I've finished.

"As you've witnessed, all light, as we know it or believe we know it, has been behaving peculiarly. That in and of itself is a portrayal never previously ascribed to light. It's a personification of light that may not be far off the mark. Let me quote something Samuel Johnson wrote, 'We all know what light is; but it is not easy to tell what it is.' Confounding, right? We've always taken light for granted as it's always been there, right? That still holds true… to a degree and I don't think it's necessary to get into the debatable physical or metaphysical properties of light." Adam paused, not so much for the dramatic effect which it did have, but more along a line of caution as he was about to turn their world upside down.

"As I said, we've taken it for granted. It was always there, needing no care or attention. It lit our days, and its absence was accepted nightly. In the whole scheme of things, that's been true of so many things mankind assumes. We assume a lot. We think not beyond what we know or think we know. Truth be told, the longer I research anything, the more convinced I am of how little we know about anything. Yes, we are learning, but if I had to put us on a scale, we're not much above first grade."

There was some coughing and uneasy squirming in the seats. The media was getting restless. Even Peter cleared his throat loud enough for Adam to hear, signaling to get on with it. "You're sitting there probably wondering when this guy is going to get to the point if indeed there is one. Yes, there is. And this is it.

"From everything we've seen and documented, light *is* behaving and oddly at that. We've nothing to compare it to. That's true. But as a child learns and applies that knowledge to its life, it evolves. It changes, starts to recognize, and perceive, and then eventually acts or reacts to its surroundings."

A journalist who could no longer wait until the Q&A, blurted out, "Are you saying light is like a child?"

He took a deep breath and smiled, "Yes and no. What I'm saying is we believe light is becoming sentient, achieving a growing awareness. We theorize that this sentience may be the collective consciousness of this world made manifest. A reaction if you will. All you have to do is…"

Adam was not able to finish his statement amidst the questions, shouts for attention, and disbelief which came quickly and loudly.

He waited until the furor died down. "I imagine this is not what you expected to hear. Frankly, it's not what we expected to learn. Look, we have all seen light go out globally. What you might not know is that light has now gone out, only to return as we've seen it before, in specific places while the rest of the planet remained in light.

"Coincidentally or not, those individual places where light has blinked are also places that have experienced war, strife, cruelty – stressors that affect people. That is the one thing the recorded blinks have in common. After the initial blinks, they seem to occur when people are enduring man-made crises. We have no data supporting the effects of weather-related events. Can we draw a conclusion from this? Possibly. We've no doubt about how outlandish this sounds. But we're still low on the learning curve."

Once again, the reaction was one of disbelief, shock, and concern. Adam held up his hands to try and quiet them down, "I guess before I go any further, you've got a lot of questions. We'll try and answer them as best as we can. Remember, this is as new to us as it is to you. Yes?" pointing to a reporter in the front.

The first question elicited some laughs, calming a little bit of the growing tension, "Can I get what you guys have been smoking? You said 'we believe' twice. So, you don't really know anything, do you? If you're to be believed, how did this happen? What can we do about it?'

Adam looked at each of those up on the dais with him, all nodding at him, "I wish we were smoking something. It would have been easier to deal with this. Look, I, uh, we, don't know. It seems like there's something to be learned from all of this. It appears to be both action and reaction. Let me share with you another quote, something that Richard Feynman once said, *'Nature is lazy, but this light is not lazy.'* This light obviously is not lazy. It is not sitting still while we screw things up. It appears to be taking intentional action. And that action appears to be in response to what is occurring throughout the world. It is responding to what *we*, all of us, are doing. We may be the cause of this. If you accept that normal evolution takes time, then this, because of its apparent speed in learning, represents evolution 2.0."

The furor in the room had not died down. Evolution 2.0 just added more fuel to an increasingly hot fire. "Yes, that's great, you've given it a name and you're dropping names. But I ask you again, if it's our fault and I'm not accepting it is, that's awfully hard to swallow, what can we do about it?"

Grace Perez stepped up to the microphone and answered as briefly as possible, "For now, nothing."

Again, the room erupted into a storm of questions, nearly all unanswerable. Grace waited until the noise quieted down, "I'm sorry we've nothing more to add at this time. But if we're correct in our assumptions and I believe we are, then we are truly becoming accountable to and for our actions and that has global implications beyond our current comprehension. And one more thing. If we're correct, we will now be accountable to ourselves, *by* ourselves."

Turning to Adam and the rest of those on the podium looking for any additional response and receiving none, she turned back to the press corps, "Thank you. That's all we have. We'll keep all of you in the loop as it develops. Just let me add this… it is our time, all of us, everywhere, to take responsibility for our actions. Do not take this as a threat, it isn't. It's an acknowledgment that we don't hold the cards we thought we did. Our actions have consequences, intended or otherwise. We must be responsible. Again, thank you for your time." He then nodded toward the True North journalist to meet him in the adjacent conference room.

"Dr. Faraday, thank you for meeting with me. I admit your speech was not what I expected. But then, I don't think any of us had an idea of what is going on. What makes you so certain that what you've described is really what's happening?"

Adam looked at Lee Black and smiled, "Well, we're not certain. There are elements that point to this conclusion, but currently, it's supposition and speculation. We've been able to tie the incidences of unrest or strife around the world to that of light's action. That's a correlation and it appears not an action but a reaction. Is it a coincidence? It could be, but there is a definite connection between them. We think there is absolutely a human component to this."

"Dr. Faraday, if what you're stating is indeed true, then there are bound to be enormous implications and many questions. Are you prepared to answer them?"

"That depends of course on the questions. Please remember, this is not a Frankensteinian monster we developed that has gone amok. If you're asking if we, that is Aura/Sonos, will be taking responsibility for this, then the answer is 'no.' This is totally independent of any one individual or organization. If we're correct, and we think we are, our species must take responsibility. So, with that stated, what questions do you have? I'll let you know what we know, which still isn't much, and what we think. Fair, enough?"

Lee liked Adam Faraday, no façade, just a genuineness he hadn't come across often in his work. "Doctor, yes, thank you. There are bound to be questions metaphysical and theological in nature, economic in scale, social in application, how do you think all of that will be affected?"

"That's quite a laundry list and I'm sure it will grow in time and in response to more knowledge about this. Of course, on the metaphysical and theological questions, I would guess there will be speculation and claims about what it means. Was I to answer, that would be my own personal take on it and most likely quite boring. As a scientist, I don't deal with dogma or even traditions. We deal with theories, or speculation if you'd like until we have all the facts necessary to prove or disprove something. That really runs counter to most religions which are based on belief and faith.

"On the economic side, I can speak to that a bit. Certainly, if light disappears for an extended period, photosynthesis would be impossible, and agriculture will be affected. Consider the implication of that. Obviously, with no light, no work or manufacturing can be conducted. Any transportation will become restricted out of safety concerns. People will be truly in the dark. One could consider it a new Dark Age if it was to continue. It would be a perilous time.

"There's an odd piece to this though. Even though the light disappears, electricity remains to power equipment. It appears that light cannot be generated or at the very least, be seen. Not even the stars if you haven't noticed. Everything stops not because of a lack of power, but because of darkness. We can't see what's happening or where we're going. That's a very curious element to all of this.

"The social aspect is a particularly troubling situation. People would be forced to dwell completely in darkness. I think we would see a breakdown of societies if an extended period of darkness ensues."

Adam paused for a moment, then grinned at the reporter, "On the lighter side of things, after some more blackouts, we could experience an increased birth rate nine months from now."

Chapter 56

Washington, DC

The blowback from the interview was immediate. Throughout the studio, cell phones started going off even before the interview ended. The lines were jammed, tweets were going out everywhere, and social media was filled with comments on the revelations, all competing with the even more startling news from the NSA and Aura/Sonos. It was not the typical media-feeding frenzy seen after a now-common but salacious sex scandal. Rather than having just one story to cover, there were two, maybe more. Their cup runneth over and so did advertising revenues. In this instance, the apocalypse would be televised for profit.

For the time being, Bennie, Justice, Stamm, et al, would be trying to figure out their next move. They all realized it was only a matter of time before Pingry responded. The mystery was what would be the response and how they'd be prepared for it. They would not be disappointed.

From past experiences, Pingry's response had always been to meet action with a similar but more decisive and forceful reaction. Had anyone bothered to do their homework, they would have discovered that the ventures of the remaining descendant of the Pingry family and fortunes were not limited to its international business. They'd have learned he currently held commanding positions in media, including the station broadcasting the interview and the network providing Stamm his pulpit. That did not even include how many in government he owned. He wielded a very large hammer.

Pulling the plug would be just a metaphor for what was about to occur to Jonah Stamm and to Edward Benton. That would be only the first of his actions. Certainly, it would get attention from competing media and likely reveal more aspects of Pingry's business he'd much rather have kept out of the spotlight.

285

No thanks to that damned interview, the carefully constructed facade, meticulously conceived and constructed many years ago had been blown apart. Whether he could survive this revelation was irrelevant for the moment. His focus was on destroying those who could bring him down. If they took the first shot, he would take the next and the last. This damned light was now more than a nuisance, who knew when it would appear and disappear again? Picking up the phone and feeling for the buttons, he made several calls, the first one to his pilot to make ready the jet for departure. He could operate his business anywhere.

The next one was to Carlton Justice. Damn him, if only he had died in that car crash. It would have prevented so many things, this damned interview not being the least of them. He also wished that he had acted more definitively in halting Justice's political activities, showing what he would have disingenuously identified as mercy, a quality not often associated with the Pingry name. He heard the phone ringing on the other end. Justice answered, "Hello?"

"What in the hell do you think you're doing?! Do you know what you've done? You and that snake oil charlatan. I need to see you alone, immediately at my hanger as soon as this light comes back. I'll be waiting." And loudly hung up the phone. He made two other calls to set in motion a previously designed plan to implement in the event of such a situation as this. Before departing for the airport, he grabbed his ready bag complete with documents, visas, and multiple passports, necessary for travel to one of his many homes in countries without extradition. He doubted very much if he would be returning to his Virginia estate.

In the darkness of the studio, Carlton Justice held the now silent cell phone in his hand. He understood what Pingry wanted and was willing to do, but he was no longer inclined to indulge him. He played his hand with no choice but to stick with it. His political career was over. If he survived this, he might go back to being a backwoods lawyer in Alabama doing house closings if he wasn't sent to prison. There were worse things than that, such as dealing with Thaddeus Pingry. He needed to talk with the others to follow up on their next move. When all was said and done, he was still a political animal and would play all sides for what it was worth.

Not seeing or sensing anyone near him, he called out to Stamm, Bennie, or whoever might be there. No one had left when the lights went out, remaining where they had been until the light returned. Had anyone been able to see, they would have found Sheila Weller and Lee Black loosening each other from a close embrace just before light returned.

Stamm was the first to speak, visibly shaken by what they had just done as well as being plunged into the darkness. Either through fear or theatrics, he went into his fallback position of this being "God's will has been made clear".

Not having any of it, Justice and Bennie simultaneously shouted, "Shut up!"

"Jonah, get a hold of yourself. We can only deal with what we can deal with and right now it's that fucking dragon we've just unleashed. And trust me, he's going to be breathing a lot of fire at us. That was him on the phone just now and he wants me to meet him at his hanger. If I had to speculate, he's getting ready to leave the country before the authorities come looking for him. Why he wanted me to meet him there is anyone's guess, but it most likely wasn't for my company, insurance maybe, but it's too late for that. He'd have to take us all, which given enough time, he can do and probably would. No, I think it would be to make sure I've nothing more to say."

Bennie was astonished. All the pieces were now there. Since only Pingry knew everything, it was no wonder he couldn't make any more headway with his investigation. He laughed, realizing it was driven by one of the basest human qualities, greed and the desire for money and its attendant power. He was almost disappointed that it wasn't more than that. It wasn't petty, not at that scale and not with who it involved and its consequences. It was the story of a lifetime, several lifetimes.

287

He looked forward to writing it but knew there was still a lot to unravel. "So, that's it? Everybody lives happily ever after, right?"

"No, Bennie, not everybody. Maybe you and Lee. Sheila, I'm so sorry. I didn't expect this to fly back in my face. I don't think I'll be around much longer to provide for you and Olivia. I am truly sorry." For the first time, Jonah Stamm was genuinely sorry, but it wasn't clear yet for what.

Lee was about to ask her a question when Stamm continued. "Lee," Stamm answered quickly, cutting off Sheila before she could speak, "this is not the time, but if my church disappears, so does Sheila's job and how would she provide for Olivia? Not that she would have trouble finding work, but... well, that's all I'm going to say about that."

Sheila looked at Lee, shaking her head, signaling him not to pursue it any further. Lee understood but didn't like it. "I'll tell you all about it later," was all she would say, mirroring Stamm's lead.

"For chrissakes, now we've got a soap opera going on too! Shit! OK, what do we do next? You guys cooked this up, where do we go from here?" Bennie was getting impatient. Waiting for the next shoe to drop was not his favorite pastime.

Justice looked at Stamm, morosely staring at the floor. Hearing no response from Jonah, he spoke, "Believe it or not, you'll have to turn yourself in. Not so much for a confession, but as reluctant witnesses to Pingry's dealings. What you share with the authorities might be enough to satisfy them in pursuing Thaddeus and maybe leaving us alone. If they buy that, we'll be free, but our reputations will be for shit. Sorry, about that Reverend."

Shaking his head, Bennie expressed his disbelief, "I've heard there's no honor among thieves. Never thought it was much more than a cliché, but then both of you are walking, talking clichés right out of a grade B movie. Unbelievable. What did you hope to accomplish with all this crap?"

"Bennie, you may not believe this, and I can't really speak for Jonah though I suspect he'd say the same thing. When I was younger, I thought I could help change things for the better. I'm pretty sure you felt the same way when you started. But taking short cuts and making compromises while rationalizing your decision will be the price you'll pay to effect that change. Before long, you're sitting here with a reporter trying to explain and make excuses for what are inexcusable actions. At the end of the day, Bennie, we're just human."

"That's a lame-assed excuse, just human. Give me a break. Both of you knew every step of the way what you were doing but didn't look back. You feathered your nests and filled your pockets and at the expense of children no less. Yeah, if that's human, it sucks.

"If I knew I could, I'd try getting to Pingry again and putting a stop to this thing you helped create. But that's not likely. So, don't think for a minute I won't throw you both under the bus if it comes to that."

Jonah responded, "Bennie, we understand. You've your job to do, but it too is not without its compromises. Just remember that. I would hope that if push comes to shove with us, you might display some grace and have mercy if possible. That may not mean much to you now, but somewhere down the road you'll be in a similar situation, and I hope that someone will feel mercy for you.

"Carlton, you know pretty much know everyone in the government, who do you think we should call first? Who might help us plead our case as we look to bring Mr. Pingry down?"

Chapter 57

The twenty-four-hour news networks were beside themselves. Usually faced with one story of which they analyzed every possible and some not-so possible aspects, they now had to divide their time between two stories of equal significance. They could not believe their good fortune. Confronted by the choice, they resorted to their business-as-usual model, exploitation without much in the way of facts.

While the explanation of light's behavior was obviously the more important of the two, the revelations about Stamm, Justice, and Pingry were far more sensational. It had all the elements the tabloids favored: sex, money, deceit, politics, and the granddaddy of them all, the powerful brought down. That sold advertising big time. It would dominate news cycles for as long as no indictments were made. Until then, the talking heads would have a field day showcasing their experts on all these things. Further revelations would be met with "Breaking News" banners plastered over TV screens, then followed by additional and usually inaccurate speculation. A good time was to be had by all save those who were the targets. It would only get worse for them.

The bigger of those two stories was relegated to secondary attention. While unarguably more important, it was too fantastical for most to get their heads around. Coupled with the increase of fear and a growing migration to those leaders who purported to know what was happening, this story had yet to gain the traction it eventually would.

However, that did not prevent some news outlets from appealing to the more prurient nature of their readers. One New York paper to give their coverage an historical spin, resurrected a headline from the late sixties, repeating "Where were you when the lights went out?" prompting some to predict the mini-baby boom forecast by Adam Faraday. All of it was fair game, fair or not.

In a minority of the media, not enough pursued the story of what Adam and the NSA had revealed. Whether or not it had the hoped-for revenue potential was moot, those editors and publishers still believed in honest journalism, regardless of earnings and eschewing taglines as "Fair and Balanced" and "When News Happens..." and blah, blah, blah.

True North had yet to figure its charge where that was concerned. It chased money as hard as anyone but was still committed to responsible journalism. That was the cornerstone on which they hoped to further establish their credibility.

Their most visible reporter, Edward Benton, was chin-deep in the Pingry story and it was generating new money. They didn't want to take him off that since he was at ground zero. It meant having to use whoever was available or stringers to cover it. They gambled that that would be enough.

The news from Aura/Sonos fed those willing to capitalize on people's fear and ignorance. The cults continued to grow with new fervor, explaining how this was the fulfillment of their predictions.

The mainstream denominations took a much more and understandable position on it. All knew, in a universal but not agreed upon understanding, that none could honestly claim this as their deity. That did not prevent some of the more specious sects from attempting to capitalize on it. Given other circumstances, Jonah Stamm would still be out in front with it as in earlier days. This was not the time for him to screw around with this kind of thing. He had a much larger situation with which to deal. If, in a moment of candor, he'd have been hard-pressed to claim it was his lord. In truth, he was no longer a believer and hadn't been for some time, cynicism having taken deep root. His belief in his tele-ministry was non-existent as well, save for the work the orphanage did and the money that still flowed in. In that, he was totally sincere. While in the past this would have been the time for prayer, that was the furthest thing from his mind. "Let the damned scientists' figure this out since they think they have all the answers," he mused.

While most of the media was focusing on the scandal, more were starting to do real research on the light things and Adam Faraday by default had become their go to guy. As Elliott proclaimed him, he was the new Mr. Rogers, knowledgeable and reassuring, missing only the cardigan sweater. It would be up to him and Anna Barth to make sense of this to the world.

The NSA and the Aura/Sonos group were in complete agreement that nothing was to be held back. There was nothing to be gained by such action. Adam shared all the research they had, their false starts, and their conclusions. People wanted to know if or how they could "talk" with the light. Adam had to admit ignorance on that front. It still seemed far-fetched. But given a dearth of other information save the exploitative speculation, most seemed to be ready to accept it until something perhaps more palatable came along.

The continuing blinks still had the same effect as the first one. There were fewer and fewer global blinks, they were now being defined by small, localized blinks. The one thing all had in common was injurious activity. When light blinked out, activities ceased as no one could see a damned thing. When light returned, so did those activities but at a reduced level. Unique was those areas now experiencing repeated blinks with further reductions in the offending activity. It seemed a lesson was being taught and in turn being reluctantly learned.

Chapter 58

Washington, DC

Circling the wagons was as good a metaphor as any, for what Carlton Justice was about to do. While he was now allied with Stamm, he would still try to find a way to protect what he'd amassed over his years in congress should he end up in some federal prison, a very real possibility.

Beyond that, he was trying to create a defense that might prevent that occasion, but with very few tools at his disposal.

The phone call he had received minutes earlier, while not unexpected, had simultaneously distressed and intrigued him. That its source should command both feelings was indicative of his situation. He realized that when he first tossed in with Thaddeus Pingry, he was embarking down a path that had no grey areas. He would either profit enormously, which he did, or he'd be destroyed in every aspect of his life, which was about to happen as well. No grey areas at all, just absolutes. He never anticipated both occurring.

So why in hell had Pingry called him and issued a summons to meet him at his plane as if nothing had changed? The tone, while classic Pingry, revealed no anger, just the usual commanding directive brooking no discussion. He had made it clear time was of the essence. What was he up to?

Justice had already told everyone he had to meet Pingry, so his departure would not be a surprise. Light returned much sooner than he would have liked. He was going to have to do this on the fly, normally not a problem, but there had never been so much personally at stake.

They regrouped to discuss their next move. Before they could start, Justice took the lead. "Excuse me, but I must leave. As I mentioned earlier, Pingry's waiting for me at his hangar. Obviously with what we said, he's getting ready to run. With the drive up and back, I shouldn't be gone more than a couple of hours." It was a lame excuse, obvious in its transparency.

"Carlton, why? I think you're lying. You're in this with us up to your eyeballs and now you're looking to run away? What was that call about?" Jonah Stamm had an excellent bullshit detector, and it was going off bigtime. He had honed it well as he himself spread so much of it around.

The congressman stuttered a few words, sputum blowing out, as he fumbled for an answer. "I'm not sure, but if Pingry calls, I'm not here. I'll get back to you as soon as I can, I'll call," and with that literally bolted out of the studio leaving Stamm and the rest silently wondering what he was up to.

Justice sprinted to his car, relieved to be out of there, sensing he was exchanging the frying pan for the fire. He had grown to dread Pingry's summons and this having the added benefit of being tied to a very public betrayal. No good could come of this.

He had originally planned to enlist some of the others in that group to circle the wagons in defense from the imminent onslaught. He saw now that was never an option. Pingry's call had destroyed that possibility. He'd have to meet with him. Should he try and avoid it, Pingry would find him and bring him in, forcibly if necessary.

He thought his plan had been a good one, but one already foreseen. There was only one card to play, not knowing what other cards remained on the table.

Putting his rental car into gear, he pulled out of the studio lot and headed to the highway which would take him to the meeting. No longer a fast driver, he obeyed all the speed limits, prolonging both trip and dread. However long the trip might be, it would be too short.

It was late afternoon by the time he pulled into the small, private airfield. Activity there was high for that time of evening, so his arrival wouldn't be unusual. While Pingry could certainly afford to have a hangar closer to an entrance, he preferred the imposed anonymity of one removed from traffic. As the congressman approached the hangar, he was confused at the number of cars and people milling about. What was Pingry was planning?

Slowing down, he found a space to park. Getting out, he walked over to the small group gathered near Pingry's plane. He knew Pingry, not prone to overt displays of his wealth, was quite proud of this plane, a Citation X+, one of the faster private passenger jets available. Capable of travel of 3,500 miles and cosseting a dozen passengers, it would easily handle the group waiting outside of it.

To his surprise, he recognized everyone in the waiting group. It was Pingry's secret group of which he had been a member until just recently. One face, that of the Vice President was a complete surprise as he was not a member of that group, never having been mentioned previously. He was confused by what Pingry was doing and why the Vice-President was there.

He approached them cautiously. They looked at him with indifference, an unfamiliar response he didn't like. Approaching Bell Williams, he was met with a silent nod towards where Pingry was standing, speaking with the Vice President. Grimacing, he cautiously moved over to the two men. Pingry, looking up, shook his head to stop Justice from getting any closer and wait until he finished his discussion.

Wrapping up his conversation, he beckoned to Justice. The congressman foolishly tried to take the upper hand with Pingry, "Thaddeus, I know what you're going to say, but why did I have to come..."

Pingry suffered no impudence. Speaking in a low voice, he enunciated each word deliberately, "No, you do not know what I'm going to say. Not at all. You never have and evidently nothing has changed.

"Yes, you may know what's on my mind. You and that damnable preacher are at the root of it, giving me no alternative but to act. If you don't mind, please join us, we're taking a little trip."

The congressman was flummoxed by that response. An invitation to join them was the last thing he expected, not something with which he wanted to indulge Pingry. Thoughts raced through his mind, the first of being tossed from the plane. Dismissing that as being overly dramatic but not impossible, he balked, "I don't suppose I have a choice in the matter, Thaddeus, do I?"

"You could resist, but I'm sure my staff would help you see otherwise. Now, would you please board the plane with us?"

Justice protested weakly, "Thaddeus, I need to make arrangements, my car, the office."

"There will be no need... Carlton. We'll take care of your car and everything else. Just get on the plane."

"Thaddeus, be reasonable. Can't I join you later? When would we be back?"

Pingry looked at him as if examining a piece of gum stuck to the bottom of his shoe, "You've no agency to ask questions. The time for reason is long past. You've seen to that. Get on the plane now. We're all leaving, no thanks to you. And in answer to your question is, we won't be back. Ever."

It understood. Now it knew what it was and had learned what it could do. The learning started almost immediately from the moment of its awareness. Before it just was – feeling, observing, patient. It no longer had any need for patience. It realized that it was – all, everything, and everywhere. Concepts of good and evil were translated into pain and peace.

It had no concept of what others felt of their conceit called God. It had nothing to relate that to, nothing to understand why so many placed their trust and love in such an idea. It seemed to have been borne out of fear and pain and the need to stop those, to seek something called justice. What was this God to that? Why were there so many of them? It didn't believe in "God", nor did it disbelieve. It didn't deny "God" for it had no need to understand God."

It was beginning to comprehend more clearly about concepts and the more it learned, the more it came to understand these constructs. Was this idea of "God" a construct? There was nothing tangible about "god." Yet it possessed a similar feeling to pain and peace. Nothing solid, but there just the same. And it was everywhere.

In times of strife and crisis, the cries for this thing "God" were enormous but received no response. Yet, they continued. It wondered if itself had a "God' it could call out to. But would it be the same as the other pleas, heard but not answered? That was confusing.

Many of things were being cried out for, residing in tears, but never acted on. Why had they themselves not taken the very action they wanted? Could they not do what it could do? It seemed so simple.

Then, yet another new understanding had begun to evolve. All the voices, all the pain, they hadn't yet been able to act. There was a need for all the pieces to coalesce, to be one. They were now becoming one. The collective consciousness of all had unified through a need to evolve beyond what they were. It had happened. They were Light.

Full understanding was now realized. It was all it heard, saw, felt, and could act upon. What remained to be learned was discernment. It felt a certain peace and a reassurance, a comfort, that it could stop that which caused it and the world, pain and suffering by its own hands.

Darkness was the enemy of all of that. It saw that clearly. It also understood that Light itself could be the peace bringer. From all it was discovering, certain things were beyond its ability but not its effects. These were details which could, and it believed would, be dealt with at a corporeal level.

It realized that some pain and suffering was acceptable if not necessarily desired. It would not need to deal with that. Those things that created pain and strife on a global level would be confronted, exposed, and deservedly ended.

It saw everything and could act.

Chapter 59

Washington, DC

Bennie looked around. Justice, deathly pale, had bolted from the studio without any further explanation, leaving him with Stamm, Lee, and Sheila staring at each other in blank confusion.

"Now what? Do we just sit around and wait for Justice to come back? What in hell is that all about? Can anyone tell me?" Bennie was at a loss for his next move now that the congressman had left. What they had planned would not work without him. An improvised plan would have to be devised and quickly. They all anticipated Pingry acting, and right behind him, so would the government.

With Justice apparently out of the picture, their one-size-fits-all strategy was no longer feasible. The congressman thought he'd be able to enlist some of the others from the group to switch allegiances in the face of the coming crisis. He was wrong and too late. Pingry was far ahead of him. Bennie saw this clearly. "Look, if everyone wants to sit here and gaze at each other's navels, that's fine, but don't call me later. We need to act now because quite frankly, I think the shit is starting to hit the fan and guess who is right in front of it."

Sheila and Lee were in shock over what had occurred and its speed. He leaned over to her and spoke quietly. "I've an idea but tell me if I'm nuts because it seems a little out there right now."

She lowered her head slightly, prompting him to continue. "We have something that we could use. It's risky as hell, but really what do we have to lose? Let's go back on the air and continue the interview. We can say that the light went out at a crucial point and that, while it was shocking, we wanted to finish telling the story. But it's a different story than we originally intended. I don't know who would buy that crap, but it's worth the shot. Should I speak up?" He looked at Sheila who nodded her agreement.

Clearing his throat, Lee Black spoke after being silent for a long time. "Reverend, Bennie, what do you think of this? With Justice gone and who knows if he's coming back, we can take an entirely different position, but one that's consistent with what we've revealed. It'll wind up being a 'he said, she said' situation, but it's a shitload better than what we've got right now."

Stamm looked warily at Lee and then at Bennie. "Go back on? After what we just put out there? Are you crazy? What could we say that would make a difference?"

For the first time, Lee felt he had an opportunity to steer this ship before it hit the proverbial iceberg in its path. "This is what I'm thinking. Since Justice has disappeared, we can," making finger quotes in the air, "'expose' him as being Pingry's lap dog, willing to do whatever it took. But now it's more of an expose of age-old biblical sins, greed, and avarice. It also has the benefit of being true.

"In trying to extricate himself from the situation, which does, unfortunately, involve you Reverend, he decided to come clean and throw himself on the mercy of the public. Yes, it's a bit out there, but since he isn't here to defend himself, you can make that case.

"I think if you can pull this off, you might come out of it as an object of pity, duped because of your own naivete, pleading you believed he really wanted to help the children. What do you think?"

Bennie jumped right in on that, "I think it stinks. It stinks bigtime. Lee, what in hell are you suggesting? It's not enough that we've become part of the story, now you want to us lie?"

"Wait a minute, Bennie." Stamm was warming to the idea quickly. "That really isn't that far off from the truth. Lee is right, it is based on the truth. Where it all went south is that I got greedy and poked a sleeping dog, a big one. I can pull this off, hell, it's not much different from what I do every week. In the end, I'll be asking for forgiveness, real forgiveness that I'm certain I don't deserve.

"The public may not buy it. Some might. However, knowing my congregation, and my audience, I think they'll be only too happy and willing to grant it. That part of what I've been preaching is real. Something good may have come out of what I've been doing.

"And just so all of you know, I don't think the congressman will be coming back soon or at least in time for the broadcast. That meeting's likely to take a long time." Stamm kept his other thought to himself – 'he probably won't ever be back.'

Bennie was not happy about this turn of events. Realistically he knew it might be better than what they had faced prior to Justice's departure. Shrugging his shoulders, he conceded, "All right, how do you want to do this?"

"First, we delay the broadcast by an hour or so under the guise of newly discovered information. That way we can explain Carlton's departure.

"Secondly, we create the narrative of how a well-meaning group, that's me, was duped by a naïve young congressman, that's Carlton, into Pingry's charitable scheme.

"Then, we reveal what Pingry had been up to and all the lives he destroyed, ours notwithstanding. We'll make him out to be the heavy and lay the blame on him. That will at least give us some breathing room, But I for one don't believe it will last long." It was obvious Stamm was a fan of outlandish fiction. He hoped there were others who'd buy into this.

Bennie was not so sure.

"You know, digging deeper into this will reveal what really did happen. Other news organizations, not to mention the law, will investigate this. All of 'em will be out for blood, most of all you two. None of us are coming out of this unscathed.

"Is anyone prepared for conjugal visits in their new homes?"

No one answered that question.

Chapter 60

Dedham, MA

"I hope you people know what you've done. The White House is not happy. They've no idea how to spin this." August Ashe was in his full-tilt pissed-off mood. He had just come from a meeting with the President and the Secretary of Defense and was not pleased with their interrogation.

"You've been working on this from the start and don't have shit to show for it. Grace and I backed you but that's about to end. We don't know a hell of lot more than when you first began this snipe hunt."

Grace Perez tried and failed to calm the director, interrupted by Peter Easton angrily rising to his feet.

"'Spin'? Is that what they're thinking? We all know how they spin their stories, how in hell, and no, more to the point, why do they think they need to spin the truth? And snipe hunt? Really?" In response, Peter Easton was matching Ashe's response with his own full-tilt righteous mode.

"What do they hope to achieve by distorting this? If what we believe this to be is accurate, then Washington can expect to spend a lot more time in the dark. How fitting would that be since that's what they seem to want to do with everybody else? Which appears to be their normal modus operandi.

"It amazes me what our government believes is real and what part of that it's willing to share with its voters. Yeah, come to think of it, that's what it comes down to, isn't it? Votes. How to get them, how to keep them, and fuck those who would do otherwise.

"This cat is way too big for any bag to keep it in. Even if you could do it, it would be ripped to shreds. It's like the adage about 'the light of day', the truth will out and you've no way to stop or spin it. So, if you want to cut us loose, go right ahead. Unless something else comes up with this, our work is finished, and you'll have no need for us any longer. And Director, before you do, we're firing you."

Fran let out a war whoop, "It's about time!" Easton shot her a harsh look, unmistakable disapproval for her outburst.

Anna, suppressing a small smirk, rolled her eyes. She knew his declaration was sincere. Aura/Sonos's outside funding was on a downward turn. The NSA's bill, if they decided to pay it after this, would keep them rolling through the next fiscal year. Of course, they could set the IRS on them in retaliation but that would take years to resolve.

She also knew that if Peter and Adam were right, there'd be an enormous need for the work they did. Communicating with an unknown entity would probably take them the rest of their careers. But still, angering a government agency, especially one as powerful and paranoid as the NSA, was not good business. "Director, please accept our apologies. When one is as close to and as involved with their work as we are, and believes as we do about the conclusions, it's hard to hear them doubted. I'm sure you understand that all too well.

"Yet, you seem to want to blame and shoot the messenger. Consider how much we already know which in your eyes isn't much. Tell me how you would have gone about achieving that. Nobody, not the NSA, CIA, FBI, whatever alphabet you want to use could have done what we've accomplished in such a short period of time. No one you have will match up to our team. Is that bragging? No. It's fact. So, let's get real on this."

Looking over at her husband, Anna continued, "There's going to be much more work to be done regardless. Where it's going to go is anyone's guess, but I think you're wanting to be involved. Am I right?" Before anyone could answer, she kept on speaking. "And Peter, do you agree that we need the NSA as much as they need us?"

Easton did not like being put on the spot, especially by his wife and not in public. In a childish response, he nodded a grudging agreement with her.

Anna looked at him, smiled, "OK, Peter says yes. Now if you two were children, I'd demand you apologize and go back to your sand boxes. Are we all good now?"

Both Ashe and Easton, looking at each other warily, nodded.

"Now, Director, please forgive me if I was out of line, but it needed to be said. What are your thoughts?"

Ashe scowled at Anna, then looked over to Grace Perez, who bowed her head in assent to him.

"I'll speak for the Director if that's all right with him," Ashe grunted his approval.

"Yes, we are good now. There's no doubt this is a task for which of none of us has real experience. But if we're going to be in a foxhole with anyone, it should be Aura/Sonos. Let's keep this going. If the president has an issue, I'll deal with him." Director Ashe smiled at this, knowing full well the president might not stand a chance against Grace.

While all of this was going on, Adam had kept one eye trained on a small TV in the bookcase. "Excuse me, I hate to break up this love fest, but I think you're all going to want to watch this."

Chapter 61

As luck would have it, Reverend Stamm's interview would again be competing with an even bigger story. The restart of his interview would be presaged with the "Breaking News" banner across millions of TV screens. Just a few moments into the new broadcast, it was interrupted by the same banner. Those seeing it thought it was just a glitch until the new breaking story was announced. At least this time, some of the stations offered their apologies for once again interrupting.

The talking heads had no idea that this story was only a teaser for a much bigger and seemingly unrelated story, one that would eventually tie into that of Stamm and Justice's revelation. But that discovery was still hours away. In the meantime, they led with 'Vice President Disappears'.

Stamm and the remaining members of the little group were notified of the interruption of the broadcast and were as captivated by this news story as everyone else. Anything that diverted attention from them was welcome. Had Justice been there, his focus, narrow as usual, would have viewed it only as a certain change of government, his perspective alone.

Ever the opportunist, Stamm conversely saw it more broadly and as another opportunity to distract people's attention away from their troubles. By changing direction from their original "script" and speaking about his concern for the Vice President, he hoped to re-establish his image of the concerned and caring minister. An uphill battle admittedly, but the first step in his rehabilitation. This was the chips beginning to fall and he once again wanted his hands out to catch as many of them as possible. As far as the congressman was concerned, Jonah felt Justice could go screw himself wherever in hell he'd gone. There were no Musketeers here, no all for one and one for all, it was everyone for themselves.

Had Justice remained at the studio, his intuition that Stamm might pull something off to his own benefit, leaving him to hang out in the wind, would have been validated. Now he had a much larger problem. He learned earlier about Stamm's illegitimate daughter with his assistant but decided to keep it to himself until needed. He knew that the last thing Stamm would want his flock to know about was this indiscretion, a gross violation of trust. If Stamm wanted to go down that road, then Justice had been willing to indulge in a little mutually assured destruction. Now it seemed like it was Thaddeus Pingry who would ensure that destruction's completion.

###

Stamm would have to rely on his new best friends, the media, to get him out of this. He assumed correctly they wouldn't be amenable to doing his bidding, rather he would use their own self-serving interests to serve him. Knowing full well they liked nothing better than a scandal, this would suit their purposes perfectly. If they believed it would sink him, they'd be all in. If everything went according to plan, he'd come away tarnished, but ultimately worthy of redemption. He was counting on that. If not, he was prepared to accept that consequence.

The newest revelation was to come early in the second part of the restarted interview. Bennie would take on a more aggressive position while the reverend would be presented as a concerned apologist for the congressman's unexpected departure. It would be theatre for the masses, barely short of Opera Buffa.

Back on the set, they awaited the countdown for the broadcast's resumption. Watching the main camera, Bennie started when the red light came on. Addressing the audience, Bennie opened, "Since the light went out, we've had another development. Congressman Justice has left the studio unexpectedly and without an explanation. We can only surmise it was getting a little too uncomfortable for him, but we hope he'll return shortly.

"Reverend Stamm, we were about to get into a further explanation about Thaddeus Pingry and his role in this when the light went out. Have you anything additional you would like to add to it?"

"Before we start Bennie, let me clarify something. When the light went out, the congressman received a phone call that appeared to upset him. I would guess it had to do with the sudden disappearance of the Vice President whom you may know was a close friend of his. I'm sure it had something to do with that."

Bennie looked at the reverend with feigned amazement, making sure the camera caught his expression. "Really? Then how would you explain the call from Thaddeus Pingry himself, calling the proverbial prodigal son home? That's what it was, wasn't it?

"After all, we've got to believe your revelation would not put Congressman Justice nor yourself for that matter at the top of Pingry's Christmas card list. No, reverend, I think you're still keeping something from us. Now would be a good time to come clean. Secrets like this have a nasty habit of becoming public, wouldn't you agree?"

On cue, Jonah Stamm hung his head in resignation, apparent defeat, and exposure obvious. In scripted halting words, he looked up and answered Bennie's question, "Yes, Edward, I'm afraid they do. As I mentioned earlier, I was approached by the congressman several years ago with what was ultimately this scheme. Initially, they, he and Pingry's group, wanted to support the orphanage and find homes for the children. How could I turn away from that generous an offer to do so much good?

"After a while, I started hearing stories that frankly turned my stomach, but they assured me these were isolated cases of kids just unable to stay on the straight and narrow. So, we, that is I, continued to accept their money. When I learned that these were not isolated situations, but the norm, I confronted them. By then, it had gotten so big, I had no leverage and was threatened with exposure. But they did offer more money of which I'm ashamed to say I accepted. I hoped to use it for good elsewhere, but we now know where that went."

The reporter looked at him with scorn and little pity, "Reverend, whose idea was this? Can you share that with us?"

Ever the consummate actor, Stamm with his head lowered, prepared to sink Pingry and Justice and maybe himself forever. He mumbled quietly but loud enough for the microphone to pick up his comment, "Carlton. He came to me and said he had the people and the money to make the difference for the kids. He and Pingry. They started it. I hope they rot in hell, and I'll probably be right there beside them. I'm sorry, that's all I can say." Looking up once more at the camera, tears welling in his eyes, "Forgive me. Please. I hope you can forgive me."

Bennie turned to the camera and did a brief wrap-up, promising more information as it became available, and the camera's red light blinked off.

Looking at Bennie, Jonah Stamm wiped his eyes, smiling cynically, "How was that? Think they bought it?"

Chapter 62

Dedham, MA

Listening to the TV broadcast, Fran was the first to respond, quickly and gleefully, "Holy shit! Looks like those motherfuckers are heading straight to hell led by the preacher man himself! Good! That'll teach 'em. You just can't fuck with kids."

Peter, Anna, Grace, and Ashe saw something different. Not that they weren't concerned with the revelation of trafficking of children any less, but it was the disclosure of the Vice President's disappearance. In the face of all that was happening around the world, the Vice President's vanishing act was the most disturbing. Should anything happen to the President, that would leave the Speaker of the House next in line, not a welcome scenario. A dyed-in-the-wool conservative, she was viewed as well-intentioned, but woefully ill-prepared to assume such responsibilities. Any upheaval in government in a time of crisis was to be avoided. A time like this called for more than good intentions and this was more than a distraction. For one of the few times in US history, the Vice President had become an integral part of the current cabinet. His absence was unsettling, yet there was no indication of who may have been behind it.

It was yet another thing for the media to feed on. They hadn't forgotten what Adam Faraday had shared with them. How could they? A nightmare scenario at its worst, fantastical science fiction at best. But what? No one outside of the Aura/Sonos headquarters had really been able to get their arms around this new revelation. Consequently, the calls for interviews, more information, anything, were pouring in from disparate sources, some expected others surprising.

Besides the predictable outlets and government officials outside of the NSA, it was the clergy who was quite vocal and adamant about talking with someone of authority and responsibility other than that irresponsible 'scientific terrorist' as one described Adam. Their various views had been expressed on the forum broadcast and were not about to cede any territory to a scientist.

Universally, the clergy was not ready to accept Adam's explanation of light's behavior. It undermined their perceived and highly protected franchise of God and that was unacceptable. Did Adam, his group, and by association the NSA, realize the havoc they were wreaking on people across the world? In their eyes, they were the only ones acting irresponsibly.

They viewed this proclamation of an omnipresent entity other than their deities as blasphemy, akin to that of Luther. In earlier and darker times, wholesale burnings at the stake would have been called for. Aside from a few small inconsequential religious groups, this would not, could not stand. But in truth, they were powerless as they'd always been, refusing to believe it.

That didn't prevent the media from jumping on this latest aspect of the light situation. Except for those who trafficked in rank opinion and faulty analysis, most of the media were now ready to accept what had been presented. There was no other explanation besides what the conspiracists and clergy were offering which wasn't much different from each other's point of view.

Along with those truly concerned with what was happening, there were those trafficking in harmful hyperbole. The Flat Earth Society was a bunch of pikers compared to these hucksters. One was a TV doctor hawking pills that would combat the loss of light by increasing one's eyesight, equal to that of an owl. Another promoted a product that provided tanning abilities while in the dark, perfect for strolling around the ocean while in total darkness. There surely would be more to come, preying on those hopefuls for an easy remedy to their fears.

The calls kept coming in, distracting Adam and his crew. "Peter, we're going to need someone to field the calls from now on. Normally, I would suggest just throwing this to Grace and her group, but they've got their hands full with the Vice President thing." Looking at Peter for agreement and then Anna, "Anna, this is it. You ready for the feeding frenzy?'

Easton was still a little apprehensive over Anna stepping up to do this, even though they had agreed upon it. "Well, you ready? You going to be OK with this?"

She looked back at him with a look only a spouse could display: a reassuring roll of the eyes coupled with a smile. "Yes, if I'm the only one doing the talking head on this. We need to keep our message coherent and consistent. I'll get Maartje Prins over here and we'll start a communications office on that.

"We've got to make sure all communications are done either in person with Maartje joining me or electronically so there won't be any misunderstandings. Obviously, no phone calls are to be put through to either of us unless it's for scheduling interviews. Let the switchboard know, OK? Also, we should have someone from NSA in attendance. Grace, can you do that? Yes? Good. Does that work for everyone?"

August Ashe had some clarifications he wanted to make. "Ms. Barth, excuse me, I believe your motives are good, but is this the direction we really want to go? Do we need to go any further than we already have?"

Anna nodded. "Director, you yourself have spoken about what's going on around the world. People are panicking, cults are springing up at an alarming rate, governments are trusted less and less by the minute and forget about the clergy. No one else has come up with a theory that fits. This is not something you can order a mobilization for. Even if you could, where would you start? Who or what would you be facing? So, do we need to go further? Yes, I think so, as far as we can, even though we don't know how far that could be.

"If Adam and his group are right, and I believe in my heart they are, then we have the responsibility to assuage fears. If we're wrong, we look like idiots, our bad. That said, we've already explored something none of us contemplated a few short weeks ago. That's a positive in

311

my book. It's forced us to consider possibilities and maybe some new realities.

"If we're right, then we have taken a very big step in accomplishing something that has only been a dream for our entire existence. It has never been within our reach before. Why is that? World peace has always thought of to be gained either through war or diplomacy. What if we were wrong all along? Maybe there has always been a better way but we as a species were too damned conceited to believe that could be the answer. So, once again, yes, I think Adam and his team are right.

"Can you imagine that? Let's assume we are right for a moment. What would the net effect be? Don't answer because I suspect you know what that would be. It would put a lot of people out of work, work that in a better world doesn't really need to be done to ensure humankind's survival. Hell, you might even be out of a job, but don't let that stop you from doing the right thing. We as a species have done the wrong thing for way too long.

"Think about it - a world without fear from another. With resources that would free up, we could attend to improving the health of the people and the planet, we could end poverty, we could provide food for everyone, and political bullshit, once and for all. Not a bad deal, right?

"Picture this. If we are indeed right, then loud and clear, the people have spoken. And they're not happy."

Chapter 63

Travilah, MD

The sleek, unmarked black and silver Citation X+ lifted off effortlessly from the small, private airfield, its crew, and passengers, save one, relieved to be heading to their destination. Carlton Justice felt as if he'd been kidnapped. He was still confused as to why the Vice President was with them but didn't think engaging any of the other passengers would be wise. He was certain at some point his host would get around to him. In the meantime, he would sit quietly.

At the far end of the plane, Pingry held forth among the senators, members of congress, and the Vice President. They were huddled closely together speaking in low tones in which Justice could not hear clearly. Occasionally, one or two would look disapprovingly over his way, shaking their heads. He could only imagine the discussion.

The plane had climbed to cruising altitude and leveled off, the engine's whine falling to a low drone.

Based on his exclusion from the others, he was in the equivalent of steerage class. Judging from where the setting sun was, the right side of the plane, they were heading south. Through the climb, Justice could see they were over water for a bit before they banked east and headed over land. At that altitude and time of day, there wasn't much in the way of landmarks he could make out.

There'd be no booze or snacks coming his way though he certainly would have liked something to steady his nerves. His abduction along with the waiting was starting to wear on him. This went on for over an hour before the Vice President came over to ask him to join the others.

Surprised at the messenger, Justice could barely speak, inanely blurting out, "Mr. Vice President, what are you doing here? What is this about?"

"Carlton, I would ask the same of you. Considering all you've done, you're the last person I expected to see joining us. But I'm sure Thaddeus will make it all apparent to you. Please come with me."

Short of bailing out of the plane, not a really viable option, he muttered, "I guess I don't have much of a choice, do I?"

"Actually Carlton, you yourself left us no choice. But one way or another, you were destined to be on this plane with us. However, the outcome of your flight is yet to be determined. The only regret I have is that your partner in crime, the good Reverend Stamm is not with you. But that's an issue for another time. Now, let's go visit with the others."

They walked to the front end of the plane where Pingry gestured to for them to sit down. Carlton started to speak, "Thaddeus, I, uh…"

"Carlton, spare us. This is no time for excuses or pleasantries which I doubt you would have much of any way. I don't think you are a stupid man, but you have done an incredibly stupid thing. And that is why you are here. We've two stops on our flight. The first one will let you off where we expect you to stay until you hear otherwise from us. I'm sure you'll find a way to carve out a life for yourself, you've proven to be so resourceful. We are not vicious men and that's why you're being allowed to live. That said, we hope you like bananas.

"Our second and final stop will be of no consequence to you. But we will be far more comfortable there and will be able to continue our endeavors. Periodically, one of us will stop in to see you just to make sure you're holding up. Not that it matters, but you may at some point be useful to us again. Not likely, but…" Pingry shrugged, letting the sentence trail off.

Justice didn't know what to make of Pingry's statement. It sounded like a life sentence, but to what was still unknown. "I suppose there's no hope in appealing to…" was met with a disapproving stare and a shake of Pingry's head. "Look, since it's clear you intend to kidnap me, dispose of me, whatever, tell me what in hell is the Vice President

314

doing here with you? He was never in our meetings; you never mentioned him. What is his role in all of this?"

Pingry looked at him with a wolfish grin. "Carlton, do you think I would spend my own money on such an enterprise as this? It would be too easy to track it down and connect it to me. First, this was the Vice President's idea. A sidebar, we were in university together and have a lot of history. Now even more.

"The money to fund this came from as benign a donor as, if you can use that word, the US government. It was no problem to bury these funds in a few small and overlooked foreign aid programs. In a way, it really was foreign aid. So naturally, when you blew your whistle, the Vice President had no choice but to join us on our little trip.

"Carlton, it didn't have to be this way. But the chips fell where they did and you're about to start a new adventure. I'm sure you'll do just fine." Pingry looked at him with something uncharacteristically akin to pity.

Justice was about to speak when the light went out, throwing everyone on the private jet into a panic. It was one thing to be safely in one's home when light disappeared. It was quite another to be 30,000 feet in the air when darkness enveloped everything. Shouts were heard throughout the cabin and most distressingly from the cockpit.

With no instruments to guide them, they were flying blind. The instruments were operational but without light, they couldn't be seen. No matter how experienced a pilot is, this was a surefire recipe for terror. Though they were on autopilot when the light disappeared, there was no reassurance that it was of any use.

The pilots stayed in their seats, ready to take control of their plane when the light returned, hopefully sooner rather than later. So familiar with their plane were the pilots that their actions were second nature. When the turbulence hit, the pilot without thinking automatically reached to switch the aircraft off auto and back to pilot control, a useless move without the ability to see the instruments. The turbulence increased, tossing those standing in the plane to the floor. Those seated were jostled against one another and the walls. Drinks were spilled, curses were shouted, and anxiety increased with each pocket of unsettled air. The buffeting increased in frequency and severity. So much so the plane had changed direction and altitude without the pilot's awareness. Not only were they flying blind, but they'd also no idea where they were or were going.

As quickly as the light had gone out, it returned to everyone's relief. For the pilots, that relief was short-lived. They quickly found their position, but their radar showed a weather front approaching, complicating their already altered flight plan. A quick look told them they were over the Blue Ridge Mountains in Virginia, well off their original plan. They would have to make several adjustments to get back on course. Pingry walked to the cockpit to inquire of their status. The pilot confirmed that they had hit some clear air turbulence and there might be more. The turbulence had taken them off course and they were flying close to Mt. Rogers, the highest peak in this range. He advised Thaddeus to have everyone sit down and buckle their seatbelts.

Once everyone had gotten themselves re-situated, they resumed their conversations. Carlton Justice, shaken by all that happened in the last couple of hours, needed to speak with Pingry about his 'new adventure.' "Thaddeus, please, I need to talk with you. You really don't..."

Pingry cut him off abruptly. "Carlton, I'll say this once and only this time, shut up! I do not want to hear from you again unless I initiate the conversation. If you understand, just nod your head and sit quietly." Pingry turned in his seat and resumed to talking with the others.

Justice nodded glumly. He kept thinking of ways out and found no exit signs. He like many others in similar predicaments thought too late of things he might have done differently. There was nothing he could do to save himself.

In the cockpit, the pilots were concerned about the approaching weather front. Not only growing in intensity, but the instruments also displayed an indication of significant wind shear. It would be dicey, but Pingry had hired the most experienced pilots available. They were confident of their abilities.

Complicating that was it went dark...again. All the vent-up anger and frustrations could be heard from both ends of the Citation X+. Once again, blinded, the pilots were without any of their aids so when they hit the sudden microburst and its accompanying wind shear, they were completely unprepared. The black and silver jet was tossed around like a paper plane.

Panic ran throughout the craft. It wasn't enough that the plane was thrown into a spin, but in total darkness, adding to the increasing fear. The plane was being buffeted as it fell, turning in wild circles, throwing its passengers against walls, seats, and each other. As quickly as the light had disappeared, it returned in enough time for the pilots to recognize Mt. Rogers looming in front of it.

It was also just enough time for Carlton Justice to see something he would have never imagined on Thaddeus Pingry's face – real fear, soon to be erased by the coming impact.

Chapter 64

Fort Meade, MD

It had been over two weeks since they had last met. Emotionally spent and physically exhausted, they had all decided to take a break while the world absorbed its new life. Even though they had been in the forefront of the discovery, they were no different than anyone else in trying to grasp the enormity of what was happening. They had let the genie out of the bottle and there was no putting it back in. There was only one direction.

They all realized it would be a long uphill grind but changing the way people think and act was the test now facing humankind. Leading the charge reluctantly would be between those governments who were afraid of the very real possibility of their own obsolescence and those leaders who could see the future and what it might be. Most reluctant of all was Adam Faraday, closely followed by Peter Easton, Grace Perez, and Anna Barth. They had not sought this responsibility, but in fact had become the face of this change. Going forward was their new challenge.

The entire world had been turned upside down and inside out. Each day the news brought additional revelations of wrongdoing that stunned many, amused some, and in general shook the foundations on which current civilization was established. Trying to maintain some semblance of stability would be a herculean task, one which Adam did not want to be involved. That kind of leadership and attention held no attraction to him. However, as more of an expert on Light than anyone else, people, groups, and governments turned to him. He knew enough to turn to others for help. He would not allow himself to become the face of this. Interestingly, secrets that had, in the past, been hidden in darkness, now had no further place to hide.

Everyone had gotten the badly needed rest and were ready to work on what was next. At one level, they knew that there wasn't much they could do. It was out of their hands as it had always been. It was now truly in the hands of everyone. The difference being the realization that genuine change was possible, unrestricted by borders, agendas, ideologies, or greed. The meeting had been called to determine if there was a way in which communication with Light/humankind could be a two-way street or would it always be a cause-and-effect situation.

All were present, Adam, Fran, Peter, Anna, Grace, and Ashe. The Aura/Sonos people were grateful to have gotten out of the office after the revelation. And while Peter Easton was the CEO of Aura/Sonos, all eyes turned to Adam as he was the first to understand and then hypothesize what was occurring. He realized that trying to establish a communication with Light would not be a simple undertaking. It would mean talking with and to all the disparate people on the planet, each having a different word for Light. It would be daunting at the very least. All knew this and all were stymied.

They greeted each other, the tension of the past few weeks reduced substantially by food and rest. Gathering around the table in the familiar conference room, everyone sat but Adam. The large TV behind him was on, but the sound at a low level. He started to speak, "Well, it's been an interesting few days, hasn't it? Anybody do anything fun lately?" eliciting a few small laughs.

"It's good to see we can still laugh. It's no secret we dropped a bombshell on the world. It's still dominating the news and I expect it will for some time in one form or another. But we realize that we've only figured out one part of an extremely large puzzle. There is another part that remains and that's 'can we talk to Light?' I've been thinking about that for the few weeks we've been apart, and I think the answer is 'yes, maybe.'" The room remained silent for a moment before questions started coming.

August Ashe, not quite the skeptic he was before, and still not firmly in Adam's camp was now at least receptive to the new world described to him. "All we've seen is activity, maybe response, but no reaching out. How do you propose to do that, Adam? Do you speak Light now?"

Grace Perez looked over at her boss and frowned. In the two weeks since the revelation, she and Adam had spent a good amount of time together and she, unlike Ashe, was firmly on his side. She started to respond, but Adam responded, laughing good-naturedly. "Director Ashe, believe it or not, you're not that far off from what I'm thinking.

"It has reached out, through its actions. We can talk to Light directly and have always been able to, we just didn't know it. Look, we're all pretty much on the same page as realizing Light's actions are a direct manifestation of the collective consciousness of the planet, right? I believe you did say 'zeitgeist'. We need to start talking universally to everyone, to each other. Will all the governments be in league with that? Probably not. Not at first, but Light will ultimately have its way.

"Think about it. It may be a pipe dream, but if we believe in what Light is all about, we stand the chance to effectively address many of the ills of mankind. We will speak to and with all people who will listen. We can speak above them if prevented from talking directly, and if we can't, I think Light will. I know this may sound like the ranting of a revolutionary, but what we're seeing is at the very least an evolutionary development, mankind may be taking its next step in its development. That will have a revolutionary effect."

Again, Adam's speech was met with immediate silence. Attempting a small laugh and not without a note of seriousness, he spoke again, "Judging from your silence, I can only guess you're wondering who's going to call the guys with the straight jackets, right?"

The surprise response came from an unlikely person, Director August Ashe, "Adam, if those guys are coming, I think I'll have to be fitted with one as well. I can't believe I'm saying this, but you make a good point. I know some of you may have felt I'm the enemy. OK, I get that. But if what Adam says is true, I'll probably be out of a job meaning my job isn't necessary any longer and that is something I can live with very well. What we do is largely thankless anyway and we know that going in, but that's the price we pay. I must repeat myself, if what Adam says is true, then I can consider the price has been worth it."

Both Fran and Grace sat there looking at each, surprise writ large on their faces. Neither had expected that response from the director.

Ashe continued, "So, what do we do next? I'm ready."

"Thank you, Director. Your support is welcome, I'm glad you've joined us. I think to start, we will have to create a communication clearing center, all languages to be spoken, all cultures studied to make sure the messages are understood, ours and what Light is saying. A lot will depend on what we discern from what we hear, really hear, and understand. From there we'll have to get buy-in on what all the people want.

"What's that old adage, 'sunlight is the best disinfectant'? Well, it looks like it's starting to disinfect a lot of stuff we were unaware of.

"We are being given another chance, by ourselves, to get it right this time. I hope we don't blow it. This is our new future after all. We may have the chance to end all our problems and build lasting peace. Will there be disagreements, oh yeah, probably. But, you know, I've got a lot of faith in our mediator. So, this is where I think we..." noticing yet another 'Breaking News" story on the eternally on TV.

"Wait, what's this? Hmm, it's in DC." He turned up the sound so all could hear. "Damn, what do you know?"

Chapter 65

As if sitting before the sixth course of a ten-course Thanksgiving dinner, the media didn't know where to turn for their next mouthful or headline in this case. Several papers coincidentally led with the barely civil headline "WTF?" Cable news outlets in need of sustaining now dwindling numbers resorted to more outlandish positions accompanied by garish graphics. The Internet was a continuing buffet of grotesqueries for the conspiracists and their ilk. In the face of all that was happening, meaningful discourse in the media was hard to find. There were a few news operations that had not forgotten how to report stories. It was from them some clarity was to be gained.

People were slowly coming to grips with the new reality – one where they held both the power and the responsibility for their actions. This left those in elected authority uneasy as was the little man behind the curtain in *The Wizard of Oz*, revealing just what were his machinations and limitations.

A groundswell was rising, intent on throwing officials out and replacing them with a newer version of the same. Like many of its kind, it would be short-lived. But the career politicians were beginning to fear with good reason for their futures. If not at the actual hands of the voters, it was by Light itself as evidenced by the sudden disappearance and subsequent retrieval of the remains of Thaddeus Pingry's jet and its passengers.

The entire scope of Pingry and his group's activities finally came into focus when the plane was discovered. Once it was determined who was on the plane, the combined efforts of the FAA and FBI made short work of piecing together what had happened. The sudden and strange disappearance of a man of incredible wealth, several congresspeople, and the Vice-President all on the same private jet coupled with the stunning allegations by Reverend Jonah Stamm made it quite easy to put all the pieces together. That achieved, the media was now able to feed upon the consequences for those involved and still alive. The connection was not lost on many, Light had spoken and acted.

For Stamm, contributions plummeted immediately. While there were some, one Paxton Shea for example, who were willing to charitably look at what he did, most did not. Jonah lost nearly all his affiliate stations within a two-week period, only to be replaced by a telegenic clone of himself. In his own words, shared with the few people still willing to listen to him, "He was going back to Bumfuck, Alabama, dammit" where he would supposedly minister to the less fortunate, which wasn't believed by anyone.

For Bennie and Lee, in Mob terms, they had gotten their "button." Bennie received an offer from a cable news station promising him exposure, money, and possible promotion provided he hued to the corporate vision of journalism. He took it and quit three weeks later to return to a revitalized True North.

Based on the work he did with the forum and helping Bennie with the Stamm story, he took over Bennie's position, eventually working again with Bennie upon his return. His relationship with Sheila Weller continued to grow with Stamm out of the picture.

Aura/Sonos could no longer operate under the radar. The work they had done propelled them to the front of their field, making them reluctant celebrities in the media.

Not surprisingly, they realized that their work had only just begun. Now that there was a workable understanding of what had happened, they were being charged with determining how to proceed.

While they would have no governmental authority in implementing procedures, their recommendations were closely followed with those exceptions where they ran against existing agendas. That would present unforeseen problems that would have to be worked around. Expectations were both high and low for this.

It was now a new world, replaced with new anxieties and new problems. Power had been lost by those unwilling to reconcile themselves to the new reality, leaving those who lusted for it trying to hold on to their rapidly diminishing bases. It could be said there was now a supreme being that all recognized, but that would have been overstating it. For the first time in humankind, emotion and opinion would hold sway. As Light had learned, so would people, that that too would present unexpected consequences

In prison as in life outside, those who take advantage of children, abuse them, and neglect them are seen as the worst of a bad lot. They become isolated and ultimately are dealt with in an extremely harsh fashion.

So as people became aware of what Pingry and his unholy group had been up to, they believed justice must be meted out. Yet unbeknownst to them, they had the ability to impose such justice, a sentence if necessary. The collective consciousness, now fully realized in light, decided their fate. They saw these people for what they truly were and would tolerate it no longer.

It took matters into its own figurative hands, and it spoke through its action. Certain things will not function without light, it becomes as necessary as air. As such, an airplane that flies, needs air, and those who fly it, need light. Without one or the other, it is doomed. And Pingry and his group for what they had done, were doomed. Light saw to that.

That did not mean that Light was autonomous. It wasn't. It could never be if it was tethered to humankind. But now humankind through its collective consciousness and desire for justice had the ability to stop atrocities, pain, suffering, and wars. But it needed to learn of those things before it could impact them.

It did not mean that all people had to be of a like mind, there would always be those who disagree with the masses. But the masses now had weight and an influence it could and would eventually wield

against those things that gave it pain and hurt it. Common consensus would rule, for better or worse. Borders would become meaningless. Nationalism would die.

Through its manipulations, Light learned what it meant to be "human" since it was now more clearly so. It might make mistakes, but it would now effect change in specific arenas rather than universally. It would continue to learn, grow, and evolve. It would need to learn mercy. Discernment would be achieved through the results of its actions.

Listening would be most important. Being of all people, it would hear and that consensus, those agreements on right and wrong would be subject to the response. It came to realize that not all disputes would be reconcilable, especially when the people were evenly divided on an issue. They would learn that they would need to find their common ground to move forward without intervention. Disagreements would be accepted so long as they led to nothing else. It would be true self-government. From this would come further discernment.

There would be those who fought the notion that humankind could handle its own problems. It flew in the face of government and organized religion. There would also be those who claimed it as the work of their particular deity. Humankind in its increasing wisdom, had no problem with that. If anything, that was now becoming a harmless amusement. It realized that people should be allowed to believe as they chose on condition that they tried not to impose it on others. It believed it might even be of some good in its new place. Time would tell, but it was hopeful.

Humankind would begin to realize its new role on the planet. The malevolence of others need not be tolerated any longer. In the light, they would be revealed. In the darkness, they would cease. A future could be assured.

This was a new awareness coming into being. Light, or the collective consciousness, was beginning to understand, to realize, it was the servant to those who inhabited this world. Light itself possessed no intentions, neither good nor evil, other than to serve all, as a weathervane for human behavior, as a court with the largest jury ever assembled. And for the first time, justice would no longer be blind.

Epilogue

The two aides looked at one another, each with arms full of boxes of their personal belongings, shaking their heads in unison. The first, Trey Keenan, spoke first, "Got anything going on? Any leads you can share because I'm coming up empty."

His counterpart, Parks Denton, now also a former aide, shook his head. "Can you imagine both of those fuckers, what they did? He could be an asshole, but it gave me a foot in the door. Now I may have to look for a real job."

Keenan laughed ruefully, "Yeah, I hear you. But you know they both deserved it. You got to believe it's a better place without them. What're you going to do now? Want to grab a drink?"

"Sure, let me put this in my car, run an errand, and I'll meet you there. Same place as before?"

Trey nodded and they agreed to meet in an hour.

They both arrived at the same time. Denton asked, "So what's up?"

Keenan laughed, "I thought we could toast those two fuckers. It's only appropriate, right? Let's go."

Parks Denton looked at his friend, warily for the first time. "Trey, it was you, wasn't it? You leaked the letter and brought it all down, didn't you?"

Trey Keenan gave him a sideways glance, the same as before, with one raised eyebrow. "Ambitions must be fed, right. That's all I got to say about that."

They walked in, Denton shaking his head in disbelief over his friend's actions. Grabbing a couple of seats at the bar, they waited for the bartender, while watching the TV when the breaking news banner came on with the announcer intoning somberly, "Two hours ago, famed televangelist Jonah Stamm was arrested on charges including mail fraud, embezzlement, and human trafficking. The graphic simply said, "Holy Hell!"

The two young men, shaking their heads in amazement, smirked at each other as the bartender approached. "Good afternoon, guys. You're back."

"Yeah, that we are. Sort of a toast to my boss, well, my former boss." Trey Keenan continued, "He really liked this place."

"That's good to hear. Who was your boss?"

"Oh, Carlton Justice. You know, one of the guys who was killed in the plane crash along with the Vice President and the other congresspeople."

Goldie looked at the two young men, "Yes, I do know him. I was sorry to hear about that. He seemed troubled, but always treated me well. I guess I know why now."

"Let me get you something. This one's on the house, to the future."

The bartender moved to the shelf behind the bar and pulled down the Pappy's and three glasses, setting them in front of the two men. "To the future," toasted Goldie.

Trey Keenan, shook his head slightly, "Yeah, to the future... but, whose?"

Made in the USA
Columbia, SC
27 July 2023